SACANDAGA
SUNRISE

My very best wishes.
Enjoy

[signature] 9-5-21

ISBN 978-1-950034-41-3 (Paperback)
Sacandaga Sunrise
Copyright © 2019 by Irene Pough

Disclaimer: This book contains graphic material that might be sensitive to readers.

For permission requests, write to the publisher at the address below.

Yorkshire Publishing
4613 E. 91st St,
Tulsa, OK 74137
www.YorkshirePublishing.com
918.394.2665

Printed in the USA

SACANDAGA
SUNRISE

Irene Pough

TULSA

ACT I

Morning has broken like the first morning.
Blackbird has spoken like the first bird.
Praise for them singing!
Praise for the morning!

—Eleanor Farjeon

PROLOGUE

New York City 2016

New York City. The lights of Broadway. The place where dreams are made and frequently broken. During the spring of 2005, Elizabeth Callison, fresh out of Syracuse University with a Bachelor of Fine Arts in Stage Management and a Bachelor of Science Degree in Directing, arrived in the city for a series of on and off Broadway directing interviews. The noise, and congestion of people scurrying from one place to the next, didn't seem to phase, the young woman who had grown up in the southern Adirondack Mountains. She was in the urban setting filled with dreams of someday making it with her name on the playbill as Director of the theatrical production on or off Broadway.

Eleven years later, Elizabeth was still working in the shadows of Tony Award winning directors. From one show to the next she continued to be open to learn from her peers and apply her craft as the assistant director. During this time, she had made a name for herself as one of the best—if not the best—assistant directors. Cast members who left a production to go on to other shows were quick to talk about Liz's work ethics, and gave her a reputation for being a no nonsense, assistant director, while working on a production. When the house lights dimmed and the curtain rose, she expected the cast and crew to be in place and do their jobs. After hours she knew how to cut loose and have fun with her circle of friends. Yes, Liz was living out her dream, and satisfied with what she had accomplished thus far in her life. That is, until a devastating blow that she never saw coming catapulted her into a downward spiral. Her dreams and life ambitions had been broken apart—shattered by betrayal of the worst kind. Liz knew that she could talk with her mother about some of what happened, but not all of her grief. She needed a confidant, someone who would listen and not judge her for how she felt. Liz knew that there was one person whom she could totally trust at this point in her life: her Aunt Amanda Newman–Wentzel.

"Elizabeth, my goodness, it is good to hear from you! How are you?" That was all her aunt needed to ask for Liz to unload her grief. Amanda listened and encouraged as Liz had hoped she would. Finally, she began to run out of steam. "Well, now, this is a mess and I see why you did not want to involve your parents at this point. Knowing my brother, he would not have been as compassionate about your situation. Having said that," Liz smiled while listening to Aunt Amanda continue on about the Great Sacandaga Lake community in the lower Adirondack Mountains. "Perhaps you should consider taking a break, a vacation. When was the last time you got away from the city? And visiting your uncle and me doesn't count." Liz responded. "Mm-hmm! Just as I thought. I'm sure you will probably not readily welcome my next suggestion. But I'm going to share it anyway." Amanda laughed at Liz's comment. "Well, even though we both know how your dad may get when he learns the truth, you might want to consider going home to visit your folks, family and friends in the area."

"Oh, Aunt Amanda, I don't know about that. Home? You really think I should go home to Mom and Dad's?"

"It's a suggestion. You know, spending time by the lake, or, in a canoe on the lake is a great way to relieve stress, and clear your mind about things. Plus, your Uncle Kevin and I will be up there vacationing with our friends at their cabin the last two weeks in July. We'd love to see you. Hint, hint!"

Liz felt her smile grow with ease. "Aunt Amanda, thank you for listening and in turn giving me things to consider. Who knows? You just might find me in upstate New York."

"That would be nice, Liz. Just remember that whatever you decide about your situation, I respect your decision."

Liz released a long, slow, breath as she ended her call. Without knowing what she was considering her aunt had suggested that she go home. Liz knew in her heart that while her parents were not going to understand and probably explode when they found out what happened, she had to go to the southern Adirondack Mountains. The Great Sacandaga Lake was beckoning her to journey home.

CHAPTER 1

Great Sacandaga Community
Eight Weeks Later

Sweat seemed to seep from every pore on Elizabeth's body as she drove the rental moving van north of Albany, New York on 187 towards Saratoga Springs. The temperature outside of the van was hovering in the low nineties, so Liz estimated that the temperature inside the cab was probably over one hundred. Shortly after she had begun her journey north on the New York State thruway, the air conditioning unit apparently decided it was too hot to work. Therefore, Liz was left with the only alternative available and opened both windows and the floor vent that sucked in all the hot road heat. Tired and road weary, Liz was in a sour mood. Not a moment too soon she saw a road sign that there was a rest area a few miles ahead. Wonderful! A bathroom! A cold drink! An air-conditioned building was just what she needed. Liz watched for the sign for the turn off into the rest area and squealed with delight, when she eased the vehicle into the right lane. She had just parked the van in the large parking space and shut off the motor when her cell phone rang.

"Hi Mom! Yes, I just pulled into a rest area on the Northway. Um, I'm a little south of Saratoga. Yes, I plan on taking Route 29 over to Route 30 and then the back roads home. No. I am not going up the east side of the Sacandaga to stop in Northville and see Caitlin and Nick before coming home." Liz giggled. "I'm sure Cait will understand that I'm exhausted and just want to get home to be with you and Dad." She listened to her mother as she slid her sweat drenched body out of the cab, locked and slammed the door shut. "Thanks for understanding. Yes, Mom. I'll be careful. And Mom— thanks for letting me crash with you and Dad."

Liz slipped her phone into her moist pocket of her shorts. Her feet slipped in her sandals as she walked on the hot asphalt to the concrete sidewalk. Her tank top was cemented to her body, causing many people to pause and look at her as she hastened her step towards the building. The blast of cold air took her breath away as she opened the door and stepped into the building. She immediately noticed the locations of the ladies' rest room and the water fountain from which she took a long, slow sip. The cold wetness in her throat did wonders to begin rejuvenating her body. A visit to the ladies' room and a cold bottle of liquid for later and Liz was back outside to complete her journey.

Melissa Callison, mother of four adult daughters and an adult son, slid her cell phone into the front pocket of her cutoff jeans. Through the years she had prided herself on having a special relationship with each of her children. She knew how to interpret mannerisms, facial expressions, tone of voice, and their individual temperament. While Melissa had not seen Elizabeth during their conversations spanning the past few weeks, she instinctively knew that something was off kilter with Liz. At the time she had shrugged it off as Liz being her dramatic self. Mel sighed as she reflected on the conversation that had just ended. Something was distressing Liz and now Melissa had that vibe, or, instinct that only a mother possesses on full alert.

"Goodness, Mellie," Jim Callison said as he walked towards her with the ease of a physically fit sixty-four-year-old man. Her husband of nearing thirty-five years with his black, graying hair, chiseled facial features, accentuating his Mohawk heritage, love of Melissa's life and her best friend knew her well. Sometimes too well. "That was a heavy sigh! Has laundry detail gotten you down?"

Melissa smiled weakly, as she glanced over at Jim and took the clothes pin, he was holding for her. "Thank you." She sighed as she hung his tee shirt. "This laundry is the least of my worries."

Their eyes met.

"Oh boy! I know that look and tone. Which one of our children has you concerned? Or, do I not want to know?" Jim lovingly and intently gazed into her eyes. He noticed the moisture on her eyelashes. This was not her normal concern. "Mellie, tell me. What is troubling you?"

Melissa took the next clothespin Jim held out to her. "Thank you. Liz called a few minutes ago."

"Lizzie! Is she still coming home?"

"Oh yes! She called to tell us that she has stopped at the rest area south of Saratoga."

"Saratoga?"

"Yes, she's coming over Route 29 to Route 30 and taking the back-way home. But, that's not what is troubling me."

"Oh boy!" Jim sighed.

"You can say that again! But, please don't." Melissa released a breath filled with concern. "I heard something strange in her voice and now I'm worried. Jim, why do you suppose she thanked me for our allowing her to come home?"

"Allowing her to come home? Mel, that makes no sense. Elizabeth knows perfectly well that she along with the rest of our children are welcome to come and visit with us whenever they like."

"I agree. And that is why I'm so concerned. Jim, something is distressing her and we both know that with Elizabeth Jeanne, anything is possible!"

Jim had a dark, ominous feeling creeping over him. He instinctively knew that Melissa was right. With Elizabeth, anything was possible! Jim carefully removed the clothespin from Melissa's fingers and dropped it into the bucket on the picnic table. Then he protectively drew her into his arms, as if to shield her from whatever life—or Elizabeth, was going to throw at them.

Back in the moving van and on her way north, Liz discovered that there was more air moving in the cab. She noticed that the trees along the highway were swaying as the breeze passed through them. Ah, relief! Besides the slight change in temperature, traffic was beginning to thin out the further north she went. Liz smiled and drew in a deep breath as she thought about summer in the Adirondacks and thoroughbred racing at Saratoga Race Track. Memories of days gone by pleasantly sprung to mind. As the second child in the Callison family, Elizabeth is fourteen months younger than her sister Caitlin. Growing up the two of them had been inseparable. They hardly ever squabbled and were known as *two peas in a pod*. Liz realized that her smile had grown and she was laughing as memories bubbled from within her weary soul, as she thought of the life they had shared in and outside of their family. Sports and competition reigned in her family, especially since her dad had been co-captain of the Great Sacandaga High School Varsity Hockey team, captain of the Lacrosse team and excelled in other sports and academics. Of course, Liz ran track and played slow pitch softball with Caitlin. She smiled as she thought of how they were great teammates always encouraging and practicing together. Then Liz sighed. "Goodness Caitlin and I had fun! Too bad our younger sisters didn't follow in our footsteps!" She grew silent as she watched the scenery change. Another sign for Saratoga. She felt something weird happen in her chest. Too many emotions to name. So, Liz allowed her thoughts to return to good memories of her life with Caitlin. Among those memories were the times they had double dated with their boyfriends. One date had been a daytime adventure when they went to the racetrack. Liz giggled as she recalled how important they had felt as they placed their very small bet on a horse that was sure to win and promptly lost. It came in last. Then, there were the concerts at Saratoga Performing Arts Center. They thought it was grand to save all their hard-earned money from their summer jobs, buy lawn tickets and sit with their boyfriends on the grass under the refreshing Adirondack night sky, while listening to their favorite musicians play their music.

While Liz and Cait were usually having fun together, there were times when life seemed very unfair, especially when one or more of their younger siblings was involved. Liz made a growling sound deep in her throat as her smile turned to a frown. Memories of complaining to her parents of multiple injustices in her family sprung to mind. She recalled how her mother would always respond with words of wisdom and a hug. A storm was brewing inside of Liz as she continued to reflect on her family, past and present. The thought of her mother, whom she had spoken to a few minutes ago, should have made Liz smile as in her past. It didn't! Life, just like when she was younger had moments when it simply was unfair, or, so it seemed. Liz released a long, heavy breath that she did not realize she had been holding. Perhaps it was a mistake to go home. Maybe she should have relocated south to be near her Aunt Amanda. She sighed. This close to home with her parent's expecting her arrival it was too late to change her plans.

Jim was glancing through the mail he was carrying as he walked up the driveway towards the house. He heard the sound of a large vehicle coming down the normally quiet country road and paused to watch whomever was passing by his home. Much to his surprise the moving van with a car in tow slowed down. The right front directional indicated that the driver intended to pull into the yard. His eyes grew larger as the hairs stood up on the back of his neck. "Mellie! Mellie, come quick!" Jim's voice boomed with excitement and concern.

Melissa, still dressed in her work clothes, a ratty old tee shirt, well-worn cut off shorts, and old sneakers appeared through the front door and onto the front porch. "Jim, whatever is it?" Mel asked as her left hand unknowingly found its way to her cheek while she bound down the steps and exclaimed, "Elizabeth!" At age sixty-four Mel was as physically fit as Jim and sprinted to his side before Liz brought the van to a stop.

"Well, Mel, it looks like you were right." Jim sighed. "Something is definitely going on with Liz, and by the looks of it she plans to stay for a while."

"Never a dull moment for us."

Melissa sighed, as they walked hand in hand to the driver's side of the van. Liz opened the door and slid onto the ground with a moan. They took one look at her sweat soaked clothes, hair falling out of her ponytail and sunglasses hiding her eyes. But the dead give-away that Elizabeth was in pain was in the way she carried herself, and her unconvincing smile.

"Oh, Jim, this is bad!"

"I see it too, Mellie. At least she's home and safe here with us. Together we'll help her through this crisis." With that said Jim opened his arms. "Elizabeth Jeanne, you are a welcome sight for this old man. Come here so I may give you a hug and get out of whatever the next job is that your mother has planned for me to do around here!"

Elizabeth sniffled and fought to hold back her tears flood gates to no avail. "Oh, Dad." She choked out. Tears streamed down her cheeks as she stepped into her father's embrace.

Jim and Melissa made eye contact silently conveying their concern, as Jim held his weeping child against his chest.

"Lizzie J, you are safe. I love you and won't let anything happen to you."

More tears fell from Elizabeth's flooded eyelids. She fought to regain her composure. "I love you too, Dad." She quietly breathed out while she hung on to her father. A moment later she turned from his embrace to her mother, who stood patiently waiting for her turn to welcome Liz. "Mom," was all Liz managed to say, before another round of tears slid down her cheeks and she stepped into her mother's open arms.

Melissa stood by the kitchen sink looked out of the window and watched Liz walking on the path leading into the woods behind their home. A few years ago, she stood at the same window and watched her niece, Summer Newman North, with her own set of troubles, take that same pathway into the woods. This time around Melissa felt different emotions as she watched her child, who appeared to have the weight of the world on her shoulders disappear into the woods. Elizabeth had been home for two hours and had not said a word about the reason for her return. Mel knew that in time, Elizabeth's time, she would tell them what she was holding deep inside her tattered heart. The sound of the garage door opening and closing did not draw Mel's focus from outside the window. She heard the familiar footsteps, and then felt Jim slide his arm around her waist. She leaned her head on his shoulder as she released a heavy sigh.

"Our children have no idea how blessed they are to have you for their mother." Jim kept his voice quiet as he continued to speak. "I moved my pickup out of the garage and moved some stuff around to make more space for Elizabeth's belongings. Since she is not in here with you, and you're staring out the window-"

"She's gone into the woods." Mel completed Jim's sentence as they often did with each other.

"Well, perhaps I should take a walk, find Elizabeth and see if she is ready to talk."

Melissa turned in Jim's arms to look into his eyes as she spoke. "Jim, I think it might be too soon."

"Mel, I understand that you are concerned, and I know how risky it is to push Lizzie before she is ready to talk."

"I hear a 'but' at the end of your sentence."

He chuckled while he gently caressed tight muscles in her lower back. "You know me too well. Sweetheart, we both know that Liz can't keep running from whatever has caused her to come home. Plus, we have to unload the van so, that it is ready for us to take it over to Gloversville to the moving company tomorrow morning."

"You have a point." Melissa stepped away from him, opened the refrigerator door and took out two bottles of water. "I suggest that you go armed with refreshments. You can tell her that I sent you with water to re-hydrate her after the hot ride north."

Jim shook his head, as his special smile reserved only for Mel found its way to his lips. "Wise woman. What would I do without you?"

"You'd be lost."

"That's for sure! I love you sweetheart, and I promise you that we will get through this situation with Liz like we always do with any family crisis."

"I love you too, Jim." She returned her own special smile that was his for the taking. "Oh, I do hate to see our children hurting!"

"Me too!" Jim gently brushed his lips over her jaw towards her lips. He tasted her sweetness, and smelled her special scent mingled with the lavender soap she had bathed with that morning. His lips made their descent to her lips. Then he sighed with reluctance as he pulled away from her, his wife, his lover and best friend.

Jim drew upon his Mohawk heritage from his mother's lineage as he walked deeper into the woods. A smile took shape on his lips as he noticed where Elizabeth had disturbed the ground as she walked along the path. He paused and listened to the sounds of nature. He noticed that a squirrel made its way along the branches from one tree to another, while a blue jay flew from one white pine tree to another as it announced Jim's presence to the woodland creatures. The sound of water tumbling over the rounded rocks on the bottom of the creek bed drew his attention, and at that moment, Jim knew where to go to look for Elizabeth.

She sat with her back to him and had not heard him approaching her. Jim stood very still while he surveyed the scene in front of him. His child was in pain. She was a victim, but, a victim of what? Jim felt his paternal need to protect rising in him, like someone submerging themselves into the water with all their might to save an injured drowning soul. But this was Elizabeth and a simple rescue would not happen with her. Yes indeed, time had taught him and Mel to tread lightly when she was injured. Without a sound Jim eased down next to her onto the pine needle blanketed ground. Neither one acknowledged the other. Instead of being upset by this, Jim simply handed her a bottle of water, then opened his bottle and took a long sip. Silence hung between them like a thick cumulus cloud. Then, like a whisper in the wind Jim spoke. "Lizzie, do you remember the time when you found the injured baby blue jay that had fallen from its nest?"

Elizabeth lowered the bottle of water from her lips and nodded. Her voice was also quiet. "Yes, it had a broken wing and I was certain that it would die."

"That's right and what did I do?"

"You helped me take care of the bird until it was healed and able to fly away."

"That's right, Elizabeth. I helped you. Today, ever since you got out of the moving van and clung to your mother and me, I've been thinking of you and that bird we rescued." He saw the confusion in her eyes, as she looked up at him. "Lizzie, it is obvious to your mother and me that you are deeply wounded. Whatever is going on in your life has caused you to feel broken inside. Now that you are home and once again in our nest, it is time for your broken spirit to heal, and in time you will soar higher than before."

"Do you really think so?"

Jim smiled as he studied his daughter's taunt features. "Oh yes, Lizzie. You know of our heritage, our faith, our spirituality passed down to us from your great grandmother, Gentle Spirit. I believe if she was here with us, she would tell you that the Great Spirit is watching over you and led you home for an important reason beyond your present pain."

"But my pain is my reason for being here." She sighed and turned her gaze towards the water.

"Liz sometimes when things in life bring you down it is difficult to see beyond the immediate situation. It is hard to even imagine that there is a bright future somewhere out there." He eased his arm around her shoulder and drew her close to him. "As tough as this is for you, your mother and I want you to remember that you are no longer alone in this situation. Rest in our family nest and allow yourself to be healed. Listen for God—the Great Spirit—to speak to you, to guide you on into the future. Then, when you are ready, take off and soar higher than you ever imagined possible."

By the time Elizabeth and Jim reached the edge of the woods, they heard the sound of children's voices in the back yard. Liz began to giggle as she listened. She glanced up at her father and noticed that his eyes seemed to be smiling, as he too listened to the commotion and the voice of authority that followed.

"Alright, you two. Stop! Nobody moves."

Liz and Jim remained quiet, as they stood together in the woods with a full view of the drama that was unfolding in the back yard.

"Now both of you listen to me and you listen really good. You both know that pushing and hitting each other is unacceptable behavior, and for that the two of you will sit for ten minutes in time out, and I expect you to think about what you've done. We are here to welcome your Aunt Liz's return to home. But, if you two insist on continuing to misbehave, we will go home. Callie Anne, you will go sit on the bench by the bird feeders to think about your actions. Nicholas Joshua Junior, you put your bottom in the chair by Grandma's flower garden. No back talk, or whining young man. Now go take your seats."

Remaining out of sight, they watched the children follow their mother's instructions with pouts and glowers at each other. "Goodness, Dad, Cait sure did sound like Mom!"

"I heard that!"

"Unbelievable! Your hearing is still as good as when we were kids!" Elizabeth burst into laughter as she stepped into the back yard. Then, she took off running towards Caitlin, who in turn ran to greet her. Their embrace, laughter, talking over each other, and genuine affection for each other caused Jim to smile. His grandchildren might be unhappy. But for right now, his two oldest girls had no problems between them. His smile continued to grow as he decided that his girls are as they always were: special. He raised his eyes towards the heavens, and breathed out a prayer of thanksgiving as he stepped towards his family.

Liz lost count of the kisses and hugs that she received from her niece and nephew, or hugs from Caitlin for that matter, during the rest of the afternoon and early evening. Exhausted from the long drive, unloading the van with Cait and Nick's help, and a full stomach from the impromptu family barbecue, Liz lounged in the well-worn wooden Adirondack chair with her legs resting on the stool. She drew in a deep breath as she watched her father throw a slow pitch softball to six-year-old Nicholas. He squealed with delight as his father Nick Sr. cheered him on to run fast to first base. Ten-year-old Callie Anne caught the ball her grandfather tossed to her and promptly tagged her brother out. An all-out feud ensued between the next generation of Callison siblings. There were tears, shouting, teasing, pushing and shoving. Liz watched her father and brother in law address the situation, while her mind slipped back to her days of youth with her siblings. Some things never change. More tears fell from Nick's eyes as he whaled in misery. At that moment, Caitlin rose from the chair and stepped in to assist with her unhappy children. Liz watched Caitlin quietly speak to both of them, she hugged and kissed them before sending them off to put the baseball equipment away and find another game to play.

"Sorry about that." Caitlin said as she plopped down into the chair next to Liz. "They don't usually misbehave like that, at least when we're here with Mom and Dad."

"You don't need to explain or apologize to me, Cait. They're kids just like we were a long time ago, or have you forgotten?" Liz softly smiled. "But then you and I never had a reason to fight, did we?"

Caitlin returned a smile while she studied her sister. She saw something in Liz's eyes that said that while she may appear to be happy, she wasn't. Her free-spirited, successful cosmopolitan sister was in pain. "Mom and Dad sure are happy to have you here." Cait said with gentleness that implied that she felt the same way. Liz made a sound that Caitlin hoped was in agreement with her. "I was warned to not push you to talk about why you are back home."

Liz exhaled. "Let me guess, Mom."

"Of course! We both know that she will never stop being Mom, and caring about us even when we might not want or need her to meddle in our lives."

"She's not meddling." Liz felt the tears pooling in her eyes and fought to reign them in, to no avail.

"Oh, Lizzie! I thought Mom and Dad were blowing your visit out of proportion. But, having seen all of your possessions that you have stored in the garage, and now you're unsuccessfully fighting to hold back your tears. This is serious! What can I do to help you?"

Elizabeth sniffled and quietly asked, "Do you have a tissue?"

"Of course! I'm a mother and an elementary school teacher. I come prepared for moments like this."

"Thanks. I need you to take a walk with me so that we can talk like we used to."

Without another word, they stood and informed their family where they were going, *alone.* Needless to say, there were two little ones who were not too pleased to be left out of their Mom and aunt's adventure. That is, until their grandfather happened to mention ice cream.

CHAPTER 2

Elizabeth moaned as she yanked the pillow over her head to block out the noise coming in from outside of her open bedroom window. Life in the country was supposed to be quiet and peaceful. She groaned as she threw the pillow across the bed. Many things in her life were supposed to be, but weren't. Liz sat up, wiped the sleep from her eyes, and stretched. Then, she glanced at the clock on the bedside table. Eight o'clock. "Oh, good grief!" She exclaimed. "Really?" She asked as she looked towards the window. "Why couldn't you birds wait to begin your singing or fighting until after I was up?" Silence. "Sure, now that I'm awake, you grow quiet. Go figure!" Liz huffed, as she slid her bare feet onto the carpeted floor. She wiggled her toes in the plush fibers and found a smile, as she fondly thought of Caitlin and her childhood when they shared that same room. The posters that decorated the walls had long since been removed, and a light shade of green paint covered their high school colors of purple and gray. A phonograph, a stack vinyl's, a cassette player and tapes had at one time had their special place alongside of the radio on a stand near the bedroom door. Liz smiled, as she looked at her phone and earbuds knowing that she didn't have to worry about either of her parents yelling for her to turn down her music. Time certainly had slipped into the future, and Liz did not feel as if she was flying like an eagle, or, the blue jay her father had reminded her about. She sighed, as she opened the dresser drawer that held her clothes once again. Since Liz was home with no one in particular to impress, she chose to dress for the day in a comfortable old pair of cutoffs, and a faded tee shirt from a vacation at Martha's Vineyard. She pulled her chestnut brown hair into a ponytail and headed downstairs. Her bare feet padded along the cool hardwood stairs, as she made her descent to the kitchen.

"Good morning." She smiled as her parents paused in their conversation and greeted her in return. Looking at them sitting in their chairs at the table made Liz feel as if she was stepping back in time. Yet, she wasn't. She saw the subtle and not so subtle physical changes in them.

"This morning, your father had fried eggs and toast for breakfast. What would you like for me to make you for breakfast?"

"Coffee is fine for now, Mom. I'll make toast or something in a little while."

She poured coffee into the mug sitting on the counter next to the drip coffee maker. Her dad had given Mom the coffee maker many years ago for Christmas. Not too romantic in Elizabeth's eyes, then, or now. But her mom had been thrilled.

"Lizzie girl, you know your mother is not going to be happy until she gets to fuss over you and make you something to eat this morning."

Her gaze passed between her parent's and at that moment, it hit her that their fussing over her felt really good. She sighed, as a smile grew upon her lips. "You're right, Dad. Mom, I'd love to have an egg."

Liz leaned against the counter where she watched her mother rise, and effortlessly prepared the egg just as Liz liked it. Plus, Melissa made two pieces of toast and lightly spread each piece with honey.

"Oh. Mom! You remember honey toast is my favorite."

"Of course, I remember what you like and don't like to eat. I bet peas continue to be at the top of your list of least favorite vegetable." Melissa's love shone in her eyes, as she watched her child process her words.

"Okay, this is scary." Liz looked at her mother with surprise, as she continued saying, "You remember way too much!"

Jim laughed, and made a comment that caused the three of them to comment and further laugh about shared family memories.

Liz took a sip of coffee, swallowed and said, "So fill me in on everything that is new here in our hometown."

Melissa settled back in her chair and began to share the local news. "And Stephen Johnson has a girlfriend."

Liz nearly choked on the coffee that she was swallowing. Then, she managed to exclaim, "A girlfriend!"

"That's right, Johnson's got a girlfriend." Jim said with a touch of disbelief in his voice.

"So, what's she like?" Liz asked, as her gaze passed between her parents.

"We have only met her once and you know that first impressions may not be totally accurate."

Liz saw something in her father's eyes and heard something in his voice, that sparked her curiosity in the mystery woman in Stephen Johnson's life. "Does Aunt Amanda know about this new woman in his life?"

Jim was taking a sip of coffee, as Liz asked her question about Amanda having knowledge of the new development in their friend's life. He coughed, as his coffee went down the wrong way, breathed in a deep breath and shook his head. "We haven't told her, so unless Johnson has told Summer and she called her mother, or Becky or Phil have been in conversation with Amanda, she doesn't know yet."

Liz sat quietly, looking at her parent's over the coffee mug as she took a sip. She swallowed and then burst into laughter. Tears began to stream down her cheeks as she fought to regain her composure.

"Elizabeth, whatever struck you as funny?" Her mother asked.

Liz wiped her eyes and drew in a breath. "Our family. The Johnson family. Think about it. Our hometown is filled with a colorful cast of leading and supporting characters. This place is like a soap opera, or perhaps a prime-time drama. Oh goodness. Oh, and our hometown story would need a catchy name. Something like Adirondack Sunrise. No…perhaps, Sacandaga Sunrise. Oh, my goodness!" Liz's eyes sparkled with excitement as she spoke. "Honestly, is it any wonder that having grown up in this environment, that I wouldn't choose to work in the theater? Oh my gosh!" Liz pushed back her chair, stood, picked up her plate and mug and took them over to the sink. "Dad, you were right! I do need to be here. No. My reason for coming home hasn't been resolved, but I have an idea and I am going to start working on it."

Before Jim could respond, Liz seemed to float from the kitchen through the door into the hall. Jim and Mel were stunned, unable to speak for a moment. Then, Melissa found her voice. "You know, Liz may be on to something about our town. My goodness, what must vacationers think when they encounter us?"

"That's a good question. Outsiders perception is one thing. But, in less than seventy-two hours after her return home, our daughter has given us an unbelievably accurate description of our community."

Mel laughed. "Yes, she has. So, are you going to call your sister?"

The most ungodly sound emerged from Jim's throat. "Yeah. I had better before she finds out and calls me, then rips my head off for not calling her."

"Smart move, Callison."

"What's Dad doing?" Liz asked as she reappeared in the kitchen.

"He's going to call your Aunt Amanda, and tell her the latest news of our community, including Johnson and his new love life."

Liz burst into laughter, as she noticed the distressed look on her father's face. She was certain that their conversation would be an interesting one.

Jim had shared his plan with Melissa, then got into his pickup and headed up into the mountain to the cabin that had been his grandmother's, Mary Freeman—Gentle Spirit. The drive up the twisty road to the old cabin brought back a flood of memories. Gentle Spirit had been his and Amanda's cornerstone during their tumultuous lives, of youth and in recent years. He sighed, as he recalled her intervention in his and Amanda's lives in January of 2010. Thirty years of estrangement between the Callison siblings had come to an end, all because a wise, loving, gentle woman had used her authority and guided them to reconciliation. Moisture began to find its way into Jim's eyes as the cabin came into view and more memories took shape in his mind. He knew, as he pulled his pickup to a stop near the porch of the cabin, that he needed the solace of his grandmother's cabin that he co-owned with Amanda when he placed his call. He climbed the steps, drew out his key, placed it in the keyhole and unlocked the door. Jim stepped inside and made a quick check of the rooms to make sure nothing was out of order. Satisfied, he returned to the porch and sat down on the well-worn glider.

"Well, good morning, Jim. This is an unexpected and pleasant surprise! How are you? Tell me what's going on to make you call me on a Tuesday morning."

Jim chuckled at the sound of Amanda's voice. He could imagine her animated expressions as she spoke. Her smile. Her hint of mischievousness in her warm brown eyes.

"Good morning, Sis." Jim sighed.

"Oh boy, a chuckle and a sigh right off the bat! Am I going to become defensive and rip into you?"

"Gee, I hope not. But I do need to tell you about something that is happening up here because it indirectly affects you."

"I see." Momentary silence was followed by her softly spoken question. "Your news wouldn't by any chance have to do with Stephen Johnson and his girlfriend, would it?"

"You know!" Jim exclaimed, and then released a loud sigh of relief.

Amanda laughed, as she imagined his expression. "Yes, I have known for a while thanks to my daughter enlightening me about her father's new love life."

"So, Johnson told Summer. Good. And I'm glad that she told you. I am wondering, since you haven't called me ranting and raving about Stephen and his girlfriend, are you okay with this?"

"Oh, Jim, first Summer was concerned about me and now you. Thank you, and yes, I am okay with Johnson finding someone to love and care about. It's well past the time for him to find happiness like the rest of us. Don't you think?" She laughed at Jim's response. "From what Summer told me her dad is getting serious, and this fall when he goes to visit her and Adam, he plans to bring his girlfriend out to Denver with him."

"Jeez, Sis, I'm glad I called you to find out what is happening up here with our family and friend."

"Glad I could help. You also should know that Summer isn't the only one who has contacted me."

Jim listened as Amanda regaled him with her account of Becky Jones—Stephen's younger sister— phone call about Johnson's new love life. "Jim, I wish everyone would stop worrying about me when it comes to Johnson. He was the love of my youth and early adulthood. My romantic love for Johnson died over thirty years ago. Unfortunately, like an annoying mosquito he is back in my life. But we also know that I am happily married to Kevin, who thankfully is the polar opposite of Johnson." Jim laughed and commented. Amanda sighed. "I guess it is kind of funny when you look at the differences in the men, I've chosen to have serious relationships with. At any rate, my past intersects with my present and my future, and it is a part of my life under my conditions. So, unless you have some earth-shattering news to share about him, let's move on to something more pleasant. How's Elizabeth?"

"Why ask me? You two talk all the time. In fact, you know why she came home. But for whatever reason she still doesn't feel as though she may trust her mother and me to share her burden with us."

Amanda sighed. "I hear the hurt in your voice, and I'm sorry that Liz is continuing to keep you and Mel in the dark about what happened to her. Jim, as much as I love you and Mel, and cherish our reconciliation," she sighed. "I will not break Elizabeth's trust."

"My faithful sister." It was Jim's turn to sigh. "Mandy, I do hear what you are saying. Even though it frustrates Mel and me to not know what is going on with Liz, I'm glad she feels as though she can confide in you."

"Me too! Hey, I am going to need to end our conversation for now and get back to work. Oh, before I forget, Kevin and I changed our summer plans. We are coming north and we will be staying up at the cabin for the week of the fourth of July instead of the last two weeks of July."

They said goodbye. Jim clicked off his phone, clipped it to his belt, and pushed the glider into a lazy slow motion. It creaked from age as it moved back and forth, and Jim allowed his mind to wander down memory lane. He felt the gentle early summer breeze against his bare arms and face. A smile brushed his lips. It was as if he wasn't alone, as if his ancestors were with him in that moment in time, Gentle Spirit and Mom. Jim sighed in contentment. He breathed in his surroundings, then slowed the glider to a stop, stood and made his way from the porch to his pickup.

"Aunt Lizzie, Aunt Lizzie!" Callie Anne burst into her grandparent's home, and began her search for her aunt. "Aunt Lizzie!"

"Callie Anne, where are your manners?" Caitlin sighed as her daughter ignored her and disappeared through the living room and into the kitchen. Cait could hear her mother greeting Callie Anne. She sighed again as she came into the Kitchen and watched her mother quietly speak with Callie. Cait was grateful that her mom was used to rambunctious children such as hers.

"Now, Caitlin," Melissa smiled knowingly at her daughter as she spoke. "You and I both know that this child is excited about her aunt being here. We also know that there was a time, or two, during your youth when you were equally loud and excited. So, take a deep breath and relax."

"Noted." Caitlin sighed and eased into a hug. "Oh, Mom, my two kids wear me out! How did you ever survive the five of us?"

Melissa hugged Caitlin then glanced out the window, and saw Callie chatting with Elizabeth, as she hung her laundry on the line to dry. "I will admit there were plenty of times when you kids tried my patience. But, after the storm passed over our family and your father and I were able to step back and reflect on what had happened, we knew that our love for each other and for each of you was what held us together." She softly smiled at her daughter and spoke with a tender voice. "Caitlin, you and Nick are terrific parents to your beautiful children. I have a secret to share with you." She saw Cait's expression momentarily change from mother to child as she had hoped. "Just because you are married with your own family doesn't mean that your father and I have stopped being concerned about you and your family. You, are my eldest child whom I will always love."

Caitlin smiled. "Thanks, Mom. I guess I needed that reminder that if you could survive us, I can survive my two!" She glanced out the window at her daughter and sister. "I think I had better go save Lizzie from Callie."

"Child, you worry too much!" Melissa laughed, as she watched her daughter and granddaughter fall to the ground and tickle each other. "It's good to see Liz able to play. Let's go join in the fun!"

Cait burst into laughter, as she listened to her mother's idea and headed outside with her. Sure enough, Mom raised her voice with feigned concern for Callie, who was laying on the ground laughing. "Elizabeth Jeanne, stop picking on that child!"

Liz immediately stopped tickling Callie. "Now wait a minute!" She exclaimed, as she hurriedly got to her feet. Caitlin was still laughing as she looked at her sister. Pieces of Liz's hair had come out of her ponytail, her shirt was no longer tucked in the waist of her shorts, and her forehead shone with sweat. "I was minding my own business hanging my clothes to dry when I was attacked by the tickle monster. So of course, I had to defend myself." She teased as her eyes sparkled with playfulness.

"Tickle monster?" Melissa fought back a smile.

"Yes, Mom. Didn't you and Cait see it sneak up and eat Callie while she was on her way out here to see me?"

"Oh dear, not the tickle monster! Lizzie, this is terrible! I thought we had slain that monster when we were teens. To think it has returned—oh goodness!" Caitlin chimed in, as she winked at her sister.

"Yeah! I thought the bugger was dead too! But no! It ate Callie in one gulp!"

"Oh Liz, we need to do something to rescue Callie before it's too late and we can't get her out of the monster."

Melissa watched Callie, as she listened to her mother and aunt. Then her daughters stepped away to whisper in a new conspiracy. Mel softly smiled as she noticed that Callie was having difficulty being temporarily left out. That is, until her mother informed everyone that it was time for the Callison females only outing on the lake on that beautiful summer afternoon. This was a special moment for all of them, one they would look back on and treasure as the years passed on from one to the next.

"Mom, why not text Dad so he knows what is happening and come along with us? It will be fun!"

"Oh, I don't know—oh, why not? Cait, you had best let Nick know where you and Callie will be. Liz, perhaps you'd be kind and grab waters out of the refrigerator and some fruit for us to take with us as a snack. I'll get my purse and lift the garage door so we can get the canoe out."

Liz could not believe it! It had been over ten years since she had been canoeing on the Great Sacandaga Lake, and even longer since she had been out there with her mother and sister. Now she was going to share the experience with her niece as well. Liz felt a strange wave of emotions, as she watched her mother slow down and pull her SUV with the canoe strapped on top into the parking lot of the J and J—Stephen Johnson and Wesley Jones—Bait and Tackle Shop. They would use their boat launch to access the lake and leave their vehicle in the parking lot for safe keeping. Melissa backed down to the boat launch, stopped and engaged the emergency break. They all got out and began unstrapping the canoe when a familiar voice was heard.

"Hey there Mrs. C! Do you need some help?"

"Hello, Peter. We'd love to have some help." Melissa addressed Wesley Jones' son, who also happened to be her son, James Junior's best friend.

Peter? Liz stepped around the SUV, so that she could clearly see who her mother was speaking to. Sure enough. The name matched the voice she had recognized. "Peter Skeeter!" Liz exclaimed, as she moved towards him.

"Izzie Lizzie!" Peter exclaimed, using the childhood nickname that he and James Junior had given her. "What are you doing here? I thought you were in New York City?" His smile grew as he stepped closer and drew her into a hug. Liz smiled in return, and thought that she felt her heart do a flip flop, as she began to answer his questions. She was so surprised and happy to see Peter that she forgot that she was supposed to be helping with the canoe. That is, until Callie Anne informed her aunt that there was work to be done.

"Oh, here, Mrs. C. Let me help for you." Peter said, as he went to the back of the vehicle to assist with sliding the canoe to the ground.

"That's alright, Peter. We've done this plenty of times before. However, I'd be forever in your debt, if you would help us get the canoe into the water, so we don't drag it and damage the bottom."

Peter assisted the women into the canoe, then gave them a shove off and watched them joyously move the vessel through the water. One woman in particular held his attention: Elizabeth. Nine years her junior, Peter had been in love with Liz when he had played with JJ at their house. She had made him feel welcome and, in many ways, treated him like another little brother. But then, there were other times when she would smile at him, talk with him and make his tender heart do a flip-flop. He thought she was beautiful. From her long brown hair, brown eyes that sometimes seemed to spit fire at JJ, or indicate she was happy, to her long, powerful legs that moved her around the track with elegant grace. Liz reminded him of the wind moving effortlessly from one place to another. She had a sense of humor that always made him laugh and a smile that could melt the ice on the lake in mid-winter. His childhood crush had secretly remained intact throughout his youth. Now Liz was back. They were both adults, and from the looks of Liz's empty significant finger, she hadn't returned home with any restrictions. Peter decided that his summer in the Great Sacandaga Community was looking up. Perhaps, it was time to see if, there might be room for him in Elizabeth Callison's life?

CHAPTER 3

Jim paused from loosening the soil by the tender plants in Melissa's small vegetable garden. It was too soon to work the ground with the hoe to oust the pesky weeds. So, he knelt on the ground and gently worked the unwanted plants from the ground. He took his cloth handkerchief from his back pocket, wiped the sweat from his brow, returned the damp cloth to his pocket and looked around the garden.

After years of talking and planning, Jim finally had taken the time and had made the garden for her in the south side of the back yard where the sun shone for the majority of the day. He heard their voices before he saw Melissa and Elizabeth returning from their walk in the woods and smiled when they came into view. Liz had been home for three weeks. She still had not said a word to him, or Mel about why she had come home. But Jim saw a difference in her. He had to wonder if perhaps her being reacquainted with Peter Jones, when his women had gone canoeing on the lake, had anything to do with it. Time would only tell.

"How was your walk?" He asked as Mel handed him her partially drank bottle of water. Jim brushed her fingers as he took the bottle from her. Their eyes silently conveyed their love for each other, while Jim gave Mel his quirky smile that had melted her heart many years ago.

"Very nice." Mel replied, as Jim took a sip of water. "The creek is getting low. I hope we get some rain before too long."

"Yeah, we do need rain." He looked down at the garden. "If this dry spell continues, I'll have to get out the hose and water our plants."

Elizabeth listened to her parents converse, as she knelt down and inspected the leaves and blossoms on the stems of the peas. Her eyes lit up with delight, as she gently separated the thick leaves. "Hey, Dad, did you see the blossoms that are hidden under the leaves?"

"Yeah, I noticed." Jim knelt down next to Liz and looked at the blossoms she had discovered. "As long as we keep up with the weeds and get plenty of water on our plants, we should have a decent crop of vegetables. Hmm." A smile formed on his lips. He laughed.

"Oh boy! I know that look and tone of voice." She laughed. "I guess I'll be picking vegetables this summer to earn my keep."

"And anything else your mother and I might need for you to do to help us." He smiled and winked at her.

Liz saw the pride in her father's eyes as he pointed and glanced around his small garden that was barely sprouting through the ground. But, at that moment, she realized something important. In all of his years of working on the state police force, he had never had the time to do something that he obviously enjoys.

"Great! Why do I feel as though I've slipped into a time warp and never left home?"

"We'll pick the fruits of your dad's labors together," Mel commented as her cell phone rang. "Hello. Jordan! My goodness, this is a pleasant surprise!" Mel's smile immediately was replaced with worry. Jim felt the hair rise on his neck as he watched and listened to Mel, as she spoke into her phone. "Oh no! Jordan, of course you may come home. By all means. The sooner the better."

Elizabeth watched her parent's silent interaction, and knew in her gut that whatever her youngest sister Jordan was saying, it wasn't good. She felt her stomach plummet to her toes, and slipped away to consider what the call would mean for her.

Showered and in clean clothes, Liz was ready to head out and explore more of the community and local towns. When she got to the bottom of the stairs, she heard her father's voice. "First Lizzie and now Jordan. What do you suppose is going on with our girls? Why won't they tell us what's wrong?"

Liz swallowed a copious amount of spit that had formed in her mouth. Then she sighed and thought, *if they knew what was going on in both Jordan's and my lives they would be crushed. Maybe Jordan won't stay too long and maybe, if things get too uncomfortable, I can go stay with Aunt Amanda and Uncle Kevin for the holiday weekend.* Liz sighed again and plastered a smile on her face just before she walked through the doorway.

"Oh good, you're right on time." Her mother said with a smile. "Lunch is ready."

Liz looked at the three place settings, her father already in his seat and her mother with a bowl of tossed salad in her hands. It was obvious that they expected her to eat with them. "Gee, Mom, I um-" Liz sighed.

"Say no more." Mel said. "I know that look. Shall we plan on you joining us for dinner?"

"As of right now, I should be back for dinner. I'll call you later to let you know what I decide."

Jim silently watched the interaction between Liz and Mel. His daughter had been acting very suspiciously since Jordan's phone call. He had to wonder if something was amiss between them, and watched for her response when he said, "Jordan should be here by dinnertime. It would be nice for you to join us."

Liz drew in a breath to calm herself from snapping at her dad. "Like I said, Dad, I'll call." She drew her keys from her pocket and headed towards the door, paused and turned to face them. "On second thought, Mom, Dad, don't expect me to be home for dinner. Jordan obviously needs you both right now. Maybe even more than I do. I'll be back later on tonight."

Liz pulled her car into the bait shop parking lot, got out, locked the door and headed towards the shop door. She opened it, and heard the bell jingle announcing her arrival as she stepped into the coolness of the building. The well-lit space smelled of old wood, fish and coffee. Of course, coffee! She smiled to herself as she recalled being a young girl and going there with her father. More often than not, Dad would have a cup of coffee with his friends, share a laugh or two and talk about things that didn't interest her. While the men talked Liz would roam through the aisles of fishing gear, or stand by the window where she would look out at the lake and dream of her life that would take her far away from there.

She walked through the aisles glancing at the well-stocked shelves, as she carefully made her way towards the counter. When she got in sight of the counter, she paused and waited for Wesley to complete his business with the customers. He surprised her when he said to the patrons, "Folks, this is your lucky day! We have a Broadway star in our midst."

"Why thank you, kind sir!" Liz smiled and responded. Without missing a step, she eased into the role of a queen, a drama queen. They all watched her in amazement. She wiped her brow with exaggeration, as her improvisation drew to an end. "But my final curtain came down and now, alas, I've retreated to the mountains to renew my strength. Hopefully with the dawn of a new sunrise I will find the strength, the courage to forge on and seek a new destiny."

The vacationers applauded and converged around her. Wes smiled as he watched her interact with the vacationers. She was patient as she answered their questions. Then she surprised him when she said, "I hope you were able to complete your transaction before I upstaged you all. This bait shop is a local landmark, and it is the best place to purchase your fishing gear and bait for fishing in the lake. Plus, not too long ago, my family and I used the boat ramp to take our canoe out on the lake. You might want to consider renting one of their canoes or row boats to go out on the water. It's a great relaxing way to enjoy the lake. At any rate, enjoy your stay." She glanced at Wes and smiled brightly. "I'm guessing Peter is working outside?"

Wes nodded and returned a smile. "He's helping Stephen down in the pavilion."

She gazed out at the lake as she walked down the path towards the bottom of the building. The gentle lapping of water against the shoreline of the lake was soothing to Liz's troubled spirit. She listened, heard two distinct male voices, and found Peter working with his uncle in the pavilion, exactly where Wes had said that she would find him. Planks of lumber and two by fours were neatly piled on the patio along with a hand and an electric saw, a screw gun, screws, a hammer and a container of various sized nails. The sound system blared classic country music from the speakers. Liz listened to Stephen singing along with Hank Williams. Of course, Peter was teasing him. Liz softly laughed when she heard Peter say, "You sound like an old crow. Caw, caw, caw! Don't give up your day job, Unc!" Peter laughed. Her smile grew as she listened to them. Liz recalled how the Johnson-Jones family had always shared something special between them. Today, was no exception. She also realized that she had forgotten that Stephen has a rich baritone voice, and that country was his favorite music to listen to. Liz sighed. It was nice that some things never changed around the old hometown.

"Hey, Lizzie." Peter called out as he stepped away from the rotted boards, they had just ripped off the southeast side of the pavilion and had thrown in the bed of Stephen's pickup. "Did you come to take me to lunch?"

She smiled at him. "Actually Pete, I was going to see if you could sneak away. But, from the looks of it, maybe lunch should wait and I should offer to help you guys instead? You know, I do have experience building sets. So, how hard could this be?" Her eyes twinkled with amusement, as she turned her gaze from Peter to his uncle. "Hey Stephen, what do you think? Could you use another set of hands?"

Johnson noticed Peter's reaction to her questions, and listened to their interaction before he spoke. "Elizabeth, you don't know how much I appreciate your offer to help me. At some point in time, I might take you up on your offer to help. Especially, if this bozo here doesn't do his part." He added, as he winked at her. Then, he glanced at his watch. "Pete, it is lunchtime. In case you didn't notice, we have a beautiful young woman in our midst. You'd be wise to take off for an hour and treat her to a nice lunch. Then, when you get back here you had better be ready to work your butt off."

"Sure thing, Unc." Peter's smile shone as bright as the sun. "Come on Lizzie, before he changes his mind!"

Stephen chuckled, as he remained standing on the patio by the pavilion door. He watched them walk up the slope towards the parking lot and thought about what had just transpired. "Ah to be young." He breathed out. "Then again, being my age and have someone special in my life isn't too bad either." With that Stephen took off his tool belt, placed it on the picnic table and walked inside the cool building to take a break.

It was after midnight when Liz pulled her car into her parent's yard. She parked next to the car that had not been there when she had left. Jordan had arrived! Great! Act two of the Callison drama was about to begin. Liz sighed as she walked towards the front door. She took in the scene around her, while preparing herself for what she might experience once she got inside. The outside light was on, as well as the light in the living room. Liz hoped that everyone had gone to bed. No such luck! She opened the door to find her father sitting in his recliner, and her mother sitting on the couch with her legs curled under her. Not the scene that she had hoped for!

"Hi." Liz smiled only to be greeted with her parent's serious expressions. Memories of her teen years swept over her. Mom and Dad were waiting for her to come home after curfew, except she wasn't a teen anymore, and she didn't have a curfew. She sighed. "I suppose there is a good reason why both of you waited up for me, even though I did call you and tell you that I was with Peter and that I would be late."

"Did you and Peter have a nice evening?"

"Yes, Mom, we did." She smiled. "He's matured into being a great guy." Liz studied their expressions and didn't know how to read them. "Is it a problem that I spent time with him? Or, that I was not here to welcome Jordan when she arrived?"

"Elizabeth, watch your tone with your mother." Jim quietly commanded, as he brought his legs from reclining position to sitting.

Liz had heard that tone of voice one time too many as a young girl, when he spoke to one of them who had crossed the line. She returned her attention to her mother as she spoke. "Sorry, Mom. I didn't mean to snap at you. If there is nothing pressing for us to discuss, I'd like to get to bed. I have plans for tomorrow and want to begin the day feeling refreshed."

"Spending more time with Peter?" Jim asked, as he placed the book that was on his lap on the table next to the chair.

"Not first thing in the morning, Dad." Liz really didn't like the way her dad was watching her, or his tone of voice. "In case you don't know, Aunt Amanda and Uncle Kevin got into town this evening." Her expression softened. "And my awesome aunt and uncle have invited me to hang out with them."

Jim raked his fingers through his hair, a sign that he was frustrated. He turned to Melissa and asked. "Did you know Sis and Kevin had planned to arrive tonight?"

"It's news to me as well." Melissa shrugged. "I thought that they were arriving on, or, after the fourth."

Liz saw the subtle movements of their eyes as they looked at each other. She had always hated it when they did that silent communicating of theirs.

"So, you spent the whole evening with them?" Mel asked.

"Well, part of it," she said with a touch of a defensive attitude, reminiscent of her days of youth. "Aunt Amanda and I spoke on the phone late this afternoon and she asked me for my help." Jim made a noise in his throat that caused Liz to glower at him. The tilt of her father's head and raising of his brow warned her to not venture any further down the silent path of opinions. "Dad, think what you want about Aunt Amanda. But I'd do anything for her." Liz sighed. Jim and Mel silently watched her. "After Peter and I had dinner at the Mayfield Diner, we stopped over to Tooley's to get a load of firewood. Then we delivered the load of firewood to Aunt Amanda and Uncle Kevin."

"I wonder why Sis didn't call me and ask me to bring up a load of wood?" Jim interjected. Liz paid him no attention as she continued on. Her eyes sparkled.

"I had asked her why she hadn't asked you. She said you seemed distracted and she didn't want to bother you. Oh my gosh! You should have been there!" She giggled at the memory. "Aunt Amanda and Uncle Kevin had arrived a few minutes before we got there." Liz giggled some more before continuing. "Aunt Amanda was still on a roll from drinking too much coffee, and had desperately needed the bathroom. We got there when she was having issues with getting her key into the lock and getting the door open. Uncle Kevin was not too much help for her with him cracking jokes about her bladder, coffee, and their journey north. Aunt Amanda was also laughing, which didn't help her situation.... Oh my gosh, they are funny!" She laughed at a memory while Mel and Jim exchanged more looks.

"My sister's funny alright." Jim's voice dripped with sarcasm.

"Wow! Aunt Amanda nailed it!" She saw her dad's brow arch once again.

"I gather she had something to say about your dad?" Liz noticed that her mother had that look that had always warned them as kids to tread lightly, or else.

"Well, yes, Mom. She said that dad would be cranky when you heard where I was, and that I had fun with them. I won't tell you what else she said." She giggled at the memory. "Oh, and Uncle Kevin's granddaughters are vacationing with them. Really nice twins. They're Callie's age, I think. At any rate, I'm tired and would like to turn in. So, unless there is something else that cannot wait until morning to be discussed, may I please be excused from this interrogation?"

Jim and Mel read her demeanor like a well- loved novel and bid her good night. However, they remained downstairs to further discuss their family issues, and what, if anything, they could do about them.

Liz awakened to the sound of her phone playing the overture to *West Side Story* and smiled, as she reached for her phone. "Good morning, Peter." She said with a sleepy voice.

"Good morning, Izzie. I hope I didn't wake you up?"

"You did, but it's okay. I should have been up a while ago." She yawned. "So, what's going on?"

"I wanted to let you know how much I enjoyed spending yesterday afternoon and evening with you and I hope that we can do it again real soon."

"I enjoyed myself, as well and would love to get together. Oh, guess what I came home to last night?"

"Your parent's waiting up for you?"

She laughed in spite of her surly mood. "You guessed it and that's not all."

"Oh?"

"Yeah, my nemesis has encroached on my time here at home."

She heard Peter release a sigh and smiled as he said, "Great! Just what you don't need, Jordan in your face!"

"That's right! The twit just couldn't stay away. So, depending on how things go around here today, I just might take Aunt Amanda up on her invitation to crash out at the cabin while Jordan is in town."

"You know, Izzie, it might be a good idea to do just that."

Their conversation continued with Peter saying all the right things to improve Liz's mood. When she clicked off her phone, she sat on her bed and reflected on how her life had changed since returning to the Great Sac Community. Peter Jones was an unexpected and pleasant discovery. Last evening while they shared dinner, Peter had told Liz about earning his teaching degree from the State University at Albany and landing his first teaching job at their old high school. They had laughed and shared stories of their college days, and things that they had done to jeopardize their studies, as well as, their triumphs. Who would have thought, that her younger brother's best friend would turn out to be such a great guy who made her heart flutter? But he did. Peter Jones was no longer a pesky little boy. Oh no! He was a fine looking young man with sandy blond hair, blue eyes that reminded her of sunshine sparkling on the lake, and a smile that made her feel as if she was the center of his world. He's smart, educated, and well, just a great guy! Perhaps, nothing more than friendship would occur between them, but that was okay with Liz. She felt cherished and that moment in time, that was all that mattered.

Liz heard the lively conversation taking place in the kitchen, as she made her way through the living room. Her good mood was taking a rapid nosedive towards sour. Of course, Jordan was sucking up to Mom and Dad! What else was new? She took a deep breath for courage just before she appeared in the doorway. "Good morning everyone." Her cheerful voice and smile received the response she had hoped for. Her parents had no idea of how she truly felt as they greeted her. She noticed that Jordan grew quiet.

"I have a mug out for your coffee," her mother said, and then continued to share what Liz's options were for her breakfast.

"Coffee is fine for now, Mom. I don't want you to put yourself out for me. If, I want something I'll make it myself and clean up as well." Liz prepared her coffee, while listening to her father and Jordan resume their conversation. She joined them at the table. "Hello, Jordan." Liz said with a touch of vinegar in her voice.

"Liz." Jordan's voice rippled with undercurrents of coolness.

Jim and Mel exchanged worried and confused glances, as Liz asked her sister, "Staying long?"

"As long as I feel like." Jordan did not waver from looking at Liz. "You?"

"Same here." Liz took a sip of coffee.

No one spoke. *Tick, tack, tick, tack.* The wall clock was the only sound.

"So, Jordan, where's Devon?" Her voice was filled with contempt.

Jordan swallowed and moistened her lips before speaking. "He couldn't get away."

"More likely he sent you away." Liz hissed.

Jim placed his coffee mug on the table. He had heard enough from listening to his daughter's conversation. "Alright! Something is obviously wrong between you girls. So, do either of you two care to share what's going on between the two of you with your mother and me?"

For a moment neither one spoke. Liz took a sip of coffee, and then glowered at her sister. "I have nothing to share at this time. How about you, Jordan?" She asked, as her younger sister glanced away from her. "That's what I thought. Mom, Dad, as I told you last night, I'm going to spend the day with Aunt Amanda and Uncle Kevin. Then, this evening I'm probably going to hook up with some old friends who are still in town."

"So, you won't be home for dinner?" Her mother asked, then added, "Caitlin, Nick and the kids, as well as Sammie and Chris are coming over for a family barbecue. I thought we'd all be together. Well, minus JJ."

"Sorry, Mom. Besides, it will be nice for Jordan to enjoy the barbecue with our family, and not have to share attention with me. Thanks for the coffee." With that said, Liz placed her coffee mug in the sink and headed back upstairs. Melissa, Jim and Jordan were still at the kitchen table when they heard the front door open and close.

Bang! Thud! Jim and Mel awakened in the early morning hours to loud noises and a blood curdling scream. Melissa reached over and turned on their bedroom light as Jim, clad in his boxers, threw back the covers and sat up. His bare feet hit the floor as he opened the drawer of his nightstand and pulled out his service weapon, and began loading it, as he headed towards the bedroom door. Melissa donned in her short sleeve cotton nightgown followed Jim to the door. Jim cautiously stepped into the brightly lit hallway. He held his weapon in his right hand, while he raked his left hand through his hair and assessed the situation unfolding before his sleepy eyes.

Elizabeth and Jordan were wrestling on the hardwood floor, pulling hair, punching, twisting extremities and yelling. Jordan cried out in pain.

"You self-righteous…....! Get off of me!"

"And have you sucker punch me, or worse? No way, you conniving…" Elizabeth spat out a vulgar description of her sister.

"Elizabeth Jeanne, Jordan Anne, that's enough!" Melissa exclaimed.

Jim and Mel exchanged horrified looks, while Liz totally disregarded her mother and continued to assault her sister. It was a slap and slug fest with Jordan rallying back using self-defense moves she had learned while growing up in the Callison family. Jim disappeared into the bedroom. He returned a moment later with a different means of intervening in this family brawl.

"All right, you two! Freeze!" Jim bellowed. The noise continued. Mel gasped as Jim lifted his weapon. Then, he fired and much to Melissa's amazement and the girls momentary shock, Jim shot them with the fully loaded super soaker water gun that he had recently taken away from Nick Jr. for harassing his weaponless sister. "I don't believe this!" Jim exclaimed as he watched his daughters, now clad in thoroughly wet night ware continued to brawl. He was certain someone was going to be seriously hurt, and so, he did the only other logical thing he could think to regain control of his family. He handed Mel the water gun, and then stepped over to Liz as she straddled Jordan. Then, he pulled her arms back and slapped his handcuffs on her, as she turned to fight him.

"Jim!" Mel's eyes had grown large as she took in the sight unfolding before her eyes. "Handcuffs?" She gasped in horror!

"You better believe it!" Jim was surprised by his daughter's strength, as she fought him.

"But, Jim, this is our daughter. You're not at work apprehending a criminal!" Mel exclaimed, as she watched her family. "Is this necessary?" Mel was afraid that Liz, or perhaps even Jim would be hurt, as she fought against her father.

"Mellie, you better believe it's necessary! Liz is acting like my sister did a few years back, and like Amanda, Elizabeth Jeanne needs to be reigned in."

Liz's eyes were spitting flames of fire ready to engulf anything or anyone in her path. "Handcuffs? I can't believe you cuffed me!" She huffed, grunted, and threw out some obscenities that would have shocked a well hardened criminal. "I bet you didn't cuff Aunt Amanda when you rescued her on the lake! And, for the record, I'm not the one you need to control." She turned then spit and kicked at her sister. "You spineless slug! You are lower than dirt!"

She said something else under her breath that no one heard thanks to Jordan finding her voice. "You started it by coming into my room and yelling at me!" Jordan accused, as she stood and straightened her nightgown.

"Me? Of course, you'll blame me, when we both know of your despicable actions that have led to you running home."

"I'm not running!" Jordan yelled as tears began to tumble down her cheeks.

"If you say so. I bet Devon kicked you out and you don't have any place to go! Do you?"

"I hate you!"

"The feeling is mutual little sister!"

Jim looked at his daughters. Their eyes were locked. It was as if neither he nor Mel were there with them. He shook his head, then sighed. Something was seriously wrong in his family, and by darn, he was just about out of patience with not knowing what the problem was. "Jordan, don't say another word. Right now, with that get up you have on, soaking wet against you, you don't look much better than a street walker. Go put on some dry clothes and then go downstairs and cool off. Elizabeth you go into your room and cool off. I don't want to find you out here unless it is to use the bathroom, and only then."

"Jim," Mel gently placed her hand on Jim's upper arm as she quietly spoke. "Liz is our daughter and not someone that you are arresting. Remove the handcuffs."

Jim saw the look in Liz's eyes. She was burning with anger and now that anger was being projected towards him. He sighed. "Lizzie, your mother is right. I overreacted to what was going on between you girls. Please turn around so that I may remove the cuffs. I hope that you will forgive me for going to such an extreme with you. It's just—" He released another sigh. "I was afraid you might kill your sister."

"I wanted to." She said as she rubbed her wrists, then turned, walked into her room and firmly shut the door. Neither Jim, nor Mel spoke, as they heard her turn the lock. But they both knew that all of the healing that had begun to happen in Liz's tattered life had been ripped open with Jordan's presence. They laced their fingers and headed downstairs to talk with Jordan, and hopefully glean some understanding of what was going on between their daughters to send them both home as enemies.

CHAPTER 4

S unrise over the Adirondack Mountains was like witnessing the hand of God gently stroking his paintbrush over his canvas with color and light as only He can do. It was barely eight o'clock in the morning when Liz drew in a deep breath and headed up the mountain in her car towards the family cabin. Woodland creatures were out in full force. A flock of Canada Geese, a doe and her fawn, turkeys, a slow-moving turtle making its way across the road and a variety of birds all seemed to be along the way to greet her. Liz smiled as she allowed herself to fully take in the scene. Life in the mountains sure was different from life in the city. She drew in a deep breath as she read the car clock and sighed. "Oh goodness! Well, I'm not going back to Mom and Dad's. I'll just sit quietly on the porch swing and wait for Aunt Amanda and Uncle Kevin to get up." Liz said to herself as she watched a woodchuck scurry into the tall grass on the other side of the old road. She slowed down as she came to the bridge over the creek and prepared to make her way up the driveway. The sun shone on the dew making the grass to look like it was littered with sparkling diamonds. She parked her car by her aunt's SUV, quietly got out of the car and headed for the porch.

The breeze made her glad that she had taken the time to throw on her hoodie sweatshirt over her tank top.

"Sadly, you remind me of myself on the day when I came here with the weight of the world on my shoulders." A sympathetic older woman's voice quietly addressed her.

Liz gasped. "Oh my gosh! Aunt Amanda, I didn't think you'd be up yet!"

Amanda smiled and chuckled lightly, as she watched her make her way up the steps. "Morning in the Adirondacks is worth getting up for and this morning's sunrise did not disappoint me."

"I see you were also enjoying your morning coffee. I'm sorry I've intruded." She said, as she approached her.

"My goodness, Elizabeth. You certainly are not an intrusion. Actually, I'm ready for another cup of coffee. Care to join me?" Her smile and her voice were equally inviting.

"I thought you'd never ask!" She watched her aunt rise from the glider, and noticed that the older woman— age sixty-two—was not moving as fast, as when she had visited her and Uncle Kevin in Baltimore. "Aunt Amanda, are you feeling okay?" Liz asked with deep concern in her voice.

Amanda smiled softly as she said, "I will be when the stiffness from the long ride wears off. But, thank you for being concerned about me. Let's go get our coffee and return to the porch to chat. Then we don't have to worry about our voices awakening Kevin and the girls."

"Sounds good." Liz giggled, as she entered the familiar cabin. Even though her great grandmother had passed, her father and aunt were taking great strides to keep her memory alive, as they cared for the cabin. She could almost feel Gentle Spirit's presence and hear her whisper *good morning,* as she looked around the great room. Amanda had made a fire in the fireplace to take away the morning chill just as great gram would have done. Soon the flame would be out and red-hot coals would burn while waiting for more fuel to be added later in the day. The smell of fresh coffee and something that had been recently baked in the old oven lingered in the air.

Liz sat on the glider, sipping the steaming hot coffee from an old chipped mug that had been in Gram's cupboard, she guessed for probably forty years or more. Amanda sat next to her, sipping her coffee and thought about the day she had sat there with Gram, so very long ago. She heard Liz release a deflated breath and noticed the moisture in her eyes. Her lashes glistened with moisture.

The silence was broken when Amanda asked, "Do you want to talk about it?"

That was all she had to ask, and Liz opened up about how she was feeling towards her sister and her parents. Finally, she paused to take a sip of cooled coffee.

"Let me get this straight!" Amanda was deeply distressed by this news and it showed in her next question. "Did you just tell me that your father handcuffed you?"

"Yes, and honestly Aunt Amanda," a renegade tear suddenly trickled down Liz's cheek. Amanda was now on high alert as she listened to Liz continue. "I'm afraid that if, he hadn't I might have really hurt Jordan. I did want to kill her. I just don't understand, what did I ever do to her to cause this to happen between us?"

Amanda sighed. Her own heart was breaking, as she quietly consoled Liz, who had laid her head on her aunt's shoulder and was crying her heart out. The sounds of voices and feet moving through the cabin towards the door brought their time together to an end. Liz wiped her eyes and nose before giving her aunt a hug. The screen door opened. Kevin emerged with a steaming cup of coffee in his hand and his two granddaughters in tow, each with a glass of chocolate milk and a jelly donut in hand. Danielle and Janelle, twins age twelve, were dressed for the day in shorts and tee shirts from their family vacation to Hawaii. Kevin in his mid-sixties was freshly showered, and shaved. His neatly combed nearly white hair and sculpted physique reminded Liz of a Greek god, a very sexy god at that. She thought that her Aunt Amanda had superb taste in men! She smiled to herself and knew that it was more than her uncle's good looks that had drawn her aunt to him. He genuinely cared about her aunt and had been a source of comfort when she needed it the most. Liz took in his attire: shorts, polo shirt and sandals. Then she noticed her aunt gazing at him with a hint of a smile on her lips, as well as hot possessiveness in her eyes that declared *you are all mine*. Liz watched him walk over to the glider, bend down and tenderly kiss her aunt. She heard their soft murmurings of good morning and felt her own heart ache, as it yearned for a love of her own.

Then, her phone rang. All eyes were upon her as she smiled, excused herself as she stood and answered her phone. Amanda, in turn smiled at Kevin as they heard Liz's greet her caller, and watched her glide away from them.

"Hey Skeet!" She giggled as she bound down the front steps and onto the lawn for privacy. "What's going on?"

"My friends invited me to a picnic at the lake and I wondered if you wanted to join me?" He asked with a smile in his voice.

"I'd love to!" Liz exclaimed loud enough for everyone up on the porch to hear. Liz glanced down at her attire as she listened to Peter. Her top was fine and she was glad that she had taken the time to dress in a pair of nice shorts and not a pair of cutoffs. "I'm not at my parent's home so don't go over there." She giggled at his response. "Right now, I'm up at the cabin with Aunt Amanda and Uncle Kevin. No. I haven't told her yet. You're right she will have something to say." Liz sighed as she listened to Peter's response. "Nope! Since I have most of my clothes repacked and, in my trunk, I'm taking Aunt Amanda up on her offer and staying here, and I was just about to tell her when you called. Okay, Pete, I'll see you soon. Goodbye." Liz released a breath of contentment as she made her way back to the porch and join her aunt and uncle.

Amanda was in the kitchen combining the ingredients for the quinoa salad when she heard the sound of tires on the gravel drive-way. "Amanda, honey!" Kevin called in through the screen door. "We have company."

"I heard. Let me guess. Jim?"

"And Melissa." Kevin added.

"Oh great!" Amanda sighed. "I bet I know why they are here." She wiped her hands, then covered the salad and placed it in the refrigerator before she and Kevin headed for the porch. Amanda opened the front door just as Jim and Mel got to the steps. "Good morning." She said as she stepped out alongside of Kevin.

"Good morning," they responded while both were obviously looking for something or someone. Amanda watched them like a hawk. She was ready.

"So, Manda-" *She wondered if Jim was trying to soften her up by using her old nickname.* "Where is Elizabeth hiding?"

Amanda met Jim's troubled stare and tone of voice with her own darkening mood. She released a sigh and then said, "She's gone out for the day and left her car here for safe keeping."

"Where did she go?" Jim demanded.

Amanda shot him a look that threatened repercussions. "Excuse me?"

"You heard me so don't play dumb with me like you used to do when we were kids. I want to know where my daughter went!" Jim's expression was intense. His eyes appeared to be black as coal. Amanda knew that fire was smoldering beneath the surface.

At that moment, Janelle and Danielle were heard coming in through the kitchen door. It slammed in their wake as they raced through the cabin. "Grandpa, will you take us to the stream so we can look for frogs?" They asked as they came through the door and immediately stopped, looked at the adults and realized they didn't know everyone and fled to their grandfather's side.

"Girls," Kevin said, "the frogs will have to wait. Grandma Amanda and I are dealing with something."

"Are you Aunt Liz's Mommy and Daddy?" Danielle asked.

Amanda softly smiled with pride, as Jim gave her a questioning glare.

"Well, yes we are." Melissa replied with a soft smile. "And who might you be?"

"I'm Danielle and this is my sister Janelle. We're twins."

"And Grandma Amanda isn't our real grandma because she isn't our daddy's mommy."

"But we like her—*love her*. More than our real grandma." Danielle added.

Amanda exchanged a quick glance with Kevin, who was equally surprised by the girls blunt honesty. She felt a smile blossom in her heart, as she introduced Jim and Melissa and the girls.

"Why did you make Aunt Liz cry?" They asked Jim and Melissa.

Both Jim and Mel looked devastated by the children's innocent question. Amanda's heart hurt for them as she responded to the children. "Girls, you know Liz appreciates your concern for her. Right now Grandpa and I need to talk with her parents about some complicated stuff." She drew them close to her as she quietly suggested, "I'm sorry but the search for frogs will have to wait. How about you girls to out into the back field and work on the Lacrosse technique I taught you?"

"But we want-"

"Girls, Grandma Amanda just finished saying that we need to have a conversation with Jim and Melissa." He gave them a wink and smile then added, "You girls need to go entertain yourselves until it's time for me to take you to search for frogs. Maybe then we can convince Grandma Amanda to join us and share some more stories about growing up here in the mountains."

"Yes, sir." They chimed in unison, hugged their grandfather, then sped off without a care in the world.

An awkward silence hung between the adults, as the girls scampered off together. Amanda sighed, as she watched Jim and Mel go over and sit on the glider. Melissa rested her hand on Jim's leg as he drew his arm around her shoulders. They were there as a united front. She glanced over at Kevin, as he settled into the Adirondack chair and then eased into the other vacant chair. Jim and Kevin began to exchange small talk, while Melissa sat quietly next to Jim looking like she had dragged a ball and chain up onto the porch with her. Tension seemed to buzz between all of them like an unwanted pesky fly.

Amanda cleared her throat causing Jim and Kevin to stop talking and look at her. "Jim, Melissa, I have a feeling that I know why you both are here. If, I'm not mistaking, it is more than simple curiosity about where your daughter happens to be this morning." She sighed as she held her brother's troubled gaze. "So, Jim, do you care to tell me why you shot and soaked your daughters with water from Nick's super soaker? More than that—why in the love of green tomatoes did you handcuff Elizabeth? When did she the innocent one turn into a felon?"

Jim's eyes darkened. His brows drew close. He began to make his familiar low growl in his throat to indicate that he was more than a tad annoyed.

Melissa gasped and breathed out, "Oh boy! Where's the spirit stick when we need it?"

Jim gently squeezed Mel's shoulder. "We don't need Gram's spirit stick." Amanda made a humph sound in her throat and mumbled something no one could understand. "Oh, moose muffins! Don't start responding in the Mohawk language, or singing like Gram would. You're not her! You're just my blessed annoying little sister.

And of course, you have heard Elizabeth Jeanne's side of what happened last night, and of course, you have taken her side and unfortunately also have an opinion." By now Jim's voice had increased in volume. His brows were drawn so tight together that they looked like one long black bristly line above his eyes. It was a scary sight! He bellowed like an old bull. "So, Amanda Kathryn," yikes he was mad! "Lay it out for us so that we may respond."

"I do have an opinion and you won't like it." Amanda's darkening eyes locked in a fiery battle with Jim. She shook her head in disgust as she spoke. "I will say you've landed in one big mess! Yes. I know what is going on between your daughters." She raised her hand to signal that Jim had best not interrupt her. "I'm surprised that Jordan ventured north at this point in her life. She's a bold one! I'll give her that!" Amanda added under her breath and then continued. "Years ago, I was justified in my being angry with you. Now, in light of everything that has happened between your daughters, Elizabeth is justified in being angry with her sister. *Tsk, tsk, tsk,*" Amanda added for good measure.

Jim straightened in his seat, as he removed his arm from Melissa's shoulders. "Unbelievable! Mellie, are you hearing this?" Jim yelled. No one responded, as Jim stood and began pacing across the porch. He stopped in front of Amanda. His eyes were spitting fury at her. "I want to know what you aren't telling me. Why is Elizabeth breathing fire and ready to kill her sister?" His eyes were flaming hot and boring into Amanda as he towered over her.

Amanda shot to her feet to even the playing field between them. Her hand shot out to push him a step back from her. Jim's eyes once again locked with hers, as he clenched his fists at his side. "You, hold up, James, dumber than dirt, Callison! Don't you even think about trying to intimidate me into sharing Liz's confidence with you. As for Jordan!" Amanda exclaimed, as she rolled her eyes in disgust. "Yes, I know all about her marital problems and what was a contributing factor to her running home. I bet she never expected to find that Liz was here! Elizabeth has every right to be angry with her sister. I will say that Jordan has been a busy young woman hell bent on destroying the lives of other people. For now, that is all I am going to say on that particular subject." She shot him a look that dared him to challenge her. He didn't. Smart man! "Now, if, you would like to sit down and reign in your temper, we can discuss your rash behavior of handcuffing your daughter. Then we can discuss the steps that you need to take to make amends with Elizabeth. Or, at least, attempt to."

By now Kevin and Mel were also standing and ready to intervene on their loved one's behalf. Fortunately, cooler heads prevailed.

Jim sighed, as he raked his fingers through his hair. "You're right." He breathed out. His brows were relaxing as the tension was easing from his facial muscles. Jim scrunched the corner of his mouth and slightly shook his head. He sighed with defeat. "Sis, even though I don't appreciate you calling me *dumber than dirt,* I'm sorry for taking out my frustration on you. Right now, the last thing I want or need is for you to be royally peeved at me."

Amanda softly smiled, and slightly shook her head as she grieved for her brother and his family. "I forgive you for acting like," she sighed, and glanced toward the back where the girls were playing. "I won't say. At any rate, perhaps, I'm not the one for you to talk with about how you reacted to your family's drama." Jim raised a brow as he listened. "Don't overreact, just listen. Please. Kevin also knows about Liz's reaction to the handcuffs and of her troubles. I think you two men should talk while I go and check on Dannie and Nellie." Her voice softened as she turned to Melissa. "Mel, if you want to blow off steam from one mother to another, I'm available."

Liz felt a sense of relief, as she sat in the passenger seat next to Peter. The wind blew through the window while Peter's playlist blared out an eclectic mix of contemporary and classic rock music. She watched the scenery as they sped down the mountain road towards the lake. "So, Peter, exactly where are we going?"

"Edinburg. My friend George Hensy's grandparent's house is right on the lake."

She smiled. "Ah, so that's why we're cutting through Northville and staying on the northeast side of the lake."

"Is that okay with you?"

"Sure! Our being away from Route 30 means less chances of my parents, or someone who knows them seeing us today." She sighed, then added, "With how messed up my life is, I don't need any more drama right now."

Peter glanced over at Liz then returned his attention to the twisty country road. There was something in her expression that troubled him. Up ahead there was a place to pull onto the shoulder where people parked to go fishing in the stream. Peter pulled in, put the car in park and then turned to face her. "I know you've got your issues with Jordan. But, Lizzie, I need to know. Are you embarrassed to be seen with me? Is it because of my age? My being JJ's friend?"

Liz saw the concern in his eyes. She reached over and placed her hand on his arm. "Oh, Peter, it has nothing to do with who you are or your age, and everything to do with my family feud."

He smiled as he held her gaze and raised his fingers to gently stroke her jaw. "Liz, that's good to know because I am enjoying getting to know you all over again. You are not the same person who left here years ago, and I am no longer the little boy you once knew." He said as he leaned in and brushed his lips over hers. Liz drew in a breath as she felt the warmth, the sizzle from his lips touching hers, and the unexpected longing for more. All too soon Peter ended their kiss. "Yes indeed, I like getting to know you and am looking forward to learning more about you. All of you." He smiled, lightly touched her cheek and then returned his attention to pulling the car back out into traffic. Peter glanced over and noticed that Liz was also smiling, as she looked out the window and took in the view as they drove to Peter's friend's grandparent's home.

The Hensy family were nothing like what Liz had imagined them to be, and their home was like stepping back in time to when the great cabins had been built on the northern lakes. She thought about how the Great Sacandaga was actually a reservoir created by the building on the Conklingville Dam. Ancient Native American burial grounds and once thriving communities were buried by the water. Liz was glad when Peter, George and his girlfriend Anna took a walk together and ended up at the secluded sitting area nestled under the trees by the lake. From there they could see across the lake to the marinas and homes that dotted the western horizon. As they sat there the breeze carried the smell of wood smoke, barbecued chicken and steaks towards them. Liz felt and heard her stomach grumble. So did Peter. He leaned over and whispered in her ear. "I'm hungry too, but not only for food."

Liz drew in a breath while feeling the heat rising in her cheeks. She turned towards him and smiled, while knowing fully well what his words implied. Peter drew her to him and gently placed his lips on hers just as Liz was moistening them. Neither one noticed when their host and his companion disappeared leaving them alone by the water's edge.

It was nearly midnight when Liz and Peter arrived at the cabin. Moths and summer bugs congregated around the warmth of the porch light with a flurry. Liz sighed, as she saw the all too familiar pickup truck parked next to her aunt's SUV. Peter shut off his car and turned to face Liz. He reached over and took her hand into his. "Lizzie, you knew that after last night and this morning leaving as you did, that you'd eventually have to face your parents. Isn't it better to go ahead and get it over with?"

"Yes, and it will ruin our day." Liz sighed with defeat in her voice.

"Nothing will ruin our day." He whispered as he brushed his lips over hers.

Liz leaned into him as she rested her hands on his shoulders. Peter gently cupped her head with his warm hands. Their lips began the dance of promise, as sparks within them lit them up brighter than the Fourth of July fireworks they had watched together by the lake. The sound of someone clearing their throat rang out in the stillness of the night and abruptly drew them apart.

"Great," Liz mumbled then said, "Dad, this is an unexpected surprise. I figured you and Mom would be home entertaining Jordan."

"Your sister went home this afternoon." He drew in a breath, while waiting for Elizabeth to respond. Silence. "Are you two going to sit in there all night?"

"No sir." Peter said. He whispered in Liz's ear before they got out of the car. They were fully aware that her father was watching every move that they made.

"Lizzie, your mother and I would like for you to come home." Jim's voice had softened a bit revealing his love and concern for his daughter. He noticed that Liz and Peter had laced their fingers together as he spoke. Interesting.

"Yes, we would, Elizabeth, and at some point, your father *IS* going to apologize for handcuffing you last night."

"Thanks, Mom. Apology or not, I'm still staying up here with Aunt Amanda and Uncle Kevin. Besides, I promised Danielle and Janelle that I'd be here in the morning to help them fly their kite."

By now Amanda and Kevin had also appeared, however they stood back in the shadows to observe the interaction between their family members. Amanda was on high alert and ready to defend Liz, if necessary. So far, so good!

"I see," Mel responded. Sadness flowed from her voice. "You could sleep in your bed and then drive up here after your aunt and uncle are up for the day."

Amanda and Kevin remained quiet. They gently squeezed each other's hand sharing their love and concern for their family.

Liz stepped over to her mother as she spoke. "Mom, I appreciate your concern for all of us. But, for now I'm staying here."

"Lizzie," her father's voice had lost all of its gruffness from before. "I'm sorry for how I reacted last night, and mishandled the situation between you and Jordan."

"Thank you for apologizing. But you should know that I am still hurt that you did that to me. Did Jordan tell you what she did to cause our fight?"

"No, Elizabeth. All Jordan told us is that you've taken Devon's side with her divorce. Liz, I certainly am not judging you for choosing to believe Devon rather than your sister. I am however concerned about the anger between you girls. What else besides the divorce is troubling you and Jordan?"

"Mom, please. Don't ask for more pain."

"No, by darn! Pain or no pain!" Jim was buzzing once again with frustration. "We're family, and-"

"Jim." Amanda's voice came from the darkness with warning.

Jim sighed, shot a remark to his sister, once again apologized to her, then returned his attention to Elizabeth. "Aright, for now, I'll let it go. But young lady before too long you and your sister had best make a truce between the two of you."

"Dad, I love you and Mom and I am sure this is difficult for both of you. But please, don't meddle."

"We love you too and will respect you wishes. Right, Jim?"

"Right, Mellie." He sighed.

Amanda and Kevin joined them by the car. They bid Jim and Melissa good night. Then turned to Liz and Peter. "We'll leave the front door unlocked for you. Good night, Peter."

Liz sighed as she watched them turn, draw their arms around each other's waist and slowly make their way to the cabin. She liked how her aunt and uncle didn't seem to worry about letting others see them show their affection for one another. Then again, neither did her parents.

CHAPTER 5

Kevin drew in a breath as he stepped out onto the porch with a steaming cup of coffee in hand. The early morning flash rainstorm had cleared the mountains and valley of oppressive heat and humidity, leaving behind welcomed relief of pleasant temperatures and sunshine. A smile touched his lips, as he recalled the first time he had been to the cabin with Amanda. It was January 2010. Kevin and Amanda had recently met, while both were vacationing at the lake as guests with their mutual friends Cassie and Andrew Phillips. In one short week they were falling head over heels in love. Then, while celebrating New Year's Eve at the community party, Amanda encountered two men from her past. She fled out onto the frozen lake and as fate, or, God would have it, she was rescued by Jim. Kevin took a sip of coffee as his thoughts continued on the events of January 2010. While Amanda was recovering at their friend's cabin, both Amanda and Jim were summoned to their grandmother's cabin to resolve their thirty-year feud that had begun in 1979. That was the year Amanda fled from the mountain community and had taken up residence in Baltimore, MD. He smiled as he tenderly thought of Mary Freeman. She was a wise old woman who knew that Amanda needed her friends to be present, as they aired their family's dirty laundry. Now, six years later their marriage was intact and their extended families were fully entwined in their lives. Kevin took another sip of coffee and drew in a deep cleansing breath. The sound of the swing squeaking drew his attention from nature to the end of the porch. Liz sat there dressed for the day in a tee shirt, cut off blue jeans, and bare feet with her tablet on her lap and a pad of paper and pen at her side.

"Good morning, Uncle Kevin." Kevin turned at the sound of her voice, and greeted her with a smile as she said, "It looks like you were having some nice thoughts."

Her eyes seemed to sparkle with happiness that had been missing a few days ago. He began to move towards her as he spoke.

"Good morning, Liz. You are very perceptive. They were good memories of the first time I came up here with Amanda and our friends. Do you mind if I join you?"

"You're always welcome!" Her smile grew, as she picked up her pen and paper to make room for him to join her on the glider. "I figured Aunt Amanda would be the first one up this morning. Is she okay?"

He returned a smile as he sat down and said, "She's sleepy from dealing with Danielle's nightmare and her wanting to join us in bed. Your aunt was not having it and spent a few hours on the air mattress with the girls. Needless to say, she's in need of rest, especially since today is the day of the great hike up into the mountain."

"Ah, yes. Caitlin has been texting with me this morning. It seems that Callie Anne can hardly contain her excitement that Mom, Aunt Amanda and the girls are going on a grandmother–granddaughter hike."

"Your dad and I have also been texting and making plans for our fishing trip to Oxbow Lake. From what your dad told me, your mom is busy packing her and Callie's day packs for the hike."

Liz laughed and smiled. "That's Mom the prepared! She loves to spend time and build memories with all of us. I do hope it's as fun as they all are imagining that it will be."

"Me too!" Kevin agreed. He glanced down at her lap, then back up at her face. "So, what did I interrupt you from doing, if you don't mind my asking?"

"I don't mind. I am looking for a job." She said brightly.

"That's good to hear." He nodded with pride for her determination to move forward with her life, and concern. "Considering that good paying theater jobs are usually found in an urban setting, where are you thinking of moving to?"

Liz carefully placed her tablet, pad of paper and pen on the well-worn pine table, that was positioned by the glider. Then she tucked her legs under her. Her face shone with excitement. "Would you believe that I found the perfect job for me right here in the north country?"

"Of course, I will believe you." His smile grew as he added, "Tell me about it!" Then, he took a sip of warm coffee. *What a difference from three months ago!* Kevin thought as he listened to Liz.

"Well, the job is with the Great Sac Community Arts Association. They are looking for a new director of operations for the G. S. Community Arts Center and a re-developer of the G. S. Summer Stock Theater." and from there Liz bubbled over with excitement, as she regaled Kevin with all that the position would require of her. Then, she enlightened him about the old arts colony, buildings that had once been utilized, and the arts association's interest in possibly revitalizing them. Liz felt that as a professional with experience on Broadway applying for the job, and someone who had grown up in the area well aware of the community's history, that she was a great candidate for the job. Kevin agreed. Also, knowing what Liz had experienced in New York City, Kevin was thrilled for the possibilities of newfound happiness, as well as, employment that were appearing for her. He had a hunch that Peter Jones was another positive incentive for her securing the job.

Liz had watched her mother, niece, aunt and step cousins disappear into the woods to begin their ascent up the trail along the stream and into the mountain. She thought about the care both grandmothers had taken of their little ones. Her mom had made sure that the girls had insect repellent on as well as sunblock, while Aunt Amanda checked the girl's day packs for necessities such as water, water-purification kits, a healthy snack and lunch. There was also a clean, dry pair of socks in a zip lock bag, and a sweatshirt in case they got a chill while up in the side of the mountain. Satisfied that they were all ready both women hugged, kissed and quietly spoke to their husbands and wished them luck on their fishing trip. Liz took a sip of lemon aide as she thought about their interaction and began to formulate a rough idea for another scene in the play that she was secretly working on. Hours slipped by. Lost in thought, the ringing of her cell phone drew her attention from her work. Caller id revealed it was her dad. "Hello." Liz said with hesitation.

"Lizzie, it's Dad." She chuckled and responded. "Okay, smarty!" She didn't hear laughter in his voice. "Have you heard from your mother, or your aunt?"

"No. Should I have?" There was something about her dad's voice that was raising her anxiety.

"We're on our way home. Well, to the cabin. Do me a favor and call me, if they get home before we do."

"Dad, is something wrong?" The hair was standing up on the back of Elizabeth's neck.

"I don't know." Liz knew from past experience that her dad was not saying what he truly felt at that moment.

"Where are you?"

"We're heading south on Route 30 just leaving Wells. Of course, I am in a hurry and now I am behind someone not willing to drive the speed limit."

"How fast are you traveling?" Liz had visions of some little old man or woman driving twenty miles an hour in a fifty-five mile an hour speed limit, and a double line not allowing her father to pass.

"Fifty-three miles an hour." His voice was laced with annoyance.

Liz burst into laughter. "Right. Those two miles an hour will make all the difference." She giggled at his response. "You know, Dad, that speed just might keep you safe!"

"Noted! Thanks, Lizzie." Again, there was something in his voice that struck her as odd.

"Don't know what I did, but you're welcome. Drive carefully and I'll let you know if they get home before you do."

Liz was pacing on the lawn, looking towards the empty path, as she talked on her phone with Caitlin when Jim and Kevin arrived. Peter had arrived ten minutes before they did and was equally concerned.

"Dad," she said as she slipped into his arms for a hug. "What's going on? Mom and Aunt Amanda should be back by now."

"I know, Lizzie. I know." At that moment, his cell phone rang and Kevin's phone indicated a text message. "Mellie, where are you?" Worry filled his voice. "What's that? You're breaking up. Hidden Falls. Callie. What about her ankle?" At that point Jim and Kevin exchanged looks of concern. "Dang cell phones. I lost the call and what I got was broken up."

"I may be able to fill in the spaces." Kevin interjected. "Amanda's brief text said they are at someplace called the Hidden Falls. Apparently, you know where they are? She also said Callie fell. Mel has been attending to Callie's sprained ankle, and that she hit her head. Melissa thinks that she may have a concussion. They're spending the night up there and will see us tomorrow."

"Da…" Jim spewed such colorful language that even Peter raised a brow with concern. "I'm sure Sis will verbally kill me for this, but I'm not waiting for them to make their way down here tomorrow morning. If Callie is injured, I'm going up there. Kevin, are you with me?"

Liz had seen that look in her father's eyes countless times before. Nothing or no one were going to stop him from hiking up the mountain to their family.

"Sprained ankle and a possible concussion? Jim, you better believe I'm with you, and you can bet Amanda will have words for both of us for being alarmists, and more colorful adjectives to describe our character!"

Liz and Peter sat on the porch and stayed out of Kevin's way as he moved from Amanda's SUV to the kitchen and their bedroom, as he prepared his backpack for the journey up the mountain. She was pleasantly surprised to discover all the items he had with him: medical kit, of course, and REM's—Ready to Eat Meals—as well as many of the same things she had seen in her Aunt's day pack and a blanket.

Caitlin and Nick had arrived by the time Jim got back to the cabin from his quick trip home to get his gear for the hike up the mountain. Jim saw the concern clearly written over their faces and drew Cait into his arms to console her, as only a father can do. He noticed that Kevin was ready with a backpack and what looked like a bed roll attached on top of his pack. Jim smiled as he recalled having heard that Kevin and a friend of his had hiked on the Appalachian Trail from Georgia north towards Maryland earlier this year. He was also glad that Kevin is a trauma specialist and would know exactly what to do medically once they got to their family. Jim hugged his daughters once more, gave them parting instructions and headed out with Kevin.

"Cait, Nick," Liz quietly spoke, as she watched them hugging and consoling each other while watching their dad and uncle head into the woods. "Everything is going to be okay. Mom is a registered nurse, and an EMS with the community ambulance service. You know she will take good care of Callie, and I can just imagine Aunt Amanda doing her part taking charge of setting up an emergency camp for the night."

"I know, Mom will take care of Callie. But so much can still go wrong!" Caitlin's voice broke. Tears slid down her cheeks. She was a wreck.

"Well, so much can also go right!" They exchanged heated words. Fortunately, Nick and Peter were able to calm them down about one degree. "Caitlin, I'm sorry. I know that you are worried, and of course I am not a mother, as you have so eloquently pointed out. But, don't forget that I happen to love you. And as your sister I am on your side, and I too am worried about Callie. You know, I'd be willing to bet that Aunt Amanda has stuff that you, or I wouldn't think to take with us. Look, Cait, all I'm saying is that Aunt Amanda is resourceful. She grew up here just like Dad, so she knows what to do up there in the mountain. Our aunt will probably build a fire to keep them warm through the night."

"If she can get a fire started. And they'll sleep on the ground, and get sick."

"And you worry too much!" Liz added more thoughts and was glad when Nick drew Caitlin away from her, so that they could pray together. She was scared for her niece, and readily stepped into Peter's embrace. At that moment, he provided the security she needed.

Darkness was closing in on the makeshift camp positioned a safe distance back from the base of the waterfalls. While Melissa had attended to Callie, Amanda put Danielle and Janelle to work assisting her with setting up their camp. First, they collected downed dry wood and made a fire for warmth during the night, and then they made a shelter against the ledge, where Callie was lying on the pine branches that Amanda and the girls had dragged to camp. The ten-year-old had a headache from her head injury and moaned in pain from her sprained ankle. Melissa sat on the ground next to her and sipped the hot tea from the aluminum lid of her thermos. Dannie and Nellie sat near the fire drinking their hot cocoa that Grandma Amanda had slipped into her day pack, and nibbled on their home-made trail mix. Amanda was exhausted from the hike and her additional physical labor in setting up their camp. She needed a few minutes to decompress and decided to spend time by herself near the stream. She was sipping her cup of tea when she heard a noise. She listened. Something, or, someone was moving down on the lower ledge behind the trees and brush. This time of night it could be anything from a raccoon to a bear. Time would surely tell!

"Identify yourself!" She called out annoyed with herself for leaving her hunting knife back in her pack, and wishing she had the old 16 gauge shotgun that was back at Gram's cabin and a couple of rounds of buckshot. She had no protection from a human or an animal predator. So, giving her circumstances, she did the next best thing. She bent down and picked up a rock, her only available source of protection. Then, she heard a voice that was music to her ears.

"Sis, it's us, Jim and Kevin. We'll be up in a minute. Amanda, keep talking so we know the path to take to come to you."

Amanda described the path that they had taken earlier in the day to direct Jim and Kevin, and was relieved when she saw their flashlights as they came around the bend through the dense trees. Her eyes sparkled with happiness as Kevin drew her into his arms. Jim heard the soft thud on the ground and looked down. He chuckled.

"What's so funny?" She asked, as she half turned her body to look at Jim, while maintaining physical contact with Kevin.

"Your rock. Very resourceful, Sis. So, what are you drinking? Water?"

"Hot tea." She yawned.

"You brought tea with you?" Jim was surprised. Then, he realized that he should have known that his sister would think ahead to bring extra food and drink with them.

"Yes. Thank goodness I listened to the quiet voice directing me this morning when I was packing for our hike."

"The Holy Spirit, or are you thinking it was Gram?"

"Interesting question. I guess it depends on where you want to put your faith. I think it was a combination of God and Gram tag teaming me," She released a weary breath. "Gentle Spirit has been with us every step of the way. I believe that God knew that we were going to need help and she came along to help me. I only wish she had told me to bring the shotgun." She snuggled into Kevin's embrace and released a weary sigh.

"Good grief, Amanda!" Jim's exclamation seemed to echo in the still of the night. "If, you had that old gun with you, you probably would have shot first and asked second."

She giggled. "Years ago, I probably would have. Honestly Jim, I like to think I've wised up with age." Jim made a comment that Amanda chose to ignore, at least for the moment. There were more pressing matters to consider. She turned her attention directly to Kevin, "Honey, Callie has had sips of water, as well as some of her sandwich. She's complaining of a headache. We used a sock we soaked in the creek to make a cold compress for her ankle. I'm not sure what else Mel has done for her. Our girls—" She beamed with pride. "They have been terrific helpers, and this evening they have had hot cocoa and trail mix."

"Hot cocoa?" Jim asked, then added, "Let me guess. Gentle Spirit?"

"Probably." Amanda sighed. She was feeling anxious and was glad that Kevin was there with her just in case she had a panic attack. "Come on you two. I know Mel will be glad to have you both here with us. Oh, and between the three of us, she's extremely worried about Callie's head injury, but don't you dare tell her I said so."

Jim and Kevin followed Amanda's lead into the small emergency camp that they had made. Danielle and Janelle sat huddled together by the fire, while Melissa was tucked under the ledge overhang next to Callie Anne, who was whimpering as she laid on the pine branch bed and had her head rested on her grandmother's lap. Kevin hugged his granddaughters, removed his backpack and got out his medical kit. He waited for Jim and Mel to complete their embrace, took advantage of the moment and drew Amanda back into his arms. At that moment, neither couple seemed to be aware of, or mind three sets of young eyes watching them.

Amanda felt the fatigue rapidly setting in on her body. Her old injuries from her motorcycle accident during the summer of 1999, the rods and plates in her legs and prosthetic hip all reminded her that once again, in her zest for life, she had overdone it. She was glad that Kevin had given her some of the pain medicine he had brought along, as well as her anxiety medicine that she took at night for her panic anxiety disorder. Amanda smiled as she listened to Kevin's quiet voice reassuring Callie that she would be fine. Her husband sure was a blessing for her entire family. She shivered, as she sat by the fire and placed another limb on top of the blazing fire. Even in the middle of summer the mountain became cold at night, and tonight it was imperative that the fire remained blazing hot for Callie and the other girls. Amanda had just pulled her sweatshirt closer to her body when Jim sat down next to her.

"Sis," Jim quietly spoke as he settled in on the ground next to her. He noticed the fatigue in her body, her eyes. He looked back at the fire, then pushed the medium size log further into the fire to burn. He turned and gave Amanda his half smile. She recognized it and gave him one of her own as he spoke. "You did good today." He saw a flash of disbelief in her eyes. "I mean it! Mellie told me how you took charge and set up camp while she cared for Callie." He glanced around at Mel and Kevin continuing to keep vigil with Callie and the other two girls. Both Dannie and Nellie had full stomachs from the sandwiches that Jim and Kevin had brought with them. Now they were drifting off to sleep on the other side of the fire on the mat Kevin had also brought with him. "Mel said that she never would have thought to make a pine bed, or move from where you were by the falls to here to use the ledge for protection. You did good!"

"Thank you, Jim. I guess it was a blessing for me to have paid such close attention to Uncle John, when he was teaching you and Sam about mountain survival." She yawned. "We sure did grow up in a different time when you were expected to do certain things in life, and I was expected to do other things."

"Yeah, we did! But, Sis, you always were a rebel!" He quietly chuckled, as to not disturb the sleeping children. "Then again, if we had not lived as Sam Callison's family and had been in a traditional family unit -"

Amanda lazily smiled, while liking where their conversation was going. "You mean as a clan with Gentle Spirit as our matriarch— which she was—I guess I'd now be the matriarch with Gram's passing and you perhaps would be the chief?"

Jim also smiled. "Life certainly has interesting twists and bends just like this stream. From one season to the next it is never the same." For a moment neither sibling spoke as both reflected on their conversation thus far. Jim picked up the stick that Amanda had been using as a poker and stirred the fire. Then he settled back on the ground and resumed his thoughts saying, "You know, it was not always easy having two different cultures blended into our family."

"No, it wasn't. But even though it did cause some of the conflict between Mom and Dad from time to time, I would not want to give up our Mohawk lineage for anything. We come from good people on both sides of our family." She sighed, then smiled and as she did her eyes danced with a sparkle of mischief. "So as the matriarch of our clan, am I forgiven for how I've cared for Liz?" Jim raised his brow in that all too familiar way that Amanda understood. She sighed. "It was worth a shot."

Jim's words that followed took Amanda by surprise, as he remained serious and poured out his concerns for his children. Amanda listened, and asked questions which Jim answered. Then, they both became quiet. Amanda stirred the fire and placed another branch on top, as both were lost in their own thoughts. At that moment, in the still of the night, she felt her grandmother's presence with them.

Liz awakened to the sound of pounding on the front door of the cabin. It had been well after midnight when Caitlin and Nick and Peter headed home. She yawned, as she sleepily made her way to the door and opened it. "Good morning beautiful!" Peter smiled, as his eyes glazed over her body covered in a tee shirt that hung to her knees and back to meet her sleepy dark brown eyes. He stepped closer and drew her into his arms, placed his thumb and forefinger on her chin and tilted it up, so that their eyes met. Then, he brushed his lips over hers while his hands, caressed her back and found their way to her round hips causing sparks of warmth to surge through Liz. Her lips slightly parted as she moaned. "Oh, Peter."

"Lizzie, woman, if you only knew what you do to me." He sighed out against her lips.

"I have a very good idea." She sighed out as he kissed her neck. "Oh, Peter what are we doing?"

"You know as well as I do, Lizzie." He quietly spoke as their bodies touched.

"Yes, I do." She drew a step away from him as she gathered his hand in hers and said, "Do you have protection with you?" He nodded and withdrew a foil pack from his back pocket. Liz smiled and almost purred as she spoke. "I'm glad we're here alone this morning. I suggest that we not waste any more time." She turned, closed the door, and secured the lock to ensure that they would have no interruptions.

The sound of Liz's cell phone woke her from her slumber. She smiled, as she gently removed Peter's arm from her midsection, then reached her phone. "Hello Cait." She whispered, only to hear her sister laugh and comment. "No. He went home. Just a minute." Liz sat up as she put down her phone, threw on her tee shirt nightshirt and then grabbed her phone and headed out into the main room of the cabin. "Have you heard from Mom and Dad?" She asked as her bare feet patted across the cool wood floor.

"Yes, they're on their way down the mountain. Now, if you don't want them to find you and Peter together as I have-"

"What do you mean as you have? Don't tell me!" Liz stopped mid-step from going to the kitchen, spun around, then flew to the door, opened it, stepped outside and looked towards the glider. Sure enough! There sat Caitlin and Nicholas with smiles on their faces. Liz moaned, "Oh great!" She moaned, as she clicked off her phone.

"Busted!" Caitlin shook her head, as her smile continued to grow and laughter bubbled from within her. "I had a feeling that it was only a matter of time before you two took your friendship to the next level."

Liz smiled and shrugged. She didn't bother to try to hide that she was a woman who had been thoroughly loved. "Oh, Cait, Nick, thank goodness it was you two who found us! Can you imagine how embarrassing it would have been to have had Mom and Dad, and Aunt Amanda and Uncle Kevin find us?"

The screen door opened and closed, as Peter stepped out onto the porch with only his worn blue jeans covering his lower half. "I think your Aunt would approve, maybe even your parents." He smiled tenderly at Liz and winked, as he slid his arms around her waist. "Good morning Cait. Nick. Beautiful day, isn't it?"

Both Caitlin and Nick greeted Peter, shared what they knew of the retreat from the mountain, and then suggested that the two love birds get dressed before their family appeared.

Three hours later the four were sitting on the front porch sipping iced tea, as they waited for their family's return. Their conversation was interrupted by the sound of a vehicle coming up the gravel drive, stopping, and then a door shut and there was a familiar voice. Liz and Caitlin both exchanged concerned looks, as they stood and waited at the top of the stairs to greet their company.

"Good morning, Stephen." The Callison sisters said in unison.

"Morning all! Caitlin, Nick, any new news about Callie Anne and how the rescue is going?" He asked, as he rested his foot on the bottom step.

"Dad got service for a few seconds and let us know that Callie will be okay. He said that Uncle Kevin approved of what Mom had done for Cal, and he has ruled out a concussion. But Dad added that she has a goose egg size bump on her head, and she is turning black and blue. He said that Mom and Uncle Kevin took turns caring for Cal during the night." Caitlin said with unspoken concern. "I'll tell you I am glad that Uncle Kevin is a trauma specialist and that he was here to help us.".

"That's good that Callie will be okay."

Liz heard something in Stephen's voice, as he spoke and saw something unrecognizable in his demeanor. Interesting. More ideas were forming for the plot of the play that she was writing.

"With a head and foot injury, how are they planning to get Callie down here?" Stephen asked.

"Dad assured me that they have everything under control. He said that as soon as they get their camp torn down-"

"They set up a camp site?" Stephen made no attempt to hide his surprise.

The Callison siblings laughed and smiled. "Cait, show him the pictures Dad sent you." Liz said with pride in her voice.

Caitlin pulled up the pictures and raved about how Amanda had come to the rescue and set up an emergency camp. Stephen saw the attention to detail Amanda had taken to care for her family. Memories. Of all the places that they could have hike to, why had they gone to the Hidden Falls? Until yesterday, that had been Johnson and Amanda's special spot. Suddenly, Stephen didn't like the direction that his thought and the conversation was going in. His friends Jim and Melissa being up at the falls was one thing, but Amanda and Kevin, they were another bucket of worms. He cleared his throat, as he raised a questioning brow. "Peter, aren't you supposed to be working?"

Peter gave him a half smile as he lazily responded. "Dad gave me the day off to help the Callison's. So, what's your excuse for being here, Unc? Checking on your old girlfriend?"

Stephen remained quiet. Liz saw something unreadable in his eyes. It caused her to wonder, as she waited. Then she heard the perfectly delivered line of a shattered man. "Same as you from the looks of it."

"I doubt it! I also doubt you told your current girlfriend where you were going this morning." Peter smiled and winked at Liz. She felt heat rising in her and hoped that her cheeks didn't betray her feelings.

The awkwardness was relieved when Caitlin and Liz's cell phones rang. Both answered, listened, squealed with glee and responded. Nick and Peter planted their feet and waited for what was to come next. Sure enough, Liz threw herself into Peter's waiting arms, while Caitlin found her way into her husband's embrace, and wept tears of joy and relief. Stephen watched Liz and Peter. Every time he saw them together it was obvious that they were enjoying one another company. Yes. Interesting things seemed to be happening this summer in the Great Sac community.

Caitlin spoke directly to Nick. "Honey, Dad said that we need to pull our SUV over to the edge of the woods, so that we are ready for Mom and Uncle Kevin to place Callie in the back. Mom and Uncle Kevin will be back there with her as we go to the hospital. Dad said that he and Aunt Amanda will follow us in his pickup. Dad assured me that if we should happen to be pulled over by the police that he will step in and address the situation for us."

"Why doesn't he just call for a police escort?" Stephen asked as he pulled out his phone.

"Good question. But, when I asked Dad the same question, he said that Callie isn't in imminent danger, so she doesn't need to be transported by ambulance, or with an escort."

Caitlin answered more questions for Nick before he sprinted off to retrieve his vehicle. By then, Stephen had returned his phone to his pocket. He noticed that Peter had lazily drawn Liz into his embrace and cupped her shoulder with his hand. He continued to watch and listen.

"Peter, Aunt Amanda wants to know if you will be able to stay here and help me with the girls? She said that, if we have plans that it is no trouble for her to stay behind."

"Lizzie, of course I'll stay here for as long as you want and need me." His voice and his eyes conveyed his devotion.

"Oh good!" Liz sighed with relief. "You will fall in love with Dannie and Nellie. But I warn you, they are pips!" Liz was smiling, as she thought of the young girls she had come to love, as if, they were her own nieces.

"Ah, Lizzie, remember I was here the night they all arrived?"

Her eyes sparkled as she laughed. "Oh, that's right! How could I forget?"

Neither Liz nor Peter noticed Stephen, as he continued to watch their interaction. Nor, did they know how far down memory lane he had journeyed in that brief moment. Unfortunately, his memory included the one woman who is currently off limits to him on multiple levels: Amanda *Callison* Newman Wentzel.

Everyone was waiting at the edge of the woods, when the weary hikers and rescuers appeared on the path. Liz and Peter held back with Stephen, while Cait and Nick rushed to the edge of the woods to greet their child and parents. They all noticed that Amanda and Kevin stood a step away from the others, and held each other close as they looked on their family reunion. Liz had to wonder what thoughts were going through Stephen's mind at that moment. Her thoughts were interrupted as she was greeted by Dannie and Nellie, who were happy to find Liz and Pete waiting for them. They immediately began sharing tales of their adventures in the woods overnight, while the others worked together to get Callie Anne in Nick and Caitlin's vehicle, and off to the hospital. Liz had not noticed that Stephen had walked over to the SUV.

The Wentzel grandchildren had just asked Liz a question when she heard her aunt exclaim some expletives that Liz had never heard before. Then, without missing a beat, Amanda started firing accusations towards Stephen. Ought oh! Liz cautioned the twins to remain with her and not approach the adults. She noticed that her aunt's eyes were darker than coal just like her dad's became when he was angry. Fire was burning underneath. Not a good sign!

"You could have called Jim, or asked Peter to give you a call when we all got down here. But, no! That's not your style." Amanda huffed with disgust. "Jeez, Johnson, you just aren't happy unless you're meddling in my life, or the lives of my family!" Amanda was exhausted and not filtering her mouth. "Remember what happened when you meddled in Kevin's and my life when we were in Denver?" She didn't wait for a response. "Daughter or no daughter!" She growled. "One of these times you will push me over the waterfall of life, and I will write you out of my life forever." She mumbled something Liz could not quite understand from where she stood.

Liz exchanged a quick glance with Peter, who also was stunned by the interaction between Liz's aunt and his uncle. It was hard for either of them to imagine those two ever being in love and creating their deceased cousin Rose, and their living cousin Summer. Liz felt warmth rush over her when Peter gently took a hold of her hand and squeezed it. They were unprepared for Stephen's response to Amanda and did not have time to cover Dannie and Nellie's ears before he exploded.

"God almighty! Mandy! You are so hardheaded! Ungrateful! I'm not meddling." His eyes shot streaks of angry towards her. Amanda was not intimidated. She stood with her feet planted apart and her hands on her hips. Her scowl beckoned him to continue with his fury, which he did! "Our daughter, and don't get smart and say something stupid about Rose talking to me from her grave."

Liz and Peter's eyes grew wide as they watched and listened. Tempers were flaring.

"For your information, not that it will matter to you, but, last night Summer called me after she spoke with Liz. Our daughter was frantic with worry about your safety. She loves you and even though she knows that Kevin is capable of caring for you, she asked me, her father, to check on you. I came here today for Summer. Not for you, your majesty!" He bellowed to inflict his own hurt on Amanda to match the hurt she had just inflicted on him. "Plus, you grumpy old self-centered hag, I came to see if there was anything, I could do to help my friends. Remember Jim and Mel are my friends, whether you like it, or approve of it. Oh, and for the record, because Jim is my friend, I will continue to be a pain where the sun doesn't shine on you and I will be here for him and his family if need be. So sweetheart, you take that snooty city attitude of yours and stuff it!" His eyes remained locked with hers, beckoning her to allow him to rant and rave some more. Oh yes! Stephen had plenty more that he would love to say to Amanda, given the opportunity.

"Well, thank you very much for that eloquent insult on my character, and may I remind you that you are equally ornery, a pain. So stuff your nasty remarks someplace equally dark! And for the record, this morning after I got service and I found fifteen messages and five voice mails from Summer, I did what any loving parent would do. I called my child to let her know we all are okay." She glowered at him while watching his expression and waiting for a response that didn't come. "Oh, so I gather you didn't have that piece of information in your arsenal when you came storming up here ready to insult me on my mothering skills!"

"No. I didn't know that, nor did I plan on insulting you." His eyes spewed a bit less angry energy as he sighed. "But you do have that uncanny ability to bring out the worst in me, and I suppose you being your hot-headed self," he paused for effect. "You yelled at Summer as well!"

Amanda huffed, but not as fierce as before. "I dealt with her." She felt moisture behind her eyes. Not good. At that moment, small hands wrapped around her bare arms, while two small bodies protectively wedged her between them and their voices yelled at Stephen.

"You, big bully! You hurt Grandma Amanda and now you are making her cry. That's wrong!" Nellie admonished Stephen.

"Yeah! You, big meanie!" Dannie added for effect, while her expression revealed her disgust.

Stephen and Amanda were both shocked by the girl's display of anger. It took a moment for Amanda to recover, and then pride set in, as she listened to the girls continue to express their opinion.

"Old people aren't supposed to be bullies! So, why are you so mean?" Nellie asked.

"Besides, she's a hero! So, you leave our grandma Amanda alone!" Dannie added, as if to dare Stephen to cross them.

Amanda released a sigh as she drew the girls close to her. "Girls, thank you for coming to my defense." She shook her head as her gaze turned from them to Stephen, who was intently watching her. "Unfortunately, both Mr. Johnson and I were wrong to yell at each other as we did. But I am proud of both of you girls for speaking out against the bullying we both were guilty of doing." She glanced past Stephen to see that Callie was secured in the back of the SUV, and saw that Jim was heading towards them. "Uncle Jim is heading this way. I need to go inside and get my purse, so that I can go with him. Are you girls okay with hanging out here with Liz and Peter?"

"Manda!" Jim called out as he approached them. "You ready?"

"Almost. I have to go inside for a minute and will meet you at your pickup." Amanda did not look at Stephen as she began to walk towards the cabin with her pronounced limp indicating that she was obviously in pain. She paused, turned and quietly spoke. "Johnson, our daughter seems to think you're happy with your girlfriend. If, that is the case, then why do you continuously reinsert yourself into my life?" Amanda sighed with fatigue as she shook her head and left him standing alone by the edge of the woods.

CHAPTER 6

Liz sat at the table with a glass of lemon-aide, her laptop, as well as a number of paper pages with notes that she had written. She sighed, stretched, rubbed her blurry eyes and rotated her shoulders. It had been two weeks since her aunt and uncle had returned to Baltimore, and left her to use the cabin during their absence for as long as it suited her needs. Liz was enjoying living at the cabin away from her parent's watchful eyes. She smiled as she thought about Peter and their adventures at the cabin thus far during the summer. The knock on the screen door startled her. She looked towards the open door and through the screen to find Peter standing there smiling at her. Then she glanced at her watch. She gasped! How could it already be five thirty?

"Peter, come in." Her smile grew as she made her way to the door to further welcome him.

He drew her into his arms and brushed his lips over hers. "Ah, Lizzie, you look tired. Do you want to postpone tonight's barbecue with my parent's?"

"Oh gosh!" Her hands flew to her cheeks with embarrassment. "I got lost in my work and -"

"And it's okay." Peter gently took a hold of a piece of hair that hung by her cheek and tucked it behind her ear. "We have time." His eyes shone with desire.

"Not that much!" She giggled. "I can be ready in twenty minutes."

"I bet you can't." Peter said with a dare in his voice. His eyes danced with playful happiness.

"What's your bet?" Liz asked. He quietly told her and she laughed. Then she gave him her brightest broad smile. "You are on Skeet, and when I win— oh this will be fun!"

Peter could still taste her kiss on his lips as she disappeared into the bathroom and he began timing her. He listened to the water as it was turned on and then off. Then Liz emerged with a towel wrapped around her, smiled and waved as she flew into the bedroom. A few minutes later the door opened and she approached him fully dressed with light makeup on her face, her sandals in her hand and her wet hair combed and hanging loose around her shoulders. "How much time did I have to spare?" She asked as she watched Peter's expression change from shock to disbelief.

"You had one minute and fourteen seconds left." He shook his head as his smile grew.

Liz sighed in contentment. "Huh! Only one minute and fourteen seconds left." She shook her head. "Gee, I'm getting slow! Oh well, I won and that's all that matters! We better get going."

Peter was still trying to wrap his head around how fast Liz had been, and the fact that he had lost the bet when he got into her car in the passenger seat. Liz driving them to his parent's home was only the beginning of her prize, and he couldn't wait to see what the rest of the night held for them. His heart seemed to leap with newfound joy that he couldn't explain to himself, let alone someone else. But one thing was certain for Peter. He knew in his heart that he had found the woman of his dreams in the one and only beautiful Elizabeth Callison.

"So, Lizzie what were you working on this afternoon that caused you to lose track of time?" He asked as she drove them down the mountain to Route 30, where they would turn south and head to his parent's house.

"After lunch I finished my outline of the story and delved into character development for my play. Some theater colleagues may criticize me for how I create, and I understand that I don't always do things by standard procedures. But I have success."

"Did you get criticized as an assistant director for not always doing your job the right way? Is that another reason for your leaving New York? I mean, besides what you told me happened with Jordan?"

Peter watched Liz draw in a breath. She kept her eyes focused on the road and the area around the outside of the car, as she put on the directional and slowed to stop at the intersection. She turned to look into his eyes. Her smile did not have the glow that Peter was now accustomed to seeing. He saw tremendous sadness in her eyes. Liz was holding back something significant that she had yet to share with him about why she had come home. Peter hated to see her like this. At that moment, it hit him. Peter Jones had fallen in love with Elizabeth Callison, and he wanted nothing more than to erase all of her pain and sorrow. He alone wanted to be her knight in shining armor who came to save the day for her. But this was Liz and she was—is—no ordinary woman. It would take time for trust to be fully developed between them.

"My job performance as assistant director was not the reason for my leaving." Liz sighed as she turned her gaze from him to look both ways and then turn onto Route 30 to head towards his parent's home. "When I spoke of my creative process, I was referring to my college days at Syracuse." A bittersweet smile grew on her lips. "Dr. Mardino would read my work and sigh," Liz softly chuckled as she fondly remembered her professor. "Just like many things that have a sequence, writing a play has sequencing. With my creative process, I tend to reverse an early step in writing my play. Dr. Mardino would say, 'if only you would reign in your creativity someday you would become a famous and sought-after play write. The theater needs people like you.' Then he would add, 'at least those who are willing to follow all of the rules.'" Liz sighed. "I am so grateful that Dr. Mardino allowed me to be myself."

"Ah, so now, I'm beginning to see a clearer picture of who you were, who you are." Tenderness filled his voice. "You are a rebel with a cause to be yourself in a world constricted by rules."

"So eloquently put by the Great Sac High School eleventh and twelve grades English teacher." Now Liz fully smiled. "Yes, and that is why I am excited about the opening for the Director of Operations for the Great Sac Community Arts Center and the Summer Stock Theater. I have the experience and skills necessary to be the director, and I will also have the freedom to be creative, and try new things to spark the community's interest in the fine arts. Maybe we could do something in collaboration with the high school."

"Wow! Liz you really are passionate about this position talking as if it is already yours."

"I just hope the arts association board is impressed enough with my resume to call me for an interview."

Peter reached over and placed his hand on her upper leg at the hem of her shorts. Her soft, golden tanned skin was warm to his touch. He watched her expression subtly change to pleasure, as she focused on the road ahead of them. "I'll be shocked if they are not impressed. We need you here. I need you here." Silence hung between them as they both processed Peter's words and what they meant for them.

Becky Jones, youngest of the three Johnson siblings, Stephen the eldest, and Phillip the middle child, came out of the back door with a tray of food in her hands. She took it over to the picnic table and then joined Wesley by the grill, where he was tending to grilling the London broil. Wes slid his arm around her waist, as she eased against his side and laid her head on his chest. He leaned down and softly kissed her hair and then laid his cheek on her head. Neither one spoke as they stood together in the early evening. Moments like this were precious to them. Their love for each other had taken bud when they were young teenagers. Wes and Stephen had become best friends and played sports together in high school. Becky had been there alongside of Amanda cheering for their sweethearts. The only thing different was that Becky and Wes did have the *happy ever after* part of their love story.

"I warned you that we should have called!" Peter exclaimed as he and Liz came around the side of the house. His smiled revealed how much he loved his parents, even when they displayed their affection for one another.

Wes and Becky stepped away from each other and looked at them. Surprise was written over their faces as they saw Liz standing there with her fingers laced with Peter's.

"Oh, my gracious!" Becky exclaimed. Her hand raised to her breast to cover her heart. Joy radiated from her.

"I should have known." Wesley added as his eyes lit up with delight and his smile grew.

"Don't tell me! Liz, are you honestly Peter's new girlfriend whom he has been so secretive about?"

Liz could not help but grin from ear to ear and nod as Becky freed herself completely from Wes and drew her into a hug. She heard Wes tease Peter and then tell him that he had made a wise decision in his choice of women to date.

Becky, grinning from ear to ear, released Liz and turned to Peter. "I guess it should have been obvious by how much time you two have been spending together! But I just never imagined it with your age difference and all."

"Mom, Dad, we had a feeling that you and Liz's parents might question our being together. That's why we didn't say anything to you until now."

"Well, I approve!" Wes chimed in. "So, Liz, do I get to give you a hug?"

"Of course!" Laughter filled the back yard as Liz stepped into Wes's embrace. She glanced over and saw Becky tenderly holding Peter's face in her hands and then pull him into a hug. Oh! She loved this family and she was excited to see what the future holds for all of them!

It was close to ten when Liz and Peter returned to the cabin, only to find her parents sitting on the porch with their feet resting on the top steps as they waited for them. Hand in hand they came to the steps, stopped and looked up into their shadowed faces. She could tell that they were not smiling and felt an edge of uneasiness. *Now what?* She wondered. A cricket chirped from somewhere on, or, near the porch, followed by a tree toad singing out in the night. Moths clamored around the porch light drawing in its warmth. Neither of her parents spoke. Not a good sign.

"Mom, Dad, this is a surprise. Is something wrong?" She used her training to mask her uneasy feeling in the pit of her stomach.

"Well, Elizabeth," her father's voice was tight with emotion. "About an hour ago we had a phone call from Becky."

"Oh no!" Peter moaned. He could only imagine how his mother had been bubbling over with enthusiasm about his dating Liz. The only problem was that she called the Callison's too soon to share her joy with them. "Please don't be mad at my mom or Liz." He pleaded.

"Mom, Dad," Liz interrupted, "We planned on telling you. Then, with everything that was going on after Callie Anne was injured while hiking, Aunt Amanda and Johnson's fall out, we just, well—"

"Neither Callie Anne, nor your aunt and Johnson are a good defense." Jim said.

"I know and I am sorry that you had to find out about Peter and me from Becky." Liz suddenly felt as if she was on a slippery slope and going down.

"Liz, it is not your fault. I should have asked Mom to not say anything until we had talked with your parents."

"So, Becky was right." The hurt was present in Melissa's voice and expression as she said, "You two are dating and not simply hanging out as friends."

Liz sighed and nodded. "Mom, there obviously is no way to rewind this day, or the past few weeks, and tell you and Dad first about our decision to date each other exclusively."

Peter had slid his arm around Liz and held her protectively close. "Mr. and Mrs. C, perhaps the next time we have something significant to share we'll have a party, or do something special to make the announcement to everyone at the same time."

"The next time?" Jim asked. His eyes remained fixed on them, reminding Liz of countless other times in her past when her father had interrogated her, or one of her siblings for some family infraction.

"Dad, we've apologized. Now, can we give this a rest?" Liz was relieved when they agreed, stood and allowed Liz and Peter to move up onto the porch with them. From there they all moved inside the cabin to build a fire in the fireplace and have coffee and dessert together. Liz realized that she had something special that just might help to pacify her parent's mood from feeling left out.

"Well, this is unexpected news!" Mel exclaimed. "I didn't know that the Great Sac Community Arts Association was looking for a new Director of Operations for the Great Sac Community Arts Center. The Summer Stock Theater has been in a shamble for years!" Melissa said before taking a sip of coffee.

Liz listened to her parent's further comment on the arts association and the community summer theater. Well, many years ago the old theater may have had its hay day. But that was not going to deter her, or wave her enthusiasm towards the prospect of her getting the job.

"Peter found out about the job opening from Stacy Potts, you must remember her. She was in school with Sammie." They nodded. "Well, she is the junior high music teacher and her mother is on the Great Sacandaga Community Arts Board of Directors. She, Stacy, that is, told Peter that they are looking for a new director, and he shared the information with me." Liz smiled tenderly at him.

Neither, Jim nor, Mel missed their exchange. Liz was definitely back and obviously planned to stay for a very long time. They also knew that the rest of the summer was going to continue to be an eventful one for their family. Both of them sipped their coffee as they watched and listened to Liz share what her responsibilities would be, if, she got the job.

"So, when will you know if they want to interview you for the job?" Jim asked as he set his coffee mug on the coaster on the old pine coffee table. He stretched, stood and went over to the fireplace, knelt down, stirred the fire and placed a log on top of the flames. His mind was processing many things that he had heard and seen this evening. Jim listened to the conversation as he poked at the fire. Liz was happy. That simple knowledge warmed his heart more than the fire in the old fireplace.

"Application submissions close the second week of September. Then they will call to schedule an interview."

"And what will you do if this job doesn't pan out for you?" Mel asked with her familiar motherly tone that Liz had heard countless times in her life.

"Well, Mom, I'm glad you asked." Liz was beaming with happiness on multiple levels. Her eyes sparkled with delight because she had a plan and direction for her life.

"Oh no!" Jim moaned as he returned to the chair he had been occupying and rubbed his chin filled with bristly stubble.

"Dad!" Liz giggled. "You worry too much! I have enough savings to hold me through winter. So, if this job doesn't work out, I'm going to apply and register for spring classes at Syracuse to pursue my masters and seriously work on writing my play."

"Syracuse? Your masters? A play? Oh, Elizabeth that is wonderful! I am so pleased to hear that you have a plan and will not be floundering around in 'unemployed no man's land' for too long!"

"Oh, Mom," she sighed, "you and Dad really do worry too much!"

"Yes. We do, Elizabeth, whether you want your mother and me to or not!" She thought she detected a bit of pride in his expression before he continued. "So, I'm wondering-"

"Ought oh!" Liz sighed, as she waited for her father to continue.

Jim raised a brow that warned Liz to keep her thoughts to herself for the time being. "Since you've been living up here and spending time with Peter, you haven't told us any more about why you originally came home. Not that you told us much to begin with."

Liz felt as though all the oxygen had been drained from her body. She realized that she had forgotten to breathe and drew in a deep breath. Finally, she spoke. "My reason for coming home has not been resolved, nor do I expect it to be resolved in anytime too soon." She held up her hand as a buffer. "And, before either of you press me any further, please, just leave it alone. Jordan has made her choices and I have made mine. We don't like each other and probably never will. I'm moving on and I am happier than I've been in years. So please, no drama. Just be happy for me." Her smile was sad and her eyes…well, they pleaded with them to drop it like a fly.

"Well, Liz, your father and I will continue to worry. But we also will respect your wishes and not press you to share your reasons for returning home until you are ready. Right, Jim?" Mel's expression warned him to not disagree with her. Liz couldn't help but smile as she watched and listened to her parents interact with each other. Then, her mother returned her attention to Peter and her. "Now that we've resolved our initial reason for being here tonight, it's time for your father and me to go home."

"It is?" Jim asked.

"Yes, it is." Mel said as she rose to her feet. "You've been so worried about our children, your sister and our friends that you've forgotten something else."

Jim was now standing next to her. He looked into her eyes, smiled as he slid his arm around her waist and whispered in her ear. Mel softly smiled as she nodded. With the acknowledgment of what was to come, he turned to Liz and Peter. "Good night, kids." His smile had said more than his words and gave them plenty to speculate about, as they watched them leave.

They listened to the sound of the pickup become more distant in the cool summer night. Speculation was short lived as they locked up the cabin, and settled in on the couch to watch the fire in the fireplace. Well, that is, until Peter drew Liz into his arms and found the tender spot on her neck below her ear and began to nuzzle her. The fire died down. The cabin drew dark. Neither one noticed as flames of desire spread between them.

CHAPTER 7

Time continued to move on from one day to the next. Liz was sitting in her parent's kitchen helping her mother fold socks when her cell phone rang. She gasped as she recognized the local 518 area code number. Her stomach did a flip flop. Nerves. Anticipation. "Hello." Her voice was calm, cool and collected as she listened to the caller. Hope surged through her as she responded. "Yes, I am still interested in the position." She looked at her mother and shared a smile with her. "This Friday at ten o'clock works well for me. Yes, I know where the community building is. Yes. Thank you for calling. I look forward to meeting with you. Goodbye."

Liz ended her call and placed the phone on the table next to her father's folded socks. Her eyes shone with excitement as she released a slow breath. "Wow!" was all she said. Mel looked at her daughter in disbelief at her reaction to the call.

"Wow and?" Mel asked, hoping to prompt Liz to say more about the call. Curiosity might kill a cat, but right now this mother had first dibs on dying from curiosity.

Liz began to smile, then started to laugh. Mel in turn began to smile as she watched her child. Liz had always been the one who had a rhythm about her. So, Mel knew that it would take time for Liz to get to the point where she would share her news. This was Liz after all, and Liz did things her way. Some things never changed. So, Mel waited. Finally, Liz drew in a breath. Then came the full smile that caused her eyes to sparkle with delight. It was hard for Mel to believe that this whole process only took seconds to be completed. Then Liz spoke.

"Mom, I'm one of the top three candidates that have applied for the job as director. They have already talked with my references and are anxious to interview me for the position."

Mel felt moisture forming in her eyes, as she stepped around the table to stand by Elizabeth. "Oh, Liz, I'm so proud of you." Proud was an understatement for what Melissa was feeling at that moment. "Please stand up so I may give you a hug."

Liz seemed to float off of the chair and into her mother's embrace. Jim chose that moment to come in from doing his outside yard work to get a drink of water. "What's going on? Is something the matter?" He asked.

"Oh, Dad!" Liz exclaimed as she stepped away from her mother. Her eyelashes glistened as she looked at him. "Everything is great!"

"Great? Then why the tears?" After all these years of living with and dealing with women, Jim still did not understand the female mind, especially when tears were involved. Then, he noticed that Mel also had tears. He sighed.

Mel went to his side and gave him a quick kiss on his cheek rather than get a sweaty hug from him. "Honey, Liz has an interview this Friday with the Community Arts Association."

"Well, my goodness!" Jim smiled broadly. "Lizzie that is terrific news! I'm proud of you kiddo." He was proud, but still confused about the tears. Women! They cry when they're happy and when they're sad. How was a man supposed to keep it all straight, and manage to stay out of the doghouse for not interpreting their tears the correct way? Jim thought that maybe he should call Kevin and discuss his dilemma with him. Then again, he decided, Kevin might be as confused as he was!

"Thanks, Dad." Liz continued to smile as she spoke. "I still can't believe I got called for an interview. Me! They are interested in me. Who would have thought it?" Liz sighed. "I have to tell Peter. He's going to be stoked when he hears my news. I guess I'll head over to the school, so I can tell him in person."

"Why head over when you can call him?" Jim asked. Both women looked at him as if he had just grown two heads. "What's wrong with calling rather than driving over to the school? You know this time of day there will be buses in and out of the parking lot, as well as kids, parents, and teachers in their cars." Jim seemed to think he had made a valid point. Only it went unaccepted by both of his family members.

"Honestly Jim!" Mel exclaimed. "How can you even suggest that Liz calls Peter? You know perfectly well, if you had something to tell me and could choose between the phone or in person, -" she gave him her don't argue with me expression as she continued, "-Of course you would tell me in person and Liz is going to tell Peter in person." At that point Jim sighed. He knew that the subject was closed between him and Mel. This was one battle he would lose. Actually, he had already lost it. Mel returned her full attention to Liz and asked, "How about inviting Peter to join with us for a celebratory dinner tonight?"

Liz was beaming with excitement. "Thanks, Mom. But I don't know how much work he will have to do this evening. You know Peter has his own homework grading essays, exams and other stuff. So, we've been keeping things rather low key during the week and play on the weekend. How about we wait on the family celebrating until I hopefully get the job?"

"Fair enough." Mel said as she placed Jim's folded socks into the laundry basket. She looked at Jim with a smile and an unspoken message.

"Oh, boy, I know that look. Lizzie since you bailed on supper, it looks like I'm taking your mother out to dinner tonight."

"Smart man, Callison." Mel teased. "I'll be ready at five thirty. Oh, and I'm in the mood for Italian."

Liz was enjoying watching her parent's interacting with each other. She smiled as she listened to them go back and forth.

"Elizabeth, now look what you got me into! I have to get cleaned up and take your mother over to Gloversville to her favorite Italian Restaurant for dinner." He sighed, then winked at her.

Liz hugged both of them and said her goodbyes. She was still laughing as she got into her car and headed towards the school. Her father may have acted like he was put out by her mother's request, but she knew in her heart that her dad would do anything possible to make her mother happy, or any member of his family for that matter.

Liz had her hair in a French braid, she wore minimal makeup, was dressed in a conservative navy-blue suit, and wore blue pumps on her feet when she arrived at the Community Arts Center. She walked into the interview with outward composure, while her insides were doing a dance routine she never heard of, and her breakfast was ready to make its grand entrance. Working in the theater really did pay off, especially when you needed to do what just might be the performance of a lifetime. Much to Liz's surprise, while the committee did have her resume in hand, the interview was more like a meeting you had with the Human Resource Department on the first day of a job. She left the interview with a strange feeling. All weekend she continued to return her thoughts to the interview. The questions she was asked. Her answers. The board members facial expressions. Their body language. Then, it happened. On Monday morning the phone call came and Liz was delighted with the news! She was the new Director of Operations for the Great Sac Community Arts Center and the Summer Stock Theater.

Breathing a sigh of relief, and a few tears of joy, Liz began to make her phone calls to share her wonderful news. Of course, her first call went to Peter, even though he was teaching and would hear her news later in a voice mail. Then, she called one of her greatest supporters. "Oh, please don't go to voice mail." She said out loud as she waited. Phew!

"Hello, Elizabeth! Is this good news?"

"It sure is, Aunt Amanda! I got the job!" Liz exclaimed. "Can you believe it? I'm the director!"

"Well congratulations! Oh, Liz, I'm so proud of you!" Liz beamed as she heard her aunt's pride in her voice. She could imagine her expression and her smile. Liz smiled as she listened to her say, "I never for a moment doubted that you would not be chosen for the position! So, what did your parents say about you getting the job?"

"I'm on my way over to tell them in person." She listened to her aunt's response and laughed. "Right. Some things are best when told in person." They chatted on as Liz made her way out of the cabin and to her car. She could imagine her aunt's smile and heard her delight in her voice as she spoke. Liz sighed in contentment. Her family was the best! Well, minus one younger sister. "Aunt Amanda before I go, I have a question."

"Ask away. Unless you want me to act in a play. That will never happen, no matter how much you beg!"

"I'll remember that!" They laughed together. "My question is about the cabin. Do you mind if I continue to live up here for a while longer? I'm really liking my privacy, and, well, you know." She couldn't help but laugh at her aunt's response. "Thank you so much, for everything that you and Uncle Kevin have done for me. I love you both."

"We love you too. And Liz, I personally can't wait to see what the summer stock theater has to offer next season. Let me know where I can send a financial donation to assist with refurbishing the theater."

"Financial donation? Aunt Amanda..." She listened to her aunt's response and smiled. "Yes, ma'am. I'll let you know." They talked for a few more minutes before regretfully needing to end the call. Liz held on to her phone as if to keep the connection with her aunt for a moment longer. Of course, she knew that it was silly to feel that way. But, at a moment like this one, well, she exhaled and smiled. One important part of her life was going right. Her family was blessed to have had things work out for her aunt and father to reconcile their differences. Aunt Amanda was truly one of her favorite people on multiple levels. Right now, she would not dwell on her debacle with Jordan. Life was going right. It was time to see her parents and then call Cait, Sammie and JJ.

"Mom, Dad," Liz called out as she came in through the front door along with a gust of leaves blown in through the front door with her. Fall in the Adirondacks! After nights with a hard frost, fall was coming on quick. The leaves had changed color and were making their annual descent to the ground. Summer vacationers were long gone. Now the fall foliage and hiking lovers were making their descent on the region, while local folks were preparing for what was to come in the months ahead. Some people tend to look at the fall season with dread that the cold of winter would soon be upon them. For Liz, this particular fall season was all about love and new beginnings.

"Good grief, Elizabeth, you were noisy enough to wake the dead!" Her father came around the corner from the bathroom with a hammer in his hand. She smiled as she glanced over his attire; old jeans and an old sweatshirt, and work boots on his feet. "Recently retired from the state police force and this is how I get to spend my time! I hope you are here to help me."

"Ah, well, not right now." She knew by his scowl that something was terribly wrong. Her father was mumbling under his breath, and the look in his eyes—well, Elizabeth knew trouble was brewing in her parent's house. But what? Was the question. "Where's Mom?" She asked with a smile in her voice.

"She was upstairs." He snapped out with a chill in his voice. Liz saw the fire in his eyes with the mention of her mother. Oh yes! Trouble had more than brewed. There was war in her parent's home and right now Liz wished that she had stayed away. At that moment, they both heard the sound of footsteps on the stairs.

"Liz, is that you?" Melissa called out as she made her descent. "This is a nice surprise," She said as she came around the corner of the living room, and into the hall where Liz was standing with Jim. "I hope you are here to help your father."

Liz looked between them. Really not good! Both of her parents were scowling at each other. Their eyes were shooting silent words back and forth. They definitely were at war. Heaven help them! "So, who bit off whose head to cause you both to be working on different levels of the house?" Liz ventured to ask. She did love to live dangerously! Neither parent responded to her question.

Instead, Melissa made a huff sound, rolled her eyes and folded her arms across her chest. Jim made a growling sound that was part of his demeanor when he was madder than an old Tom turkey. This caused Liz to laugh, only to have his expression transform into his glower that the Callison children had learned to avoid at all cost while growing up. "Oh goodness, Dad, you're obviously in the dog-house and ready to take me with you!" Then she turned her attention to her mother. "Mom, is it really that bad?" Her mother's expression had not changed since Liz was a young girl. It was the one that said, 'I'm ready to throttle you!'

"Ask your father!" Mel snarled. Her eyes shimmered with anger.

Liz gazed between them and sighed. "You know what? I really don't want to be a part of your drama! So, I am going to pretend that I just walked in here, and the two of you are happy to see me. I'm going to share my news, and then I'm leaving so that the two of you can get back to being mad at each other."

Liz's words made an impact on Mel. She sighed, then said, "We're sorry, Liz." Her mother looked at her with a smile that Liz saw right through. Yes. Her parents were at war with each other and she knew from growing up in their house that a truce was not in the immediate future. "So, is it about the job? Did you get it? Oh, I hope so." She added as tenderness began to shine in her facial features.

"Yes, Mom, Dad, I got the job!" For a brief moment, the whole mood in the Callison home changed. Well, while they were hugging and congratulating her, that is. Then Liz asked, "Will you two do me a favor?"

"What's that, Lizzie?" Her father asked through the scowl that had returned to his face.

"Please make up with each other, so that later on when I come back here to chat, I won't have to feel like I'm walking on a mine field." They exchanged a look that Liz did not know how to interpret. Probably just as well, she thought. "I'm heading over to meet with the Arts Council Board Chairperson and then get started on my new job. I'll call you before I plan to return." She gave them both a hug and then disappeared through the door, only to have more leaves blow in as she exited.

Jim sighed as he raked his fingers through his more salt than pepper hair. The morning had begun so peaceful and then they had received the phone call and that had changed everything. He looked into Mel's sad eyes and felt stabbing pain in his heart. He knew that he alone had caused her sadness. "Look Mellie, Lizzie's right about us needing to make peace. How do we expect our girls to work out their differences, if we can't work through this? I said I was sorry for my outburst. What else do you want me to say?"

"Honey, I know that you are sorry, and I understand why you and Stephen are angry."

"But?"

It was Melissa's turn to sigh. Their family had been through so much pain and turmoil that stemmed back to August of 1979. She was beginning to doubt that they would ever be able to totally move on from the demons of the past that continued to lurk in their lives.

"The one person who has a right to be angry hasn't said a word to us. Don't you think we should follow her lead and keep quiet? What gives you and Stephen the right to condemn Junior at this point in his life?"

"Mellie, I can't believe that you are siding with a felon who not only raped my sister but other women as well! He's a criminal!" Jim yelled. He was wound up tight all over again. Memories of his shattered sister, and his own betrayal all those years ago were front and center in his mind. Amanda might call Junior McGrath a slimy slug, but Jim had other words soaring through his mind. At that moment, he wanted to rip the man apart for what he had done to all of them! His voice conveyed just how hot with anger that he was. "And before you respond, what's to say that once he is out of prison that he won't do it again to someone else? I don't believe for a minute that he is reformed."

"Jim, unlike Shannon Green, Junior McGrath has obviously complied with his sentence, and he did whatever was necessary to be considered for early parole. Perhaps instead of being angry about something you can't change, you should contact Amanda to see if she knows about this? See how your sister is feeling about this turn of events. And, think about this. Perhaps, you need to be the supportive brother to her instead of fighting with me about something we can't change. What do you think of that?"

Jim hooked his hammer into his tool belt and slid his arms around Mel's waist. "Sweetheart, of course you are right! I'm sorry for reacting as I did. You of all people did not need to hear my anger. Please forgive me."

Mel clasped her hands together around Jim's waist. "Oh, Callison, I know you rant and rave like this because you love your family, and of course, I forgive you." She laid her head on his chest and listened to his strong heartbeat. "Making up is so much better than arguing. Don't you think?" She softly smiled as he gently took her chin between his thumb and index finger and tilted her chin so that their eyes met.

"I agree." His voice had lost the gruffness as he suggested, "Let's do something we haven't done in a long time on a peaceful afternoon." His eyes no longer held anger. Deep desire and warmth of a different fire had replaced the other heat.

Melissa immediately recognized the difference. She smiled and licked her lips as her heart jumped with expectation. "You're right! We haven't made up like this in a very long time, and we had better lock the door just in case one of our girls decide to stop over while we are upstairs fixing our marriage."

Jim smiled and began to chuckle. "Do I need to bring my tool belt?" His eyes danced with anticipation. He laughed at Mel's response, gently took her by the hand and escorted her up the stairs.

Liz had no idea of what her parents were up to, as she drove over to the community arts center. The council chairwoman arrived and greeted Liz. They went inside to attend to some more details, specifically the handing over of the keys for the building and the set of keys for the buildings at the old art colony. Ah, yes! The old art colony and the amphitheater that Liz had heard numerous stories about as a child and teen had always intrigued her. She had always felt a yearning in her heart to do something with the vacant buildings.

Now, as the director of the arts council, she would have that opportunity. The chairwoman talked Liz's ear off as they made their way to the old community arts colony, that was located up in the side of the mountain, about two miles from the arts center. The buildings, built in the early 1950's were nestled in the side of the mountains on the western side of the lake. They had not been used since the early 1980's when funding was drawn from summer stock theater, as well as the community arts association, due to the recession and lack of community interest in the fine arts. Liz was filled with enthusiasm, as she looked around and saw potential, where the chairman of the arts council only saw an eyesore that needed to be torn down.

"I'd like to begin my tour by looking at the amphitheater." Liz was buzzing with excitement within, while she appeared totally composed.

"The amphitheater? Why there?"

"Well, since the theater has been exposed to the weather for years and it was neglected proper care, it will need to be refurbished and up to code before our summer theater season can begin."

"Oh, you won't be able to have this monstrosity operational by then." The chairwoman spoke with a bit of disdain in her voice.

"Let's reserve judgment until after I've fully inspected all of the buildings, have made my evaluation, and I've submitted my recommendations to the council." Liz smiled, while not revealing how she felt about the chairperson's tone and remarks. She paused and made notations of her observations, as she moved through the cement bleachers crumbling from years of neglect and being exposed to the elements. "It's too bad that these bleachers had not been made of granite. We could have saved money right off, if that had been the case." Liz had predicted that she would get a comment from the chairwoman and she did. It was obvious that the council chair did not hold the same enthusiasm that Liz did. At that moment, she had to wonder why the woman was on the council, if she didn't want to see the theater succeed? Oh well! Liz was enthused and, at that moment, that was all that mattered. She cautiously walked down the steps into the orchestra pit and withdrew the keys from her pocket to unlock the side door that lead under the stage to the stage stairs, dressing rooms and storage area. The hinges squeaked as the door swung in, and a musty, damp smell from water seepage and being closed up for so long greeted them. Sunlight lit a few feet into the dark cavern under the stage. Then, there was noise and movement. Liz gasped while the other woman shrieked. A bat flew through the door, and soared past them directly towards the woods.

"Well, that was exciting!" Liz chuckled and smiled. Her eyes shone with excitement. "I wonder what else I'll find in here?" Liz said as she peered into the darkness and made a notation to bring a flashlight with her the next time, she came out there.

"You aren't seriously planning on going in there?" The woman gasped. Her eyes still held the horror of the frightening greeting and escape of the bat.

Liz's eyes continued shine with excitement. "Not today! But, yes, I certainly plan to explore the rooms and passageway and see what we have here to work with. You know, just because the colony and amphitheater hasn't been used for a while, that doesn't mean it doesn't have potential to once again be a prominent part of our community." She glanced at her watch. "It's nearly four o'clock and there is more to see before we head back to the arts center." Of course, she had no complaint from her companion.

Liz was still smiling as she pulled into the high school teachers parking lot, and felt as if she could soar up into the sky and touch the clouds. For the first time in months she felt as though her life was at peace. Her new job was going to be a challenge that she was prepared to meet, and her love life? Well now that was an unexpected gift that she had received upon moving home. She scanned the cars that remained parked in the lot and found Peter's car in his designated parking space. It was too beautiful of a fall day to remain in her car and wait. So, Liz got out, walked over to Peter's car and immediately hopped up on the hood to sit and wait for him. A light breeze blew with a hint of fall in the air, while the sun warmed her shoulders. In a matter of minutes, she saw Peter emerge from the building with haste and determination in his step, as he approached her. All of a sudden, he recognized her and sprinted the rest of the way to her. Liz was giggling with joy as he flung his bag of work to read and correct onto the hood of the car. He cupped his hands around her jaws and lowered his lips onto hers. Tenderness quickly gave way to longing as his tongue beckoned her to open her lips for him. Fireworks burst forth in her heart. It felt so right to be there at that moment with Peter. Then he ever so slightly pulled his hungry mouth from hers.

"I could easily get used to this." He murmured as his lips toyed with her lips and jaw. Gentle strokes that caused Liz to suck in a breath. The man was wicked and she loved every minute of it!

"Mm. So could I." Liz breathed out, lost in the moment.

"Hey, Mr. Jones, no making out in the parking lot!" A wise senior called out as a group of students approached them while cutting through the teacher's parking lot to the general school parking lot.

Liz felt heat rising in her cheeks. She watched Peter collect himself Then she drew her lips together to attempt to not laugh as the teens teased Peter and he responded to them. She noticed the teens not so subtle eyeing her over. Now she smiled.

"Hello, everyone. I'm Liz Callison. I guess it was weird for you to see us in an embrace here in the school parking lot." They responded and there was laughter before Liz continued. "Actually, Mr. Jones and I have been friends for a longtime. He graduated with my brother James Junior, aka JJ Callison."

"JJ Callison? I've heard stories about him playing on our hockey team." That statement opened up a more in-depth conversation lead into the next question. "You mean your father was the Jim Callison? The guy whose picture is in the athletic trophy case in the hall?"

"Yes, that's my dad. The legendary Jim Callison athletic superstar of our school." Liz said with a touch of pride. She knew in her heart that her dad was a superstar in other ways as well. Those other ways were what truly mattered for Liz.

Peter seized the moment and interjected, "Ms. Callison graduated from our school a few years ahead of her brother and me. Actually, Liz was not only known for her own athleticism, she also participated in our high school drama club."

Liz smiled and nodded. "Yes, I did. Drama, the theater is very important in my life, and what you saw happening with Mr. Jones and me was simply him congratulating me on my new job with the Community Arts Association and Summer Stock Theater." She smiled a bit more brightly and winked.

"I am?" He hadn't intended on questioning her and quickly recovered, and cleared his throat, while his own smile grew. "Well, yes I am congratulating our new Director. You might be interested in knowing that after graduating from Syracuse," he saw the teens look impressed with Liz's college education. It was time to add the juicy information that Peter was sure would impress them. "Liz worked on Broadway until this past summer when she came home to us."

"Oh wow! Broadway? For real? Why'd you give it up to come here?" They all wanted to know.

From those first responses and questions more interest and questions were thrust upon Liz. Peter listened to his students and intently watched Liz engage in conversation with them while ideas for collaboration between his English department and the community theater soared in his mind. Finally, Peter glanced at his watch and noticed the time.

"Ladies and gentlemen, I hate to be the bearer of bad news, but it's time for us to break this party up and head home. I'm sure that you all will have a chance to speak with Ms. Callison in the future."

His gaze met hers. Sheer pride shone in his eyes. Liz smiled at Peter and the teens gathered around them. Then she said to all of them, "In a couple of weeks there will be an official gathering to introduce me to the community as the new director. All of you and your friends are welcome to attend."

"Wow! Like you really want us to come?"

That question, bad grammar and all, led them into another discussion about how the teens felt insignificant and unwanted in the community. When it was once again only Elizabeth and Peter by the car she sighed quite heavily.

"This is supposed to be a time of celebration for you. What's wrong Lizzie?"

"What those kids said about our community…it's obvious that not too much has changed since I was a teen. Well," she had a sparkle in her eyes that made Peter stand up a bit straighter and listen. "I have some ideas and I intend to use my new position of authority to do good in our community."

"Lizzie, sweetheart, I also have some ideas." He gently hooked a piece of hair behind her ear, then allowed his finger to linger on her jaw.

"I think we have different ideas at the moment." Liz smiled.

"Mine are two-fold. An idea for here at school and us when we are alone." He yawned and stretched. "I'm so proud of you landing the directorship. You are going to be just what our community needs. Tonight, we have to celebrate. Where would you like to go for dinner?"

"Hmm. Choices." Liz scratched her head, grinned and then jokingly added. "Oh, that's right, this isn't New York City with a gazillion choices for dine in or take out. Hmm. What will the young heroine decide to do? What will be her knight's fate?"

"Lizzie!" Peter exclaimed while unable to refrain from smiling at her improvisation. "He's going to keel over from hunger! Then pitifully go limping to his mother and beg for her to come to his aid."

With a stone face she said, "Trust me, your mom will see right through your whining and send you back to me." They burst into laughter, hugged and decided where and when to meet, before leaving in opposite directions to get ready for their evening together.

Liz's days were filled with reviewing the records of successful fundraising, and community events that had been done by the Arts Association in years past. She understood that one of her immediate tasks was developing fund raising and new programs that would renew and generate people's interest in the arts, easier said than done. Of course, she utilized her family as a sounding board for her ideas. Chief among her listeners was her aunt who having worked on fund raising for the not for profit where she works had some ingenious ideas for fund raising at the arts center. It also helped for Liz to have Peter as a sounding board for new artistic ideas, as well as his willingness to help her out on the weekend at the old arts colony.

It was a sunny, crisp Saturday when they slowly made their way down the pothole filled gravel road from the main highway. Old hardwood trees had shed their leaves taking on a ghostly appearance alongside of the road, while white Pine trees loomed from behind providing coverage for woodland creatures. Liz's overactive imagination caused her to laugh out loud as Peter slowed to stop in front of the old mess hall.

He turned, smiled and gazed towards her. "Okay, Liz, one minute we are having a totally rational conversation and then for no apparent reason you burst into laughter. So, please tell me, what struck you so funny?"

Her smile grew as she gazed into his eyes with a hint of mischievousness and delight. "Okay, Peter. I know this is going to sound ridiculous. But for just a moment allow your imagination to run free. Just look around us. Think about what you see. For me," Liz's whole demeanor seemed to change, come to life in a new way, an artist's creative way. "I quite vividly see a scene unfolding before my eyes. The trees and these old buildings," her hand swept through the air to punctuate what she was seeing, "are a wonderful backdrop for a murder mystery."

Peter glanced out of the window just as a gust of wind shook a few remaining leaves from a Maple tree. He watched them tumble to the ground as he quietly spoke with a hint of apprehension in his voice. "You know, Liz this was the place where a Sacandaga lumberman had met his death many years before the art colony was built..."

"I remember the story. Peter, did you know that many of the artists who stayed here and performed on stage reported mysterious things happening throughout the summer theater seasons?" Liz's imagination was kicking in. She felt her heart rate increasing, as Peter picked up and continued on with the story.

"Yes, I heard that a woman felt as if someone had their hands around her throat..." His eyes quickly moved from Liz to the area outside of the car and then returned to gaze at her.

"Yet no one was on stage with her at that particular moment." Liz's voice revealed an ominous feeling that Peter picked up on.

"Another time..." Peter began with a hint of secretiveness in his voice. Suddenly he stopped speaking. A shadow moved past the mess hall towards the amphitheater. "Holy crap!" Peter exclaimed. "Lizzie, did you see that?" Peter was dead serious. All color had drained from his face.

They remained in the car, unable to move as a sense of doom blanked them. Neither one spoke. The wind blew. Leaves continued to fall from the trees.

Finally, Liz found her vice. "Yeah, Peter that was weird." Liz felt a sudden chill on her neck, but shook it off. "We both know that there probably are many reasons why we saw that shadow. So, even though I jokingly planted the original idea, let's not allow our imaginations and an old legend to spook us. Ghost or no ghost, I have a job to do up here and I intend to do it." She glanced back out of the window at their surroundings, seeing nothing out of the ordinary. "You know, Peter,"

"Ought oh!" Peter said with major concern for what Liz might be thinking.

She giggled. "Aw come on! All I was going to say is that in the future we might be able to use the shadow and the legends of ghosts to our advantage to spark interest in the summer theater. People might simply come out of curiosity to see if this place really is haunted."

Peter released a sigh of relief that Liz didn't have a more outrageous idea. "That's true." Peter was not smiling as he turned from looking out of the window to meet her gaze. "But, Lizzie, after what just happened, I know that I would feel better if you didn't come up here alone."

Her eyes softened as she reached over and touched his chin. "Peter, some women might take offense at your concern, but I don't. But, having said that, don't think that I'm a wimp who is going to run to you every time something odd or in-explainable happens around here. I appreciate you sharing your concern for my safety with me. Do you have any idea how scary it can be to walk alone late at night on the streets of New York City, even in a good neighborhood? In the theater district where I called home for over ten years?" From that question Liz regaled Peter with a couple of incidents that had happened to her. One in particular would have been avoided, if, her boyfriend had shown up to walk her home as he had promised.

"I hope you dumped the idiot for being inconsiderate." She told him what happened, easing his mind. Then he responded, "You never have to worry about me standing you up, and treating you as he did, Liz."

"I know, Peter." Their eyes spoke of unfulfilled desire and longing as she said, "You have grown into an amazing man, and you are in an entirely different league from him."

With those words, Peter gently placed his hands-on Liz's jaws, leaned in and brushed his lips against hers. She tasted of coffee and lips gloss as she leaned into his touch. Liz rested her hand on his chest. She felt his muscles and steady heartbeat through his sweatshirt. By now Peter had increased his pressure on her lips. She slightly opened them, inviting Peter to take more, and he did. All of a sudden there was a knock on the driver's side window. They pulled apart and looked, while fully expecting to see a familiar face. But, no one was there. Still, the romantic moment had been shattered. They regained their composure and decided to get out of the vehicle before they lost their nerve. Hand in hand they walked across the compound to begin their walk through of the old mess hall and storage area. Liz had ideas to generate community interest and involvement with restoration. Today's project would provide Liz with knowledge about whether her idea was a go, or it should be scratched. Of course, the weather and the apparent resident ghost may further alter her ideas. She hoped not!

CHAPTER 8

Warm fall days gave way to cooler temperatures and finally the weather turned downright cold. Winter was making its descent upon the mountains. Work that had begun at the arts colony was put on hold until spring. Now Liz gave all of her attention to the community arts center. The first event that she had organized for Halloween, featuring artistic work of the Great Sac High School students, was a success much to the amazement of some of the council members. In years past the council had not considered having the youth display or, for them to perform at the center. Liz was thrilled at the response she had received from parents, teachers and community members as they viewed the student's various forms of artwork. One conversation in particular had stayed with Liz. It made her smile as she recalled hearing the couple say, *it is wonderful to see the creativity of our youth. I cried when I read Leah's poem, and Mark's carving of the eagle in the round piece of pine was amazing. Charlie did an outstanding job playing the banjo. It sounded like he should have been down south in the mountains, rather than up north with us.*

While the cold weather ended outdoor work projects at the arts colony for Liz, it ushered in cold weather events at the arts center, and winter sports at Great Sacandaga Community High School and other schools. It was a gloomy Saturday morning. Peter was chaperoning the hockey team at an Adirondack High School Hockey Tournament up in Lake Placid, New York, so Liz was alone at the cabin. A fire was blazing in the fireplace making the space warm and cozy, while the sky was spitting sleet that was forecast to turn to snow later in the day. With a mug of coffee in her hand, Liz read the lake scene that she had just completed in the second act of her play. A smile graced her lips as she realized that her play was coming together in ways that she had never imagined. However, Liz was concerned that the transitions between the past and the present, and the merging of two different generations in her story might be too complicated, or confusing for the audience. Time would tell. A noise outside drew her attention to the front window. She placed her mug on the coffee table, stood and stretched, then walked over to the window to look outside. She drew in a breath in surprise. Someone had ventured up the mountain in a vehicle that did not appear to be suitable for driving in winter weather in the north country. An ominous feeling swept over Liz as she studied the unfamiliar car. She checked the door to make sure that it was locked. Okay. No. It was not okay, because whomever was in the car was not alone. Someone was getting out the passenger side. Oh, good grief! Liz watched her dad, of all people close the passenger side door and say something to the driver who was still hidden because of the side of the cabin. Now, what in the love of cheesy rice was her father doing out on a day like this in someone else car? Why hadn't he driven up the mountain in his pickup? At least that had four-wheel drive! Liz sighed as she watched her dad wait for the driver to join him. Her dad appeared to be in a good mood, all smiles and laughing at something that was said. Well, that was a good sign! Then, she saw who the driver was when Uncle Kevin came into view. A smile burst onto her lips as she unlocked the door, flung it open, and stepped out onto the porch to greet them.

"Good morning, Dad, Uncle Kevin. Where are Mom and Aunt Amanda?" Liz shivered from the cold, as she waited and watched them proceed carefully along the slippery walkway to the steps.

They both returned a greeting as they came up the steps, and onto the porch. "First, your aunt informed us that she was abducting your mother for a girl's day out. Then, she informed me that she was stealing my pickup which she promised that she would return dent free, and that we were to fend for ourselves." Jim was not smiling.

"Girls day out! In this?" Liz's eyes revealed her own concern. "Dad, Uncle Kevin, you both do realize that you drove up here in sleet that is supposed to change over to snow, and the two women whom I treasure most in the world, with the exception of Cait, are out someplace in this nasty weather? Why isn't Mom driving them in her SUV?" Liz was deeply concerned.

He scowled and grumbled, and then he said, "I told you, Elizabeth, your aunt abducted your mother and stole my pickup."

Liz looked from one man to the other, in disbelief at what she was hearing. They were normally sensible, smart men. But, this morning, given what her dad had just told her, Liz had to wonder how many brain cells they were functioning with. "Why didn't either of you two stop them?"

At that moment, a gust of wind pelted them with sleet, as they stood on the porch. It was Kevin who responded. "Liz, I too have come to treasure your mom. And as for your aunt, the love of my life, well, I've learned to choose my battles with her. This girl's day out weather and all was one battle I was sure to lose."

"You and me both!" Jim interjected while rolling his eyes. "I should call the barracks and report that my truck was stolen."

"Dad, you can't do that to Mom and Aunt Amanda!" Liz's eyes darted between her father's eyes and his hands to see if he withdrew his phone from his pocket.

"Lizzie, you worry too much! I said I should, not that I would. I shudder to think of the war that would cause with my wife and my sister."

"And I'd be in the thick of the battle with you." Kevin added. Liz listened to them carry on about her mother and aunt. They were not painting a nice picture of either of them. Then Kevin shared words of wisdom from his years of working in the medical field, and as the director of the trauma emergency department. "So, as the director of the arts association you will have to learn to choose your battles wisely."

Liz took a moment and mulled over their words. "Thank you both for your words of wisdom. I'll remember that. So, Dad, since you two were left to find something to do, you obviously decided to come up here to spy on me. Were you hoping to catch me and Peter having a little fun?" Liz bit her lips while attempting to hide her smile. She shivered as she turned to open the door for them.

Jim chuckled. "Lizzie girl, you are scaring me….sounding a bit too much like your sassy aunt!" Liz smiled with satisfaction for what she accepted as a compliment, even though she knew that was not her father's intention. "For your information little girl, I spoke with Wes and I know Peter's with the hockey team. But, nice try." His smile and the teasing in his eyes warmed Liz's heart.

Still, Liz didn't know if she should be flattered, or upset that her dad was so accepting of Peter spending so much time with her, and obviously had an idea of how they spent their time. She decided that some things were best left alone. Her intimate relationship with Peter was one of them!

"So, Uncle Kevin," she said as she closed the door. "What brings you and Aunt Amanda north at this time of year?"

Kevin moved within the familiar space with ease, removed his coat and placed it on the coat hook by the door. He turned and walked over to sit in the chair he liked that was positioned near the fire. "Yesterday we got a flight in to Buffalo, rented a car and went to the state prison for Junior's appearance before the parole board."

"Oh!" Was all Liz said, as she watched her father and uncle exchange glances.

"Since we were up here in New York, it made sense for us to stop in and see your parents, then go to Albany to return the car and catch a flight home."

"That is great!" Joy shone in Liz's smile.

"Yeah, it's great, alright!" Jim, on the other hand, was not smiling. "Your aunt informed me that they are here to make my life miserable for the weekend. She says it's so I'll appreciate how good I have it with your mother after they have gone home."

Liz burst into laughter. She could hear her aunt saying all that and more. Then, she grew serious. "So, Uncle Kevin, did Junior get his early parole?"

"No, and he is crushed. Junior has worked hard and made commendable strides in his life while serving his sentence. But, the two young women who pressed the charges against him, that led to his conviction were also there. They provided updated victim impact statements and, well, even with Amanda's victim impact statement and her statement regarding the counseling that she has been providing Junior through her letters, the board looked favorable towards the other women. Amanda is a little hot, to say the least, by this outcome."

"Of course, my sister is hot!" His cheeks revealed that he also was a tad hot. "Remember, Kevin, I grew up with the woman. I know firsthand what happens when she gets a bug up her -" Jim cleared his throat. "Well, you know! Lizzie, this is another example of how your aunt won't just let the judicial system do its job."

"Jim, that's unfair!" Liz saw something in her uncle's eyes. She had never seen him look so serious, and wondered what he might say if she wasn't present.

Then her dad lashed out. "No, it's not Kevin. I know we hashed this out last night. But I still don't agree with my sister. You know what Junior did to Amanda. How could you agree to defend him?"

Liz remained quiet, as she watched and listened to her father and her uncle. She had a feeling that once word spread about Junior not making early parole, and that her aunt was defending him that more people would be sharing their opinions. Little did the men sitting with her know that they were providing Liz with ideas for the of her characters in her play.

"Jim, you better ease up on your opinion of Amanda before you see her later on today. As Amanda reminded me, she forgave him, and everyone deserves a second chance, especially if they prove that they sincerely want to change their life for the better. We both have seen Junior striving to change and that's why we contacted the lawyer."

Liz took advantage of her father remaining quiet for the moment. She could tell that he was deep in thought. That was encouraging! So, she quietly asked, "Uncle Kevin, are you and Aunt Amanda paying for a lawyer for Junior? Even after what he did to her and the others?"

"No, we did not hire a lawyer. But we have secured a public defender to work with Junior on his appeal." He sighed. "So, now we're here to unwind before heading back to Baltimore."

"Well, I'm glad that you are here." Liz sincerely meant it. She smiled and inquired, "How about some more coffee, and perhaps a piece of pumpkin pie to go with it?"

"Pumpkin pie?" Her father asked. Liz smiled, nodded, and then stood while he exclaimed, "Child, you've been holding out on us!"

Sunday morning a light blanket of snow covered the road leading to Jim and Melissa's. Liz could see from the tracks in the snow that others had also ventured out on this cold, early winter morning. She drove cautiously and knew that it was only a matter of time before the town plow got to her parent's road. A smile graced her lips as she answered her blue tooth. "Good morning, Pete. How did we do?"

"Morning, Lizzie." He yawned. "We won. Four to three. Sorry it took so long for me to return your call. I have to say, we made the right judgment call staying at the hotel last night, rather than coming home in the dark on slippery, snow filled roads. I only wish I had bars on my phone so I could have called you."

Liz heard voices in the background. She giggled. "It sounds like the guys are still celebrating over their win."

"Celebrating is one way to put it! I wonder if our dads were this crazy?"

"Our Dad's?" Liz asked with laughter in her voice. "Have you forgotten that you and JJ also played varsity hockey?"

"Oh yes, Lizzie I do remember." Peter grew quiet.

"Hmm. I'm hearing a story or two that obviously cannot be told with young ears close by."

"Yeah. Exactly." Peter yawned into her ear, then asked, "So, how is your morning going? Did we get much snow?"

"It's still snowing. We have about three inches of wet, heavy snow on top of the layer of ice we got yesterday. The roads are a mess, even though the town and state plows have been out. I'm heading over to my parent's house to see Aunt Amanda and Uncle Kevin before they head home." Their conversation continued on with ease, until Liz turned into her parent's driveway. "Well, Pete, I'm here at my parent's house. It looks like Dad has been busy this morning and has their drive all plowed out. Promise me that you'll drive carefully when you get back to school. Okay. See you later. I love you too."

Liz sat for a moment in the warmth of her car and looked towards her parent's home. She had been home for five months. So much had changed in her life during that time. But still, some things had remained the same. Her younger sister, Jordan, continued to be the sore spot in her life. Still, if it hadn't been for Jordan, Liz would be in New York City and she would not have a challenging new job, or Peter in her life. With a sigh in her heart, Liz got out of her car and raced through the snowflakes to the front door. Laughter greeted her as she stepped through the door. Slipping out of her outerwear, and kicking off her wet boots by the front door, Liz sought out her family.

"Good morning, Liz —Lizzie—Elizabeth." They all greeted her with smiles, asked about the condition of the roads, and if she had heard from Peter. Liz spoke with a smile in her voice, as she answered their questions while she made herself at home, got a mug from the cupboard and fixed herself a cup of coffee. Joy radiated from her as she approached her aunt, and leaned down to give her a hug.

"Well, now," Amanda said, while reciprocating with a hug of her own. "This is a nice surprise to see you this morning. What brings you out on this snow?"

"I am on a mission. First, show me the fingernails ladies." Liz flitted from her aunt to her mother owing and awing, while listening to their comments about their fun time together. Not only did they do their nails, they had lunch together, and bought some new clothes.

"Elizabeth," her father's voice interrupted the women's conversation and drew everyone's attention to him. "You said that you are on a mission. I sincerely hope that you did not come over here simply to see your mother and aunt's painted fingernails." He gave her his *I'm not thrilled that you came out in this nasty weather* look. Liz knew that look all too well! No. Her father was not thrilled with her. She knew that it wasn't because she had come over to his home. The problem was the weather and his concern for her being out in the bad weather, instead of being safe at the cabin.

"Dad, thanks for being concerned." Liz eased over to him and rested her hand on his shoulder. He in turn raised his hand to rest on hers, gave it a gentle squeeze and then lowered his hand to his coffee mug. "My mission is two-fold. It includes Aunt Amanda and Uncle Kevin." Everyone's eyes were on Liz as she spoke. "Aunt Amanda, I know it's snowing, and you do have to leave for Albany before too long."

"I hear a but coming." Amanda was smiling as the others chimed in with their understanding of the unspoken but. There was laughter from everyone except Liz. "Oh, Elizabeth, I'm sorry." Amanda was still smiling. "We did get carried away with our teasing. What were you going to say?"

"Well, I was going to say you grew up here, so you know how winters are-"

"And?" Amanda asked with a twinkle of delight in her eyes. Her niece had come so far from the shattered weekends she had spent crying on her and Kevin's shoulders. She was glad to see how Liz could respond to and hold her own with their family's teasing and sense of humor. There was something else that Amanda had seen in Liz's eyes, her demeanor. Until now, she had not recognized what she was seeing. Pride. Accomplishment. A new positive sense of self-worth. Peace. Belonging. Liz was finding herself.

"And, even though the weather is rotten, I hope you have time to join me for the nickel tour of the community arts center, and the arts colony before you and Uncle Kevin leave."

"Elizabeth, use some common sense!" Jim exclaimed. "Today is not the day to be traipsing around on snowy dangerous roads showing your aunt and uncle where you're working. Besides, Amanda knows where the arts colony is."

"Dad, please stop being Aunt Amanda's bossy big brother for just a moment." Liz's eyes implored him. Melissa softly chuckled and smiled at Liz's description of Jim. "Aunt Amanda and Uncle Kevin are capable of telling me no, if they don't want to go over to the colony and center with me."

Amanda raised a brow as she glanced between Liz and Jim. She sighed, while tapping the end of her polished fingernails on her coffee mug. She did know where the old arts colony was. During her and Jim's youth it had been a popular spot for teens to sneak into with their dates and make out. So, of course she had been there with Johnson, and yes, they had made out in various locations. That memory was a rather sad one. Love gone wrong. Yet, no one knew what she was feeling at that moment in time. She cleared her throat as her gaze swept over her family. Her smile was soft and her voice clear. "Liz, your dad is right." She held up her hand as Jim opened his mouth to speak. "Years ago, I was a frequent trespasser at the arts colony along with others from this fine community." Amanda smiled as she looked straight at Jim. Liz saw something pass between their eyes. Oh great! They were doing it again, conversing without saying a word! Fortunately, Amanda broke the moment of silence in the room. "Tell me, Elizabeth have you had any more encounters with the phantom?"

"Amanda!" Jim's exclamation was accompanied with a scowl. "Don't encourage Elizabeth's imagination to grow from old community folklore." His eyes were taking on a darker shade of brown.

"Oh Jim! Come on!" Amanda gave him a challenging look. "You and I both know that there are kernels of truth woven into the folklore. Remember, a lumberjack did supposedly die out there in the mountain, and there is also the story Gentle Spirit told us when we were kids."

"Another story! Gentle Spirit had a story? Great gram's stories were always the best!" Liz exclaimed. "Dad, why is this the first I'm hearing about it?"

"Because it's just a story the old woman told us to try to scare us into behaving when we were teenagers."

Amanda snickered, then raised a brow. *Tsk, tsk, tsk!* Jim glowered at her.

"Liz, your father is partially correct about Gram. She wanted us to be aware of the stories of our people, our Mohawk heritage, and I do believe that there is something to Gentle Spirit referring to the area surrounding the community arts colony as the place of the troubled spirit. You know, there may well be other spirits besides the lumberjack roaming around in the area."

"That is quite possible." Kevin interjected and gave Amanda a wink, while Jim grumbled his annoyance at Kevin's supporting of Amanda. "Look at Gettysburg, PA for instance. Ever since the war people have reported seeing ghosts in the area."

"That's right." Amanda agreed. "So, there may be spirit's here. Ah, Jim, remember our conversation as we sat together by the fire up in the side of the mountain?"

"We both agreed that was Gram." Jim tipped his chin down, as if, to dare Amanda to dispute his words.

"Mm-hmm!" Her eyes sparkled. "We both know that there could be other spirits at the colony."

"Other spirits? You mean besides the lumberjack?" Elizabeth was curious about the new story of the community's history. She was captivated by the way her aunt shared the story. Eventually, it came to an end.

"I still think Gram embellished the story of the French- Indian War." Jim shook his head in disbelief.

Tsk, Tsk, Tsk! Amanda responded.

Liz giggled as she listened to her father and aunt further exchange their opinions on the subject. She had to wonder if she and her siblings were half as entertaining as those two?

"Thank you both for sharing your thoughts on the arts colony." Liz said as she helped herself to another piece of coffee cake.

"Feel free to call me at any time, Liz. You know I will share anything I know to enlighten you about our family's past." Amanda stretched and looked into her coffee mug. Empty. Not good! At that moment, Mel stood and quietly spoke to Amanda before walking over to the counter to make more coffee.

"Thank you, Aunt Amanda. You know, Dad, if you'd be more forthcoming, I wouldn't have to call Aunt Amanda as much." Once again Liz giggled, as her father shared a remark that only drew more comments from her aunt.

"As enjoyable as this is to hear about the past, Liz did invite us to see the art colony and arts center. Perhaps, since the snow is hindering our going to the amphitheater we could go to the arts center and see the current artist's showing that you told us about. Then, we can make plans to come visit the arts colony in the spring?" Kevin suggested.

Jim immediately supported his suggestion, while Amanda slid her hand onto Kevin's leg to silently thank him for intervening. Liz agreed, said her goodbye to her parents, and went on outside to brush the new fallen snow from the windshield, and warm up the car for their excursion. Her aunt and uncle appeared just as she was getting into her warming car.

Liz should have known that her disappointment about not being able to take them to the art colony would be short lived thanks to her aunt. On the way to the art center Amanda regaled her and Kevin with more stories about the community dating back to the French-Indian War. During that time, and in the years after many of their ancestors had lost their lives. Their villages had been uprooted and clans were displaced as more white settlers stole ancestral lands. Gram's cabin was on land that had been in their family's clan for generations. Of course, Liz's imagination soared as she pictured longhouses standing in a group in the area where the cabin rests in the open field on the side of the mountain. Liz listened and wondered why her dad had never shared any of this family history with her. Did he even care about their family's past? Her aunt did, and her willingness to share family history meant the world to Liz.

The snow was letting up as she turned into the arts center parking lot. Liz smiled to herself as she ushered them into the building, turned on the overhead lights, answered their questions and watched them as they walked hand in hand through the local fiber and weavers show.

"Wow! This is amazing, Liz." Amanda sighed as she looked around the room that held a display of large and small loom and handwoven pieces from an eclectic array of materials, as well as, various sized reed baskets that had been strategically placed to show off their simple beauty.

"Liz, I agree with your aunt. This work is truly amazing. I am wondering, are any of these pieces for sale?" Kevin asked.

"Good question, Uncle Kevin." Liz beamed with delight. "Some pieces are strictly for show and other pieces are here on consignment."

"Consignment?" Amanda asked from the other side of the room where she was admiring a wool spread that had been hand woven on a loom.

"Yes. The Great Sac Community Arts Assoc. makes a minimal profit off of the sales of the items that the crafters are selling." Liz responded. "I'll get you a brochure that has a bio of the artist and the cost of their pieces. Then, if you are interested in purchasing anything you can either call them directly, or give me a call and I'll set it aside for you."

"Thank you, Liz." Kevin shifted his gaze and glanced out the window. It was still snowing but was changing to that mix in the precipitation that the meteorologists had called for. He also noticed that Amanda was looking intently at a rag rug. Kevin had a sneaky feeling that they were soon to be the owners of the rug. Where they would put it in their apartment? He had no idea! Still, the weather was of utmost concern. "Amanda, sweetheart, I know that you are enjoying yourself. However, the weather is changing, and I do believe we should get going."

Liz and Amanda agreed. They closed up the center, got in Liz's car and headed back to Jim and Mel's. The roads were slick in spots where the snow was covered with an icy mix. By the time they had pulled into the drive and Jim and Melissa's, Amanda and Kevin decided that they should prepare to leave for Albany to allow for a slower drive to the airport.

It was late afternoon when Liz received a call from Peter to tell her that he was at the school. He was glad to be back in the valley, and filled her in on the treacherous ride down through the snowy and icy mountains. There had been three accidents: one fender bender and the other two more serious ones that required medical assistance. As if the accidents weren't bad enough, at one point they had to take a detour do to downed tree limbs and power lines obstructing the road. Peter was man enough to admit to Liz that he had been scared, and did a lot of praying for their safety. So, now that he was at the school and could breathe a sigh of relief, he declared that it would take a blizzard to keep him from driving up to the cabin. Right now, the only thing holding him up was the last two students who were picked up by their parents. Liz was smiling as she listened to Peter share of his adventures and his desire. She too wanted to see him. But his safety was equally important. So, she told Peter about her experience of driving on the local roads earlier in the day, and that she would understand, if he simply wanted to go to his apartment and meet up with her tomorrow evening. By the time they ended the call, Liz was buzzing with anticipation for what the night promised to bring. After all, Peter had said that only a full-blown nor'easter would keep him from coming to see her.

One half hour later Liz heard a loud thump outside. She breezed through the cabin from the kitchen to the front window and from there she looked out towards the drive. There was Peter, no hat on his head—she recalled how often he would come into her parent's house as a teen without a hat on—hunched over with his coat collar pulled up to keep the snow from hitting his neck. He had a large gym bag slung over his shoulder and looked tired and in need of adult company. Her company. She opened the door, as he came to the steps and stepped out to greet him. Peter dropped his bag onto the porch, grabbed a hold of Liz's upper arms and drew her into his embrace. His jacket was wet and cold, and sent a chill through her sweater. Her slippered feet didn't fare much better, as she felt the chill of the wood flooring on the porch. But Liz made no attempt to leave the safe harbor of his embrace. Peter's desire was made evident as he lowered his lips onto hers. He nibbled on her lower lip causing Liz to moan and then sigh. Her mouth responded.

"Peter, I think we should go inside." She finally breathed out.

"I agree." He quietly said with a hint of reluctance to break their hold on each other.

Peter drew back from her, bent and picked up his gym bag. Then he gently gathered Liz's hand into his, as they entered the cabin. Once inside the warm space it was like entering another world. The fire blazed and crackled shedding soft light in the room, while the aroma of homemade chicken soup, cookies, and muffins mingled with the wood smoke. Peter removed his coat, hung it on the hook, and turned to find Liz stirring the fire before adding a new log. He kicked off his wet shoes, peeled off his damp socks and walked over to her. He placed his socks near the fire, then held out his hand and said, "Lizzie, come sit with me and tell me about your weekend."

No further invitation was necessary. They snuggled together on the couch, and soon put discussing their weekends on hold, as another conversation opened up between them. Their bodies sizzled with hunger as their mouths meld together. Oh yes! They both had much to say to the other. Each understood the other's needs, while their hands were busy with their own conversation. The day had quietly slipped away to night. The fire that had blazed was almost down to embers, when they awakened together on the couch with an afghan covering them. Their clothes that had been removed with haste, were mingled together on the floor by the couch. "Ah, Liz, I didn't mean to-"

Liz placed her finger on his lips. "Am I complaining? Did I protest when we were making love?"

"Well, no!"

"That's right, Peter. I have no regrets. Every time we make love—especially what we shared today is better than a glass of the finest aged wine."

"I'm better than wine?" His eyes sparkled with mischievousness.

"Oh yes!" Liz smiled and stretched in sheer contentment, and as she did the blanket fell away. "Goodness, we better stoke the fire, or we will need more than a blanket and each other to ward off the cold."

Peter's gaze slowly made its way over her body. A knowing smile crept over his lips. "Mm Lizzie, you are amazing. I'm so lucky to have you in my life." Peter leaned down and picked up the tangled pile of their clothes. "As soon as I find my briefs, I'll stoke the fire."

Liz fought back a smile while attempting to sound serious as she asked, "Do you plan on using your briefs to stoke the fire? If you do, they won't last for too long." The absurdity of her question and comment caused Peter to stop pulling the underwear up his legs. He turned to look at her and saw the mischievousness in her eyes. Her sense of humor was a breath of fresh air. Peter responded, causing Liz to burst into a round of laughter. Tears pooled in her eyes causing her lashes to shimmer with wetness. Liz finished pulling on her clothes and socks, stood and stretched. With the smile of that of a well-loved woman, she turned the light by the chair from dim to bright, then headed to the kitchen to prepare a light meal for them.

It had been a few weeks since Peter had stopped into his dad's and uncle's business. One reason was that he didn't need to have his uncle meddling in his life. The other reason was that he had simply been busy, and when he had a few spare minutes from his demands of teaching, he was with Elizabeth. Night crept over the valley like a thick winter blanket. The freezing temperature, leafless hardwood trees all indicated that winter was there for the long hall. Soon the lake would be frozen solid enough to hold the weight of a vehicle, and ice fishermen would dot the frozen water. Peter slowed down his car, put on his directional and eased into the bait shop parking lot. His dad's and uncles' pickup trucks were in their usual parking places. Yes, indeed, anyone in the community, perhaps the county, for that matter, knew that the two men always parked in those two places. He smiled as he remembered one time when someone had parked in his uncle's spot. Uncle Stephen was livid! His smile grew as he recalled the words that had been exchanged when Stephen had entered the bait shop and confronted the person who had the nerve to take his spot. Then, Peter chuckled as he thought, *only Mr. C would have guts enough to park there and live through Uncle Stephen's repercussions.*

Peter knew most of the regulars who came to the bait shop, but tonight there was an unfamiliar car in the lot. He noticed that it was a very nice car, an expensive fairly new car at that. When Peter opened the door to the shop, the bell jingled as he stepped inside. He heard his uncle and dad laughing, as well as a woman's voice. He was just about ready to speak when he heard his dad call out. "Well, my goodness, Peter! This is a pleasant surprise!"

"Hey, Dad. Uncle Stephen—ma'am," he responded as he closed the door and walked through the aisles of fishing gear to the counter where the adults were congregated.

"Hey, Pete! How's life at good old Great Sac High these days?" Stephen asked while lazily cupping his hand onto Belinda's shoulder and drawing her closer.

"Great, now that I'm a teacher and not a student!" Peter smiled and responded to his uncle's comments. "Actually, Dad, I'm here to have a conversation with you." He looked at his father as he spoke. "It's a father-son thing. Later when the time is right, we'll include Mom. For now, I need to talk with you. Alone." His eyes shifted towards his uncle and then back at his father.

"A private conversation? This must be something serious." Stephen was watching his nephew. He had some ideas and ventured a guess. "You wouldn't by any chance have played too close to the fire and got Elizabeth pregnant?" Stephen asked.

Peter thought there might be a touch of smugness in his uncle's tone and expression. He also was more than a bit annoyed and had a response. "Pregnant?" Peter slightly shook his head, as if, in disbelief. "I should have known that you would immediately think something like that, given your track record and all." His tone was judgmental, just as he had intended.

"What's that supposed to mean?" Stephen had released his hand from Belinda's shoulder and was now standing straight. His eyebrows were drawing together.

Wes had remained quiet, listening to their interaction and didn't like where it was heading. "Son, choose your words wisely." Was all he said, while knowing that Peter was wound up and ready to fire back at Stephen. Which he did.

"For your information, Unc, I unlike you, take responsibility for my girlfriend. We have an understanding with each other."

"Son -" Wes spoke with authority, only to go unnoticed by Peter.

"Unc you are the last person who has any right to stand there and judge our relationship. Love, respect, trust and friendship are the basis for our relationship, not sexual gratification that comes second to the other. Of course, our faith is also important to us. I bet you didn't know that we are going to church together." He saw the surprise in his uncle's expression. "I guess Mom and Dad being respectful of Liz and me didn't tell you that we all have been in church together on Wednesday nights." He watched Stephen turn to his father for confirmation. Wes nodded. "That's right, Unc. We are building a lasting relationship that is more than lust and sexual gratification. From what I know of your past and present, I don't think you ever truly loved or respected Amanda. If you had, then you would have believed her over those two so called friends of yours. You know, I pity you Unc. Until recently you've been alone because instead of taking responsibility as a man, you ran a classy woman out of town. You didn't deserve Amanda." There was a tone in Peter's voice, perhaps disgust as he spoke. "I sure do hope you are treating Belinda," he nodded towards the woman at Stephen's side, "better than you ever treated Amanda. I guess time will tell." Yes, Peter was on a roll. Wes gave up trying to stop his son and listened. He noticed things, important things. Over the summer and fall Peter had matured, and at that moment, Peter was protecting his woman. A surge of pride swept through Wes as he listened. "Mom and Dad raised me to be different from you with how I treat women. I've seen how Dad loves and cares for Mom. Even though my relationship with Elizabeth is none of your business, I will say that I am following my dad's example and she is not pregnant. When and if she does become pregnant, it will be because we both are ready and want the child to be in our shared lives."

Silence hung in the air between the men. Their eyes were locked, poised for further battle. It was Belinda who quietly spoke. "Stephen, much has been said. Perhaps we should excuse ourselves and give Peter time alone with his father." No one noticed the wetness clinging to her eyelashes.

Stephen sighed. His nephew had just challenged him as one man to the other. Unfortunately, for Stephen, Peter had shown great wisdom and maturity. He also had ripped open memories that Stephen didn't want to acknowledge at that moment. His voice revealed his wounds as he spoke. "Yeah, Belinda I guess we had better go." He turned towards Wes and said, "I'll see you tomorrow. Tell Becky I'll call her later." Stephen held Belinda's coat for her. He didn't say another word, as he took her hand and escorted her from the shop.

Neither Wes nor Peter spoke until after the door was closed and they were alone. Wes withdrew the money from the cash register and prepared to count the drawer. Then he turned to face his son. He was not smiling. His voice revealed that he was in full father mode. "Well, son now that it's the two of us, suppose you tell me what has your butt on fire to the point that you acted like a total jerk with your uncle?"

Peter didn't respond to his father's question. He simply pulled a small jeweler's box from his pocket and placed it on the counter in front of his dad. Wes looked at the box then at Peter as a knowing smile began to creep onto his lips. Peter nodded towards the box. Wes remained quiet as he reached out and picked it up. He opened it and saw a beautiful diamond surrounded by rubies and sapphires set in a white gold band. Wes cleared his throat and sniffled.

"Well now," he sighed. "I certainly can understand why you wanted to keep this private between you and me." Wes couldn't help but smile. "Son, I approve of the woman you have fallen in love with. Elizabeth Callison certainly comes from a fine family, and it will be a joy to welcome her into ours. Now about your choice in engagement rings?" He saw a look of concern sweep over Peter's face. He chuckled. "Son, it's beautiful! So, when do you plan on proposing to Liz?"

"Later on, tonight when we're at the cabin." Peter was grinning from ear to ear as he picked up the box, closed it and slid it into his pocket.

"Sounds good." Wes said as he nodded with approval, and then asked, "I do hope you plan to tell Jim and Melissa before your mother?"

Peter's eyes grew bigger as he nodded. "That is for sure! Especially, with the hot water we were in when they found out from Mom that we are dating!" He glanced at the wall clock and began to zip up his jacket. "I better get going."

"Hold on a minute." Wes was no longer smiling as he had been only a moment ago. He nodded towards the chair Peter had just vacated. "We have another matter to discuss. An important matter!"

Peter sighed and slid onto the stool by the counter. He knew what was coming. One half hour later he left the bait shop knowing that his father was right. He had been disrespectful of his uncle, and he did need to apologize to him. To make matters worse, he knew that before too long he was going to hear about it from his mother. Peter released a long, slow breath as he started his car. Even though it had been tough for him to have his dad criticize how he had spoken to his uncle, he also had given some good advice for dealing with the Callison family. He started his car to warm up and pulled out his phone, dialed and waited for Liz to answer.

"Hi Pete. Did you have a nice visit with your dad?"

"It was okay for the most part." He released a breath. "I had some words with Uncle Stephen and, well, I need to apologize to him."

"Ought oh! I can hear it in your voice that it was beyond not good!" Liz knew that Peter needed to unload his feelings. So, she quietly waited for him to continue.

"Liz, we said some really nasty things to each other. He pushed my buttons. But that's not why I called."

"Oh?" Liz had an ominous feeling. "Please, don't tell me you can't keep our dinner date."

"Don't worry, Lizzie dinner is still on for tonight at the restaurant up in Speculator." He chuckled at her response. "But I was wondering if we could meet at your parent's house, instead of me driving up to the cabin to pick you up."

"At my parents?" Liz's radar went up at Peter's odd request. "Peter, what are you up to?"

"Nothing major, Lizzie. It's just that something's come up, and I need to talk with your dad about our hockey team." He waited for her to respond. Silence.

Liz had taken her phone from her ear and was looking at it in total bewilderment. Then, she put it back to her ear and said, "Peter, let me get this straight. You want to talk with dad about hockey?" He responded. "Tonight?" Liz gasped. "We'll never get out of the house if you get him started on hockey!"

Peter laughed. "Oh, Lizzie, you need to trust me. Our conversation won't take too long and we'll get out of there in time for dinner."

"Alright." She sounded skeptical as added, "I'll see you in about fifteen minutes at my parent's."

"Great, and Lizzie," his voice was quiet, filled with emotion.

"Yes, Peter?"

"I love you."

"I love you too." He could tell that she was smiling just like him when she said "goodbye."

CHAPTER 9

Peter took a deep breath for courage as he turned into the Callison's driveway. The front porch light illuminated the walkway that was cleared of snow, and cast shadows on the snowbanks bordering the walkway. Christmas and holiday decorations had been removed since the last time he had been there with Liz. Now the house stood as a safe haven against the stark bleakness of winter. Peter drew in a breath of courage as he parked near the garage. As he approached the steps, Jim opened the door and stepped out onto the front porch to greet him. In the darkness of early evening, with the light shining behind him, he looked quite formidable as he stood looking down at Peter.

A smile touched the younger man's lips before he spoke to the man that he held in high esteem. "Hey Mr. C. I mean Jim." Now that Peter was a young adult, many things had changed in his life. How he showed respect to his elders was one of them. It was taking Peter some time getting used to being less formal with the man who he hoped would be his father in law.

"Peter, welcome, come on in out of the cold." Jim said as he held open the door. "I must say Lizzie surprised me when she called me, and said that you needed to stop by and talk to me about the hockey team. Between you and me," he raised a brow as a hint of a smile touched his lips as he continued. "My daughter didn't sound too thrilled about this, and she said that we were not to talk for too long." Peter responded and they both chuckled. "So, what is the urgency in this visit?"

"Sir, I actually kind of lied to Liz." He quietly said as he entered the Callison's home. He remained in the entry way and waited for Jim to firmly close the door. Peter noticed similarities in how Jim and his dad, well how most of the men in the north country dress: thermal underwear shirt covered by a flannel shirt with the sleeves rolled up to just below the elbows, blue jeans, and work boots in his feet.

"Oh?" Jim responded, as he once again raised a brow. He motioned for Peter to go on into the living room.

"I wanted to talk with you privately before she gets here, so I used hockey to throw her off." Peter gazed around and saw that Mel was nowhere in sight. Jim was suspicious, but remained silent as he watched Peter fumbling with his jacket and pull the box from his pocket. "I just talked with my dad, but not my mom." He sighed. "Mom's going to kill me for not telling her yet. But I wanted to do things right by you."

Jim allowed a half smile to make its way to his lips. He had a sneaky feeling that he knew what was coming. The box Peter held in his slightly shaking hand confirmed it for him.

"Mr. C—I mean, Jim…later on tonight, I plan to ask Elizabeth to marry me and, well sir, I'd like your blessing."

Jim thought he saw small beads of sweat at Peter's brow, while his Adams apple bobbed up and down. He swallowed back the emotions that he was feeling, as he decided that one emotional man was more than enough to contend with at the moment. He silently took the small box from Peter, opened it, and gazed at the sparking stones, which he expected would be glistening on his daughter's finger before the night was through. If it wasn't, he'd be totally shocked.

Jim cleared his throat of his emotions, and then allowed himself to fully smile. He closed the box, handed it back to Peter as he said, "So I gather you don't have any intention of talking with me about hockey."

Jim watched Peter's eyes dance with excitement.

Then, Peter sighed with relief. "Actually, after I used hockey as my reason for coming here, well, I did some thinking, and I would like to know if you would be willing to mentor our guys on our team?"

"Well," Jim chuckled. "Peter, I'd say yes, even if you weren't proposing to Liz." He continued to smile, as he saw Peter release a sigh of relief. Ah, young love. "Besides," Jim added with a smile, "helping out with the school hockey team will get me away from the house and Mel's 'honey do list!'" Peter snickered. And was about to respond.

"I heard that!" Melissa exclaimed as she came into the living room from the kitchen. Jim had just enough time to wink and whisper, "welcome to the family," before Melissa stepped next to them.

"Good evening, Peter." Her smile was warm and welcoming. Peter returned his own greeting that included a hug. "Liz spoke with us and said that you were stopping by to talk with Jim about hockey." She noticed that Peter had unzipped his jacket but hadn't removed it. Interesting. Then she noticed their silent exchange. Her radar went up. If two men were ever to look like the cat that had just swallowed the canary? Those two were guilty as sin of something. The question was, what? For now, Melissa would be patient with them. But before the night was over, she was determined to know what they were up to.

"Yes, ma'am, and you and Liz—when she gets here—will be glad to know we've already dealt with the hockey issue."

Mel shook her head as she studied Peter. "It must not have been too important for you two to have resolved the hockey issue this quick." Her gaze passed between the elder and younger man. Oh yes! They were up to something!

"Actually, Mellie," Jim was grinning with pride. "It is rather important. At least, I think so, and now that I am retired this will be a great way for me to use my time and continue to do something positive for our community."

"Don't tell me that you are going to be a coach." Her expression was priceless. Jim couldn't help but chuckle as Mel continued. "I was just getting used to having you home. Now I'll never see you!"

"Mellie, honey, relax. Yes, I'll be working with the team, but not as a coach." Mel sighed with relief. "Peter has asked me to be a mentor for the hockey team."

"Oh, Peter, that is a wonderful idea!" She listened to them exchange some ideas for the team practices. Then grew concerned. "Jim, you can't be serious about having the team practice on the lake. And you want to lace up and skate with them! Are you crazy? You'll fall and break your neck! Then I'll end up transporting you to the hospital. Then you'll come home and—Oh no!"

Jim couldn't help but laugh. He shook his head and drew her into his embrace. "Sweetheart, I'll be mentoring. The only reason I may be on skates is to demonstrate for the kids should how they should do a particular technique."

Mel sighed. She still was not convinced about that wisdom of Jim going out on the ice on skates. For now, she'd let it go. "So, Peter, have you asked your Uncle Stephen to be a mentor as well?"

Peter cleared his throat. "Ah, no ma'am. As of tonight, Unc and I are not on speaking terms."

"What?" They asked in unison.

At that precise moment a vehicle's headlights shone in through the window. Liz had arrived and for Peter, not a moment too soon. For the time begin his annoyance with his uncle was forgotten. He watched outside and saw her wave at them as she looked through the window. When Liz came in through the door, she was delighted to find her mother there to greet her. Then her eyes swept across the entry way and into the living room. She noticed Peter's drawn expression as she greeted him and her father's features that indicated that he was upset. Hmm. Now what?

"Did something else bad happen, besides Stephen Johnson being a jerk?" She asked in disgust. At that moment, Melissa and Jim's eyes met, and they exchanged a worried look.

"Elizabeth!" Her mother gasped. "Peter had just begun to tell us about his troubles when we saw you drive in. So, I gather you know what transpired between Peter and his Uncle?"

"You better believe I do and the man is lucky that I was not with Peter when he said it." Liz's smile had been replaced with a scowl that meant she was extremely unhappy. Her eyes had changed from warm chocolate to dark brown, an indication that danger was smoldering underneath.

Jim groaned as he listened and watched the fire igniting in his daughter's eyes. If Liz lost her temper over whatever Johnson had done…heaven help them all!

"Lizzie, we all know that my uncle will never change. He says what's on his mind and sometimes people are hurt by what he says." Peter quietly consoled her as he wrapped his arm around her shoulders. "Let's not allow Unc to ruin our night. We have time before going out for dinner. So, let's sit and unwind a bit and visit with your parents?"

"That's a splendid idea!" Mel exclaimed. Jim chimed in with his own pleasure in hearing that they wanted to—well, that Peter—wanted to spend more time with them.

Jim seized the moment to ask, "Have you two done any more work on the buildings at the colony?"

"Not this week, Dad. We have too much snow for outside work, including working on the amphitheater stage. Although, I've been out there with the electricians who appraised the work in the cabins, outer buildings and mess hall. Now they are writing up their bids for the board to decide on who will do the work." Liz said, as she slid out of her coat, took Peter's jacket along with hers and hung them on the hooks by the front door.

She walked back over to Peter and noticed him exchange a peculiar look with her dad who simply nodded. Hmm. Those two were up to something. Hockey? Liz didn't quite know how to interpret their visual exchange. Just as Liz was ready to sit on the couch, Peter slipped his hand onto hers. She stopped and looked at him. Mel had been saying something and gasped as she saw Peter drop to one knee. He had the small box in his hand and opened it. Mel drew her hand to her mouth as tears pooled and then slid down her cheeks. She sniffled. Jim looked on with mist in his own eyes. He also sniffled then released a long sigh. His smile grew as he watched his daughter's expression change from questioning to amazement, while Peter slipped the ring onto her finger.

"Elizabeth Jeanne Callison, my beautiful Izzie Lizzie, I fell in love with you before I knew what it means to love someone. When we were young, I'd live for the day that JJ would invite me over to play with him just so I could be close to you. Then when you graduated from high school and left us, my heart was shattered. Oh yeah, I dated through high school and college, but my beautiful Elizabeth, no other woman has ever ignited my heart on fire as you do. I love you, and hope that you will say yes and marry me. Please Lizzie. Be my wife, my lover and most of all my best friend for life."

Liz's mouth had dropped open at some point during Peter's declaration of his love and intent. Her eyes lashed shimmered with wetness and her face glowed with joy. She slowly recovered, closed her mouth, swallowed and found her voice. "Oh, Peter." She brushed away the tears that had taken liberty to stream down her cheeks. "Wow! I never saw this coming." Her smile spoke first. Then she said, "Yes, Peter. Yes. I love you and I'd be honored to be your wife, your lover and have you as my best friend." Peter rose to his feet and kissed her, as if Mel and Jim were not in the room with them. It didn't matter because Jim fully understood what it's like to love so tenderly and deeply as he eased Melissa into his embrace. Then he kissed her with a promise of what they would share later when they were once again alone. They drew apart when they heard Liz say, "Thank you for including Mom and Dad in this special moment and proposing to me in front of them." Then her smile slipped as she asked, "Does your Mom know?"

Peter shook his head. "My Dad knows, and he's been sworn to secrecy until we told your parents. I had planned on proposing to you later on tonight when we were at the cabin. But," he shrugged. "It just seemed right to do it now. I hope you're not disappointed that I didn't wait until later when we were alone?"

"Oh, Peter, you worried for nothing." Liz gently touched his cheek, while her eyes and smile tenderly held him. "This was perfect!"

Laughter, more tears, and plenty of hugs were passed around before Liz and Peter left for the evening. When it was quiet once again in the Callison home that had nurtured Liz to become the woman she is today, Jim drew Melissa into his arms. They stood together in the middle of the living room holding each other close. Two hearts beating as one. Husband and wife, lovers, best friends, parents. For a moment both were quiet, lost in their own thoughts. Finally, Mel sighed.

"Care to share what's on your mind?" Jim asked against her head while his strong hands gently stroked her back.

"I'm overcome with happiness for Elizabeth and Peter." Jim could relate to Mel's feelings in his own way. For Jim, his lost injured child that had returned last summer was making great strides in healing. She was just about ready to soar off from the nest. If only he knew what was the problem between her and her sister, then they could make peace and be a loving family once again. Mel sighed. "You know Jim, it was pretty gutsy of Peter to propose to our most unpredictable daughter in front of us. What if she had said no?"

Jim chuckled. "Mellie, I doubt there was even a remote chance of that happening. If there had been, Peter never would have taken the risk of her saying no in front of us!" Jim grew silent then said, "You know, Mel, I have a feeling that the Great Spirit and Gram may have had a hand in all of this."

"Oh, Callison, God does work in mysterious ways. I'm also sure Gram was smiling down on Liz and Pete. Who would have thought when Elizabeth arrived home, with the weight of the world on her shoulders, that so much would have changed for her?"

"I sure didn't expect this!" Jim shook his head in disbelief as a smile once again crept onto his face. "Peter Jones is to be our son in law!"

"That's right. Our daughter is getting married to a terrific young man." Mel sniffled back the tears of joy that threatened to cascade down her cheeks. "Come on into the kitchen and I'll get our dinner on the table."

Word quickly spread around the valley that Elizabeth and Peter were engaged. Of course, both Becky and Melissa decided that their children should have an engagement party. At first both Elizabeth and Peter were reluctant to the idea and for good reasons. Time. Liz was fully involved with working on a gala event to raise money for the summer theater season, plus she had events scheduled at the arts center, and Peter was busy teaching as well as coaching hockey. So, the two decided that it would be best to leave the engagement party preparation in the caring hands of their mothers. Of course, Liz had given them a few suggestions, and she informed them that she and Peter would have final say in their plans. Both Melissa and Becky had a laugh about Liz and her inability to give up control. Oh yes.

Liz was a director through and through. As the plans were underway for the party, so was the Great Sac community grape vine. The gossip that was initially spread, no thanks to one Stephen Johnson who just happened to share his suspicions about Liz and Peter needing to get married before a baby arrived, grew by the day like a bad weed. Needless to say, there were some very unhappy people in the Great Sac Community. Especially one Elizabeth Callison, Melissa Callison and Becky Jones for starters. Jim and Wes had taken Peter under their fatherly protective wings, and had guided him in how to handle the community gossip. Of course, Stephen had received a thorough chewing out by Amanda when she caught wind of what he had done to her family, Peter included.

Finally! The day of the party had arrived. It was a cold late winter morning. Becky was bundled up in her winter coat, hat and a scarf over her mouth to protect her delicate asthmatic lungs from the bite of winter air. She was in a good mood, as she walked into the bait shop with a bag full of decorations for the downstairs pavilion. She paused after closing the door and listened. Trouble! Colossal trouble! By the sounds of it, Melissa was going up one side of Stephen and down the other. Oh, good grief! Now what had her brother done? She listened.

"I know for a fact that you were one of the main instigators who started the rumor about Liz and Peter. Buster, right this moment I do not care if you are one of Jim's oldest friends." Melissa's expression dared Johnson to interrupt her while she was on her tirade. "I also don't care if you are Becky's brother and Wes's brother in law. Friendship and family ties do not excuse your behavior. I know that Jim has already spoken with you, man, to man." She held up her hand to stop him from speaking, since he obviously hadn't listened to her first warning. "Don't even begin to think that you're off the hook with me by default just because you and Jim had a chat." She hissed in disgust. Becky's ears perked up even more because she had never heard Melissa hiss and growl before this moment in time. Oh yes, Becky fully recognized maternal instincts alive and well in her friend. "How dare you take the liberty to make an unfair assumption about my daughter and Peter?" Melissa took a half step towards Stephen causing him to take a full step back. Her eyes were dark with the threat of a full-blown angry explosion. "What gives you the right to judge them, as if you've never sinned?"

Ouch! Becky and Wes both sucked in air with that question. Melissa was fully enraged with anger, like and old gunslinger with a fully loaded and drawn six shooters ready to be fired, and there was no stopping her from firing her words.

"Just because you are a preacher's son doesn't make you a saint! Oh, you are too much! You know? For years I've defended you! I was willing to look beyond your actions that drove my sister in law away from here. I was willing to chalk your behavior up to being young and not knowing any better. But mister…Amanda has been right in so many of her opinions of you. You don't think, or care enough about other people's feelings before you speak. You hurt others to protect yourself from being hurt. How long do you think it will be before Belinda wises up to you and leaves you? I know I certainly wouldn't blame her if she left you. Johnson, I don't care if you are Peter's uncle. You stay away from my daughter and my sister in law, and heaven help you if I should catch wind of you uttering one syllable or word against them. Or any other member of my family for that matter!"

"What?" Stephen's mouth dropped open in disbelief.

"You heard me, Johnson! Right now, I am thoroughly ashamed to call you my friend, and of this moment, I declare that the female population of the Callison family including, Amanda, is off limits to you." She finished with adding some other things that made Becky's eyes pop in shock.

Stephen drew in a breath. His eyes studied Melissa's expression and her posture. Sadness engulfed him, for he knew that she meant every word that she had just spoken. "Wow! Melissa, I never expected you to hold such a low opinion of me." He said while not caring if anyone heard the anguish in his voice.

"Well, right now I do because you disregarded and perhaps ruined my daughter's reputation. I also happen to know that Elizabeth's very disappointed in your opinion of her. She'd like nothing more than for you to not attend her and Peter's engagement party."

"I see." Hurt permeated Stephen's voice. He drew silent.

"No, you don't. Even though Liz is hurt by your behavior, she loves Peter, and thinks the world of Wes and Becky. Unlike you, she would never intentionally hurt any of them. So, since you are Becky's brother, and Peter's uncle you are still invited to the party."

What a mess! Becky had heard enough and let her presence be made known to all of them.

"Melissa, excuse me. I couldn't help but overhear your discussion with my brother. I must say that under these circumstances, it is mighty gracious of Liz to welcome him." Becky said as she walked down the aisle towards them with purpose in her step. She was not smiling. In fact, when her eyes locked with her brother's fury spilled from them. "Unfortunately, I agree with your assessment of my brother. Apparently, time hasn't taught him a blessed thing, at least where the Callison family is concerned!"

"Thanks for your family loyalty." Stephen mumbled with a note of sarcasm.

"Lose the attitude with me, big brother! You're in boiling hot water with me. But then, this is not the first time. Is it?" Becky snarled as she stepped close to Wes, who slid an arm around her waist. With Becky being this angry at Stephen there was no telling what might further happen between them, and the last thing Wes needed was for Becky to haul off and clobber her brother.

"What are you getting at?" Stephen asked, while Wes simply shook his head, sighed and tightened his hold on his wife, who was vibrating like a steaming pressure cooker that was almost ready to blow.

"Don't play dumb with me! I know you haven't forgotten about what happened between us after Amanda left here in '79." Silence. "Hmm. Am I mistaken? Oh no, I see it in your eyes. So, don't try to pretend that you don't remember my wrath! Remember what it was like for those ten years when I made you pay for how you hurt Amanda? Remember what it was like when I excluded you from my life because I was angry with you?" Becky glowered at Stephen.

"Oh, no!" Wes moaned. He knew better than to interrupt his wife when she was on a roll with either of her brothers. He also knew that Stephen was rapidly approaching the desolate area beyond Becky's doghouse. If Stephen was once again banished to that area, life was going to be rough for all of them.

"Sis, you can't be serious?"

"Try me!" Becky glared at him with a chill that could have instantly frozen the equator.

"Becky," Mel interrupted. Sadness radiated from her as her gaze swept through the group. "I think it might be a good idea for both you and Stephen to cool off with some distance between you. You know, before one of you says something that—well, you know. So, perhaps we should go downstairs and get to work on the decorations and set up the tables as we planned?"

"Thanks, Mel." Wes quietly said, as he hugged Becky, who quickly kissed him and then glowered at her brother, before heading with Melissa to the door leading down to the pavilion.

Elizabeth was glad that she had graciously turned over plans and preparation for the engagement party to her mother and Becky, so that she could spend all her energy on her work. Even though she was not directly involved with the preparation, like any good director, she knew what her cast and crew was up to. Unfortunately, one of the minor cast members, appeared to have a chip on his shoulder and had been doing his best to upstage everyone in the Great Sac Community. As of that morning, that problem was dealt with. Unfortunately, another unforeseen problem had suddenly risen and Liz was in a foul mood by the time Peter got to the cabin. He opened the door, stepped in and was surprised to find her pacing in front of the fireplace with a medium size log in her hand. Not good! Especially when he heard her mumbling about what she'd like to do with the log.

"Hey, sweetheart!" Peter cheerfully greeted her, as he shut the door to keep out the cold. "Did I do something wrong?" He asked as he unzipped his coat, hastily hung in on the hook and cautiously approached her.

Liz stopped pacing, stilled the log she held in her hand and looked at Peter. Her eyes were smoldering with heat that signaled fire lurked below. What was the cause of this dark mood? He had no idea, but Peter sincerely hoped that he was not in her line of fire when her anger fully ignited. She sighed and tossed the log into the chair beside her, as he stepped closer and drew her into his arms. Liz lowered her head onto Peter's shoulder as she drew in a calming breath, then released it.

"Oh no, Peter!" Sadness was loud and clear in her voice as she spoke. "My sour mood has nothing to do with you." She sighed, as she burrowed against him. Peter tightened his hold on her as he brushed his lips against her hair. She smelled of lingering floral shampoo from her morning shower and wood smoke. His Lizzie.

"Hmm. Since I'm off the hook, then let me guess. Jordan? Uncle Stephen?" He felt her body stiffen against him. Not good!

"Both!" She huffed while clinging to him. "Your uncle, I can deal with. But, that lousy little sister of mine—that cretonne from another planet has decided that she should make an appearance at our party!"

"What?" Peter gasped in shock.

"Yeah, the twit is on her way north as we speak." He felt Liz vibrating with rage as he held her close. "She received a personal invitation. But we both know that I certainly didn't invite her. Guess who did?"

"Not your mom?"

"No! My mom knows better than to interfere, but not my wonderful meddling Dad. Oh no! Even though I told him not to butt in, dad being dad, he didn't know enough to stay out of this!" She huffed, as she pulled away from Peter's embrace. "Dad has this idea that Jordan and I can resolve our issues just like him and Aunt Amanda." Liz sighed.

Peter also sighed. He could see the writing on the wall. His well-meaning, soon to be father in law had basically dumped a lake full of good intentions onto a pair of sisters who were nowhere near ready to make amends. And now, their party was on a slippery path to being a disaster.

"No wonder you are upset." He sighed. "Well, Lizzie, our family, meaning both of ours, will drive us crazy, if we allow them to." His eyes tenderly held hers as he spoke. "Right now, I for one don't give a rats fanny about your sister or my uncle. They are who they are. We are who we are, two people in love, who happen to have some very interesting and often times annoying family members." He drew her close to him. "Let's not allow our two thorns to ruin our special night. Our moms have joined forces and worked hard to make this night special for us. So, let's focus our energy on our loving family and friends who will be celebrating with us."

Liz returned to Peter's embrace. His lips tenderly brushed hers while Liz's hands moved to the back of his neck. Then they heard a noise outside, their romantic moment was gone, as they turned to look towards the window into the darkness and they saw the reflection of a light shine through the window. Someone was parking their vehicle in the driveway. They exchanged a worried look and then went to the door, opened it and stepped out onto the porch, where a familiar voice that made both of them smile.

"Elizabeth, Peter! Goodness sake, for two intelligent, well-educated young people right now you both are 'dumber than boot jacks' standing out here in the middle of winter without a coat on! Get inside before you catch your death of cold!" Amanda was softly chuckling, as she and Kevin made their way up the steps.

Greetings, hugs, and laughter filled the cold, early evening of winter. Liz sniffled back her emotions as she clung to her aunt and they made their way inside the cabin. Amanda could read her niece like a well-loved novel and knew something else had happened to upset Liz. In no time at all both Amanda and Kevin had been brought up to speed on the latest drama unfolding in the Callison-Jones family saga. Needless to say, Amanda was in solidarity with Liz and vowed to defend her and Peter at all cost. What was her meddling brother thinking by inviting Jordan to the party? Time would tell.

Jim and Melissa were at the pavilion with Wes and Becky to greet the guests before the arrival of the guests of honor. Even though they all were unhappy with Stephen, they agreed that they would do their best to include Stephen and Belinda. After all, Belinda really was not at fault in any of this mess, and they really should try to get to know her before casting any more judgment against her. They paused from their conversation with Stephen and Belinda when they saw the pavilion door open. Smiles crept onto their lips, as they saw Liz and Peter step into the pavilion with Amanda and Kevin at their side. Melissa immediately noticed the expressions on both her daughter and Amanda's faces. Not good! Jim also noticed the expressions. His smile faded as he quietly groaned. Unfortunately, Jordan had called to inform them that she was about an hour away, and she would in fact be at the party. An ominous feeling, similar to the one Jim had on New Year's Eve 2009 and New Year's Day 2010 when he found out Amanda was missing on the frozen lake, was churning in his gut. At that moment, he was regretting the decisions and actions that he had made during the past couple of weeks.

"Dad. Mom!" Liz exclaimed as they came together and exchanged hugs. "Everything is beautiful! Thank you both for everything that you did to make this night special for us."

By now Wes and Becky had also made their way over to welcome their son and soon to be daughter in law. Amanda and Kevin held back to observe the interactions and smiled. They had seen Liz at her lowest point in her life. Now, despite the imminent return of her sister, she glowed with happiness. They also noticed that Peter had his hand gently, and protectively cupped around her waist. A smile touched Amanda's lips as she watched them.

"They make a beautiful couple." Kevin softly shared with Amanda.

His breath tickled her ear, causing Amanda to giggle, then sigh, as she leaned against him. "Mm. That they are and I am happy for them. But my love I happen to be biased and think that what we have is more special than what any other couple has."

Kevin gently released his fingers from Amanda's and slid his arm around her waist. He brushed his lips against her ear. His words were intended for only her to hear. "Sweetheart, I won't challenge you on the point. I love you." She giggled and felt the heat rise in her as Kevin shared more of his feelings with her.

At that particular moment, Jim stepped away from Liz and Peter and approached them. His eyes scrutinized Amanda's demeanor and Kevin's possessive hold on her. Jim shook his head, as a lazy, knowing smile slipped onto his lips. "I'd say welcome, but looking at the color in my sister's cheeks, and your expression Kev," Jim chuckled. "Maybe I should advise you two to skip the party and go up to the cabin for your own private party?"

Amanda cleared her throat, as she gave Jim a look that warned him to say no more, then slipped into his arms for a quick hug. Gentle teasing and laughter floated between them. Before too long Melissa joined them and was embellished with praise for the party. No one commented on the incidents with Stephen or the impending arrival of Jordan for fear of breaking their festive mood.

Liz and Peter moved through the guests greeting and thanking them for sharing in the evening with them. Every time the door opened Liz unconsciously held her breath, then sighed when Jordan did not appear. Her smile grew as Caitlin and Nick entered the pavilion.

"Caitlin, Nick, I'm so glad that you are here!" Liz exclaimed while Peter greeted Nick and mouthed 'thank you' to Caitlin.

"Of course, we're here, silly!" Caitlin's smile grew as she spoke. "Do you honestly think with or without Dad's meddling that we would miss this special moment?" Cait couldn't help herself as a tear of joy slid down her cheek. "Think about how weird it would be for you if your matron of honor skipped your party. That certainly would add fuel to the Great Sac Grape Vine, and we don't need that. Do we?"

Liz was able to see the humor in Caitlin's words as she pulled her sister close. She sniffed back her own emotions as her eyes began to water. "Ah, Caitlin I do love you. I'm so blessed to have you as my sister and my dearest friend." Liz whispered. "Please help me to not kill Jordan, if and when she shows up here tonight?"

"Oh, Lizzie. Don't you worry about our little sister. Remember? We're two peas in a pod and I'm here for you." Caitlin smiled and gave Liz the family nod that means *You can count on me!* Liz sighed with relief, as Caitlin continued on as her bossy eldest sibling self. "Now go and enjoy yourself. Oh, and before you do," she pulled Liz closer and whispered, "Did you happen to see Stephen's expression? Is he sulking?"

Liz burst into laughter. "Yeah! I hear that Mom and Becky gave him more of an ear full earlier today. He's in their doghouses along with being in mine." Caitlin joined Liz in laughter as Liz added, "Plus, Aunt Amanda knows what else he did!" Caitlin raised a questioning brow. Liz's smile grew as she said, "Oh yeah, I ratted him out!"

Liz had begun to relax as the evening progressed. Her brother James Junior and his girlfriend Elise had arrived from Boston half an hour before the party began. As they chatted, bringing each other up on events happening in one another lives, they both realized and regretted having allowed so much time to pass since they had last seen one another. Liz's disappointment was short lived as JJ and Peter embellished Elise with stories of how they had once been an annoyance in Elizabeth's life. Of course, Liz had her own stories to share. Having made their way around the room greeting their guests, Elizabeth and Peter were once again with JJ and Elise.

"I must confess that I was surprised to hear that you two had hooked up last summer." JJ raised his lips to form a smile that reminded Liz of their father when he was pleased with the outcome of a family situation. "Now that I see you two together," his eyes twinkled with delight. "Mom and Dad are right." Liz raised a brow as she listened to JJ continue. "Izzie Lizzie, you did good, Sis." His gaze passed from her to Peter, who stood next to Liz with his arm protectively around her waist. "Peter, old buddy welcome to the family! Who would have thought that one day my best friend would be my brother in law?" Laughter and loving teasing passed between them helping to ease Liz's tension.

A few minutes later Samantha and her husband Chris arrived. More introductions and family greetings were made. Liz had to wonder why she had stayed away from her family and hometown for so long? She watched her younger sister by only a couple of years and her husband interact with JJ and Elise. They had a special younger sibling relationship that Liz didn't share with them. She was determined to not feel envious of them, especially since she had her own special exclusive relationship with Cait. Still, Liz was realizing that being away for so long that she had missed out on memorable moments with her family and friends. She allowed herself to smile as she listened to Peter and JJ tease Sammie and share memories of their youth with Chris and Elise. Even Caitlin, who had found her way to them, got in on the fun sharing what it was like to be the eldest and have to put up with all of them while growing up!

Laughter and smiles filled the pavilion, as Liz and Peter left their family and once again mingled with their other guests. Some folks were sampling food from the tasty morsels of food on the buffet table. Sparkling wine and soft drinks were passed around, while the band played jazz music for listening enjoyment. At the appointed time the band announced that they were going to play a special song for Liz and Peter. The crowd oohed and awed, as they took the dance floor and began their official engagement dance together. Before the song ended their parents had joined them on the dance floor. It was a real celebration, and of course the moment was captured on their guest's phones and cameras. Liz and Peter didn't seem to mind as they only had eyes for each other.

Then, the door opened. Liz drew in a calming breath. She may be the guest of honor at the party, but a sinking feeling in the pit of her stomach. She knew that she was about to be upstaged by her younger sister. A chill swept through the room, as Jordan stepped inside and closed the door behind her. Her coat was pulled snug around her, but Liz could see that the make up on her face was applied in an attempt to hide the tautness in her face. Her eyes were bloodshot, and dark circles not well hidden under eyes revealed that the months since their last meeting had not been too easy for her sister. Too bad! Liz did not feel one ounce of pity or sympathy for Jordan. Her sister had caused their family too much misery by her actions. The love of family and blood may bind them. But in Liz's heart that was all it did! Jordan was a mean-spirited woman whom Liz did not like, or want to have anything to do with. In an instant Liz's expression began to turn from joyous to murderous. Like a deer blinded by headlights, Liz saw only her sister. She was ready and standing her ground. Peter eased his arm around Liz as she sucked in air.

"Lizzie, sweetheart, lean on me!" Peter whispered to her. "It is going to be alright."

Liz released a breath. At that moment, she realized that Caitlin, as well as her aunt and uncle were standing next to her. Then, it happened. Jordan made eye contact with Liz. Her smile was for appearance only as she marched towards her.

"Breathe, Elizabeth." Her aunt softly spoke from behind her right shoulder. "You got this! Remember what we talked about. Remember what you and your counselor talked about. You are in control."

Liz did have control over herself and the situation. She broke away from her safety net and stepped towards her sister. Her eyes spewed deep burning resentment, and her clenched teeth gave warning to all that she was on a mission, as she passed through the space that separated them. Peter followed and was standing slightly behind Liz as she came face to face with Jordan. He knew from Liz's body language that it was not going to be a pretty scene between the Callison sisters. Of course, Peter was feeling defensive towards Liz and wanted to protect her from Jordan. But he also knew that Liz would not appreciate his interference at that moment.

"Jordan, I am sure Mom and Dad will be glad that you made it to Peter's and my engagement party." Liz's expression and voice did not reveal how she was feeling towards her sister. She was certain that her parents had seen Jordan enter, and that they were making their way to them to intercede, if necessary. But she hoped that they would stay out of it, because Liz, while being angry with Jordan, was calm and in control and she had things to say, party or no party.

"Elizabeth, regardless of how we ended things last summer and how we still feel towards each other, I'm glad Dad invited me to come here tonight. We have more siblings in our family, and despite how we feel towards each other, it will be nice for me to see everyone else." Her eyes darted around the room as a smirk formed on her lips. "I have to admit that I was surprised to hear about your upcoming nuptials. I guess congratulations are in order on your engagement to Peter?" She speculated as Peter took his place next to Liz and slid his arm protectively around her waist. He was not smiling as he watched and listened to their interaction.

"Thank you, Jordan." Liz smiled as she turned her gaze to Peter and said, "We are very happy." Then, in a blink of an eye, Liz looked back at Jordan. Her expression turned cold as ice as her eyes bore into her sister. "Unlike Greg, my former boyfriend for eight years, of course you know who I'm talking about." She watched Jordan shift her weight as she spoke. Good. Let the little weasel squirm. Liz was just getting warmed up with her arsenal of words for her sister, and she was not going to stop until she decided that she was finished. "I know that I can trust Peter to be faithful to me and not take you, or any other woman to bed."

Silence had fallen over the room to watch the altercation between sisters. Someone gasped. Jim and Melissa had made their way over to their daughters in time to hear Liz's declaration. Jim felt Melissa slip her hand into his, as he glanced around and made eye contact with Amanda, who nodded to confirm his silent question.

Jim sighed out a deflated breath as the magnitude of Liz's words penetrated deep into his core. Family betrayal had once again reared its ugly head on a new level. Now everything was making sense to Jim. No wonder Amanda had been so defensive of Elizabeth! No wonder Liz had wanted to kill Jordan last summer! What a mess! He released another heavy sigh, as he returned his gaze to his daughters, and listened, poised to intervene if necessary.

"What's the matter Jordan?" Bitterness laced every word Liz spoke. "Last January you had plenty to say when I finally caught you in bed with Greg." Someone else gasped. Liz didn't notice. Her eyes had taken on a darker hue. Trouble lurked in the hidden depths. "I see by your shocked expression that you didn't expect me to call you out in front of Mom and Dad and our hometown community. Too bad! I'm not keeping this secret any longer. I am moving beyond you and your hateful and selfish adulterous actions." Liz noticed the tears pooling in Jordan's eyes. She pursed her lips and shook her head in disgust. "Tsk, tsk, tsk! I must say, tears are a nice touch, Jordan. Especially, if you were on stage in a dramatic play. But this is real life and little sister you need to understand some important facts. I've learned and grown through your betrayal. I have been taking care of myself and talking with my core support group to assist me with moving through my grief." Liz noticed the subtle worry that passed over Jordan. "You look surprised. Did you honestly think that I would not tell anyone the truth of what you did to me? Did you honestly expect me to take with me to my grave how you, my own sister, ripped my life apart?" Hot flames of anger spewed from Liz's eyes, while she spoke with controlled anger in her voice. "Peter and Caitlin have known about your adulterous ways since last summer." A brief half smile crept onto the edge of Liz's lips. "Hmm. You should have known that I'd turn to Caitlin as my sister, my confidant and best friend. Unlike you, I know that Cait is a woman of fine integrity. I trust her with my life." At that moment, Liz felt her sister reach over and gently squeeze her hand, then release it. "Caitlin isn't the only person I trust with my life. With how things progressed between Peter and me, it was only a matter of time before I confided in him. A word of warning, even though you don't deserve it—you don't want to know what Peter really thinks of you. Let's just say, it's along the line of what Aunt Amanda might say." Someone made a comment. Jim moaned. Amanda snorted. None of it phased Elizabeth as she continued. "At any rate, both Caitlin and Peter have been amazing sources of comfort and strength, as I have been healing from what you and Greg did to me."

The stark realization of Liz's words was penetrating deep into Jordan's conscience as she gazed over at Peter and Caitlin. She gave up trying to control her tears that trickled freely down her cheeks. How could something that had started as simple flirting grow into adultery and sever her family and her marriage?

"Is that true?" Jim quietly asked Caitlin, but wasn't answered as Liz continued. He watched and listened to his child in disbelief. This couldn't be happening all over again. It had to be a bad dream. A nightmare. Liz's words confirmed that he was wide awake witnessing and participating in his family's pain.

"Actually, Jordan, Aunt Amanda and Uncle Kevin have known about everything that happened between us before anyone else in our family." She watched Jordan look at their aunt and uncle. Devastation radiated from every fiber of her sister's body. "That's right. They know everything that you did, you little skunk! They even know things that you didn't know at the time, or anyone else for that matter. As least, until now. Oh yes! There's more." She watched Jordan draw in a breath. Was it fear that passed over her sister's eyes? Liz didn't know and she didn't care. It was time to fully call her sister out even if it meant airing all of the Callison family dirty laundry before the people of the Great Sac Community. Liz was beyond caring about keeping up appearances.

"While you and Greg thought you were so sneaky having your affair in my bed, I found out that I was pregnant with his child." Gasps were heard. Jordan's eyes grew larger while her face suddenly lost all color. She looked like death warmed over as reality hit her. "Yes, Jordan. I was pregnant with Greg's child! Needless to say, my joy was totally shattered when I found the two of you in bed together. Before I actually knew I was pregnant, or that you were sleeping with Greg, I had been talking with Aunt Amanda on the phone about what I suspected. So, after I found out I was pregnant and that he was cheating on me with you, I went to Baltimore to be with Aunt Amanda and Uncle Kevin to regroup and figure out what I wanted to do about my child, and the mess you and Greg had caused. Both Aunt Amanda and Uncle Kevin cared for me while I cried my heart out."

Liz did not realize that her father was holding her mother, who was softly weeping. Nor, did she realize that her father had tears in his eyes as he too grieved for his family. She glanced over at her aunt who gently smiled and nodded. Drawing in a breath, Liz continued, "Aunt Amanda shared with me what it was like for her to be a single mom, both her joys and her struggles in raising Summer alone." Liz paused and once again gazed at her aunt who gave her another slight nod of encouragement. Then, Liz returned her eyes to face her sister. "During my stay with them, God made the decision for me. I had a major miscarriage and was hospitalized overnight. My baby would have been a boy." An unwanted and unexpected tear slid down her cheek. "Every day I thank God for Aunt Amanda and Uncle Kevin. They were gracious, loving and mostly non-judging as they took care of me. They allowed me to visit them multiple times after that, as I mourned the baby I had lost. Aunt Amanda was a blessing." Elizabeth swallowed hard as she silently commanded her emotions to stay at bay, and refused to cry as she continued, "- Since, she knows firsthand what it feels like to miscarry. In her wisdom and loving care, she hooked me up with one of the counselors at her center. While my counselor," Liz chuckled, "Who also happens to be named Liz, helped me with my grief, and other stuff, it was Aunt Amanda who led me to consider taking a leave of absence. She suggested that I take a rest and refocus on life here at home in the Adirondacks far away from the lights of Broadway. So, I embraced Aunt Amanda's wisdom and came home to Mom and Dad, and I found Peter waiting here to accept and love me for who I am. Like I said, I know that I can trust Peter to be faithful to me and not take you to bed. Having said all that, I do love you, but only because we are family. But, Jordan, I don't like you as a person, and I still haven't forgiven you for betraying me." Liz shrugged as she made no attempt to hide her grief. "Who knows, maybe thirty years from now I'll be ready to forgive. We can always hope."

At that moment, Jim and Amanda exchanged a sad glance, as Liz's words hit them. Thirty years. Heaven help them! That's the last thing their family needed.

"Now, Jordan if you will excuse me? This is Peter's and my engagement party and we have other guests to attend to! Enjoy the party." She began to move, then stopped and looked Jordan dead in the eyes. "And Jordan, take my advice and leave our male guests alone. All of them!"

Liz had not expected her mother to take a hold of her arm, and block her from moving away from where she was standing. She turned her gaze and saw the tears in her mother's eyes. The pain. "Oh, Elizabeth, my precious child." Mel sniffled as her hands gently stroked Liz's jaw.

"I'm sorry, Mom." Liz's voice was ragged. "I didn't want you and Dad to have to ever find out what had happened between Jordan and me." Liz sniffled. "I should never have unloaded on her as I just did. Now the whole community knows and you and dad-"

"Oh, Elizabeth, my precious child, don't you worry about your father and me. We will survive this mess." Melissa's voice and feather soft touch gently stroked Liz's tattered emotions. "Honey, right now my concern is for you and your sister. You said what you felt was needed to be said, and I don't blame you for that. Unfortunately, it was said in front of the whole community." Liz began to open her mouth to speak, only to have her mother place her finger on her lips to silence her. "But, as we know from past experience, this isn't the first time the community has known about our family's dirty laundry." Melissa sighed. "I guess Johnson and your aunt did a good job paving the way for you and your sister."

Liz sniffled and sighed. "I'm not sure Aunt Amanda would like to hear that. But, now do you see why I've clung to Aunt Amanda?"

"Yes, I do and I'm sure, that we'll talk more about this family betrayal and your grief after tonight. Now, as you said to Jordan you need to find your beautiful smile and go enjoy your party with Peter." Mel quietly spoke to Peter then turned to her other family members. Amanda and Kevin were standing alongside of Jim, who was listening to Caitlin quietly chastise her younger sister. Jim's expression was a mix of disappointment, anger, concern and other familiar Callison emotions that did not surprise her.

"Jordan," Melissa's tone said it all. "You, young lady, have made quite an entrance. Don't even consider removing your coat, or consider causing any more of a scene than you already have by showing up here. You will come outside with your father and me, where we will further discuss our family issues in private." She added with her mother's expression that warned Jordan to not speak.

Liz watched her parents leave the pavilion with Jordan just ahead of them. She shook her head, as a wave of sadness sweep over her. One selfish act by her sister had caused a ripple effect that had torn their family apart. Liz sighed just before a quiet voice of reassurance lifted her spirit.

"Liz, you know that what happened here tonight was not your fault. The truth had to come out."

She turned and stepped into caring arms. She leaned her head on his chest and breathed in his spicy aftershave cologne. "Uncle Kevin, thank you for being here. I honestly don't know how I'd have made it through everything had it not been for you and Aunt Amanda."

Kevin gently hugged her. "Liz, you are welcome. As we told you last spring, we're family, and we will always do whatever we can to help you and the rest of our family. I don't know if you realize it, or not, but you have claimed a special place in my heart. I hope that despite everything that has happened between you and Jordan, that you will be able to find a smile and enjoy your special night with Peter."

Liz sniffled. Her emotions were a mess! She drew in and released a weary breath as she stepped out of Kevin's embrace.

"Lizzie, are you crying again?" Peter asked as he stepped close to her.

She sniffled, as her uncle handed a tissue to her. "Thank you, Uncle Kevin, and yes, Peter I seem to have sprung a leak in my eyes. My emotions are a mess."

Kevin quietly watched their interaction. Then he handed Peter a few tissues. "Liz seems to be a lot like her aunt. Since, they are so similar, here's my advice for you, Peter. Keep a well-stocked supply of tissues in your pockets at all times."

"He exaggerates! I don't always need a tissue." Amanda huffed in feigned annoyance, as she eased next to Kevin and slid into his embrace. Kevin chuckled as he leaned over and whispered in her ear. Amanda's eyes sparkled with mischievousness as a smile graced her lips. "Oh my! Sweetheart, you have a date." She cleared her throat, then slid her tongue over her lips before speaking to Liz and Peter, who were watching her with amusement. "If you both will excuse us? My husband owes me a dance, for starters." She glanced past Liz then said, "Besides, Liz, your parents are heading your way. Ready or not, you need a moment. A private moment with them."

Liz tried to smile as Peter slid his arm protectively around her waist. He was her anchor in this turbulent time in her life. How blessed she was to have found him here waiting for her! Still, Liz knew that her aunt was right. She did need to talk with her parents. Before she could say anything, her father was at her side, drew her into a bear hug and whispered in her ear. She sniffled back her emotions as she squeezed him tightly, while he placed a light kiss on her hair. Then it was her mother's turn to cradle her in her arms. Liz felt the gentle rocking of her mother's body, as she too whispered things for only Liz to hear. Their shared response to her outburst about the cause of the feud between her and Jordan surprised her. Her parents didn't ridicule her for tearing into her sister. Instead, they expressed how much they loved her and mourned for her loss—their shared family loss. At that moment, the conversation she had with her dad on that miserable summer afternoon shortly after returning home came to mind, she straightened in her mother's arms and looked at her father.

"Dad," her voice was soft, filled with emotion as she looked up at him. "Remember the conversation we had the day I returned home? The one about the injured bird?"

She watched his eyes and was not disappointed by what she saw. This wasn't her dad who had pelted her with a water gun and handcuffed her in the upstairs hallway. This was her dad who was her protector, the one who had her back. Her father whom she knows loves her.

"Yes. I do, Lizzie." His voice was quiet, filled with emotion. She thought she might see moisture on his eyelashes. "Now, do you understand what I saw in you?"

"Yes. But I don't understand how you knew how broken I was?"

He looked into her eyes with such amazing powerful love that Liz was momentarily speechless. She felt her own eyes moisten.

"In time, if God, the Great Spirit, has anything to say about it, you will have a child of your own and then you will. For now, your fiancé is patiently waiting to celebrate your engagement party with you." He shifted his eyes towards Melissa who released her arms from her. "And I'd like to dance with your mother."

Liz watched her mother's expression change from mother mode to wife as her father reached out his hand out to her. She sighed as she watched her parents. The look that they shared was all that Liz needed to see to understand not as a child, but as a woman longing for her soul mate. Peter. She turned to find him patiently waiting as he tenderly smiled and held out his hand for her. Then, without a word they moved into each other's arms and moved to the beat of the music.

CHAPTER 10

Morning in the valley began with an explosion of light in the eastern sky: brilliant red, orange, yellow, a touch of purple and robin egg blue. Snow blanketing the mountainous terrain sparkled with the dawn of light. The temperature hovered at a balmy twenty degrees with no wind, a welcomed, pleasant change for the residents and visitors of the Great Sac Community. Amanda stood on the porch of the cabin gazing out over the valley blanked with snow. Evergreens dotted the barren landscape with splashes of color, while the sun shone on the evergreens and dormant hardwoods casting shadows on the barren land. Amanda drew in a deep breath, released it while watching water vapor escape from her mouth, then raised the mug of coffee to her lips. It was a good morning. Kevin had risen early, prepared for a day of ice fishing with Jim on the Great Sacandaga Lake, and had left with Jim shortly after sunrise. A smile brushed her lips as she thought about how many things had changed in her family since her return in 2009. Even though she and Kevin didn't get north as much as they would like, when they did come north from Baltimore, the time that they spent with Jim and Melissa and their family was special for them. Today would be a guy's fishing day, and Amanda would be helping Melissa and Becky clean up the pavilion from last night's party. A snort escaped from her, as she thought about Jim and Kevin ice fishing. Amanda couldn't help but smile because she knew in the deep crevices of her heart exactly why Jim had not invited her to go fishing with them. They both may be in their 60's, but sibling competition still reigned between them. So, Amanda knew that Jim was probably afraid that she would have shown him up by catching more fish than him. Well, when they were young, she was the better fisherman. Amanda laughed at her own politically incorrect usage of the word 'fisherman', in her thoughts. It didn't matter to her. She knew in her heart that she was the better one, so, why would now be any different? Amanda sniffled, as she felt moisture forming in the edges of her eyes. "Thanks Gram!" She breathed out, then returned to her thoughts about her family. Their grandmother had reminded them that she was the matriarch, the wise one whom they needed to listen to. She had done a good thing by bringing them together to confront their conflicted past. Amanda brushed a renegade tear from her eye, as she thought about the new Callison conflict. Now, without Gram and her wisdom, who could help Elizabeth and Jordan reach a point where they could talk out their differences, and hopefully find forgiveness and reconciliation? Amanda sniffled again, and shook her head as she thought, *thirty years is a waste of time. You lose so much by harboring anger and hatred.* She breathed out, "God, please help my nieces learn from the mistakes their dad and I made. Please help them to come to a place of forgiveness and reconciliation before it's too late for them." Amanda wiped away another tear with the back of her gloved hand. She sighed, looked down into the valley, then turned and walked back into the cabin to prepare for the rest of the day.

Melissa and Becky had just arrived at the bait shop and were standing by Becky's car when they saw and heard Amanda pull her SUV into the parking lot. Both women smiled and waved as she pulled the vehicle to a stop next to Jim's pickup.

"Good morning," she called out as she emerged from her vehicle and headed towards them.

"Good morning!" Both women responded.

"Sorry I'm late. Your pastor was a little long winded."

It was then that they both noticed Amanda was not in her normal, relaxed attire when she visited the area. On this cold winter morning she wore a traditional camel hair winter coat. Of course, her head was uncovered. She wore fine leather gloves, and her legs were covered with dark dress slacks and leather boots donned her feet instead of her insulated hiking boots.

"You were serious!" Melissa exclaimed.

Amanda smiled as she nodded. Her eyes sparkled as she said, "Oh yeah! And let me be the first to tell you both that while he had a good message. Well, he's not Reverend Johnson. Now that man could preach. Short. Sweet. Right to the point."

Becky snorted with laughter. "Oh Mandy, you of all people should remember that my dad could be very long winded. Have you forgotten the day we both fell asleep during his sermon?" Becky asked, then coughed.

Amanda smiled warmly at them, although concerned for her friend. "Becky, I do remember that time. Right now, that doesn't matter. You're coughing concerns me." Worry took shape on her brows and in her eyes as she shifted her gaze between Becky and the gravel with hidden splotches of ice. "Should you be out here in the cold? You know, with your asthma?" Amanda questioned.

Once again Becky coughed and wheezed. "I'm okay. Really." She smiled brightly as Amanda stepped next to her. "But thanks. You always did watch over me like a mother hen. I guess I can blame my mom for that by insisting that you take care of me."

Amanda looked at her sheepishly. "It's because we all loved you and we still do!"

"Yes, we do love you." Melissa confirmed. "Once we're inside I want to hear more of this story about you two falling asleep in church. I gather you both were old enough to know better?" She couldn't help but smile, as she watched their eyes meet and their expressions light up with delight. Oh yes! Those two women had been quite a pair. Looking at them and listening to them sharing their shared memories, Melissa knew that they still were quite a pair. And the best part of them being together was that they welcomed her to be a part of their shared lives. Yes indeed! The three women together were a formidable threesome and the men in their lives knew that, and loved them for who they were.

At that moment, a breeze kicked up. All three women shivered and headed for the door. Amanda continued on as 'mother hen' when they got to the door, and made sure Becky entered first. The bell jingled to inform Wesley of their arrival. "Good morning!" He called out with laughter in his voice.

"Good morning." They returned as Amanda shut the door behind them.

"Where's my brother?" Becky asked as they walked down the aisle towards the counter where Wesley was sorting a box of lures to be marked and put on the shelves.

Wes's smile immediately disappeared with Becky's question and a round of coughing. "Do you have your rescue inhaler?" Becky nodded as she pulled it from her pocket. Wes slid his arm protectively around her as she used her inhaler. When he was certain that his wife was out of imminent danger, he answered Becky's question. "Stephen called to inform me that he was going to be late this morning." His voice implied more than his words had said.

"So, I gather he wasn't alone when he called." Becky snarled, stepped out of Wesley's embrace and wheezed. "He better not intend on bringing Belinda over here with him and offer her assistance with cleaning up downstairs."

Just as those words were out of Becky's mouth the bell on the door jingled as the door was opened. Everyone turned to see who was entering. Amanda moaned and made eye contact with Melissa as Johnson and Belinda walked in.

"Good morning!" Stephen called out as he shut the door. "Chilly morning!" Johnson added, as he escorted Belinda up the aisle towards them.

"Chilly alright." Amanda said under her breath. Becky snorted, coughed and returned a comment for only Amanda and Melissa to hear.

"Wow!" Melissa quietly responded. "Remind me to never be on both of your bad sides at the same time."

"Oh, Mel, honey, you are so right. We're worse than an EF5 tornado when we're both mad at the same thing or person at the same time." Amanda stated with a totally sober expression.

"That's for sure! Now I have to act like I like the woman." Becky smiled brightly then turned to the newcomers. "Good morning, Belinda." She immediately turned her gaze to Stephen. "So, brother, I see you finally decided to drag yourself out of bed and get to work." She was not smiling. Not a good sign—especially when she threw her jaw to the side. "Good thing my husband, who is father of the groom to be, and who had a right to sleep in is the responsible one of this business partnerships and got to work on time." Both Johnson and Wesley simultaneously raised a brow, as Becky continued to glower at him. "Better late than never, I guess. At any rate, you need to go out to my car and bring in the plastic totes that are stacked on the back seat."

"I do?" Stephen's tone and bristly expression indicated that he did not appreciate his sister's belligerent attitude.

"Yes. Unlike Wes, you still have on your coat, so it makes sense for you to go back outside and bring our supplies inside for us. My car is unlocked. It's right here near the door." She gestured with her hand to accentuate her point. "So, don't act as if I asked you to walk down to the lake and bring a collapsible ice fishing shack and gear back up here." She coughed.

"Becky, you've already used your rescue inhaler." Amanda quietly interjected as she gently placed her hand on Becky's upper arm. "Don't let your ornery brother drive you into a full-blown asthma attack that sends you to the ER. It is obvious that Stephen doesn't feel up to helping you. So, let him be." She shot him a quick look indicating that she was not pleased with his attitude. "You go rest and take care of your breathing. I'll go out to your car and get the totes, and to save time I'll carry them down to the patio door. Then, when we are ready for them, we can bring them in through the sliding door."

"Thanks, Mandy." Becky and Wes said in unison as she turned to head out the door.

Amanda looked over her shoulder, giving them a smile as she said, "Glad I can be of assistance." She closed the door behind her, held on to the doorknob for a moment longer as she drew in a calming breath. Being at the bait shop two days in a row, Johnson's attitude, his girlfriend—memories—all were churning inside Amanda. She felt as if she was on the slippery slope of a panic attack. Amanda knew the signs. Even with her relaxation techniques and medication, it was only a matter of time before the panic exploded in her. She only hoped that it would be later when she was alone with Kevin in the privacy of the cabin.

By the time Amanda got to the patio door of the pavilion with the first load of totes, Becky had unlocked the door and was opening it for her. Becky's expression said a long novel's worth of feelings. Amanda smiled, winked at her and drew in a calming breath as she stepped into the pavilion. Sunlight shone in through the door warming the area, as Amanda placed the totes on the floor alongside of the table near the door. Melissa had already gotten out the step ladder, was standing on the third rung of the ladder and was busily removing tape from the wall that was holding up a row of streamers. Becky had turned on soft instrumental music. Amanda listened and smiled to herself as she recognized a familiar old hymn that spoke of loving God and others. Leave it to Becky to strive to be the peacemaker in a tense situation. She drew in a calming breath, then breathed out a quiet prayer.

Amanda shed her coat, then noticed that Stephen and Belinda had found their way down from the bait shop and were standing by the door to the broom closet. She was well aware of the unspoken tension in the room. Still, Amanda was determined to make the best of it, as she quietly moved around the room carefully taking down and folding paper wedding bells and cardboard wedding theme decorations. She had just handed Becky her first collection of decorations when they all heard Stephen comment to Belinda, "Sweetheart, here's the spot I've told you about. I'm grateful that Amanda controlled her temper last night and didn't leave any new spots of discoloration on the cement floor."

Amanda was mortified by Johnson's tone of voice, his words and Belinda's response to him. She commanded herself to breathe and began her techniques for deescalating a panic. There was a mutual sound of sucking in air between Melissa and Becky as they looked on in horror. Amanda placed a hand on Becky's arm, then shook her head as Becky was ready to speak. "Becky, please, stay out of this. And don't feud with your brother on my account." Amanda sighed. "Some things never change. Your brother and me, well, we are obviously one of them. It seems no matter what, we're destined to hurt each other in some way." Amanda saw the pain in Becky's expression. She released her hand and drew her friend close. "Honest. I'm okay."

Amanda drew in a slow calming breath as she stepped away from Becky. She looked around the pavilion, fully aware that Stephen was watching her. He had no idea how much his words had wounded her, nor was she going to tell him, at least at that moment. Right now, Amanda needed to take care of herself. She drew in another breath. "Mel, Becky, since you have additional help with Johnson and Belinda being here, I'm going to excuse myself and go see how Jim and Kevin are doing with their ice fishing."

By now both Mel and Becky were gathered around her in solidarity. Becky glowered and made what sounded like a growl as Stephen said, "You better be careful and watch for thin ice so you don't fall in. Again!" Johnson chuckled as he remembered their shared past.

"I'm sure you'd like that! Wouldn't you, Johnson? Lucky for me my husband is already out on the ice should I encounter a moose, or thin ice and need rescuing." Amanda gave Melissa a forced smile as she said, "Text me when you're ready to go." As Amanda turned to head for the door, she heard Johnson say, "Yeah you go on and run away, Calli old girl, you're good at that!"

Amanda stopped, pivoted around, glared at Stephen and stepped towards him. Fire spewed from her dark eyes. Her breathing, clutched fist and stance indicated anger or a panic attack was imminent. Both Melissa and Becky sucked in collective breaths, while Belinda looked stunned and not sure what to say or do. Amanda didn't notice them. Her vision was focused on Stephen like having a deer in the scope of her rifle, and poised to pull the trigger. "If you had been the man that you claimed to be back then and now, I wouldn't have needed to run. Would I have?" Amanda's words dug deep into him as she intended. She shook her head in disgust. "But then, not taking responsibility for yourself and blaming others is what you do best. *Tsk, tsk, tsk!* Stephen, for your information, today I'm not running away. This morning I'm running to my husband, who loves me, and who will do his best to take care of me. I'm going as well as to my brother, who has proven to me that he does have my back. You had better be glad I'm going."

"Oh?" He saw something unreadable in her eyes that warned him that he was in danger.

"Yes, Stephen, because if I stay here any longer attempting to talk with you, there will be no hope of ever repairing our tattered relationship." Amanda didn't wait for a response. She turned, walked out the door and headed towards the frozen lake.

The sound of laughter, the pleasing aromas of apple pie mingled with fresh caught fish frying, and the bickering between Callie and Nick, all greeted Elizabeth and Peter as they entered through the front door of her childhood home.

"Aunt Lizzie!" Callie exclaimed, as she scrambled from the couch to greet her aunt. "You missed the excitement." She announced as her arms hugged Liz's waist.

"Grandpa and Grandma are mad at Mr. Johnson." Nick announced as he got to his feet and joined them.

"Oh?" Liz asked them as she exchange a worried glance with Peter, who shrugged while knowing that with his uncle anything was possible.

"Yes, and Aunt Amanda told Grandpa to stay out of it. Whatever it is?" She looked beseechingly in hopes that somehow her Aunt Liz would telepathically know what was happening. "Even Mommy and Daddy were told to butt out by Aunt Amanda! I thought Mommy was going to cry."

Oh boy! Apparently, Jordan's drama hadn't been enough for their family. Now Stephen Johnson was in the thick of it with the elder Callisons. Major trouble! Liz sighed, as Peter slid his arm protectively around her waist and she leaned into his strength.

"Yeah, and Uncle Kevin had his arm around Aunt Amanda, like you two," Callie added a comment while Nicholas shot an accusatory scowl at his older sister for interrupting him as he continued, "and he kept telling her to breathe." His expression turned serious, deep in thought. "Aunt Liz, I'm confused. Aunt Amanda kept talking. So, wasn't she breathing?"

His confused expression touched Liz's heart. She stood straight and opened her arms to embrace her nephew, who readily accepted her invitation. Then, she quietly assured both children that Aunt Amanda would be alright, but she and Peter would check on their family, just to make sure. Before heading to the kitchen, Liz suggested that they finish their checker game, or find something else to do to entertain themselves until dinner was ready.

As Liz and Peter came to the kitchen doorway, she was unseen by her family, with the exception of Caitlin. From where Liz stood, she was able to make eye contact and communicate with her sister, as they had done on countless occasions during their past. The slight shake of Cait's head and her expression told Liz that Callie and Nick had been correct in their assessment. Something was definitely wrong between the Callison and Johnson families. Liz and Peter still hadn't been seen by the others, so Liz was able to mouth more questions to Cait, who nodded or slightly shook her head. Fortunately, the sound of laughter indicated that for the time being the family elders were moving on from the previous storm and were now engaged in sharing family stories of days gone by. Liz quietly listened to her father. Aunt Amanda denied his statement, then giggled, only to finally admit that he had been correct. Her dad and aunt never ceased to amaze her. They loved and fought. But in the end when it mattered most, they confirmed the old adage *blood is thicker than water.*

At that moment, Melissa crossed the kitchen from the stove, where she had been working, and caught sight of Liz and Peter as they stepped forward. "Oh, wonderful!" She exclaimed. "Elizabeth and Peter, you are right on time. Dinner is almost ready."

"Hello everyone!" Liz smiled brightly as she and Peter fully entered the room. Greetings and laughter filled the kitchen. In a matter of minutes both Liz and Peter were brought up to speed on the days drama that had unfolded at the bait shop. Without a word spoken between them, Liz and Peter laced fingers, as they listened to her mother describe what she'd like to do to his uncle. Ouch!

The sound of Amanda's cell phone caused everyone to pause in their conversation as she answered the call. "Hello, Summer." Of course, there was a chorus of hellos to follow from their family gathered in the kitchen. Amanda laughed at her daughter's response to their family joining in on their conversation. Then Summer made a direct comment that only Amanda was privileged to hear. Both Jim and Kevin took notice that Amanda's whole demeanor changed in an instant. Her brows grew together. "Excuse me? What did you just say to me?" She asked Summer while mouthing "sorry" to her family, and rose from her chair to head for the family room to speak privately with her daughter. "That's what I thought you said. Oh really? Is that so?" Amanda huffed. She drew in a calming breath as she listened. Summer was on a roll and so was she! "Summer Newman North, you had best lose that tone with me." Panic had been replaced by anger, as Amanda continued. "Don't give me that! You obviously have spoken with your father and have chosen to take his side."

Jim and Kevin had just arrived at the family room door in time to see and hear Amanda as she paced the room and spoke to Summer. What they saw was alarming for both of them. Her normally warm chocolate eyes were dark with angry hot fire ready to consume her body. Her left fist was clenched at her side. With her earlier altercation with Stephen and now Summer, Amanda was like a dormant volcano ready to explode, and they were ready to intervene when necessary.

"Apparently Johnson's word is golden for you and my word is nothing better than crumbling shale on the side of the mountain. Tsk, tsk, tsk. Well, my dear daughter, that's the way it appears to me, and Summer let me warn you, choosing sides between your parents may have lasting major consequences for all of us." Amanda flexed her fist as she listened. "Yes. I'm serious. And let me add, I do love you and whether you believe it or not, I even forgive you for what you've said to me. However, as you know I do have a long memory. Oh yes, I do! As of now with your attitude and your low opinion of me, there is nothing more to be said between us. I wish you and Adam happiness in life and with your father. Goodbye, Summer."

Amanda ended the call and released a sob, as tears raced down her cheeks. "Amanda." Kevin's quiet voice was like the light from a lighthouse pointing the way for a wave beaten ship on a fog ridden river. She turned and slipped into his embrace and wept. Jim gently touched her shoulder, made eye contact with Kevin, nodded, then returned to the kitchen. Later he'd be there for Amanda, if she chose to talk with him about this latest mess in their family.

A few weeks after the engagement party the gossip about the Callison family had finally quieted down. Liz was relieved that her parents were once again out of the town's spotlight. But all was not peaceful in the Great Sac community. There had been a double homicide in a prominent family—drug related. Now everyone's attention was focused on another family and their community in grief.

Peter was busy teaching during the week and spent time after school with the hockey team and the newly formed varsity drama club. Of course, his weekends were spent with Liz, unless the school had an overnight away hockey game. During this time, Liz had provided Peter with valuable insight and guidance in the creation of the drama club. The students who had signed up to participate in the club were ecstatic to find out that Liz would be helping them with their spring production. Some of those same students had shown an interest and were helping Liz at the Community Arts Center.

Stephen Johnson was keeping a low profile after spreading his rumors about Liz, as well as his newest altercation with Amanda, and was still earning forgiveness with his sister and the Callison women residing in the north country. As part of his amends for his actions, he graciously plowed the roads and parking lot at the arts colony, drew in a load of gravel, and filled the potholes in the road. With the road improvements, Liz was able to have the contractors work on the electrical rewiring and general indoor construction on the outbuildings throughout the winter.

"My goodness!" Jim exclaimed, as he got out of his pickup a few days after the road had been repaired. "Elizabeth, you did good by getting Johnson to fix the road. Now I don't have to fear that my shocks will wear out, or worry about breaking an axle when I drive in here. But child," Jim gave her his familiar look causing her to pay attention, "Remind me to never be on the receiving end of needing your forgiveness!" Liz laughed with relief that he was teasing and not upset about anything. Sometimes, like at that moment, she needed her father's sense of humor. She responded, causing Jim to also laugh as he pulled her into a bear hug. "This place is really starting to take shape." He said as he released her and gazed around the little community of buildings.

Liz's smile grew as she drew in a breath as her eyes moved from her father, who seemed to be beaming with pride, to the buildings. At that moment, even though the sun was shining bright warming them, the wind kicked up and reminded them that it was still winter in the Adirondacks.

"Thanks, Dad! It means a lot for me to hear that you are pleased with what I am attempting to accomplish here." She eased her gloved hand into his, as she had done countless times as a child. At that moment, that was exactly who she was. His child, and with everything that they had been through during the past nine months, she was so glad that they had endured the storm that could have ripped their family apart. She felt his gentle squeeze, just as he had always done when she was a little girl and would hold his hand. "Let me show you what we've been doing inside the buildings."

Jim smiled as they walked towards the cabins that would house the cast and crew during the summer theater season. Every once in a while, she would pause, take a small pad of paper and pen from her pocket, scribble down a note and then continue on their way. He watched and listened to her speak with enthusiasm as he asked countless questions. Liz proved without a doubt that she was in charge of the situation and had sound answers for him. "So, Dad, this is the cabin that has me concerned." She said as they stopped in front of the refurbished door and she slid the key into the new lock. "As you can see, we've taken great strides to save money and maintain the integrity of the old arts community. When the weather warms up, we will be painting it, so that it blends in with the other buildings and nature's backdrop." Liz glanced at her father as she opened the door. The hinges that had squeaked last fall, had been oiled, or replaced and moved with ease. She noticed something in his eyes as they stepped over the threshold. Concern? Hesitation? Curiosity moved her to ask, "Dad is something wrong?"

He looked at her with an expression Liz was not accustomed to seeing on him. Her father was quiet, gave her a slight shake of his head as he moved into the cabin. The sun peaked through the limbs of the evergreens that blanketed the cabin and through the window casting light and shadows. Jim released a slow breath as he looked at her.

"Lizzie, remember last November when your aunt and uncle visited and we had the conversation about lingering spirits?"

"Of course. We talked about the legends of the lumberjack and the French and Indian War. I also remember that you were not too pleased with Aunt Amanda sharing so many stories with me. Dad, what has prompted you to ask me this?" Liz felt her heartbeat increasing as she watched and listened to her father.

Jim walked further into the cold, barren space. As he looked around, he could begin to picture how his daughter would turn it into an inviting space for the visiting theater troupe or other artists. He also felt something. It was unsettling.

"You and I both know that I am not as keyed into our Iroquois-Mohawk ancestry and legends as your aunt is."

"Yes, I know." Her voice was quiet as she studied her father's demeanor.

He cleared his throat as he gently smiled at her. "I think that before too long, we should invite your aunt to come up and visit here. You know, to check things out. Now, child, don't give me that look! I didn't mean to worry you." He sighed, removed his cap from his head and ran his fingers through his hair. "It's just that, I've been feeling something since I got out of my truck. The feeling is stronger in here and, if, you plan on having people stay here, and there is a lingering spirit here, then we need to make sure that spirit, if there is one, is okay with you and the others being here."

Liz released a breath that she had not realized that she was holding. Her dad had raised some valid concerns. So, since there is no time like the present, she pulled out her cell phone and speed dialed her aunt.

"Good morning, Elizabeth!" Liz smiled as she heard the genuine pleasure in her aunt's voice. "This is a nice surprise to hear from you! How are you?"

"I'm great, Aunt Amanda! And before you ask, yes, Peter is great too!" They laughed and shared other greetings and inquiries about one another. "Actually, Aunt Amanda this is not a purely social call."

"Oh?" Liz heard her aunt's intake of air and then her concern when she asked, "Are you in crisis again?"

"No. Honest Aunt Amanda, I'm good. Right now, I'm at work and Dad is here with me at the arts colony. Right!" Liz giggled as she looked at her father who had been nosing around the space, paused and shot her a look that said a number of things. "I think we both just got caught and are now in trouble."

"He gave you that look. Didn't he?" Amanda's tone was filled with amusement.

"Oh yes!" Liz snickered. Her father made a guttural sound while her aunt, who had obviously heard him as well, sighed and commented. Sometimes. Like right then, her family cracked her up! There were so many traits and nuances that clearly defined who they were. "At any rate, Dad and I have been talking about the town folklore dealing with spirits and Dad, if you can believe it? Thinks that you should come up and visit the arts community. Really. I'm not lying! Okay! Here, Dad." She stretched out her hand with the phone and beamed with delight. "Aunt Amanda wants to talk with you."

Jim drew up the corner of his mouth, tipped his chin down and sighed, as he took the phone from her. "Hey Sis. Yeah, I have to agree with Lizzie. Something is going on around here. I don't know. It is hard to describe." He listened and huffed. "You know you are annoying. Touché. No, Amanda. Nothing in particular happened. It is just a feeling that I keep getting. It's, as if, someone is watching us. I can't shake it and it is stronger in this cabin." Jim nodded, as he listened to Amanda. "Exactly, Sis. No. You know I am not a full believer like you, but I will give credence to what Gram taught us. Thanks, Amanda. Listen, you have a good day and tell Kevin I send my regards. Okay. Here's Liz." He gave her the phone and then walked around, snooping to see what other repairs had been done to the cabin. The old electric wiring hung in disarray overhead going to the light fixture that would need to be replaced. Jim didn't worry. He knew that the cabin, as well as the other ones that would house the troupe would be repaired and up to code before the summer season. He opened a door, walked into the full bath and stopped dead in his tracks.

"Lizzie," Jim called out. "Come here."

"Dad, what-" Liz didn't complete her question, as she stepped into the bathroom. "How in the world did that window get open?"

"I was going to ask you the same question." He was not smiling. His expression emphasized his concern.

"Dad, this is too weird. I know for a fact that the window was closed and locked, because I closed and locked it myself after it was installed." Liz looked at her father for reassurance, only to have him respond.

"Great!" He sighed and shook his head.

Liz also sighed heavily. Something weird was definitely going on, and for once she was glad that her dad was in the thick of it with her. Now there was no way for him to discount her stories about the arts community.

Later that night, Liz, exhausted from her day's work, laid snuggled against Peter's chest as they lay together on the couch. Upon returning home, thoroughly chilled through, she had built a fire in the fireplace. Then she showered and changed into sweatpants and an old pullover sweatshirt of Peter's that he had conveniently left there during one of his visits. Peter held her close as he lazily caressed her arm, causing surges of warmth to charge through her body.

"Mmm, I love nights like this when we are together and nothing crazy is going on in our lives."

"Shush, Lizzie, or you will jinx us." With that said, Liz's cell phone rang. "See. I was right! I recognize that ringtone. Here we go!" Peter moaned as the mood was fully broken and Liz sat up to answer her phone.

"Aunt Amanda at this time of night! Hmm. This could be good, or, I won't say." She told Peter as she picked up her phone and cheerfully answered it. "Hey, Aunt Amanda! First, I called you, now you're calling me. I hope everything is okay with you and Uncle Kevin. Are you by any chance planning to come visit?"

Liz listened to her aunt and heard a touch of laughter as she said, "We're both fine. But, thank you for asking. You must have learned that trait of expressing concern for loved ones from your mother, and certainly not from your father." Liz responded and they both laughed. "You are right. I am looking at this from a younger sibling's perspective and yes, your father can be considerate. At any rate, I hope I did not interrupt your evening with Peter?" Liz looked over at Peter, who was caressing her neck, and making it difficult for her to pay attention to her aunt. Her breath caught and didn't go unnoticed by her aunt who said, "I see. Hmm. Please tell him that I apologize for interrupting your quiet moment together."

Liz couldn't help but giggle. She knew perfectly well that her aunt was smiling and probably enjoying herself. "Pete, Aunt Amanda said she's sorry for interrupting us." Her voice was thread with anticipation of what was to come.

Peter made a noise that caused Liz and her aunt to laugh. "She's not sorry." Peter said, as he eased his fingers to Liz's neck and found the spot that he knew would drive her nuts. Her rapid intake of breath did not go unnoticed by the old woman on the other end of the phone connection.

"He's right, Elizabeth! Tell him this is payback for him and JJ heckling at Kevin and me."

Liz flicked his fingers from her neck and came to a sitting position, bringing the blanket that had been covering them with her. Her expression turned serious as she responded. "Hold on a minute! Okay, my phone is now on speaker to make it easier for me to talk with both of you. So, I'm obviously missing something important that happened between you all before I returned home. Pete, when did you and JJ heckle Aunt Amanda and Uncle Kevin?"

"Ah, jeez!" Peter was also now in sitting position and securing his share of the blanket. "Amanda, don't you ever forget and forgive anything that's done to you?"

Liz was scrunching her eyebrows together, as she listened to both conversing, as if she wasn't there.

"Peter, I do forgive, but forget?" There was laughter laced in Amanda's feigned annoyance. "Perhaps you should ask the older men of the north country about my memory!" She sighed.

"Actually, Elizabeth," the male voice took them both by surprise. "I too clearly remember your brother and Peter interrupting our special moment." She watched Peter sink his face into his hands and moan, as her uncle joined in the conversation. Oh yes. Pete was busted! Liz was smiling. She loved it when she had speaker phone conversations with her family in Baltimore. Tonight, was no different.

"Okay, Uncle Kevin, by the mortified posture of Peter and the comments from you and Aunt Amanda, this had to be good, so fill me in on what happened." Liz folded her legs under her as she listened to her uncle, heard her aunt interject comments and watched Peter as he attempted to defend himself. Laughter and teasing had definitely replaced their romantic evening. Family. Half an hour later Liz ended the call, unfolded her legs and turned into Peter's arms.

"Skeeter, you and JJ are lucky she has forgiven you!" Her eyes danced with laughter as she attempted to sound serious.

"I know. But, honestly honey, we were just teens having fun."

"Mm-humph!"

"Ah, come on Izzie. Don't tell me that you wouldn't have thought that it was gross! There we were, J and me skating on the lake in late December and then we see an old couple sitting on a rock by the frozen lake and making out like -"

She gently placed her hand on his chest. "Don't finish that! Remember, I've seen them together." Then she allowed herself to smile. "As you all shared, it was at the beginning of their relationship and I bet it really wasn't that different from you and me. I bet they were tender, exploring."

"Exploring, all right!"

"Peter!" She exclaimed as he drew her down onto the couch and began to kiss her, while his hands found the end of her sweatshirt and then her bare skin. It was time for their own exploring and more!

CHAPTER 11

I t was a sunny, warm Saturday morning. Spring had finally sprung. The trees were budding and leafing out with a vengeance, woodland creatures were emerging with their newborn young, and birds that had headed south to avoid winter's fury had once again returned with their familiar songs. A smile graced Liz's lips as she drove with ease into the art colony. While the winter had been a stormy one on multiple levels, she was grateful for the crushed shale that had been drawn in and leveled out on the road thanks to Stephen Johnson. If it hadn't been for him, Liz would be driving through mud, while dodging potholes, ruts and hoping to not get stuck along the way. She pulled next to her father's pick up, stopped, shut off her car, gathered her clipboard, car keys, colony keys, and got out to greet her dad and other workers assembled in the parking lot.

"Morning boss!" Jim called out with a smile in his voice. Elizabeth smiled brightly, as she approached him. Everything about her said that she was the one in charge, and that she was the right person to be the executive director of the community arts program. He wasn't surprised that Elizabeth had a gift to bring people together for a common purpose. Even the community's staunch pessimists were beginning to change their tune, about Liz's inexperience in non-for-profit work, with the programs and events being held at the community arts center. Jim had been impressed when Liz used mailings, postings in various stores and social media to notify the community of renovation costs, how the community could assist with funding, volunteering, and her timeline for completion of all major projects before summer stock theater would open. So far, through creative community events and donations, she had nearly raised all of the necessary funding for immediate arts colony repairs. Liz was a people person and had managed to form a diverse group of volunteers. Of course, some people might think that Jim was rather biased in his opinion of his daughter, and he probably was. But Jim didn't care what others thought. He knew how far Elizabeth had come in her life since she arrived home last summer with the weight of the world on her shoulders. Now she was proving to herself, more than anyone else, of what she was capable of doing with her life. Jim wrinkled his nose, as he sniffled back his proud emotions.

"Good morning, Dad! I won't tell Mom you called me boss." Liz giggled, as she watched him make a comment to one of the other workers before turning his undivided attention on her.

"Lizzie J," His expression was serious, while his eyes contradicted him with mischievousness. "Your mother already knows that you're the boss over here, and she knows that she will always be the undisputed boss at home." A hint of a smile took shape on his lips, as he continued. "Just so you know, little one, your mother did give me her 'honey do list' to complete on my way home from here, and a word of warning, Elizabeth Jeanne, I do not intend to end up in her doghouse! So, how about you tell me what you have planned for us to do and then we get started?"

"Oh, Dad!" Liz's smile had grown as she listened to him. "You crack me up!" She noticed his brow arched. She giggled. "Okay. I won't tease you anymore. For now!" She added with another soft giggle. "Folks, we need to unlock the outer cabins, so that the window frames can be painted and the floors sanded down, buffed, and then resealed." Liz turned to five adult volunteers who stood by them. "If you all will come with me, I will unlock the mess hall door and show you where the supplies are located for those jobs." Then she turned her attention to her father. "Dad, after I get this work crew situated, and Peter arrives with his drama club teen volunteers, the rest of us will go over to the amphitheater where we will be working."

"Sounds good." He nodded in approval at her attention to detail. "I'll help carry supplies over to the cabins."

"Actually, Dad, we have a utility cart to put the smaller stuff on. So, the only thing that needs to be carried over is the buffer."

Fifteen minutes later, Liz and Jim were making their way down the stairs to the orchestra pit in front of the stage when they heard voices calling out. "Hey, Lizzie, Mr. C, I mean, Jim! Beautiful day! Isn't it?"

Liz and Jim looked up to see Peter along with seven of his drama students standing at the rear of the cement bleachers. She quietly laughed, as she listened to her father's response that was intended for only her to hear, while they waited for Peter and the youth to join them.

"Hi Pete!" Liz's smile laid claim on him, even though they had been together not too long ago. She heard her dad quietly clear his throat, which caused her to blush. "Good morning ladies and gentlemen. I'm glad you all could come and help us this morning. Did Mr. Jones explain how non-glamorous our work is at this point?" She laughed at their responses as well as her dad's comments, and knew in her heart that this would be a memorable day. "Believe it, or not, an indoor theater that has been neglected can be just as dirty and strenuous to clean up as this open theater is."

Jim watched and listened to Liz as she answered questions and explained what their goal was for the day. He saw the look of determination in his daughter's eyes to complete the strenuous, dirty, work that was required to make the arts colony a viable part of the community once again. Liz was on a mission and Jim hoped the young people were going to be able to keep up with her. Actually, at that moment, Jim hoped that he was going to be able to keep up with her!

"Okay, Dad," her eyes sparkled like a star-lit night as she said, "I am making you the captain of team one." A smile tugged at her lips.

"Hey, now! How come he gets to be the captain of team one?" Peter asked with feigned outrage of Liz showing partiality towards her father and not him. "What are we? Chopped liver?"

"Ewe! Mr. Jones we're not liver. You maybe, but not us!" one of the students stated.

Liz giggled as she took in Peter's wounded expression, and saw the looks of amusement on the faces of the students. "Peter, trust me. You and your great team will like the name I give you."

"Oh?" His eyes held hers. It didn't matter that they had an audience. His love for Liz shone through in his facial expression. Neither one noticed her dad's look of amusement as he watched them.

"Yes, you are the captain of the Great Sac High Drama All Stars. It is a great honor to be an all-star." Liz looked serious. Only her eyes revealed the fun that she was having at that moment in time. Peter and his team were quiet. The teens watched him as his look of contemplation transformed into a nod of agreement. "We accept. All Stars we are!"

Jim was paying close attention to the interaction between Liz, Peter and the students now being known as all stars. His team was disgruntled by the other team's declaration, and they were determined to prove that they were the number one team. Oh yes, the competition was on! So, Jim huddled his team together and told them something for only them to know. Liz watched suspiciously. Then, she saw the smiles emerge on their faces, and knew that her dad, in his infinite wisdom, was the ideal captain who knew exactly how to rally his teammates. She sighed to herself, as she imagined what he must have been like as a teen leading the high school sport teams on to victory. Her dad! Her hero!

"So, now that our teams are set, I will show you captains where you and your team will be working." Liz glanced down at her clipboard, then up from the pit to the amphitheater stage. She made a notation on her paper. Then, she looked up at the all-star team and said with a tone that stated she was the director, "Pete, you and your all-stars will be up here working on the stage. In the back of the stage you will find the backdrops and set pieces. Be careful when you pull out the backdrops and set pieces. With how long they've been neglected, they may fall apart. See what we can salvage, repair and reuse. Plus, identify any stage repairs that need to be made." Liz fielded more questions then turned towards her dad, only to spin back towards Peter. "Oh, and before I forget, someone will need to go to the mess hall and get the large broom and dustpan to sweep off the stage. Sometime after today we will refurbish the floor."

Liz had noticed her dad's expression as she gave her instructions, and she instinctively knew that he was going to have a response to her next directions. "Dad, you and your team will be working with me down under the stage in the storage rooms and dressing rooms. We will pull everything out of storage, so that we can give the props a good cleaning, and determine what is salvageable, or, if it needs to be thrown out."

"Has the electrician been down there to check the lighting?" Jim asked. His concerns were evident in his voice and expression.

"Ah," Liz drew in a breath and slowly release it. "Well, that's -"

"Say no more!" Jim exclaimed, shook his head and sighed. "Team one you called us?" He looked at the teens who would be working with him and calmly stated, "Team suckers is what we are." He glanced over at his daughter with a raised brow, tilted down chin, sighed, then looked back at his team. "Come along with me. I have a couple of lead cords, flood lights and drop lights in my truck that we can use to bring light into the dungeon."

"Hey now!" Liz exclaimed. "It's not a dungeon!"

"If you say so boss!" Her father responded, then headed off in the direction of the parking lot with the teens in tow. He was prepared and had more equipment than the lead cords and lights to bring for this job that was sure to be messy and very dirty.

Liz unlocked and opened the door to the lower passageway under the stage. She was glad to not be greeted by any bats or other residents inhabiting the once forgotten space. Only damp wetness greeted her. Not good! Liz was not feeling too optimistic about the condition of the props that most likely had been stored in cardboard boxes. Years ago, at the end of the season, the stage crew probably had anticipated another season and had seen no reason for placing the props in water resistant containers. Liz hoped that despite the years of neglect that they could salvage a few things. The sound of young voices along with her dad's drew her attention to the once crumbling concrete steps that had already been repaired.

"Here, Lizzie." Jim held out a drop light that he had turned on for Liz to use to see by.

"Thanks, Dad." She said as she turned off her flashlight and attached it to her tool belt and with- drew her work gloves from her back pocket. Jim smiled, as he watched her dressed in scuffed up work boots, old jeans, a tee shirt with an open plaid flannel shirt over top, a down vest, and a baseball cap on her head. Liz was right in her element as she took a hold of the drop light. "Alright ladies and gentlemen, follow me down this hall to the end rooms where we will begin our task for the day."

"Excuse me, Liz, do you expect us to clean out every room while we are here today?"

"You're Kellie. Right?" The teen nodded. "No. We certainly won't get through every room today. It simply makes sense for us to start in the back and move forward. From darkness to light."

"I like that. It works." Kellie smiled. "From darkness to light."

"Speaking of darkness and light," Jim inserted, "Derick has another flood light for us to hopefully hook up here in the hallway, so we won't kill ourselves trying to see to get out of here."

"Thanks, Dad!" Liz slid over and placed a quick peck on his cool stubble free cheek. "I knew you were the right leader for this team—leading by example. Okay, team, let's get started." Liz had taken a step when all of a sudden there was a burst of laughter. "Kellie, what struck you? If, you don't mind my asking."

"I just got it!" She giggled. "You told Mr. Jones that your dad is the captain of our team, and you just called Mr. C our leader. But you are our real captain. We're your team and that is what makes us number one!"

There was laughter and comments from the others.

Then Jim spoke with quiet authority, and perhaps a touch of amusement in his voice. "Young lady, you would be wise to restrict your observation to within our group. We wouldn't want to hurt Mr. Jones' feelings, now would we?"

"No, sir!" Kellie smiled. "Oh, I am so glad that I joined the drama club, and I get to work with the fun group!"

Liz allowed a soft smile to grace her lips, as she listened to the others join in with laughter and joking about the fun that they were already having on their team.

"We'll see how much fun you think this is in a few minutes." Jim said under his breath.

They were having fun. As soggy, musty cardboard boxes of props, and larger props were drug out into the hall, one of the boys, Michael, began to sing *The Music of the Night* from *The Phantom of the Opera.* His voice was hauntingly beautiful sending a chill down

Liz's spine. Voices were hushed as they all fell into a rhythm of working together under her supervision and her dad's leadership. From the Phantom's song, the music turned to classic Rogers and Hammerstein *Oklahoma*, or, more precisely, *Poor Jud* from the musical. Liz was amazed to hear how Michael's baritone voice blended with Aiden's tenor voice. Her heart soared, as she began to consider the possibilities of what the drama club could do with their raw talent.

All of a sudden there was a blood curdling scream from the room across from where Liz was working. "C- Man—Mr. Callison! Oh my god! I'm going to be sick!"

Jim was already at Kellie's side, when Liz ran out of the room and into the hall. The young girl standing in the hall was shaking and had lost all the color in her face. Liz saw her dad place a hand on Kellie's shoulder to steady and console her.

"Kellie, what's wrong?" His concern was genuine as he watched her look up at him. Terror. Her eyes held terror. From what? Jim felt the hair rise on his neck. It was suddenly eerily cold in the hall.

"I think I found a real body. A real dead body. Not a prop! Oh god, I'm going to be sick."

Liz was now standing next to Kellie. She gently pulled her close to hug her, as she and her dad exchanged concerned looks. She shivered as a chill came over her. Then, Jim calmly spoke to them. "I'll go in and see what we have in there."

"Okay. Thanks, Dad."

Liz quietly spoke to the teens gathered around her in the hall. At that moment, she was thankful that her dad was a retired state police officer, and that he would know what to do, if, there really was a dead body in the room.

Jim made his way into the dimly lit room. The drop light that had been hung against the interior wall by the door cast shadows on the walls. Jim drew in a breath as he walked further into the space. Then, with the aid of the flashlight he had in his hand, he found the area where Kellie had been working. His light centered on scattered and intact human bones, that until that morning had been wrapped in a blanket and canvas tarp. Human remains. Death. There would be no more work in that room, or any room under the stage until an investigation was completed. Jim closed his eyes and prayed for whomever had been placed in that room—a room with secrets. So many questions. Would they ever have all of the answers to this mystery? Jim doubted it. He turned off the drop light and walked out into the hall.

"Dad?" Liz quietly asked.

"Yes, Lizzie. We have uncovered human remains. Everyone outside. I have to make calls and," he sighed, "for now all of you are to remain in the orchestra pit. Elizabeth Jeanne, you are to go and send Peter's crew home. Also, the others who are working in the cabins need to leave the area. Only you, and our team, are to remain here in the colony, until the police get our statements and tell us we may leave."

She had heard that calm, commanding voice many times in her life, and knew that her father had just superseded all of her authority as the theater director. At this moment, as a retired officer of the law he was in charge. Still, the thought of having to remain there without Peter was a bit disconcerting for her. "Dad, can Peter stay?"

"Elizabeth." He tilted his head and raised that one brow.

"I know, Dad." She sighed. "You know what is best. But you can't blame me for trying!"

Jim raised the edge of his lip, with his look that said, *"nice try!"* He then moved away from them and began placing his calls. He continued to observe the teens, while he spoke on the phone. Kellie had shed a few tears which was understandable considering the trauma she had just experienced. Derick sat next to her and slid his arm protectively around her. There was no laughter, as Jim had grown accustomed to hearing. They all spoke quietly, as if to show respect for the deceased. It was a touching scene in the midst of the grave situation.

Liz reappeared with bottles of water for all of them, and Sheriff Phil Johnson by her side. She felt some relief knowing that her dad and Peter's uncle, the county sheriff, would handle everything.

"Phil, glad you came." Jim greeted him without a smile, as Liz normally saw when he greeted his friends. It was interesting for her to observe her dad, as if he was still on the state police force.

"Dad, excuse me." Liz interjected. "Just so you know, Peter has left along with the other teens. He wishes that he could stay. But he too understands why he had to leave. This is just too creepy. A dead body under the stage." Liz shivered, then felt her father slide his arm around her for comfort. She sighed as she thought, *there's nothing like having your dad with you to make a really bad situation a little better.*

Liz and Jim's interaction didn't go unnoticed by Phil. His friend may be a recently retired State Police BCI—Bureau of Criminal Investigation—officer, but right at that moment, he was a father—a loving, caring father. An unseen smile touched Phil's heart, as he continued to watch their interaction and spoke. "Jim, I'm glad that you were here with Liz and the kids when they found the body." He saw Jim give Liz a gentle squeeze, as she continued to lean against him. A wave of sadness swept over Phil. Years ago his wife and twin daughters had gone on a school trip to Boston. The group had just begun their journey home when the school bus and a tractor trailer collided. That day when they died, he'd lost his world, and now he strives to find joy and fulfillment in helping other families remain intact, whether they are family, friend or strangers. His voice was somber to meet the gravity of the day. "The State Police, D.A. and coroner are on their way…" Phil updated Jim on the particulars as to why it seemed to take so long for everyone to arrive. They chuckled as they made comments about people Liz had never heard of. Yet there was no frivolity in their voices. By now Liz had regained her composure, checked in on the teens in their midst and continued to watch them interact. Both men were in their element, just as she had been in her element, until the body had been discovered. She listened as Phil added, "Kind of like the old days, before you retired. Isn't it?"

"Yeah," Jim sighed. "Unfortunately, Phil, I believe in my gut that this is a homicide. That body's been there for a long while. Long enough for the blanket to be rotting away. Maybe one of the state's cold cases…I just hope that the feds won't need to be called in before this is through."

"Ah, jeez! Callison, you just love to throw gasoline on a fire! Don't you?"

"Not really." Jim sighed, removed his cap from his head and ran his fingers through his hair. "I'm just telling you my thoughts from what I observed when I was down there."

Phil had heard that tone of voice and had seen that look in Jim's eyes from the time they had been in high school. No, scratch that! From the time Jim and Phil's older brother Stephen had become friends as children. Jim saw things most others missed, well, unless you were Jim's sister, Amanda. At that moment in time, Phil, didn't have time to go down memory lane. He needed to be sheriff.

"You got my attention." Phil paused and turned to Liz. "Liz, I know this is tough for you and unfortunately, it is going to get tougher before it gets easier, for all of us. For now, how about you go sit with the students? While your dad and I go down and secure the room. If we're not back up here when the others get here you can show them where we are."

"Sure, Phil. They're a great bunch of teens and I don't want this horrible scene to deter them from the theater. Maybe I can help get their minds on something more enjoyable while we wait together." Liz turned, took a step, then turned back and said, "Phil, thanks for being here."

Phil stepped over to her and drew her into a hug. "Liz, you don't need to thank me. As sheriff, family friend, and more importantly as your future uncle, I will do everything in my power to get this resolved as soon as possible for you."

Phil could not help but smile as he felt Liz hug him back while whispering her thanks and calling him Uncle Phil. *Yes indeed,* he thought. Peter did alright in hooking up with Elizabeth Callison.

Later that afternoon, after all of the drama students had given their statements and been released, Liz handed over a second master key for the rooms under the stage to Phil and was finally allowed to leave. Of course, she asked for permission and received it to go and secure the other buildings before she left. She slowly walked towards the cabins and mess hall when she felt a presence near her. She paused and turned around expecting to find her father behind her. Liz gasped. No one was physically next to her. She heard her father's, Phil's and other law enforcement people's voices and saw them congregated by the amphitheater. Then she watched the County Coroner pull away in his official county vehicle with the corpse. She felt a cold chill and sighed.

"Okay," she said in a near whisper—a theater whisper. "I wish I knew if you are a man or a woman so I could give you a name. I really hate calling you something like 'hey you' when I know that you were someone who had a life and for some reason you are lingering here." Nothing. Silence. Liz sighed. "Well, be silent then, and come on, if you must. I'm on a time limit to check things out and then leave. Now, you haven't up to mischief, have you?" She asked, as if expecting an answer from the resident spirit. Liz quickly and efficiently walked through the colony observing, making mental notes of what still needed to be done, and feeling a sense of great accomplishment in the midst of tragedy. Unlocking the door to her car she allowed herself to smile and quietly breathed out, "Please behave yourself, and do not cause any trouble for the police, while they do their investigation. I'll see you when they say that I can return."

Liz found herself smiling, as she slowly eased her car down the gravel road to the main road. She hit the phone book on her car touch screen, selected and dialed Peter's number.

"Hey, beautiful!" His voice filled Liz with yearning to be transported at that very moment from the car and into his arms. "What a crazy day! Are you heading home any time soon?"

"Crazy is one way to describe it. I am on the main road about a mile from Route 30." She yawned. "Oh, Peter, I am exhausted. I want a hot shower, to snuggle in your arms, and I don't feel like cooking dinner."

"Well, Lizzie, I will be glad to snuggle with you and even pick up dinner for us. Anything special?" He laughed at her response, which helped to lighten Elizabeth's tattered spirit. They spoke for a few more minutes then hung up. Liz turned off the radio to quiet her mind and focus on driving home. Well, driving and the events of the day, which brought her aunt to mind. Yes, in due time, she would have to contact her aunt and fill her in on the drama being played out at the art colony: the dead body and the resident ghost-spirit. But, not tonight. Liz needed to process everything that had transpired before she was ready to talk with others. Well, others besides Peter.

Liz arrived at the cabin in the late afternoon daylight. The sun had nearly completed sinking behind the mountain. She slowly made her way up the porch steps to the front door, unlocked the door and stepped into the old cabin. The furnace was completing its cycle providing minimal heat. So, Liz shed her coat, hung it on the coat rack, and headed over to the fireplace. Placing her hand over the ashes she was disappointed to find that the fire had completely gone out. Time to build a new fire and warm up the cabin.

When Peter arrived, the fire was roaring and the cabin was toasty warm. Liz had showered and was changed into gray sweatpants, a hunter green thermal top, and wool socks donned her feet. She greeted him at the door with a light kiss as she reached out to take the pizza box and bottle of wine, allowing Peter to come in and close the door behind him. Upon entering he eased out of his leather bomber jacket, and left his work boots by the door. Peter also had changed from earlier in the day, and was wearing clean blue jeans and a blue flannel shirt. He stepped over to Liz, who had placed their food on the coffee table, and gently pulled her into his arms. Liz wrapped her arms around his waist and laid her head on his chest. He smelled of spice aftershave and lingering soap from his shower. She smiled as she breathed in his familiar scent, and felt centered for the first time since the body had been discovered in the room under the stage.

"That was a heavy sigh, Lizzie." His quiet voice and his gentle rubbing of his hands on her back soothed her tattered spirit.

"Mm. I guess it was." She sighed out her fatigue.

"Sweetheart, you go ahead get settled on the couch, while I go out into the kitchen and get our plates and wine glasses."

Peter's willingness to take care of her touched Liz's heart. By the time Peter returned to the living room Liz had the television set for the movie that they planned to watch. Throw blankets and pillows were in easy reach for them, should they want to use them. Soon after the food and a couple of glasses of wine were consumed, Liz fought to keep her eyes open. Peter held her close, as her eyelids closed for the last time. So much for the movie! She was sound asleep in his arms.

It didn't take long for Liz to rebound from the discovery of the remains at the arts colony. Nor, did it squelch the flourishing of the Community Arts Center programs, from arts enthusiast's participation and the attendance of the inquisitive. The Spring fundraiser was held and raised the remainder of the money needed to finish renovations at the arts colony, that is, when the police completed their investigation and allowed her back on the site. At night curled up on the couch next to Peter, or sitting at the table with him, Liz spent time working behind the scene assisting Peter with the drama club. All that was about to change.

Walking into the high school office, for the first time as an alumnus of the Great Sacandaga High School, and as a community member sharing her professional expertise with the drama students was a surreal moment for Liz. Even though it was after school hours when Liz had arrived at the school, strict security measures were in place. Unlike her high school days, Liz was not able to walk through the rear auditorium door and enter the school. A wave of sadness surged through her, as she thought about how scary the world had become for students, even as they were engaged in after school activities.

Liz quietly waited for two women, one being the principal and the other a teacher, to complete their conversation. A smile tugged at Liz's lips as she eases dropped on them, and she recognized the principal's voice. Mrs. McCoun. The older woman had been Liz's high school guidance counselor, and someone whom Liz highly respected. She smiled as she thought about how she and her peers would refer to their counselor as '*the apple of my eye*'. Mrs. McCoun had never chastised Liz or any of her peers for teasing her simply because her name also happened to be a variety of apples. Instead, Mrs. McCoun would chime in and respond, "Yes, I am and don't you forget it!" Her eyes always had a hint of playfulness that Liz would respond to.

The two women completed their conversation. As the other teacher began to turn, she gave Liz a cursory smile and then fully recognized her. "My goodness, Elizabeth Callison, I was hoping I would run into you!"

"Mrs. Yliad!" Liz beamed with happiness. "You're still here!"

The older woman laughed and smiled, then responded. "Yes, I am and I've been hearing good things about you as the Director of the Community Arts Center. I also have heard that you plan on revitalizing the summer stock theater program." She smiled at Liz as she added, "You always were a go get-err, so I'm not surprised by your undertakings. Tell me, how are you handling the shock to finding skeletal remains at the old art colony?"

"Honestly, it was creepy! Fortunately, I have plenty of other work to keep me busy so I don't dwell on it." Liz sighed as memories flashed before her. "But honestly, sometimes it still creeps me out."

"That's understandable, Elizabeth. I hope you have someone to talk with and process this traumatic experience with." Mrs. McCoun tenderly interjected.

Mrs. Yliad nodded in agreement, as she looked at Liz with fondness in her eyes. "Elizabeth, I hear that you are going to be spending some time assisting Mr. Jones with the Drama Club." Liz nodded. "Sometime I'd like for you to come in and share some of your experiences working on Broadway with my freshman and sophomore English classes."

"I'd be honored, Mrs. Yliad. Now, if you both will excuse me? I am late for my meeting with Mr. Jones and the drama club."

Liz stood in the rear of the auditorium and watched Peter as he sat on the stage with students gathered around him. In that moment, it was as if she had stepped back in time. Memories flooded over Liz like spring rush when the winter snows melted up in the mountains and came racing down the streams to the valley floor. She too had sat on that stage as a band and chorus member, and she had participated in the traditional junior and senior class plays as well as the annual school musicals. It was on that stage that Liz had fallen in love with the theater. Now her life had come full circle. No longer was she the student. Today she returned as a teacher in her own right—a mentor for a new generation. The sound of Peter's voice directed at her brought Liz from her thoughts to the present.

"Good afternoon, Miss Callison. Please, come join us."

Liz didn't wait for a further invitation. Especially when Kellie, Aiden and Michael's voices rose collectively to welcome her as well. She took her place on the stage floor with them, immediately crossing her legs, placing her legal-size pad of paper on her lap and withdrawing a pencil from somewhere in her ponytail. Everyone took notice, especially Peter.

"Liz—Miss Callison." He cleared his throat, while his eyes softened for a split second as he gazed at her. Liz noticed. Nodded and squelched a smile as the students looked on. "This afternoon's meeting is informal. I intended for this meeting to be for you and all of my drama students to get acquainted. We do not have work that requires you to be taking notes."

Now Liz did smile as her gaze passed from Peter to the students gathered around them. She cleared her throat. "Well, Mr. Jones thank you for clarifying your expectations for this meeting. I apparently misread your intentions during our previous conversations, and as a result of our previous collaboration I have come with information to present to the drama club this afternoon."

She noticed the eyes that were attentive to the interaction between her and Peter. She also noticed the change in Peter's demeanor.

"Oh?" Peter asked with a touch of a challenge in his voice.

Liz drew in a breath as she recognized Peter's 'oh', and what he was saying to her. In that moment, Liz had unintentionally hurt his feelings. She sighed to herself and made a mental note. *Peter may be an English teacher and high school drama teacher, but he also has a hidden theater heart and temperament. Life sure is getting interesting.* Yes. Liz mentally admitted to herself that she had overstepped her authority by indirectly assuming leadership. She was, and will be for years to come, a director. Sharing that responsibility, even with the love of her life, does not come easy for her. But somehow, she needed to do immediate crisis intervention and smooth over the situation with Peter.

"Yes, Mr. Jones." While there were plenty of things that Liz would like to share with Peter, she was well aware of their audience. "I have here in my notes that you gave me the authority to use my contacts and gather necessary information on two dramas to be presented to these fine young people for their input and final decision. Now, Kellie, Derrick, Aiden, Michael, Sandie, and Scott already know about my attention to detail as the Director of The Great Sac Community Arts Center and Summer Stock Theater."

"Yeah, and she has adventures that are better than a haunted house on Halloween." Aiden quietly said only to have others comment.

Liz was surprised to hear that other students who had been working with Peter on the amphitheater stage, while they were encountering the corpse, were actually disappointed that they were not a part of her group. She glanced at Peter and realized what his body language was indicating. Peter was not too thrilled with his students remarks about the Saturday's adventures at the arts colony. Oh boy! She had a lot of cozy-in up to and consoling to do later when they were in private to soothe his tattered ego.

"I sincerely doubt there will be any more adventures quite like the last one at the colony. At least, I hope not!" Liz sighed. "At any rate, Mr. Jones, as the drama teacher this is your turf. You are the director and I do apologize for obviously misinterpreting your directive. I came here ready to share my findings with all of you." She looked directly at Peter, not smiling, but questioning his desire. "Again, you are the director, and, if you'd rather I wait until another day to share my findings, or that I simply give you this information to review and then share with your students..." Liz masked her hurt feelings with a smile, "I'll understand." She drew quiet.

In fact, the whole auditorium was quiet. Everyone's eyes were on Peter. It was his call.

"Miss Callison." His voice was crisp, causing Liz to raise a questioning brow. "Thank you for your apology, and please accept my apology in return for our apparent miscommunication on my expectations for today's meeting."

At that moment, Liz didn't think that Peter was too apologetic. It sounded to her as if he had lapsed into full teacher mode and was speaking to her as if she was one of his students. Well, that was going to change! But for now, she'd hold her tongue. Later, Peter just might get an earful from her, instead of her stroking his ego and cozy-in up to him, as she previously thought he needed.

"Please, Miss Callison, go ahead and share with us what you have put together thus far." He said with lack of enthusiasm.

"Alright." She gave him a half smile and a nod before turning her full attention to the students gathered around them. "After Mr. Jones shared with me your dreams and goals for your drama club, I got to work and contacted a few people I know both on and off of Broadway." Liz saw the questions in their eyes. Oh yes! They wanted to know about her adventures of living in New York City and working in the theater district. But that would have to wait until another day. "The first person I spoke with is Dr. Mardino, my mentor and former adviser from Syracuse." She smiled warmly. "I see by your expressions that some of you are surprised that I chose to go first to a former teacher, and not a former theater friend and colleague on Broadway. Well," she shrugged, "It was a no brain-err for me to call him. I trust his judgment and his guidance. If I didn't, I would not have asked for him to assist me with my play."

"You're writing a play?" A wide-eyed young woman asked.

Liz's eyes sparkled as she smiled at the teen. She noticed that the youth had a dab of freckles under her dark blue eyes, minimal makeup donned her face, braces shimmered on her teeth, and her clothes were designed to hide her figure. A wave of sadness filled Liz, as she imagined that the young girl had probably faced ridicule from her peers at some point in her life about her weight. Life could be a challenge for those who were not a part of the in group for whatever reason that might be. Unfortunately, physical appearance ranked at the top of the list. By being judged and left out due to prejudicial attitudes, talent and intelligence often goes untapped and unacknowledged.

"Yes. I am and sometime I'd be glad to share more about it with you. For now, we have other things to discuss." The teen smiled and nodded. "So, here's what I've put together..."

Questions, excitement, and laughter filled the auditorium, as Liz presented her proposal for the spring theater production. When she felt that she had completed her presentation and honestly answered all of their questions she turned to Peter and said, "Mr. Jones, if you are in agreement with the students, I will make arrangements to have the scripts of Thorton Wilder's play, "*Our Town*" sent to you here at the school. In the meantime, it would behoove you to schedule try outs for the play." Liz swallowed. "Sorry. I had a momentary lapse into director mode."

Peter's slight nod allowed Liz to release a sigh of relief. She quietly watched Peter address the students, and then dismiss them. It didn't surprise her when Kellie came over to speak with her about showing her oil paintings at the Young Artists Craft Vendor fair being held at the arts center in two weeks. Kellie has an amazing talent—a true gift—one that needs to be further developed. For now, Liz was keeping her ideas for future displays of the talented teen's art to herself. Hopefully, Regina Sullivani, a friend of Liz's who works in a small New York City gallery would be able to come and see Kellie's work. When, and if, things progressed as Liz hoped that they would, well, then she'd share her idea with Kellie.

"Miss Callison?"

"Yes, Amber." Liz smiled as she asked, "How may I help you?"

"Were you serious when you said that you'd talk with me about writing plays?"

A soft smile remained on Liz's lips as she nodded. "Besides writing stories, do you write poetry as well?"

Liz saw the joy begin to radiate from the teen's eyes. Her expression turned from pensive to relaxed. Tenderness filled Liz's heart as she watched and listened to Amber.

"I only write short stories. So far, I've submitted two of my stories to teen writing competitions, but they weren't good enough to win." Her voice trailed off. Liz's heart ached for her.

"Amber, unfortunately, rejection is a major part of professional writing, whether it is a short story, a novel or a play. Any of the arts, for that matter, are highly competitive. Perseverance and a tough skin are vital for self-preservation."

Amber sighed. "I guess with my soft skin I'll bleed to death before I'm out of high school."

"Hey now!" Liz gently placed her hand on Amber's shoulder, "Defeatist attitudes are not welcome in my presence. As artists, we are all winners! You included, Amber."

Tears shimmered on the teens eyelashes. She sniffled. "You really mean that. Don't you, Miss Callison?"

"Yes, I do." A noise drew Liz's attention away from Amber. She noticed Peter was the only one remaining in the auditorium with them. "Looks like Mr. Jones is ready to go. So, you and I also need to get going."

With that said, they joined Peter in the rear of the auditorium and left the school together. When Liz and Peter remained alone by her car, watching Amber leave in a nondescript used car, Peter turned to her. He didn't touch her. His backpack was dropped onto the hood of his car, hands were jammed into his jacket pockets as he shifted his weight from one foot to another. Peter cleared his throat, then spoke with remorse. "Lizzie, I'm sorry for acting like a jerk in front of the students. I think one part of me was proud of you and the other was jealous of you."

"Oh, Peter, thank you for apologizing. I too am so sorry because you probably were entitled to feel upstaged by me walking in there with my production proposal and rehearsal outline."

"Well, maybe a little—oh alright— a lot!" He declared with a smile. Then, Peter gently cupped Liz's jaws and drew his mouth to hers. At that moment, Liz surrendered to his lead. And what a lead it was! His body weight pinned her against her car, and his hands slipped inside her coat, while his mouth and tongue devoured hers. A moan escaped from Liz's lips as her cell phone rung and broke the moment.

CHAPTER 12

After a long and at times frustrating month, Elizabeth finally received notification that the police investigation at the arts colony was completed, and she was free to resume work on all the buildings and grounds. Today was the first day back on site, and her first order of business was the amphitheater stage area. Liz took her time reviewing the work that Peter and his crew had completed on the stage, noted what still needed to be completed before her theater was ready for the summer troupe, and had begun to make her descent on the stairs into the orchestra pit when she heard familiar voices. She stopped so quickly that she nearly fell down the stairs, and grabbed onto the rail to regain her balance while a smile took shape on her lips.

"Aunt Amanda, Uncle Kevin!" She exclaimed, as she raced back up the stairs and aisle to greet them. "What are you doing here? Do Mom and Dad know that you are here? Silly me! Of course, you let them know that you planned on coming! Didn't you?" Her face radiated with joy as she reached her aunt.

Amanda's smile grew as she softly laughed, opened her arms as she said, "Oh, Elizabeth, yes, they know. Let's begin with a hug and then we'll talk." Liz didn't require any further encouragement as she stepped into her embrace. Then it was her uncles turn for a hug. Kevin responded to Liz's questions with a chuckle in his voice, "Elizabeth, we're staying with your parent's."

"Oh!" Liz was surprised by this news. Elizabeth looked deep into her aunt's brittle chocolate eyes and saw tremendous pain. Something major was going on.

"We have some things to discuss with them and well," Amanda's voice faded off. Elizabeth waited. The moment of silence seemed to hang on forever. "Let me add that right now, as much as I enjoy sharing life with you, your dad and I need each other as brother and sister—our family. When the time is right, you and your siblings will be informed about what is unraveling in our lives."

"Wow! I guess now I might have an idea of how left out the others feel when Caitlin and I exclude them." She gave them a half smile, sighed, then asked, "Since whatever is going on is none of my business, how about I show you both around the colony? We've done a lot since you were last here. Well, until we found the body."

Joy radiated from Elizabeth, as she showed her family around the stage of the amphitheater, while explaining about all the renovations that had been made, and still needed to be completed before a theater troupe could perform. Then, she led them down the stairs to the passageway that held the storage rooms and dressing rooms. Liz told them about the previous lack of lighting, and how her dad approved of the new reset hall lights in the rehung sheet rock that still needed to be painted.

"And here is where we found the body." Liz said with a quietness in her voice that conveyed a sense of reverence, or respect for the deceased.

For a moment, no one spoke. Liz and Amanda exchange glances as they silently asked each other, *"Did you feel that?"* Their nods confirmed what they each knew. They were not alone.

"I know we've discussed the experience you and your dad shared with the students, but being here, seeing the room, I can only imagine how terrible it must have been for all of you." Amanda quietly breathed out, while taking a hold of Kevin's upper arm. Without saying a word, he understood her need, eased out of her hold and drew her close to him.

"It was beyond terrible, Aunt Amanda." Liz breathed out as the memory swept through her. "I honestly don't know what I would have done, if, Dad hadn't been here with me. You should have seen him take control of the situation. Dad was wonderful with the students," she swallowed, "with me. And you should have seen him with the array of police who descended upon this place. Dad might be retired, but he's still a cop through and through."

Amanda, and Kevin nodded in agreement. They, along with Melissa knew just how involved Jim continued to be in the situation. Earlier in the day, after they had arrived at Jim and Mel's during their conversation, Jim revealed that he had been spending time over at the police barracks. Needless to say, Mel was not too pleased to hear that Jim had been withholding information from her about his whereabouts, and the fact that as a retired BCI officer he was unofficially involved in the investigation. The human remains found down in the storage room confirmed that the person was murdered. With the evidence collected at the crime scene it was believed that the murder was committed somewhere else.

Amanda remembered Jim's words, as if, he was standing next to her and speaking to her. *The M.E. has completed her exam and she is able to confirm that the person was a male. She believes that he was in his mid-forties and that the murder probably took place around forty to forty-five years ago.*

"Forty years? Oh my, we were teens. It couldn't be! Could it?" Amanda breathed out while reaching out for Kevin's hand. Her thoughts had her reach out once again. *Jim, when will they know* who the person is? How will they find suspects and a motive if it was in fact a murder?"

"*Those are good questions, Sis. After the initial investigation is completed, it will probably be classified as an unsolved cold case.*"

Amanda remembered Kevin asking, about how the person was murdered and Jim's response. "*Blunt force trauma to the back of his head and his neck was broken.*" He sighed as the magnitude of the situation hit him and Amanda knew why. "*I've been holding back some important information since Liz and I found the body. Important things that both Phil and I saw. We decided it was best to keep it to ourselves—that is the police forces involved in the investigation, and D.A.'s office—until we had absolute proof.*"

"*Proof of what?*" Amanda asked. She carefully watched all of the subtle body signs being given from her brother as he spoke.

"*There was a thin silver chain around the victim's neck.*" Jim's eyes shimmered with wetness as he maintained eye contact with Amanda, who sniffled as her eyes held Jim's with a mixture of pain, and unspoken understanding. Jim cleared his throat. Then drew in a breath. "*When the coroner moved the body, we found a medallion. Of course, it had to go with the body, so I didn't get to look at it right then. But in my gut, I knew. Since then, as I already told you, I have been working with the BCI and DA. After we saw the inscription on the military dog tag, I gave a sample of my DNA.*"

"*I'm going to be sick.*"

"*I felt the same way, Sis.*" Jim quietly consoled. "*I felt the same way. Then, I was angry on multiple levels. Our father Samuel Callison the second was murdered and stashed in the room where his murderer had hoped that he would never be found. Now we know what happened to him. I just wish Mom could have known this before she died.*"

"*Me too!*" Amanda quietly wept. "*Me too!*"

"*Oh goodness!*" Mel found her shocked voice. "*Jim, when will the police release your father's identity to the media?*"

"Next week."

That was all that had to be said to set into motion the family events that were to take place.

Amanda returned her focus to the present, listening to Liz and Kevin's conversation. "Liz, what are your plans for this evening?" She quietly asked, causing Liz to look at her with concern.

"Peter and I are planning on a quiet night at the cabin. But, Aunt Amanda, you are not acting like yourself. At least, how you normally appear to be." Liz had an ominous feeling, as she looked at her aunt. "Something major is wrong. Isn't it?" Her eyes searched her aunt's for answers. She sighed. "Should we plan on being at Mom and Dad's?"

Her aunt nodded, closed her eyes to force back tears and swallowed. Liz's ominous feeling immediately turned to a sense of doom as she watched her uncle protectively draw her aunt to him.

Samantha's pregnancy was causing her life to be a day by day event. How she felt dictated what she did, or if she even left her bed. Melissa had talked with her an hour before the other family members arrived and knew that she was not feeling well. So, Jim and Amanda decided to go ahead and share their news with Caitlin and Liz, as well as Summer, JJ and Jordan through video chat. Liz stood with Peter, Caitlin and Nick by the grill in her parent's back yard, where they were tending to the London broil that was cooking on the grill. The older sisters were anxiously awaiting the arrival of their pregnant younger sister, Samantha and her husband Chris to arrive for the family picnic and meeting. The air was cool on that spring evening requiring most everyone to wear a heavy sweater or jacket. The Callison grand children were busy entertaining themselves inside watching a movie on the large flat screen television in the family room. Liz glanced over at her parents, aunt and uncle.

Their voices were kept lower than normal. There was no gaiety or teasing and laughter between them.

She could only imagine the mix of emotions that they must be feeling with finally knowing their father's fate. Murdered. Liz also grieved for her grandmother, who had died not long after their grandfather with never knowing what had happened to him. Grandfather Callison's death—murder— was being classified as an unsolved cold case. So really only one part of the family mystery had been solved. Liz shivered, not from the cold, but from how unfair life continued to be for her dad and aunt.

"You okay?" Peter quietly asked, as he slid his arm protectively around her. She laid her head on his shoulder as she turned into his embrace.

"I was just thinking about Dad and Aunt Amanda." She sighed. "First, they lose their brother Sam in Vietnam, then grandpa vanishes and then grandma dies from metastatic breast cancer. Now they know how he died, but not who murdered him and why. Oh, Peter, it's so unfair!"

"I agree Liz. It is unfair. For all of us!" Peter gently stroked her cheek as he brushed a kiss on her head of soft hair. "To think that your dad discovered his own father's remains. It is mind boggling!"

Caitlin quietly interjected, "Look at Dad. I can't even begin to imagine what he must be going through, to have had his dad disappear, and then years later discover that he had been murdered. And look at Aunt Amanda. We all know how tough she usually is. But right now," Caitlin sighed. "She looks so fragile, like an old twig that would break if it was stepped on."

Nick closed the lid of the grill, placed the long-handled fork on the side tray and reached over to ease Caitlin into his arms. "You all are correct. We can't imagine what this is like for them. But I will say Dad and Aunt Amanda are pretty remarkable with how they are handling all of this."

At that moment, as if on cue, their father called over to them to inquire about how much longer the meat would have to cook. Then he asked, "Do you four want to come join us?"

When they were all together Jim cleared his throat. "Sammie is not feeling well. Apparently that little one she is carrying is running a marathon inside of her, and she's glued to the bed, when she's not having a conversation with the toilet. So, she won't be joining us."

Both Cait and Liz made comments pertaining to their sister's condition. Jim looked from one daughter to the other. He recognized their behavior from years gone by. His *two peas in a pod!* Jim knew all too well that they were up to something, and it may have to do with their sister. If that was the case and Sam wasn't feeling too well, she might not appreciate her big sisters being around her. So, he began his fatherly interrogation in an attempt to discover what his girls had been up to. Of course, Amanda made light of it, only to be admonished by Jim.

"They don't need any encouragement from you!" He did that quirky raise of his lip, causing Amanda to smile. He was so predictable!

"Oh please," Amanda rolled her eyes. "Like you and Sam never shared information between the two of you, or conspired to do something, especially when told not to. Don't bother to pretend that you were a saint when I certainly know better!" Amanda's eyes shimmered with unspoken knowledge. Her lips were ever so slightly turned upward. Oh yes! She had stories!

"Is that so, Aunt Amanda? Do tell us about our dad's conspiring and misbehaving! Did he get in trouble for scheming with Uncle Sam?"

Amanda's eyes twinkled with delight, as she watched her nieces take defensive stances, folding their arms over their chest and tipping their heads to the side. At that moment, there was no mistaking that Cait and Liz are Jim Callison's daughters. Her smile grew as she licked her lips and responded. "I'm not tattling on him. You'll have to ask your father for the details." Her eyes met Jim's. He was not smiling, but Amanda was and her smile grew to full size as she said, "Sometime ask him about our father's socks that disappeared off of the clothesline. Or, about Mom's brother, Uncle John, knowing that Gram and Mom had planned a surprise birthday party for him."

Everyone heard a rumble of laughter coming from Peter and turned to him. "Peter, what hit you?" Liz asked.

"Amanda and your family!" Peter was grinning from ear to ear as he said, "I am so relieved to know that JJ and my actions are not the only ones that she has kept a running record of."

"Trust me, Peter. That one," Jim was not smiling as he pointed at his sister, "She has a memory like an elephant."

Amanda stopped smiling and feigned displeasure when she spoke. "Hey now, when did this evening turn into pick on Amanda day? And for the record James Callison, if I am an elephant then you certainly are a Jack -"

"Okay, Sis. Noted!" He cleared his throat. "We do get off track. Don't we?"

Amanda nodded, as Melissa commented, causing them all to laugh.

"Dad," Caitlin spoke up drawing their attention to her. "I gather what you and Aunt Amanda want to share with us is of importance. So, we'll be serious now."

"Thank you, Caitlin." Jim raised a brow as he looked at her, and held back the smile he was feeling towards his eldest daughters. There was no doubt that Jim loves all of his children. But these two daughters? There always had been something special about them that set them apart from the others. Right at this moment in time, they truly were a blessing.

"Everyone. Amanda and I have decided how we want to handle our father's death after it go public. We will have Dad's bones—what's left of them—cremated and the ashes will be buried next to our mother in the family plot at the cemetery. Since the majority of the people who knew Mom and Dad have moved away or died, we feel that a grave side service will be best."

"What about calling hours?" Caitlin asked. "Remember, Dad, we have friends who will want to extend their condolences to us."

"Caitlin," Amanda's voice quivered as she spoke. "That's a good question, and we have that under control. We are inviting family and friends to join us after the committal service at Gram's for an open house with food and fellowship to celebrate our father's life."

Liz watched her aunt draw into herself. Breathing. Finding her inner strength that had undoubtedly carried her through other adversity in her life. Then, she glanced over at her father. She wasn't surprised to find that he too was drawing on his inner strength. Liz had to wonder if they knew how similar they truly were as brother and sister?

It was a cloudy somber day with the threat of rain later in the day. The cemetery staff had erected a tent over the Callison burial site. Many floral arrangements were placed near the opening in the ground and by the headstone. Liz clung to Peter, as she watched and listened to her father. The gravity of his words pierced her heart.

"Sis and I want to thank you, Rev. Smith, for sharing God's words with us, and for all of your help in this time of grief. Only a few of our friends gathered here with us knew and remember our dad, and know what we went through as a family when he disappeared. Only a few of you, along with Sis and me, remember what it was like to watch our mother, who had been our rock of faith, having buried her first-born son, who died while fighting in the Vietnam War once again be thrust into despair with the disappearance of our dad. The grief our family experienced -" Jim felt his emotions crumbling. As he drew in a breath, he felt a gentle hand touch his arm. He looked over to see Amanda's watery eyes sharing his pain, providing him with the strength to continue. "-So, we thank you for being with us both then and now. Yes, now that we have Dad's remains, we have some closure to our family mystery. But Amanda and I have found ourselves reflecting on the brutally and unfairness of Dad's death. We can only imagine the horror he must have felt when his life was ripped away from him." Jim paused. He drew in a breath, and as he did, Amanda gave his arm a light squeeze. "Our brother Sam's death seemed to be the catalyst that changed Dad from being a humorous, fun loving, generous man to an angry, abusive man with his family. Unfortunately, Dad tended to take his anger out on Mom and Amanda. We figure that I was probably not abused because I was his only son he had left. Why he took to hurting Mom and Sis we will never know. Regardless of his actions in that year before his death, he was our father. We loved him. The good and the bad Sam Callison the second, and no one deserved to die as he did. Even though we don't know who murdered our father, or why it happened, we are thankful to have some closure to the family mystery. We are thankful for our family, and also for you our friends who have grieved with us, and cared for us throughout the years."

Liz turned into Peter's arms and wept. She had no idea that her other sister's in attendance were doing the same thing with their husbands. Then the sound of quiet singing drew her attention to her aunt. Liz listened. She realized that her dad had joined her in singing the somber melody. They were obviously singing something that their grandmother had taught them. Liz was filled with amazement. Even though their dad and aunt were Christians by faith, at that moment, they also chose to draw into their maternal family heritage for spiritual comfort in their time of grief.

Liz found that she needed a few moments to herself, to mourn the grandparents she had never known, to mourn the uncle and cousin she had not known, as well as her beloved great grandmother who had been the center, the rock, the gentle guiding spirit of their family. Quietly she stepped away from Peter, Nick and Caitlin to visit the other family grave sites. Liz lifted her head towards the sky and drew in a deep breath. Then she slowly released her breath as she took a step, only to stop. She gasped, as she overheard the conversation that was taking place by her cousin Rose's small gravestone. There stood Summer, Rose's younger sister and Stephen Johnson's girlfriend, Belinda. Her cousin Summer Newman North and her husband Adam North had traveled from Colorado to be with the family. Up to that point, neither her father, or her aunt would say why Summer and Adam were staying with her father, Stephen Johnson, and not the Callison family. Now, Liz had a good idea of what was going on.

"That is unfair." Liz stated with clear annoyance in her tone of voice.

"Excuse me?" Belinda asked. Her surprised expression would have been priceless, were it not for the gravity of the family's reason for being there.

Liz glowered first at her cousin and then at the other woman. "Who do you think you are trash talking my aunt like this? And you!" She pointed her finger at Summer. "You, Aunt Amanda's living daughter saying unfair and hurtful things about your mother. Shame on you, Summer!"

"Liz, you only heard the last part of our conversation." Summer said defensively. Her normally warm brown eyes were taking on a darkening hue indicative of fire smoldering from her view.

"I heard enough. You were bashing my Aunt with information you obviously obtained from the one and only Stephen Johnson. The Great Sac Golden Boy!" She rolled her eyes in disgust. "It is obvious that neither one of you have bothered to consider Aunt Amanda's feelings."

"Don't you think Mom has told me about my sister, the rape and her leaving here?"

Elizabeth was livid with Summer for her remarks. Heated words were exchanged between the two cousins, while Belinda interjected her defense of Stephen and his part in the saga. Neither cousin acknowledged her presence. The family feud was hot with anger. Fire blazed in their locked eyes.

"So, Liz, since you are apparently Mom's golden niece, perhaps you'd like to enlighten me with what you think you know about my parent's grief and pain?" Summer snarled.

Liz shook her head. She sighed. "I really do pity you, Summer. You are the golden one in your mother's eyes. She loves you to the outer reaches of the universe and far beyond. That woman would tear up the world to protect you if need be. And yet, you apparently don't know her at all!"

More heated words were exchanged. Neither woman realized that by now their family had slowly made their way around them to see what was going on.

"Right now, you are just about as low as my sister is in my eyes and heart. I love your mom almost as much as I love my parents. Aunt Amanda is simply someone whom I know I can trust to listen to me, counsel me, and have a great time with. She has provided me with rock solid emotional support at my lowest time in my life. She understands the hell I've been through because she too has walked through her own hell, and she has risen from the ashes to breathe new life. Yes. We have a bond. Yes. We have shared things in confidence. But Summer I will never take your place in her heart. Nor, do I want to." Liz drew in a breath. Then she dropped her bomb. "I have nothing more to say to you, except, don't expect to get an invitation to Peter's and my wedding." Then Liz turned to Belinda and snapped, "And you! I don't give a flying monkey if you are my fiancé's uncle's girlfriend. You lady had better learn to keep your mouth shut. Especially when it pertains to my family."

Liz gave the two women one more glower for good measure, then turned to step away from her cousin's grave. Peter stepped forward to meet Liz and extended his hand that she readily latched on to. No one spoke for a few moments as they quietly slipped away from the crowd.

"Mom!" Summer gasped in surprise. "How much did you hear?" Tension hung between them as dark and as ominous as the clouds overhead.

"Enough." Amanda's quiet voice revealed how deeply her heart was hurt, and the sadness in her eyes confirmed it. She sighed. "I warned you that there would be consequences for your words and choosing sides between your father and me. For you to accuse Elizabeth of claiming your place in my heart was unfair." Her eyes shimmered with wetness. "So, you honestly believe that I do not have enough love in my heart too include my extended family along with you? Summer, in these years since we discovered the truth about who your father is, our relationship has greatly changed. I honestly don't know you anymore. Right this moment, as I look and you and listen to you speak, I see your father, not my Sunshine. Today I not only grieve for my parents, but also for both of my daughters whom I have lost."

Amanda did not wait for Summer to respond. She turned, took an unsteady step, and reached out her hand to Kevin's extended hand that drew her close to him. Summer raised a hand to wipe away her tears, while her other hand cradled her stomach that was in knots.

The rain had held off until late afternoon. A few close friends who remained at the family cabin were seated or stood with family under the protection of the large tent. A long table that had been borrowed from the Bait Shop Pavilion held remnants of food and drink.

During the afternoon, Liz had enjoyed hearing many people share stories about her grandparents. The rain drops that were hitting the tent reminded Liz of a drumbeat. Then she noticed her aunt and her dad conversing with Callie and Nick, as well as some of their friend's children. Liz watched and listened. She moved closer and heard her dad singing. His feet were moving. Then, Aunt Amanda joined in gathering the girls behind her. They were dancing. Then the boys followed the instructions and began moving behind her dad. Liz was enthralled by what she was witnessing. In all her years of life she had never seen such a public display of her family's Mohawk heritage as she saw today. When the dancing stopped her dad and aunt hugged and smiled. Of course, young voices begged for more, only to be sent off to entertain themselves.

Liz was lost in thought about her family. Since her confrontation with Summer at the cemetery, they had given each other a large berth. She gazed around and noticed that her cousin and Adam, had been standing with the Johnson family on the opposite side of the circle of onlookers. Of course, Summer had withdrawn from the Callison family, and sought protection from her father! Liz watched Summer wipe away a tear, as Adam quietly spoke to her. Interesting.

"Oh, dear. Do I sense more trouble brewing?" Peter quietly asked, as he whispered against Liz's ear.

His voice and breath caused Liz to draw in a quick breath. She felt the hair on her arms rise, as her body responded in anticipation of more to come. Peter lightly stroked her bare arm eliciting a quiet moan from Liz.

"Jeez, Peter." She breathed out. "Here I am observing your uncles and our cousin, thinking about how our families could be the northern Hatfield's and McCoy's, and you are seducing me right here in front of everyone!"

"We're not the H's and M's. And Yes, my precious Elizabeth. I am seducing you." He gently blew against her ear, while gently stroking her arm and sending a shiver through Liz. Peter lazily smiled as he whispered, "You live to be scandalous with me."

Liz turned into his arms and whispered back as Peter's lips gently came down on hers. "Yes, I do!"

Hours later, Liz laid in Peter's arms in her bed at the cabin. She was secretly glad when Aunt Amanda and Uncle Kevin had informed her that they were continuing to stay with her parents. But tomorrow morning they would be up to the cabin. They, including Jim and Melissa, would be there to open up the loft that had been closed off after Jim had graduated from high school. Amanda was itching to discover what things of her mother's had been tucked away up there. Now was the time to begin sorting through family memories. Liz knew that her aunt was hoping to find her mother's wedding gown so that she could see it. Liz also was hoping that it was up there. If so, she had plans to use it in the gown that she was creating for hers and Peter's wedding. She felt Peter's hand gently caress her jaw and chin.

"Lizzie, I can tell by your breathing that you're wide awake, and that your brain is in overdrive. Care to share with me what you are thinking about?"

"Mm. Just about today. I really should not have allowed Summer to rile me as she did. But, Peter in so many ways she reminded me of Jordan. I wanted to ring her neck." She sighed. "I guess I probably should discuss my thoughts with Aunt Amanda. I'm kind of wondering if I maybe projected some of my anger towards Jordan onto Summer?"

"I don't know. From what I heard of the argument, it sounded like Summer deserved to get your anger towards her. Plus, your aunt held her own and got in some powerful words that also rattled Unc."

"Oh?"

"Yeah. Dad told me that Unc didn't have much to say for the rest of the afternoon, except to Summer and Belinda."

"Still, I probably should have kept quiet and followed in Dad and Aunt Amanda's example with how they were conducting themselves. Dad and Aunt Amanda really surprised me, with how open they were to allow us to see their vulnerability as adult children grieving together for their father. Our family has endured so much pain and suffering over the years. Oh my!" Liz breathed out as she felt Peter's hand gently grazed over her neck on down to the top of her nightgown. The tips of his fingers brushed against her skin at the top of her gown. She felt his warm breath on her neck. Her breath hitched. "And now you are distracting me from my thoughts and I am glad."

"Good." Peter quietly spoke as his fingers lazily slid further down on her skin under her nightgown. "I plan on distracting you a lot more before this night is through. I love you Elizabeth Callison. Now and forever."

With that said, Peter's lips found Elizabeth's slightly opened lips. Gentleness turned to urgency. They gave of themselves to the other as their desire grew to the point of no return. Their passion burned in a scorching blaze of desire. Then, in total abandonment they cried out as they reached fulfillment together. Satiated and lying in each other's arms, gently stroking one another as they drifted off to sleep.

Liz carried her morning cup of coffee through the cabin to the front door. She quietly opened the door and stepped out onto the porch looking out into the valley far below. The sun had long since risen to usher in a new day. Birds cheerfully sang out mating songs to one another, while a Cardinal whistled to his mate. Unfortunately, his mate was not answering him. *Poor guy! Must be in the doghouse.* She thought. Still lost in thought, Liz turned and gasped.

"What are you all doing here?" She asked, as her gaze passed between her parents and her aunt and uncle. Liz also noticed that they each held a travel mug in their hands. They obviously had brought their own coffee. She shook her head and smiled as she walked over to perch herself on the porch railing near them.

"We're here to work." Jim said with a twinkle in his eyes.

Liz sighed, then took a sip of coffee.

"I told your father and aunt that we should call you first to make sure you kids were up!"

"And why didn't you, Mom?" Liz saw her mom shoot her dad a pointed look. Oh boy! Something was up. Dad had that look that indicated he was close to being in Mom's doghouse.

"Because he hid my phone and won't tell me where it is."

"Oh, Dad!" Liz exclaimed. "You do like to live dangerously. Don't you?"

Jim shrugged, as if, he wasn't too worried about any repercussions from Melissa. "I was just thinking about the conversations your mother and I had recently regarding how life used to be when we didn't carry phones around with us. We survived just fine!"

"Yes, we did." Mel acknowledged. "However-"

Oh no! Liz saw the sparks start to appear in her mother's eyes.

"That was before I was working as an EMT and needed my phone in case there is an emergency." Jim started to speak only to be silenced by Mel. "And I do recall how glad you were when Amanda, and the children and I were up in the mountain, and we were able to communicate with you when we needed your help. So, buster, unless you want to be sleeping on the couch tonight, you had best produce my phone."

Liz watched her parents. Her mother was not teasing. If her dad was smart, he'd return the phone before too long.

Much to everyone's amazement, Jim pulled the phone out of his back pocket and handed it to his wife. Then, without uttering a word of apology to Mel he turned to Liz. "So, Lizzie is Peter still in bed? Or, can we go on inside and get started?"

Liz was dumbfounded by what she had just witnessed between her parents. She had to wonder why her dad hadn't apologized to her mom. Plus, she noticed that her mother had not thanked him for returning her phone to her. Yes indeed! Something was amiss in Callison Happy Land!

"If you all will excuse me, I will go in and inform Peter that we have company." Liz did not wait for anyone to respond. She turned and disappeared through the open door, allowing the screen door to firmly close behind her.

Amanda cleared her throat as she looked over at Jim. "I think I'll take a walk out to the old barn and look around to see what treasures there might be hidden under the dust and dirt. Kevin, would you like to join me in my adventure?" Her smile and gaze were fixed on him.

"Of course, sweetheart." Kevin said as he rose from the chair. He reached over and took Amanda's hand into his. He drew her palm to his lips and kissed her. Then he said, "Every moment of our life together is an adventure. I'll go anywhere with you." His eyes held hers. At that moment, it was as if their family had disappeared and they were the only two people on the porch.

The sound of giggling drew everyone's attention to the screen door where Liz and Peter stood together. Amanda recovered and said with a twinkle in her voice and eyes, "Go ahead and giggle. Some day you both will be our age. When you do reach this age, I hope that you two will be uninhibited enough to show your love for each other in any situation. It is truly a wonderful thing to find your soulmate. When you do, the life and love that you share is a daily adventure."

No one said a word as Kevin leaned over and tenderly kissed Amanda on her lips. Then, with fingers laced together they silently walked down the steps to the path leading to the barn. Jim cleared his throat, as Liz and Peter emerged from the cabin. He turned to Melissa reached over with his thumb and forefinger and gently held her chin. He looked deep into her hurt eyes. His voice was filled with sorrow as he spoke.

"Mellie, I'm sorry for trying to tease you in a way that hurt your feelings. That was never my intention. Please forgive me for being— you can fill in what I am—I should have known that you would be concerned about not having your phone and not being able to get an EMS call if need be. That was obviously one of my more stupid jokes."

Mel sighed as she placed her hands on his shoulders. "Oh, Callison, what am I going to do with you?"

"Love me?" He asked.

"I always have and always will." She softly smiled at him. "Let's go see what Amanda and Kevin are finding."

"Knowing my sister, it is probably trouble!" Jim winked at Mel as his smile grew. He pulled her into his arms and kissed her soundly on her lips, taking Mel's breath away. Then, with his arm around her shoulder, he tucked her close to his side, and guided her to the steps.

Liz and Peter remained on the porch and watched them disappear from their sight. Then, Peter turned to Liz. His smile grew as he looked into her warm chocolate eyes. "I think we just had a couple of lessons about love."

"And humility." Liz sighed with contentment. "I hope that when we get to be their age that we too will be uninhibited as Aunt Amanda said, and openly express our love for one another."

"Why wait?" Peter asked, but did not wait for an answer. He gently cupped Liz's face, touched his lips to hers. Liz's hands found their way to Peter's shoulders as his hands found their way to her back. They were lost in the moment. No one else existed but them. Well, that is until they heard the clearing of a throat. Liz drew out of the fire of desire, while needing a fully charged hose from the local fire department to cool her down. She attempted to step back from Peter, only to have him pull her tee shirt up revealing bare skin as he removed his hands from her body. Liz sighed as her aunt stepped up onto the porch.

"You know, I usually am annoyed that my old bladder doesn't work as good as it used to." Her eyes twinkled with mischievousness. "But seeing the two of you lost in your moment reminded me of Kevin and me on the rock."

Peter moaned. "Oh great!" He shook his head and sighed with defeat. "Look. Amanda, J and I were seventeen year-old jerks who thought we were bad asses. Are you ever going to let me live that down?"

Amanda winked at Liz then smiled at Peter. "Someday." She said as she disappeared into the cabin.

"She's not going to let this go. Is she?" Peter asked Liz with a note of defeat in his voice.

She laughed. "Not in a million years!"

Whoop, whoop, whoop! Something brushed past Liz's head as she stirred awake in the bed. Peter was breathing quiet heavily, lost in a sound sleep. She listened. There it was again. *Whoop, whoop, whoop!* Fear. Dread seared through her as she recognized the sound. Cringing while certain she knew what to expect, she turned on the light next to the bed. It swooped. Liz screamed.

Peter bolted up into sitting position. His eyes bulging with panic. "Liz, what's wrong?"

"Look over there!" Liz was pointing to the window and curtain rod. There, clinging to the screen was a bat that was apparently trying to make its great escape. "Oh, Peter it swooped right over top of us. I could feel the brush of its wings as it flew by us. We have to get it out of here! Now!"

Peter heard and saw the panic in Liz. She was so cute in her disheveled state. But Peter knew better than to comment about how cute she was at that moment in time. Liz was looking to him to be her hero. How? He had no idea! Still, he had to do something. So, Peter threw back the sheet and swung his legs onto the side of the bed. He reached for his blue jeans that he had tossed in the chair and pulled them on over his tight-whites. Standing next to the bed, he looked tenderly at Liz. She was usually so brave, but the bat had really shaken her. There would be no teasing her over this.

"Lizzie, I'm not sure." *Whoop, whoop, whoop!* At that moment, the bat decided to stretch its wings and take a lap around the room. "Holy crap!" Peter exclaimed. "Okay. We either call my folks or yours and ask them what to do."

Liz looked at her watch. "Peter it is two o'clock in the morning. We can't call either of them."

"Well, how do you propose we get rid of the critter?"

"Um." By now Liz had slid over to Peter's side of the bed. Her old stretched out tank top and sleep shorts barely kept her decent. At that moment, modesty was the farthest thing from Liz's mind. "We'll call my parents." Liz had not taken her eyes off of Peter as she spoke. Then she realized that her phone was out of reach. She was starting to reach across the bed when the bat took another fly through the room. Liz squealed like a stuck pig and flew to the door. "You call my parents. I'm out of here!"

Peter wasted no time and was out the door with her. He immediately closed the door and headed out into the great room of the cabin, while Liz turned on every light in the room. Then she went into the kitchen and turned on the lights in there as well.

By the time Jim, Melissa, Amanda and Kevin arrived, it looked like a party was in full swing at the old cabin. The sleepy foursome was emerging from the pickup when Liz came bursting through the screen door and sprinted down the steps and path to Melissa's arms.

"Oh, Mom!" Liz buried herself closer to her mother's breast. "My encounter with the bat under the stage was nowhere near as scary as having a bat awaken me from my wonderful dream. It was right near my face."

By now Peter was also with them. "We're sorry for waking you all up over the bat. We just didn't know what to do."

Amanda yawned, as she stepped away from Kevin towards the cabin. "Well, you stick with us and you will learn. So where exactly is Dracula hanging out?"

"Oh, Aunt Amanda! That's not funny!"

Amanda snorted. "Yes, it is! It's a bat. They are nocturnal creatures. Obviously, it must have found a way into the loft from outside. Today when we opened the door and were snooping around up there it probably made its escape into the cabin. Elizabeth the poor thing only wanted to get outside. Who knows? There might be a whole family living in the loft."

"Oh no!" Liz moaned as she stepped from her mother back over to Peter's arms for protection.

"Come on, Sis. Let's go see if we can convince the cabin vampire to find a new home."

An hour later the two windows in the loft and the door were firmly closed. The screen window in Liz's bedroom was back in place and the backyard light had been turned off.

"Well, that was fun!" Amanda yawned and stretched.

"You have a warped sense of humor." Jim said as he too yawned.

"Okay, bat heroes." Mel quietly said, as she looked at her daughter who was barely able to keep her eyes open. Liz was leaning against Peter, who was sitting in the chair and holding her on his lap. "These kids need to get some sleep. And I have a bed calling my name."

Amanda and Kevin agreed with Mel and were heading for the door when Jim spoke up. "Peter, if another bat should appear from hiding, do us a favor."

"Sir?"

"Don't call us! Call your parents."

Peter looked sheepishly at Jim. "Yes, sir. I guess it is only fair to share the adventures between our families."

With that, Amanda seemed to come to life, fully awake. She shook her head as she looked from Jim to Peter. "No, Peter, don't call either set of parents. You all need your rest. Call your uncle and not Phil. You call Stephen Johnson. He likes to be the hero. Call him mister know it all—coming to save the day!"

Jim and Kevin exchanged looks that said a thousand words, rolled their eyes, and shook their heads. Some things never changed.

CHAPTER 13

Summer burst upon the Adirondack's. Somehow, even with a very tight budget, a murder investigation, rain, a multitude of other small glitches, pessimistic board members, Liz was thrilled to have a theater troupe pulled together to stay at the arts colony and perform on the amphitheater stage. Plus, many of the students from the high school drama club were volunteering to work as stage and lighting crew and hold box office positions. Some students had even auditioned and were to be extras in the performances. Needless to say, Liz was on a theater high. But, not so high that she did not understand that at any moment her high could plummet her into turmoil with an unforeseen glitch-crisis.

Liz arrived at the arts colony at seven in the morning. There was a heavy dew on the grass, and the sun was shining brightly already warming the day. In no time at all, the parking lot would be filled with cars, trucks and people—paid theater people from cast to crew. Liz got out of her car, grabbed her backpack, and went to the rear of the car. She opened the trunk and began removing boxes of food and beverages, and other supplies. By her third trip to the mess hall and her small office space, Liz had a large pot of coffee brewing in the sixty-four cup electric coffee pot. Boxes of baked goods, cups, and condiments were on the counter. She expected the caterers to be there by nine and then take care of lunch and dinner until the end of the production run.

The sound of a vehicle in the parking lot drew her attention to the outdoors. Liz picked up her clipboard filled with notes, her travel mug of warm coffee and headed for the door. A squeal of delight burst from her as she saw the doors of the SUV open. She saw six actors emerge.

"Elizabeth. Hey, beautiful!"

Liz was smiling and laughing, as she responded with her own greeting to her friends and former theater mates. She placed her things on the trunk of her car and hugged each of her guest artists for the summer production.

"Elizabeth, darling," Jonah, a tall, light haired man who had emerged from the back seat said, as he slipped his arm back around her shoulder. "You look fantastic!"

"Yes, love you do look considerably better than when you left us." Blaine, a dark haired, slim, medium height man added.

"Life here in the mountains must be agreeing with you." Natasha a petite, whimsically dressed woman Elizabeth's age chimed in. "Dare I guess you haven't been pining away for the man you lost to your despicable sister?"

"Oh, I know that look!" Annie chimed in. "She's in love!"

Lost in familiarity and conversation with her friends, Liz did not realize that Peter had arrived. Nor did she see him standing off to the side observing her with them. Liz felt alive with renewed energy that had been dormant for a long while—a long year.

"So, when the rest of the cast and crew get here, we will have our first production meeting. Until then, let me give you all the nickel tour, and get your cabin keys, so you can get settled into your homes for the next six weeks. Oh, before I forget, I have pots of regular and decaf coffee on, as well as cold beverages and food for breakfast in the mess hall."

"Coffee!" They all exclaimed.

"Ah, Liz you are the best!" Andre unwrapped his arm from Natasha, leaned over and kissed her on the lips.

That did it! Peter had seen enough. "Good morning!" He called out as he walked over to Liz and her theater comrades.

"Peter," Liz slid from where she stood between Jonah and Andre. "Everyone, I'd like for you to meet Peter Jones. And before you ask, yes. He's the reason I am so happy up here in the Adirondacks. Peter, these are my dearest friends who were—are—the best people. They're the best crew and cast to work with."

Liz watched the interactions as the men and women introduced themselves to Peter. During the past year Liz had learned how to read Peter's body language. Today was no different. Something was off with Peter. He smiled, but insincerity lurked in his eyes. Liz thought that she heard a coolness in his voice as he shook their hands and welcomed them to the Great Sac Community. That was not the warm, friendly Peter that she was used to being with. Then, he looked at Liz and she knew that something was more than off. It was terribly wrong! Liz sighed.

"Perhaps you all would like to head over to the mess hall for breakfast? You will find that there are bathrooms in there as well. Peter and I will be along in a minute."

"Oh, wonderful!" Alexis exclaimed. "Come, darling." She said as she wrapped her hand around Jonah's arm. "Elizabeth, we'll go entertain ourselves. You take as long as you need with your man." With that said, they moved along together towards the mess hall while raving about their summer theater adventure in the mountains.

Liz drew in a centering breath as she watched her friends depart from them. Then she turned her gaze and zeroed in on Peter. "Alright,

Peter." Liz quietly and pointedly said. "Something has changed since you and I left the cabin this morning. Let's have it! What is wrong?"

"I'm fine." His eyes that Liz read like a well-loved book, betrayed him.

"Bull!" Her eyes were beginning to smolder with angry fire towards his unwillingness to tell her what was wrong.

"You have a lot going on with your cast that is already here, and the cast and crew that are going to arrive shortly. If I stay, I am only going to be in your way. So, I'm going to head out."

Liz felt the tension sizzling between them like bacon slapped down on a hot cast iron skillet. She was beginning to see glimpses of Greg in Peter and she didn't like it. No. In fact, she was not going to travel down that road again, if she could help it.

"Peter, you need to tell me what is wrong, so I can fix whatever the problem is between us." She held his gaze. Concern filled every pore of her body.

Peter shook his head. His finger grazed her cheek as he quietly responded. "We can't fix our problem while standing here in the parking lot."

"Why can't we talk out whatever the problem is here and now?" Liz felt her stomach turning sour. She felt moisture forming in her eyes.

"You have people waiting for you to direct. I'll see you later." Peter began to turn to leave.

"Peter." Her voice broke. Oh yes! Different time—but it was Greg all over again. Their love was breaking apart like a piece of shale carelessly thrown to the ground and splintering apart. Crumbling before her.

He paused and turned back. "Lizzie, I don't want to get into it, especially with an audience. But I will say that maybe you've been too hard on Jordan." Peter's words cut through Liz like a dull knife ripping and shredding her as it passed through her.

"What in the world?" Tears streamed down her cheeks. "How could you go from loving me when we were alone at the cabin to standing here and throwing Jordan at me?" She gasped. "Oh my gosh. You flippie–dippie–idiot!" Liz exclaimed. She didn't care who heard her. Peter's words had been the match that set her anger ablaze in her. "How could you? You got me all wrong! I am not my sister by a long shot!"

"Aren't you as guilty as her? I trusted you and yet I arrive here I find you in another man's arms and I saw that kiss you exchanged with what's his name."

"Andre." Liz whispered through her shock.

"Yes. Andre. Let me guess, he tongued you. Didn't he?" Peter asked with disgust.

"No, Peter. Andre did not tongue me. Oh my gosh! You are head of the drama club, but you know nothing of the theater world, at least the world I've lived in for years. Andre and everyone else are my friends, they're part of a theater family. But you obviously would rather think I am a tramp all because I was happy to see and welcome my friends. Who knows where that overactive mind of yours is going? I sure don't." Liz drew in a breath. "But I do know that if you don't trust me anymore, especially with my theater family, then I don't want you in my life. I need a partner that I can trust, and who I know will trust me no matter what he sees, or thinks he sees. You are obviously not that man. I'm just glad that I realized it now before I said, 'I do'." Liz fought back her tears as she slipped her engagement ring from her finger and thrust it into Peter's hand. "You know the way out of here. Goodbye, Peter."

Liz turned away from Peter and greeted the new road weary arrivals of the theater troupe with a smile on her lips and a broken heart. Then she immersed herself in her work, as she had told Peter she would do.

Wes and Stephen had just finished their morning coffee when the bait shop door opened. The jingle of the bells indicated that the door was being opened with a force. They waited. No greeting. Just the door slamming shut and the bells ringing out their alarm indicating that trouble had arrived.

"Hey!" Stephen called out. "What did that door do to you?"

"Go to..." Peter yelled back.

Wes sighed, as he lowered his cup to place it on the counter. The expletives that he had just heard from his son were totally out of character for Peter. The expression on Peter's face, the devastation in his eyes all indicated that it was obviously time for a father-son chat. His voice was calm yet firm enough to get Peter's full attention. "Son, you seem to have a dark cloud hanging over you today. I was heading outside to do some work. Care to join me?"

"Yeah, Dad! That would be great." Peter grumbled, stopped and stood looking at the fishhooks. "I should have known better than to let her hook me." He said under his breath.

Wesley and Stephen exchanged knowing glances. Neither one spoke. They simply shook their heads in full commiseration with whatever had happened to fully upend Peter's world.

"Let's go." Wes said with concern as he placed his hand on Peter's shoulder. Peter mumbled to himself as his father to lead him outside. Wes released his son's shoulder as he closed the door with less force than it had been opened. Neither spoke as they headed down towards the lake and over to a quiet spot that was good for meditation and deep conversations. "Have a seat." Wes said as he gestured towards the fallen tree.

Peter sat down on the log stretched his jean clad legs out in front of him and looked out over the lake. Wes quietly stood for a moment and prayed for guidance before sitting down next to Peter. He knew that look on Peter's face. His son was in pain—shattered pain.

"So, do you want to talk about what happened between you and Liz to make you nearly rip the door from its hinges? Or, don't I want to know?" Wes quietly asked.

Peter accepted the invitation and told his dad everything that had happened from the time he arrived at the art colony to the moment that he left with Liz's engagement ring in his hand. The stones sparkled in the sunlight as he held it up in front of them. Yet the happiness that Peter had felt earlier in the morning when it had sparkled on Liz's finger was gone. Gone like a warm summer breeze that had instantly turned to the cold chill of winter.

Wes released a heavy sigh. "Hmm." He sighed again. "Well, son, you got yourself a mess, and I definitely have an opinion."

"But?" Peter asked as he looked over at his father, then looked out at the lake, while sliding his work boot across the pebbles on the ground.

"Well, life has taught me that women, especially those with a burr up their fannies don't think like we do. I think in this situation we need to have your mother involved in our conversation to give us a woman's perspective. She may be able to shed some light on this mess for us, and be the one to guide you in how you should go about apologizing to Liz."

Peter stopped scuffing his foot over the ground. He looked at his father in total surprise and exclaimed. "Me apologize? Are you crazy? I'm not the one who ended our engagement!" Peter was now standing. He leaned down and picked up a handful of pebbles. Anger, pain and hurt all spewed from him as he threw the pebbles one by one into the lake.

"Son, come along." Wes said, as he waited for Peter to send his last pebble hurling into the water. Peter did not protest. Once inside the building Wes informed Stephen that something had come up and they were heading home for the day. "And no! Don't think it, or say it! Peter did not get Elizabeth pregnant!" Wes called out as he shut the door behind him.

Becky was sitting at the kitchen table, sipping a cup of black coffee. Summer pollen and the humidity were raising havoc with her breathing. She had already used her rescue inhaler for what she considered a normal attack, and her cell phone was on the table in front of her, just in case she had a major attack and needed medical help. She was surprised when the door opened and her two favorite men walked in together. Immediately Becky noticed their grim expressions and naturally was concerned. She placed her cup on the table and stood as she asked, "What's wrong? Did something happen to Stephen or Phil? Are you both okay?" Her questions flowed from her as she began to wheeze and cough.

Wes immediately was in front of Becky taking her hands into his. "Your brothers are fine. But, you're not! Becky honey," his voice resonated with concern as he looked into her drawn face. "Do we need to go to the ER?"

Becky drew in a weak breath and coughed some more. She shook her head as she eased into Wes's arms, then lowered her head onto Wes's chest and wheezed as she fought to breathe with ease. "I'll be alright. Honest."

"Mom, are you sure you are okay?" Peter also suffered from asthma, except not as bad as his mother did during the summer months. His asthma normally kicked up in the cold of winter. Regardless of when it reared its ugly head, asthma was nothing to fool with. "I think you should go to the ER."

Becky turned from Wes to Peter. "I am okay. Really." Wes studied her drawn features. Becky might say she was okay, but Wesley knew his wife would put her love for family before her own medical needs. He remained on high alert as Becky said with labored breath, "Before you two came in I used my rescue inhaler, was sipping coffee

231

and now I am beginning to feel better. So, tell me what has brought you two here at this time of day?" She drew in a deeper breath which helped to ease some of Wesley's concern, then asked, "Or, don't I want to know?" Becky had an ominous feeling, as her gaze passed between her two men.

Peter raised his fisted hand, turned it palm up and opened it for Becky to see what he was holding.

"Oh no!" Becky exclaimed as she began to cry and wheezed. Her baby was in crisis, and she needed to be Mom. Right now, she didn't have time for a medical crisis, as she moved from Wesley's tender arms to gently pulled Peter into her embrace. "Oh, honey, I'm so sorry." She felt Peter tighten his hold on her as her eyes met Wes'.

He shook his head, while watching her like a hawk as he said, "I told Pete that we needed to come home and talk with you about his and Liz's demise. You know, sweetheart, maybe you can help Pete and me, for that matter, to try to understand why Liz reacted as she did. As much as I hate to admit it," Wes slightly smiled. His eyes held a twinkle of mischief, "We need your help from a woman's point of view and all that."

Becky realized full well what her husband was up to and returned her own smile, while her eyes said, *"smart man,"* then she said to them, "Of course, I'll help in any way that I can." Becky sniffled and wiped her nose. Her breathing was still quite shallow as she moved from her men to the sink. "This is obviously going to take us some time for us to sort out, so I'm making us a fresh pot of coffee. Are you two hungry?"

In no time flat, fresh cups of coffee and plates of coffee cake were on the table in front of each one of them. Over the next hour Peter shared what had happened and listened to his parent's advice.

"Thanks for listening and," Peter sighed, "For pointing out where I made a stupid mistake with Liz. I love her so much and now," Peter's eyes were shimmering with wetness. "I've probably lost the best woman to walk this planet."

Becky quietly handed Peter a tissue that he had not requested. But he took it anyway and used it. After he had wiped his nose, Becky silently took Peter's hand into hers with calming tenderness that only his mother could provide him with at that moment.

Wes released a heavy sigh, then said, "Son, don't give up on Liz too quickly. As you move forward and work towards repairing your relationship with her remember," he paused and sighed. "She is a Callison." Becky made a comment and coughed as Wes continued. "Having known her family my entire life, I can tell you that her father and her aunt do not readily forgive or forget."

Peter nodded. He knew from stories that he had heard, and knew from firsthand experience that Liz's aunt had an unbelievable trove of memories stashed in her brain. "Yeah, Dad, I have a feeling that Liz is a lot like them."

Wes nodded, then said, "Son, I've seen the way Elizabeth looks at you. There is no doubt in my mind that she loves you. But winning her back—now that will not be easy. Elizabeth is deeply wounded and you've got your work cut out for you."

Becky sighed, sniffled, and wheezed. "Your father is right. Liz trusted you to be different from her former boyfriend who broke her heart. But rather than talking with her, you accused her of being unfaithful to you, and in doing so, your words have ripped her wounded heart back open. Son, Liz may still love you, but without honesty, communication and trust between the two of you there is no lasting relationship. Sadly, in many ways you and Liz remind me of your uncle and her aunt." This caught Peter's full attention as she continued. "Amanda may love my brother, but it will be a cold day .... before she will ever trust him again." Becky released a deflated sigh and shook her head. "It looks like my initial concerns for you and Liz are a reality as the Callison-Johnson saga continues with the next generation."

"Becky," Wes calmly spoke as he lowered his cup to the table. "While there are some similarities, Pete and Liz are not Stephen and Amanda by a long shot." Peter began to speak, only to be silenced again by having Wes raise his voice one decimal. "Young man, the first thing you need to do is to remember who you are, how we raised you, and be the man your mother and I have taught you to be."

"Yes, sir. I know I have to apologize to Liz for comparing her to her sister." Pain and regret oozed from Peter's voice as he spoke.

"And for being jealous of her friendship with men with whom she has a shared past," Becky pointed out with her familiar motherly tone that suggested Peter pay close attention to her, "Just like you have female friends that Liz does not have a past with."

"Right, Mom. But that is going to be a lot harder to admit and get over."

Peter sighed, as his mother gently took his hand into hers and tenderly squeezed it. Her breathing was labored, her face drawn with worry and fatigue, but her eyes shone with love. It was the love that Peter needed at that moment in his life.

"Admitting to yourself that you are jealous is the first step you need to take to repair your relationship with Liz and Pete, when you do talk with Elizabeth," she paused to draw in a much-needed breath. "Be honest with her and let her know how you felt— how you feel. Son, also be willing to listen. Don't just hear Liz. Listen to what she has to say to you. Admit when and how you've been wrong. Let her see how much you love her."

Peter leaned over and hugged his mother. "Thank you. I love you, Mom."

"I love you too, Peter." Becky kissed the top of her son's head, as she had done countless times throughout his life. The scent of shampoo lingered in his hair, along with his familiar scent that identified him as her son. "It is going to be okay. You'll see."

Peter released his hold on her and a breath. He looked across the table to his father who was quietly watching them. "Dad, thanks for taking time to sit and listen to me earlier today. You were right. We did need to come home and talk with Mom." Peter attempted to find a sad smile as he finished speaking, turned his gaze to his mother, and then to his father. "What would we do without her?"

"I reckon we'd be mighty miserable." Wes' love for Becky shone in his eyes as he smiled at her. Her love shone back at him. Then, Wes turned to find Peter intently watching them. "Son, what are your plans for the remained of your day?"

"Now that things blew apart with Liz, I don't have any plans. Well, I guess I should go over and ask Mr. C to go up to the cabin with me so I can get my stuff that is there and take it to my apartment. Why, Dad? Did you need me to do something for you?"

"Actually, son I could use your help scraping the paint on the windowsills, so that I can get them repainted." He tilted his head towards Becky as he added, "I'd also like for you to be here in case your mom has an asthma attack and needs help."

Becky began to protest that she was fine and didn't need a babysitter, only to begin wheezing and coughing. The attack intensified and her face drained of all color while taking on a blue hue. Air was going into her lungs, but it was not coming back out. Peter was immediately on his feet moving to the bathroom to get the nebulizer for his mother. Wes was at Becky's side feeling helpless, rubbing her back, while knowing that there was nothing else that he could do to ease her pain.

An hour later Becky was in the air-conditioned living room in her recliner, resting. Wesley sat in his chair reading the latest mystery novel by his favorite author. Becky opened her eyes, looked over at Wes and felt a tear forming as she thought about how blessed she was to have a husband as kind, loving, caring, and simply as good as him. Then, as she heard the step ladder being positioned against the house her heart grieved for Peter and for Liz. She quietly prayed for them and hoped that God would guide them through this storm in their relationship and bring them back together. Then she added, *"If that be your will, Lord."*

Becky sighed, causing Wes to look up from the book that he was reading. He dog eared the page and closed the book.

"You had quite a rest. How are you feeling sweetheart?" Quiet concern filled his question.

"Exhausted, but able to breathe easier." Becky weakly smiled at him. "Oh, Wes, I am so thankful that you and Peter were here to help me through my attack."

Wes leaned over and gently took a hold of Becky's hand, giving it a slight squeeze. "You and me both! I hate to admit it, Becky, but every time you have a severe attack, I am afraid that you will die on me. Becky," Wes drew in a breath. Terror and wetness filled his eyes. "Honey, you are my world and I love you more than you will ever know. I honestly don't know if I'd have the strength to live, if anything were to happen to you."

"Oh, Wes, I do love you. For better or worse, till death we do part." Becky tenderly smiled, then squeezed his hand, as she drew in a breath, then felt her lungs push the air back out. Another crisis had been avoided.

The sun had slowly risen over the eastern shore of the Great Sacandaga when Jim pulled his pickup to a stop in the bait shop parking lot. It had been years since he had time to go fishing on a summer weekday morning. In fact, it had been so long that he couldn't remember the last time he had been able to relax and spend time fishing. Jim was not counting the winter ice fishing day that he had spent with Kevin at the lake. Jim got out of his truck, stretched, and drew in a deep breath of cool morning mountain air. He locked the doors and slid the keys into his worn jeans pocket. Then he picked up his pole and tackle box and took off towards the bait shop door to buy some minnows and worms.

"Morning!" Jim called out as he entered the bait shop. Silence. Well, now that was weird Jim thought, as he saw Wesley and Stephen standing together by the coffee pot. Neither one acknowledged him, and he knew darn well that they had seen and heard him enter. So why the cold shoulder? Something was wrong. Jim mulled it over and by quick process of elimination Jim decided that his sister must have said, or done something to annoy Stephen and cause Wes to have joined forces. Time would only tell and now was the time to find out, so Jim could get on with enjoying his day.

"Let me try this again. Good morning."

Silence. Then Stephen's eyes met Jim's. He nodded, however, he remained silent as a marble statue. Jim was reading their expressions and did not like what he was seeing.

"Have you come to rub more salt into our family's wounds?" Wes asked with a frosty mid-winter chill.

"Wes, Johnson," Jim's eyes passed between them. "I'm obviously missing something here since neither one of you seem too happy to see me. What's this about salt in your family's wounds? Has Amanda done something to tick off your family?"

Stephen released a heavy sigh. "Your sister's another bucket of worms that we won't touch this morning. But then again, after what has happened between Amanda and Summer, her lighting into Belinda and me, perhaps we should begin by discussing your sister's influence on your daughter."

"My daughter? I have four daughters." Jim continued to study his friend's expressions. What had his sister done now? He'd find that out later. Right now, he had a more pressing problem. "Do you mean Elizabeth?" Jim noticed Wes' demeanor change, yet again. Anger was churning in his friend. Oh boy! Jim felt that old familiar feeling deep in his gut—the one that signaled impending doom.

"Don't play dumb." Wes snarled. "You know exactly who Stephen means."

Well, that was totally out of character for Wes!

"Do you care to elaborate, so that I know what has put such a rank decomposing dead bear up your butts?" Jim asked a tad louder than he had intended.

"Your daughter ripped my son's heart out, and your precious Elizabeth is going on with her life as if nothing happened."

"Wes, what are you talking about?"

Jim was totally confused. The last time he had seen or spoken with Elizabeth, she was blissfully in love with Peter. Unfortunately, Jim realized that was two weeks ago. It was also obvious that Melissa didn't know about whatever had happened, otherwise she would have said something to him by now. At that moment, the bait shop door opened and a large family entered. Wes immediately drew away from Jim to take care of the customers who wanted to rent canoes. That left Jim and Stephen standing quietly by the coffee pot.

"Johnson, I honestly am in the dark here. So, no more beating around the bush. Tell me. What happened between Lizzie and Peter?"

"You honestly don't know. Do you?" Stephen quietly asked.

"No. But I'm beginning to get the picture loud and clear." Jim sighed. "I gather my daughter broke up with Peter?"

Stephen nodded, released a breath and shook his head. "Peter's a mess." His voice was quiet. "Plus, Becky's been having a tough time with her asthma. She's been in the ER two nights this past week alone. Wes is worn out worrying about both Becky and Peter."

"Oh great!" It was Jim's turn to sigh and shake his head. "We all know how rough it is when Becky has her asthma attacks. Then Liz breaks up with Peter." Jim looked Stephen straight in the eye as he continued. "I honestly did not know that any of this had happened. Exactly when did Lizzie break up with Peter?"

"Two weeks ago."

"Two weeks? I know that Mellie has talked with Liz and to my knowledge, she never said anything about breaking up with Peter." Jim grew quiet. Then he made a guttural sound that Stephen had come to recognize over the years as *'Callison just put the pieces of the mental puzzle together.'* Jim sighed. "Well, now I understand why my daughter has only contacted me through text messages. Oh, she's a sneaky one!" Jim did that classic Callison lift of the side of his mouth, shook his head, then said, "Well, I'll see what I can find out from her and let you know what her reason is for breaking off the engagement."

"Thanks, Jim." Stephen drew in a breath, glanced out the window towards the lake and slowly released his breath. "Great day for fishing. Do you still plan on going out on the lake?"

Jim looked at the sun drenched deep blue water with hardly any waves lapping against the shoreline. Then slowly turned back to his friend. "No, not today. I've overstayed my welcome with Wes, and I now have different fishing to do." He slightly shook his head with regret. "Thanks for filling me in on what is going on with Liz and Peter."

"Wish it had been better news."

"Yeah, you and me both. See you around."

Noise filled the arts colony. Time flowed by quickly for Liz as she was surrounded by those who loved the theater as much as she does. Liz began her days meeting with Jonah, the assistant director, and Blaine, the stage manager, as well as her volunteers, to assign them their work for the day. She enjoyed watching the cast and crew members move through the daily routine. Without fail someone would play a joke on her, or do something to make her smile.

Liz had just walked out of the mess hall door, when she heard someone yell from the over at the amphitheater. She knew from the daily schedule that the lighting and set designers were working together on stage. Then she heard more noise from the stage area. Time to check things out. Liz clutched her clipboard to her chest as she took off on a run. When she arrived at the stage, she found the crew untangling the new ropes that had been purchased for the curtains.

"What happened?" Liz asked as she approached the stage.

"Well, besides the lighting shorting out, someone decided it would be funny to tangle up the new curtain and rope we planned to hang this morning."

"Oh boy!" Liz blew out a breath through pursed lips. At that moment, she felt a tickle on her neck. She groaned, closed her eyes and shook her head. Liz had an eerie feeling she knew exactly who thought it would be funny to tangle the ropes, and she had a feeling that the short in the lighting could also be explained. However, Liz also knew that there was no way she could tell her theater troupe about the resident spirit.

The day drew to an end. Notices were hung on the board informing the production team of their schedule for the next day. The cast had been informed of their evening meeting with the assistant director, music coach and choreographer. It was time for Liz to head home for the night. Liz was in her car heading down the old road to route 30 when she allowed herself to look at her hands and empty finger holding the steering wheel. It had been two weeks but her breakup with Peter seemed as fresh as if it had been that morning. Pain. Grief. Anger began to surface once again as Liz replayed in her mind the confrontation that she had with Peter over her friends and colleagues. Liz huffed as a colossal mixture of emotions churned within her. A tear slid down her cheek. Then another. Without a second thought, Liz slowed down, made a three point turn in the road and headed back towards her parent's home.

Melissa had just sat down at the kitchen table with Jim to have an evening cup of decaf coffee and dessert when they heard the porch door open. They both looked over at the door and gasped as they saw Liz emerge through the doorway. Without a word they stood in harmony and moved towards her.

"Oh Liz, honey!" Mel quietly exclaimed, as she held her weeping child and shared a concerned look with Jim, who now had his hand resting on Liz's shoulder as her weeping turned to sobbing.

"It's over!" She managed to exclaim between sobs.

Jim knew from what he had learned earlier in the day and shared with Melissa, that over probably meant Peter. But, then again, something could have happened to the theater and that would be as devastating for Liz, as her broken relationship with Peter. Jim felt a stabbing pain in his heart. Jim watched and listened as Melissa gently rubbed Liz's back and gently consoled their child. He was amazed to see how Mel still had that magic touch as only a loving, caring mother possesses. The wailing and sobbing soon became whimpers. Then sniffles to finally quiet. Still, Mel did not speak or demand answers to the multitude of questions that she and Jim had for Liz. Instead, she continued to console her.

"I know you hurt." Silence. "Life hurts." Silence. "In time your pain will cease." Silence. Liz drew in a deep breath and slowly exhaled. Silence. "Would you like to tell us what happened?"

Jim watched. Listened. He was amazed at how quietly Mel spoke to Liz. More than that, he was amazed when Liz drew in another deep breath, nodded and stood up straight. Then, she raised her left hand to show them her empty finger. So, Wes and Stephen had been right. Liz, his wounded 'little bird' had once again returned to the nest, and now she was finally ready to talk with them and they were ready to listen. Dessert was forgotten, as they made their way into the family room to sit together on the couch to console Liz's broken heart and discuss the demise of her engagement to Peter.

It was after eleven that night when Jim and Mel finally fell into bed. Jim sighed as he lay beside Mel stroking her bare arm. Her head rested on his bare chest, while her hand rested on his abdomen.

"I love you, Callison." She breathed out.

"And I love you, my sweet Melissa." Then Jim brought his hand up to her jaw. Gently raising her chin, he lowered his mouth onto her lips. Mel sighed out against his warmth. At that moment, their bodies didn't need any prompting as they meld together in the perfect rhythm of a well-known love song. Each took and gave in perfect harmony, as they climbed together, reaching the summit of their love and clinging together, as they cried out in total ecstasy. Then, Jim cradled her in his arms and gently stroked her soft body as they fell asleep in total contentment.

Hours later, Jim awakened to find Mel lying next to him texting on her phone. He yawned, then leaned over to kiss her. Her morning kiss brought him joy that could not be matched by anything in the world. Still, he knew from his mate's expression that something important was already going on in their world.

"So, let me guess. Elizabeth?" Jim lightly began playing with the top of Mel's nightgown that she had put back on at some point during the night.

"You guessed—oh!" Mel gasped. "Oh, Jim. After last night, I figured you would be exhausted."

"You figured wrong, sweetheart. Retirement has its perks!" His eyes sparkled with mischief as his fingers lightly touched her skin, arousing her as he spoke. "Is Elizabeth still in crisis, or can she wait?"

"She can wait." Mel breathed out as she placed her phone on the bedside stand. Then she turned and laid in sweet surrender to the love of her life.

One day slipped into the next with rehearsals, coaching, choreographing, set construction, costume design and other preparation for their summer production. Finally, Liz was able to get back up to the cabin before midnight. It was dusk. Nocturnal creatures were stirring. Peepers and tree toads sang out. Liz felt restless as a black bear not ready to concede to slumber. Fully aware that bears were roaming in the woods and not to be played with, she decided to walk only as far as the stream to sit and think about anything and everything. She found a spot not too far up the stream with a flat rock that jutted out into the stream. It was a perfect spot to dangle her feet into the water. She sat down, removed her sneakers and socks and tentatively stuck a toe into the water. Liz gasped. The water was freezing cold! She shook her head and wondered how in the world her father and aunt ever had the courage to swim in that water? Liz surmised that there was only one explanation. They both had to be certifiably crazy! She remained on the rock with her feet dangling above the water and allowed her mind to wander.

Darkness had fallen. Lightening bugs lit up the night sky. Peepers and tree toads serenaded Liz as she made her way back to the cabin. Back inside Liz locked the kitchen door, turned off the light, went into the living room, locked the front door and went to bed expecting to have another night of fitful sleep.

Liz was shocked when she awakened to the sound of her alarm clock. She went through the motions of preparing for her day, while formulating a plan for how she would execute her commitments and her new mission. The drive down the mountain to the arts colony should have been uneventful. It wasn't.

There had been a major car accident one half mile south of the old road on Route 30. Liz stopped and waited in line to be allowed past the scene. Liz saw the community rescue squad and knew that her mother would be there with the other crew members. That didn't trouble Liz. As the police allowed her to pass by the scene, she caught a glimpse of one car in particular. It looked like Peter's car. Panic filled her. Liz was torn. As angry as Liz felt towards Peter, she wanted to stop and see if it was him in the accident and if he was alright. But she needed to continue on to the arts colony to her day's work.

Once Liz was able to safely pull off of the road, she called her father. "Dad, do you know who was involved in the accident?" Panic was reaching its peak in Liz.

"Not yet, Liz. Why do you ask?"

Liz explained to her father what she had observed as she slowly drove past the accident.

"I see." Jim did see considerably more than Liz had shared with him. "I will make some calls and let you know what I find out. In the meantime, you be careful and get to work."

"Thanks, Dad." Liz sighed as she ended her call and drove on. She continued to feel uneasy about the accident. Fear led her to use her blue tooth to make another call. One ring and she heard the familiar voice.

"Good morning, Elizabeth. This is a wonderful surprise! I figured with everything you have going on with the community theater that you'd be too busy to call. What's going on?"

"Aunt Amanda I don't want to ruin your day, but-" A tear slid down her cheek.

"But you need to dump your burdens in a safe place." Amanda sighed. Her heart ached for her niece. "I'm glad that you called me. I gather this has nothing to do with the theater, and everything to do with Peter and your broken engagement."

Liz swiped away another tear as she drove. She sniffled. "You know me too well."

"Oh, sweetie," Liz almost smiled as she pictured her aunt talking with her. "Tell me what's troubling you."

Amanda quietly listened to Liz share her horror, her fear, her heartache. By the time they said their goodbyes Liz felt the necessary calm that she needed to get through her day. Family. Liz actually smiled, as she drove into the arts colony ready to get to work with her other family.

Jim put his phone back in the clip on his belt and finished loading the dishwasher for Mel. He wiped down the counter and gazed around the kitchen to make sure that everything was in its proper place. Satisfied, he stepped over to the coat rack and took his cap from the hook and placed it on his head. He withdrew his keys from his pocket and headed for the door. It was time to take a drive.

Jim backed his pickup out of the garage with his thoughts on Melissa and the crew attending to the accident scene. Right then, Jim had mixed emotions about being retired and not immediately knowing about who was involved in the accident, and the severity of the accident victims. He sighed and did as he always had done while working. He prayed for the first respondents and for the victims. It took only a few minutes for Jim to be out on the road heading to the bait shop. Traffic was lighter than normal on that bright sunny summer morning. Jim was glad as he went past one landmark after another. Relief swept over Jim as he put on his directional, slowed, and pulled into the bait shop parking lot and saw both Wes and Stephen's pickups in their usual spots. Jim eased his pickup into the spot next to Wes' truck, shut it off and got out. He headed towards the door with quickness in his step.

Upon entering the shop, he heard raised voices. Jim paused. What he heard was not good. Jim quietly moved on towards the counter, where Wes and Stephen were exchanging heated words. He listened.

"I have more than enough of my own family problems to worry about. But you—you take the cake! No wonder Mandy is so royally pissed off with you and Summer! How could you do that to her? Hasn't she endured enough pain from you to last a lifetime?"

Stephen responded with colorful words that would have made his mother gasp with embarrassment, if she was alive and there with him. Wes was shaking his head in disgust, as Jim stopped in front of the counter. Jim's gaze swept between them. Trouble had obviously brewed to a cataclysmic explosion.

"Sorry you had to see and hear me tare into this jerk!" Wes huffed as he glowered at Stephen.

Then he looked back at Jim. "I'm actually glad that you are here." Wes's eyes were now filled with sorrow. "I'm sorry for ripping into you about Liz. I had no idea that you didn't know."

"Well, Wes, I'm also sorry for how things are turning out for all of us. How's Peter getting along?"

"He's still a mess." Wes sighed. "Would you like a cup of coffee?"

Jim nodded and helped himself to the last of the pot. He turned off the coffee maker then returned to the counter. By then, Stephen had stomped out of the building without saying a word to either of them.

For a moment neither man spoke. They simply sipped their coffee and allowed one another time alone with their thoughts. Then Jim sighed. He placed his cup on the counter, looked out at the lake, then over at Wes and said, "Wes, you said some harsh things to Stephen in defense of my sister. While I appreciate you defending her, shouldn't you be more concerned about your relationship with Stephen. You know, as brothers in law and as business partners?"

"Nope!"

That was all Wesley said. Short. Sweet. Right to the point. Wes was not smiling. Neither was Jim, for that matter!

"Jim, I'm tired and deeply concerned for my family. I have a son with a broken heart, and a wife who has been in the hospital emergency room multiple nights during the past three weeks for her asthma. This morning Stephen opened his mouth and I lost it! How dare he ridicule Amanda? When she's done nothing to cause his retribution. He'd rather blame her than admit his culpability in their past. His stomping off countless times in 1979 didn't solve anything between them, and it certainly won't now!" Wes sighed, drew in a breath and continued. "As for this business? I may have to seriously consider selling out to him and moving Becky to a drier climate more conducive for her breathing. Not that I want to, but Becky and her fragile health is my primary concern."

"Wes, you've made valid points, and I sure do understand you loving and thinking of Becky over your business. I'd go to the ends of the earth and back, if it meant making Melissa's life easier for her."

The phone rang. Wes answered it, allowing Jim time with his thoughts.

"Sorry about that. You were saying?" Wes asked she clicked off the phone.

Jim returned his thoughts to their previous conversation. "Actually, Johnson sidetracked me from my initial reason for being here. I came to find out where Peter is this morning."

Wes saw the worry in Jim's eyes. "He's home, helping his mother and me. As I said before, Becky had another major asthma attack and ended up in the hospital emergency room again last night." He saw the relief in his friend's eyes as he yawned. "Peter's been a god send working around the house doing outside work for us, and being near Becky in case she has an emergency."

"So, he's home?" Jim felt some relief as he asked and waited for confirmation.

"Yes. Good grief, Jim! What's wrong with you?"

"Not what I had feared, that's for sure! Elizabeth called me after she went past the accident that Mel was called to earlier. Well, Liz saw both vehicles and one just happened to look like -"

"Peter's car." Wes understood and finished Jim's sentence.

Jim sighed in relief. "I guess I should have known things were okay when I walked in and saw you lacing into Johnson as you were." He shook his head. "What a day this is turning out to be!" Jim exclaimed. Wes nodded before taking his last sip of coffee and Jim added, "I'm glad to know that Pete's alright."

The two men allowed their conversation to turn to unimportant bits of information about things happening in their community. Then they returned to a more pressing topic for both of them. Their children. Together they devised a plan that they thought just might work in bringing their kids back together.

"You know our wives are going to kill us, if our idea backfires." Wes sighed. His physical and mental exhaustion was getting the best of him.

Jim nodded. "Yeah, but at least we will be able to commiserate together."

Peter whistled as he scraped the frame of the kitchen window. The sun beat down on his bare back. Sadly, it was the only part of him that felt warm. Since Liz had broken off their engagement, a sense of coolness had taken residence in him. Peter wanted nothing to do with anyone or anything outside of his parents. He heard the sound of tires crunching on the gravel drive, looked up and saw his Dad's pickup followed by an equally familiar one. What in the world was Mr. C doing there with his dad? Peter moaned. Jim Callison was the last person he wanted to see. An ominous feeling swept over Peter like a thunderous dark cloud. He stopped his work and got down from the ladder to find out what was going on.

"Hey, son, the house is looking good." Wes said, as he smiled with approval.

"Thanks Dad. Hey Mr. C." Peter greeted them both with a smile that he really was not feeling. They stood together in the sun-drenched yard totally unconcerned what the sun's UV rays were doing to their skin. It was there the men commiserated with Peter and shared their idea with him. At first, he simply looked at them in amazement. Was he feeling the effects of the hot sun? Or, had they lost their heads? Then, as he mulled over their idea, and listened to their quiet remarks, a smile took shape on his lips. "You two are brilliant!"

They both laughed.

"Well, Son, I don't know about brilliant. But we have had a few more years of practice with the female population when they are pissed off. So, we thought we might be able to help you."

Peter was silent. Then worry took shape on his face, throughout his body. "Do Mom and Mrs. C know what your idea is?"

"Oh, heavens no!" Jim exclaimed. "They'll kill us for sure, if they know that we are helping you."

"Meddling is what Becky will say we're doing." Wes added.

"Yeah, as if they never meddle." Jim chuckled.

Peter couldn't help but smile. "So, you two are willing to get in trouble with mom and Mrs. C to help me dig myself out of this hole I'm in with Elizabeth?" Peter saw them both nod. "Okay. So, when are we going to begin operation win back Liz's heart?"

Both men smiled as they said in unison, "Now!"

Wes watched Peter get into the pickup with Jim. He knew that it was a risk that they all were taking to interfere in Peter and Liz's tattered relationship. But his son was desperate and, well, sometimes a dad just had to lend a hand. Wes was turning towards the house when Becky emerged through the door.

"Hey, beautiful!" Wes smiled as he gazed into Becky's troubled eyes. "How are you feeling?" He asked as he strode towards her.

"I am feeling better." Becky drew in a cautious breath. So far so good. "What did Jim want?" She quietly asked while watching his eyes. "Why did Peter leave with him?"

Wes sighed. Becky was suspicious. He knew that if he was not extremely careful, their plan would explode before they even got through phase one.

"Jim and Peter went to retrieve a step ladder from Jim's so that I can help Peter with this project." He watched her eyes. Phew! Becky accepted his answer. "Honey, would you like to go for a ride? How about we go out for lunch?"

A smile crept onto Becky's lips. "That will be wonderful. While we are out, we can swing by the pharmacy to get my prescription that is ready."

Jim and Peter were both amazed to see all the vehicles that were parked in the designated lot for employees and artists, as well as the visitor's parking lot. They heard music, singing, saw people practicing scenes under the shade of the trees. Jim had dropped the pickup's manual transmission into second gear and was slowly creeping along while watching for pedestrians. Both he and Peter saw Liz at the same moment. There she stood. Her expression indicated that she was all business. She had a clipboard in one hand, and her other hand on her hip. She wore no makeup, and her hair was pulled back into a ponytail under her favorite baseball cap. A bright green tank top, and blue jeans covered her body and her work boots were on her feet. Everything about her said, "I'm the boss." Jim smiled to himself, as he eased into the one remaining parking space, that happened to be next to Liz's car.

Liz had seen her dad pull in. She was happy, until she saw who was with him when they emerged from the pickup. Strain was in her voice as she greeted them and asked, "So what can I do for you?"

Someone interrupted to ask her a pressing question before either of them answered. Jim watched her glance down at her clipboard. She looked back up at the man and smiled, answered his question then turned back to them. "Sorry. We're one week away from the curtain going up. So, this is a rather busy time for us. So, you were about to tell me what brings you both here?"

Jim noticed her discomfort. Good. She should think about the young man standing next to her. "Well, Lizzie, I've managed to get myself into another job and I need my extension ladder. I figured before heading up the mountain to the cabin we'd stop over here and see if I had left it over here by any chance." He watched Liz. Oh yes. Their presence was raising havoc with her.

"Gee, Dad, I think that you are out of luck. I -" She paused, deep in thought. "Actually, I know that you are out of luck. Don't you remember? The ladder was used at the cabin when," a tear formed in her eye. Liz drew in a breath to steady her unraveling nerves. "When the bats got in." She sniffled and fidgeted. "If there is nothing else, I really do need to get back to work."

"Actually, Liz," Peter's voice made her pause a she began to take a step. "When your dad and I are up the mountain, I'd like to go in the cabin and get the clothes and things that I left there."

Jim watched the interaction between Liz and Peter. It was obvious that Peter's presence was shaking Liz to her core. Good. Jim could only hope that his daughter would wake up to what she has with Peter before too long.

"Of course, you may go in and get your belongings." Her eyes began to mist. Darn. Just what she didn't need. Fortunately for Liz one of the stage crew called out to her. She responded, then returned her gaze to Peter and her dad. "If you both will excuse me. I do have to get back to work."

Jim and Peter left Liz to return to her responsibilities of directing, while they progressed to phase two of their plan. They made two important stops before heading up to the cabin. Of course, one involved food and liquid nonalcoholic refreshment! Jim was feeling rather pleased with how things were progressing after they made their second stop. He only hoped that their plan would not explode in their faces. If it did? Jim knew that there would be no living with the women of the north country! Heaven help them! Especially, if the women called in his sister for reinforcement! He knew that Amanda exploding in anger would be worse than a nuclear bomb detonating, and Jim certainly didn't need that!

CHAPTER 14

Liz arrived home as the sun took its final dip behind the mountains of the western horizon. Exhaustion filled her as she trudged up the front steps onto the porch. She turned the key and opened the door only to be greeted by an unexpected overpowering floral smell, that just about knocked her back out the door. Turning on the light, she was greeted by a bouquet of summer flowers. An unwanted tear escaped and plunged down her cheek as she wiped her eyes with the back of her hand. Suspicion catapulted her across the room to the table that held the flowers. Liz bent and smelt the luscious fragrance. Then, she picked up the envelope that had been carefully leaned against the vase. Her legs became weak, drawing her down onto the couch.

After allowing herself to have a good cry Liz wiped her eyes, stretched and stood. She sighed, as she looked at the flowers, felt the sadness of another love gone wrong, and headed towards the bedroom. Turning on the light, Liz was greeted by another surprise. While Peter had been at the cabin with Jim to collect his belongings, he had placed a single rose bud in a vase next to the bed. That did it! Liz's tattered emotions had reached their final breaking point. She gave in, collapsed onto the bed and wept, eventually falling asleep.

The next morning Liz looked and felt terrible. Even a good dose of makeup was unable to hide her drawn features from everyone's attention and concern. Finally, by noon Alexis, Andre, and Jonah all requested an emergency meeting with Liz. It didn't take long for her dear friends to pry the necessary information from Liz to fully understand what was going on with her.

"Would it help for me to try to talk to Peter for you?" Andre asked, with sadness in his expression for the pain he had unintentionally caused for Liz. "You know, explain how difficult it can be for outsiders to accept the family atmosphere that is created within the theater community?"

Liz gasped. "Good heavens, no, Andre!" Her eyes widened with alarm, then softened as she added, "But, thank you for trying. Until last night I hadn't had any contact with Peter." She sniffled then turned to Josh. "I've put things off for long enough. It's time for me to deal with Peter. Jonah, will you take over for me for the rest of the day?"

Jonah smiled and nodded with approval of what Liz was going to do. "You take as long as you need."

Liz nodded, wiped away a random tear, then handed over the keys and clipboard to him. Then she turned and headed for her office to gather her belongings. It was time to get her personal life in order.

Peter had just finished painting the second story window frame outside of his parent's bedroom, when he saw a familiar car turning into his parent's yard. He gathered the paint can into one hand, and held on to the rungs, as he carefully made his way down from the ladder. Hope. Trepidation. As well as, a surge of other emotions that sped through him as he watched Liz get out of her car and approach him.

"Elizabeth." His voice was a bit shaky, uncertain of what she would say and do. His eyes held hers, as if to attempt to see into the hidden depths of her mind.

Liz attempted to smile. But one would not form. Instead an unwanted tear slid down her cheek. That seemed to be happening a lot lately. "Hello, Peter." Her voice was shaky. She glanced at the empty paint can and brush that held remnants of white paint in the bristles. "I, ah, didn't mean to take you from your work. I guess I should have called." He remained quiet. "I'll leave." She began to turn.

"Is that what you want Liz?" He asked, causing her to stop and turn to once again face him. "I mean, to leave without telling me why you took time from you precious theater and drove over here to see me?"

"Peter, I came over here to thank you for the flowers you left me up at the cabin, and hopefully begin to mend our difference. But now -" Liz could not hold back her emotions for one second longer and burst into tears. "Darn it! Why did you have to ruin it by having that accusatory tone in your voice? And then, there's your posture that betrays your true feelings. Don't even begin to think that I can't read you like a well-read book! Yes, Peter Jealous, UN-trusting Jones, the theater is precious to me and always will be. It's my craft. I'm not giving up the theater, or my friends for you or any man for that matter!"

"Liz, I am sorry for saying those mean things to you when your theater friends arrived. Please believe me when I tell you that I know in my heart that you are nothing like your sister. For a moment I went insane with jealousy. I didn't want to see any other man touch you." Pain radiated from Peter as he continued to speak. "Lizzie, I'd give anything to be able to take back my words."

"Peter, I know that you are sorry. I am too. But, Peter," Liz sighed. Tears were forming, but she didn't care. Let them fall. She was emotionally exhausted, and she didn't have the energy to put up a brave front. "You broke my trust to the point that I can't step back into a relationship with you as if nothing happened between us. For now, it's probably best if we sever all ties. Maybe in the fall when things begin to quiet down, we can decide together if we want to work on rebuilding our relationship."

Liz could see that Peter was having a difficult time accepting her response to his peace offering. She knew deep in her heart that too much was a stake for both of them. What they shared had to be more than a fantastic, satisfying physical relationship. Where was their faith and trust in each other? Where was their love? Liz sighed, as she looked tenderly into Peter's troubled eyes. Her voice was quiet forcing Peter to have to listen carefully to her.

"Peter, I'll be honest with you. I trusted you to be faithful and have faith in me as your partner. Without trust between us," Liz sighed, "We have nothing to build our life together upon. Love without trust doesn't last." She held up her hand, as Peter began to speak. "Please, allow me to finish. Look at our parents. They love and trust each other. Trust has been a necessary building block and continues to be vital in their relationship. Now think for a moment about my Aunt Amanda and your Uncle Stephen. Their love died for many reasons. But when you peel off the layers of their relationship you find that the core reason why their love died was that he broke her trust. Yes. She forgave him for what he did. But she lost faith in him, and what they share at this point in their lives is more tolerance than anything. Aunt Amanda doesn't trust him -" Liz slightly shook her head. Her eyes were filled with sadness. "-And I don't trust you!"

"Wow!" Peter looked at her with amazement.

"I won't settle for superficial tolerance in our relationship. If we are to be a couple, then we start from scratch. We rebuild, but not until the summer is over. I have a show to put on and events planned at the arts center, so my time is tied up until after Labor Day weekend. Plus, we both need this time to figure out exactly what we want and don't want in a relationship. Goodbye, Peter."

With that Liz turned and walked away without turning back. She knew if she did, she'd give in and meld into his arm, leaving the problems that had separated them hanging between them.

Stephen Johnson sat by the window in the air-conditioned bait shop facing the lake as he took a bite of his Italian hero. He was actually glad that Wes had needed to take Becky to her doctor appointment. Now he had some quiet time to reflect on his life that has been in turmoil since Sam Callison's funeral. It had been a shock for Stephen along with everyone else to find out Amanda and Jim's father had been murdered and disposed of in the old amphitheater. Summer and Adam's time with him and Amanda could have helped bridge some of the tension between him and Amanda. Unfortunately, it hadn't. The altercation between Elizabeth and Summer, while they all were at the cemetery had a ripple effect on his and many others lives. Stephen had just swallowed a bite of sandwich and taken a sip of coffee when the door jingled open informing him that a customer had entered.

"Be right with you!" Stephen called out as he wrapped his sandwich, wiped his mouth and stood. It was then that he heard and saw who had entered.

"Take your time, Johnson." Jim returned as he walked towards the counter. His footsteps revealed that he was a man on a mission.

Stephen sighed. His day was going from bad to worse. "I'm over here, Jim, eating my lunch." He sat back down, but did not unwrap his partially eaten meal.

"Looks to me like you're finished for now." Jim observed his friend and his unfinished sandwich. Stephen's eyes looked tired as if he hadn't had a good night's sleep for months. His face was drawn.

"Yeah, I lost my appetite." Stephen didn't elaborate as to why, picked up his cup and finished off his lukewarm coffee.

"Let me guess. Women problems?" Jim pulled up a stool and sat down. He watched his friend's expression, his eyes, the slight movement of his jaw.

"Something like that." Stephen sighed. "It seems to be the common dilemma facing the men of my family."

Jim waited to see if Stephen was going to say anything else. He didn't so Jim filled the quiet void by adding, "I think you might be the only one. At least, I hope Peter's flowers began to repair his relationship with Liz. Then again, knowing my daughter, she probably isn't making this easy for him. I guess time will tell."

"If Liz is taking lessons from Amanda on how to treat men—well, heaven help us!" Stephen huffed with disgust in his voice. He shook his head and turned to look out over the lake.

Jim felt a wave of sadness in his heart as he listened to Stephen make grunting noises. At that moment, Jim had no idea what was really wrong, but he decided to take a stab at the most obvious, since Johnson had already accusingly mentioned his sister. "I gather things are still dicey between you and Mandy."

"Of course, they are!" Stephen snapped. "She'll never change!"

'*Neither will you*,' Jim thought, then sighed. "Johnson, let me ask you a question." Stephen nodded, giving Jim his permission to ask. "I'll get around to Manda in a bit. For now, let me ask you a question based on my observations throughout the past year. Are you happy?"

"Sure. Why wouldn't I be?" Stephen locked eyes with Jim challenging him to argue with him.

"Well, we've known each other a long time and been through a lot together." Stephen made a quiet reply. Then Jim continued. "After Manda left in '79 I hoped that someday you would find a woman who would fill your world with love and happiness. I'm pleased that you are dating—apparently rather seriously— this time around. But Johnson something seems off to me when I see you and Belinda together." Jim raised his hand to stop Stephen as he began to open his mouth. "It's something unsettling that I can't quite put my finger on. What I do know is that you've changed since you've been dating Belinda." Jim shook his head. "Don't even try to deny it. We've all seen the change in you."

"All?" Stephen's brows were drawing close as he asked and listened to Jim continue.

"All," Jim nodded. "Poor Tom just about holds his breath every night until closing time in hopes that you don't come into the pub with your girlfriend. He sees a lot and even he is concerned about you. And then, there's your own brother, Phil. When's the last time you've seen or talked with him?" Stephen responded with a puzzled look as Jim continued. "I happen to know that Phil works and then goes home, so he doesn't have to risk running into you and your girlfriend. Johnson, haven't you wondered why other friends and I don't stop in here as often as we used to?"

"I guess I figured you all were busy." Stephen responded. His expression suggested that he was pondering over Jim's comments.

"Too busy to stop and shoot the breeze? No." Jim shook his head. "You've changed, and not for the better."

Silence hung between them. Jim removed the cap from his head and placed it on the table. He sighed. "Stephen, when we were at Dad's committal service in the cemetery, I didn't hear all of the exchange between Liz, Summer and Belinda. So, I asked Liz to tell me what happened. She won't say." Jim gave Stephen his pointed look, that said a lake full of unspoken thoughts that were better left unsaid. "I know that Amanda is equally upset, and she won't say anything other than that you and Summer have shown your true colors, and that you and Belinda deserve each other. Trust me, you don't want to know exactly what she thinks of Belinda." Jim drew his brows together in their familiar way, as if, to place an exclamation point on his next words. "Sis, just might be right on this one."

Jim saw Stephen wince. Good. He didn't wait for Stephen to respond.

"Amanda also assured me that you two Johnson's," Jim was on high alert noticing each and every grimace and body movement in Stephen as he digested his words. "And your girlfriend are not going to chase her and Kevin away from coming home to visit me and my family. I will tell you that was a relief for me to hear. Mandy and I have a lot of lost time to make up between us, and I rather enjoy having her back in my life. My sister's done alright for herself living down in Baltimore. Kevin's a good man, who loves Manda, and he has unexpectedly filled a void in my life—a missing piece since Sam died." For a long moment Jim grew quiet. Then he looked Stephen straight in the eyes and said, "But, my friend, now you need to listen very carefully to what I have to say. I love my family, and I will defend each of them at all cost—even the cost of our friendship. I will not tolerate you, your daughter, or your precious girlfriend hurting any one of my family members."

"Are you threatening me, Jim?" Stephen asked as he rose to his feet. His expression was unreadable. That didn't matter to Jim, as he also rose to his feet. He replaced his cap on his head. His eyes shimmered with underlying heat. Fire. Yet, his voice had a quiet unnerving chill as he said, "No, Stephen. It's not a threat. It's a promise. I'm taking care of my family."

"But not, Summer?" Stephen asked with bitterness in his tone of voice.

Jim shook his head. "Summer? I really don't know your daughter—my niece." There was a quiet noise in his throat. The familiar noise that made Stephen stay on high alert as Jim continued. "But I do know that if she continues to hurt her mother, I will be calling her." Jim's chin was now tilted downward. His darkened eyes pierced into Stephen like a sharp deadly arrow. Not a good sign. "And if I do—she'll wish to the high heavens that we had never met."

"That won't be necessary." Stephen closed his eyes as he sighed. His life was spiraling out of control. Then, he met Jim's gaze with grave sadness. "I'll talk to my daughter." Stephen glanced out the window at the lake, then looked back at Jim. "Jumpin' Bullfrogs! This is a mess!"

"Yeah! And only you have the power to clear things up and make them right." Jim shook his head. "I know my way to the door. See you around. Enjoy your lunch." Jim left Stephen speechless and headed towards the door. The sooner he was away from Johnson the better.

Stephen was still reeling from what had just transpired between him and Jim as he sat down on the stool, released a deflated breath, and once again looked out at the lake. The lake usually gave him a sense of calm. Not today. If anything, it seemed to be laughing at him for the fool that he had been for so many years. He closed his eyes and immediately reopened them. Open or shut eyed, he saw one woman in his mind. Not Belinda. Stephen sighed and picked up his phone. He opened his contacts and selected the number that he really didn't want to call, but knew in his heart that he had to call and try to make things right again.

In no time at all he heard a quiet, "Hello."

Silence. There was no cheerful greeting. Not even a snide remark that Stephen would have welcomed. Silence.

"Amanda. I—do you have time to talk?" Stephen asked with his own quietness to match hers. The normally confident man was totally unsure of himself.

"I will give you five minutes, Stephen. No more." Now her voice was as chilly as the stream that ran by her family cabin up in the side of the mountain.

"Fair enough. I called to say I am sorry for the things that were supposedly said about you by Summer and Belinda and overheard by Liz."

"Mm humph." Silence.

Stephen sighed. He ran his fingers through his short hair on his head, then pounded his fist on the counter. "Dang blast it woman! I knew you would not accept a simple apology and you'd expect me to gravel and plead for your forgiveness." His volume of his voice had risen with his frustration.

"Oh, I hear an apology for what you are assuming that Summer and Belinda said. But, Johnson you have yet to admit that you were the instigator." He began to speak only to be cut off by Amanda. "You and I both know that you have not apologized for what you said to them to spur them on to belittle me." Her tone was flat. There was no emotion as he was used to hearing in her voice.

"Mandy, this is such a mess!" He sighed. "Ah, Mandy, please believe me. Honestly, I never intended for you to be hurt when I told Summer and Belinda things about Rose and our demise."

Stephen closed his eyes, as he held the phone to his ear. He could picture Amanda's expressions. The fire in her eyes. The sadness that he had put in them. The thinness of her lips as she held back her feelings. Or, perhaps the way she drew her top teeth over her lower lips, while she was listening to his feeble attempt to grovel for forgiveness. Amanda. His lost love.

"But I was hurt." Silence. "Again." Amanda sighed. "And poor Elizabeth was shattered to know that you thought so little of me to accuse me of—oh forget it! I'm done, finished rehashing our past with you. I accept your apology as it was given. Now please, Stephen, do us both a favor. Forget my phone number and leave me alone. Your five minutes of my time are over. I have work to do. Goodbye, Stephen."

He listened to the click, the severing of their call in his ear. Slowly he lowered his phone and sat there holding it in the palm of his hand. He looked at it in disbelief. Amanda had once again walked out of his life. He cursed and cried out to the empty room. Stephen was afraid. This time, not only was Amanda walking away from him, if he didn't do something drastic to change the situation—well, Stephen knew deep in his heart that he might also lose Jim, his best friend. Then, to make matters worse, in the end, Stephen might even lose his own family if Becky and Phil decided to take Amanda's side in the latest Johnson-Callison fiasco. What a mess! At that moment, the next song on his playlist cued and he heard Merle Haggard woefully ask, *Are the good times really over…*

Stephen groaned. He needed to get out of there. He needed time away, alone to think. He picked up his phone and dialed Peter.

"Hey, Unc. What's up?"

"I need to know if you are busy painting, or if you could come over and take care of the shop for me for a while?"

"I'm finished painting, and now Mom and Dad have me washing windows, inside and out." Stephen laughed and commented. "Yeah, go ahead and laugh, Unc. This summer I'm getting a whole new perspective on my parents. Do you know that they conspire together to come up with work for me to do for them?"

Stephen laughed harder, as he listened to Peter regale him with the woes of being the only child and available to do unpaid work for them.

"Hey, Peter, I happen to know that your folks appreciate all that you're doing for them. I also am grateful for your willingness to help your dad and me here at the bait shop."

"I know you do, Unc. Give us about fifteen minutes and I will be there to take care of things for you."

"Thanks, Pete." Stephen ended the call, stood up, placed his phone in his back pocket, picked up his unfinished lunch and empty cup, walked over to the garbage can and dropped both in the can. Then he went behind the counter to busy himself as he waited for Peter's arrival.

"Liz, it's good to see you." Stephen gave her a smile that he wasn't feeling, as they met on the arts colony green under the shade of an old maple tree. She returned a smile that lacked the warmth it once had held. Someone called out to her. Stephen watched her respond. Everything about Liz's demeanor seemed to change in an instant. He saw joy radiating from within as she gave direction to her crew member. Then, she returned her gaze on him and Stephen saw something unreadable, yet cautioned him to proceed with caution.

"Liz, I decided it was in my best interest to come here to the arts colony to see you, so I have a witness or two. Not that I'm sure it will help me any." He added, under his breath, as he glanced around at the others who were nearby and seemed totally disinterested in his appearance. Stephen drew in a breath and slowly exhaled. "Liz, I know about your father, Wesley, and Peter plotting together. I'm not here for them."

"Oh?" Liz's eyes seemed to bore into Stephen as if to read his mind.

"No, I'm not. I came here to apologize for my part in the conversation that you overheard between Summer and Belinda, and has somehow mushroomed into a colossal mess between our families."

"A colossal mess is a good way to describe what has happened between all of us." Liz' eyes scanned the community then rested back on Stephen. She saw his troubled eyes and knew in her heart that he was sorry. But she also knew that she was only one piece of his regret. "Look Stephen, while I appreciate your apology, you don't need to ask for my forgiveness. This conflict is between you and Aunt Amanda. You two obviously still have things from your past that you both need to reconcile."

He noticed everything about her demeanor and there was no denying that she may have forgiven him, but she also was a Callison through and through. Undoubtedly, Liz would remember the altercation for a very long time to come. His voice oozed with regret. "After the brow beating, I received from your dad and your aunt, I don't think there is too much hope for Amanda and me to ever put everything behind us. And now your dad's and my friendship are up in the air."

At that moment, Liz began to feel sad, almost sorry for Stephen. He appeared to be filled with remorse over what had happened at the cemetery and in very recent conversations between her dad and aunt and him. "Stephen, you and dad have been friends since before I was born. I'm sure that with time, he'll come around and forgive you for whatever you did to upset him."

"Well, time will tell. Right now, it seems that the only hope I have is to make things right with you and maybe Jim. If I'm that lucky."

"Don't you think you should try to make peace with Aunt Amanda?" At that moment, she honestly felt sorry for Stephen.

"Peace with Amanda? Not likely." He sighed and shrugged. "My crazy heartburn life with Amanda goes on. His eyes were filled with sadness. "And trust me, there are not enough antacids throughout the world to calm down this raging volitional heartburn mess between us!"

"Well, maybe in time things will improve." Liz said with more hopefulness than she felt.

"Ha!" Stephen exclaimed. "Not with Amanda it won't. This time there will be no forgiveness."

Until this afternoon, Liz had not realized just how precarious things were between her family and the Johnson family. For her to be on the outs with Peter was one thing. But Stephen and Aunt Amanda and her dad—well, Liz had a very sickening, ominous feeling where they were concerned.

"I probably shouldn't tell you this, but Aunt Amanda and Uncle Kevin will be in the area for the grand opening of the new Great Sac Summer Theater. Perhaps you should consider extending an olive branch of peace towards her."

His expression softened, as his frown was replaced with a slight smile. "Do me a favor and hold on to that optimism for me. And between you and me, it will take more than an olive branch with your aunt. In the end, I just may have to concede defeat. Thanks for listening, Liz." He glanced around and nodded towards a crew member heading in their direction. "Looks like you're being summons. Take care, Liz."

"You too, Stephen. I appreciate you coming up here to clear the air with me."

Liz remained standing on the green and watched Stephen walking back to his pickup, as she waited for the crew member to meet up with her.

ACT 2

Life is a journey, not a destination.
Ralph Waldo Emerson

CHAPTER 15

Liz arrived at the arts colony and found cast members and crew gathered in front of the mess hall. Concern filled her a she gathered her things and got out of the car. She waved as she started towards them.

"Good morning, Josh. What's going on?" She asked, then glanced over at the people congregated in the parking lot and making their way towards her.

"I wish it was a good morning, Liz. We have a problem." Liz had worked with Josh for years and knew when he was teasing, or when he was being serious. She felt the hair stand up on her arms and the back of her neck. Not good. She sighed. "Let me have it! Tell me what's wrong."

"Last night some strange things happened before and while Marco and Sarah were practicing their duet on stage."

"Oh?" Liz saw the intensity of Josh's expression. Yes, he was an actor as well as her assistant director, and could portray just about anyone he felt like being. But the man who stood with her was not acting. Something had seriously shaken him. "Well," Liz released a long, slow sigh. "You might as well tell me what happened, so that I can address it and then we can continue with our days' work."

"Marco was singing and doing his dance routine when he felt, as if, something perhaps like a pair of hands was clasped to his waist. It was so intense that he looked around to see if someone had sneaked onto the stage and was shadowing him."

Liz turned her gaze to Marco, who had just arrived next to them and was nodding in confirmation. With her hair pulled up into a ponytail, she could easily feel the tickle on her neck. She reigned in a smile that begged to appear on her lips, as the humor of the situation took shape in her mind.

"That is definitely interesting," Liz said as she gazed around the stage. "Did anything else out of the ordinary happen?"

"Well, now that you mention it," Sarah said in an almost accusatory tone, "I don't appreciate the stage crew hiding my handbag and parasol, so I didn't have my prop for the racing scene."

There was grumbling among the stage crew members that were standing with them. Liz heard their comments and said, "I'm sure there is a logical explanation for why the props were not on the table. Actually, Sarah, rather than accusing without proof, let's be glad this flub happened now while we are still practicing and not on opening night. From here on in we all must be diligent to make sure we have props and set pieces ready for each scene change. Right?" She glanced around at cast and crew waiting for their responses. Some people commented while others simply nodded in agreement. After all, Liz is the director and no one at this point in the season wanted to fall out of her good graces.

"Ah, Liz," Josh responded for all of them, "Last night's rehearsal issues weren't the only thing that happened."

"Oh?" Liz gave Josh her look that clearly said, *Cut to the chase. Let me have it!*

"Andre," Josh had turned his gaze from Liz to him as he said, "You should be the one to tell Liz what you experienced."

"Alright, when Natasha and I went back to our cabin the lights wouldn't work."

Liz asked the obvious question. "Did you check for a blown bulb?"

"Of course," Andre responded with a deadpan expression. "Liz, before you begin to ask about all of the other obvious things we should have done, yes. We checked everything, and nothing was out of the ordinary other than no power in the cabin."

"No electric at all?"

"None."

"Did anyone else experience the same issue last night?" She addressed the crowd gathered around her. Some commented while others simply shook their heads.

"The freaky part is that an hour later everything was back to normal. Everything worked from the lights to Natasha's blow dryer turning on by itself."

"And I don't remember leaving it turned on." Natasha added with a troubled look.

First shadow dancing, then props were misplaced. Now something else was amiss besides the tickle she had on her neck. Liz had a sneaky suspicion she knew exactly what had happened, as a smile crept onto her lips. There had been so much unhappiness woven into her summer, today Liz welcomed the news of the arts colony spirit's apparent antics.

Josh noticed her amused expression, as his own expression changed from a frown to a full-blown scowl. "Are you laughing at us?"

"No, Josh, not by a long shot. But I do think it's really not as bad as you think." She patted his arm.

"Give me a minute." Then Liz turned her attention to the crowd of cast and crew intently watching them. "Hey, everyone, grab yourselves a cup of coffee while Josh and I confer on what has happened here." No one argued about have another cup of coffee, or extra time to relax before beginning the day's rehearsal schedule. Then she turned to Josh. "Okay, let's go and while we're heading over to the theater," she sighed, "Well, I'm going to tell you a story."

Liz watched the color drain from Josh's face, as she nodded and told him about the resident ghost and what had happened to her family, as they walked over to the amphitheater. At first, he said nothing, then, he found his voice and asked her questions. Liz graciously responded to each one. As they made their way onto the stage, Josh grew quiet. He watched Liz as she quietly stood on the stage for a few seconds. Then she stepped away from Josh and turned towards stage left. "Good morning resident spirit. Are you here this morning?" She slowly turned to look at the rest of the empty stage. Silence.

"This is crazy!" Josh exclaimed, and shook his head in disbelief.

Liz tenderly smiled with understanding, but didn't comment to him. Instead, she directed her conversation to the spirit while gazing around the vacant stage. "I'd like to talk with you about your mischievous behavior last night." Silence.

"Liz, you can't honestly believe that some voice is going to be heard from some ghost that you think is living here!"

"Think what you want, Josh. I happen to have great respect for him or her. I want our resident spirit to know that we are only going to be here for a few weeks to do our performances, and that we do not want to cause him or her any displeasure."

"Yeah, well, what about the displeasure it is causing us, disrupting our practice. What's it going to do during our production? If it keeps on, we might not even have a cast or crew to put on the show."

"Thank you for your input. I happen to think we have a friendly spirit. Perhaps even our protector." She turned from him once again and said to the empty stage, "Do you hear me, spirit? I'm defending you because I think that you are friendly— a lonely spirit who wants to play. Oh yes, I have not forgotten about the bathroom window you opened last winter, or how you scared Peter and me when you tapped on my car window. To tease me is one thing. But to traumatize my -"

Josh gasped. "Did you feel that?" His face had once again lost color. He looked as though he was going to pass out from fright.

Liz laughed. Her eyes sparkled with joy. "Hi spirit. Yes," she giggled. "I am ticklish. It's a family trait." She glanced around, still smiling, then sighed. "Spirit, thank you for appearing. But, from now on until the end of the season, which will be Labor Day Weekend," Josh began to interrupt her only to be shushed before Liz said, "Please restrict who you're playing and teasing with to me. I really need these people to stay and do this summer theater production. I promise you that if you will stop traumatizing them, then I will renegotiate things with you after Labor Day. Do we have a deal?"

The stage was quiet. Liz smiled as she remained quiet and waited.

"What did you expect, Liz? Did you think that he or she was going to talk to you?"

Liz opened her mouth, but before any sound came from her an image of a man and woman dressed in circa 1800's clothing took shape on stage right near the backdrop. Liz gasped. "Oh my!" She breathed out. "A couple. Josh, we have a couple residing here!" Liz was filled with joy, awe, and wanted to move closer to them. But Liz remained next to Josh, as she watched them turn and pass through the backdrop.

"Oh my god!" Josh exclaimed, as color vanished from his face.

Liz took pity on him. "I know this is shocking for you. Not everyone believes that there is a spirit world beyond our comprehension. But I do. There are legends about lingering spirits that go back to the French and Indian War and further yet. My aunt has shared stories with me that she learned from our grandmother who was a full-blooded Mohawk. The spirit world is very much a part of my family. Today is the first time I've actually seen our resident spirits. Oh my gosh! Josh, this is so exciting for me!" Liz's eye shone with excitement as she giggled. "Aunt Amanda is going to be so jealous that I got to see them before her."

"Ah, Liz, I'm glad that you are excited and all. But what are we going to do about them?" Josh was amazed by everything he was experiencing. A part of him wanted to run for the highway and head back to New York City. He honestly didn't know what to think about what he had just encountered, or what to make of Liz's apparent acceptance of the spirit.

"Nothing." Liz 's expression revealed how absurd she though his question had been. "They lived here. Apparently for quite some time. We came here without their permission and have been disrupting their spirit lives. Actually, I came here stirring things up and then we found my grandfather's corpse hidden under the stage and -"

"You are really loving this!" Josh looked at her in disbelief.

"You better believe it! Having resident spirits here with us makes our summer theater unique. Now what we have to do is continue with our work while being respectful of the spirits. I honestly don't think that they mean us any harm. I think they are actually enjoying having us here with them."

"Not everyone is going to be happy to know that we have ghosts among us."

"Let me handle it. You just reassure folks that everything is okay. Tell me of anything interesting that happens and I'll address it with our spirits."

The rest of the day flew by for Liz. After the morning encounter with the spirit couple one thing remained clear to her, the spirits were actively participating in the daily life of the arts colony residents. Since her morning conversation with them, they more openly made their presence known. Fortunately, Liz was their target for their jokes. Shortly before heading to her car to go home, Liz wandered over to the empty stage. She stood there for a moment. Quiet.

Liz drew in a cleansing breath and released it. Then in a stage whisper she said, "Good night, spirits of the arts colony. Have a good rest and please leave my cast and crew alone. See you both in the morning."

Liz remained still. She heard nothing but the sound of peepers and tree toads beginning their evening songs. Liz smiled, then quietly and slowly walked off the stage. As she took one step onto the walkway, she felt something brush her cheek. "Good night." she whispered.

On the way to her car Liz pulled out her phone and speed dialed her aunt. Unfortunately, her call went to voice mail. Liz replayed the events of the day in her mind, and things to be done in the days ahead as she drove down the highway. A squirrel began to dart into the road but decided it was wiser to wait and not play *dodge the tires*. Liz laughed out loud as she watched it sprint across the road behind her. She had just turned north onto Route 30 when her phone rang. Answering it through her Bluetooth Liz regaled her aunt with the day's adventures with the theater troupe and the resident spirits.

"I'm impressed that they revealed themselves to you. They must really like you."

"Aunt Amanda, I have to admit that I like them too. They have a great sense of humor and seem to be enjoying having us with them." Liz giggled as she listened to her aunt. "I can't wait for you and Uncle Kevin to be here on opening night and hopefully meet our resident spirits." Liz felt a wave of concern when her aunt didn't immediately respond. She waited.

"Actually, Elizabeth, I was going to call you later on this evening. Unfortunately, as much as we'd love to share your special moment with you, we're not going to be able to join you for opening night."

All the joy that Liz had been experiencing vanished, and was apparent as she spoke. "You're not! Well, why not?"

"Elizabeth, are you whining?" Amanda asked with a touch of a chuckle in her voice.

Liz sighed. "Yes, and pouting! If Cait saw me right now she'd ask me if I've been taking lessons from her kids!"

"Hmm. I have a feeling Cait's kids could probably take pouting lessons from you and your siblings." They laughed and responded to each other's comments. Then Amanda said, "I'm truly sorry, Elizabeth, but your uncle and I have another family commitment that is taking us to the southwest, to Tucson, Arizona—rather than the northeast."

Liz listened to her aunt as she explained the medical crisis Kevin's sister Cora Beth was facing. Then she quietly responded, "Oh, Aunt Amanda, please tell Uncle Kevin and his family that I am praying for his sister. For all of you." She smiled at her aunt's response. "You know hearing about Cora and her battle to live makes the misery in my life seem rather trite."

"Trite? Oh, Liz, you've had a right to be in misery, and my dear niece your emotional heartache has been as real as Cora's physical pain and suffering."

Liz released a sigh. Then, with a touch of a smile in her voice she said, "Aunt Amanda, you are so good for my ego. Thank you."

"You're welcome. Now tell me what else is going on besides the resident spirits."

An hour later Liz got out of her car that she had long since parked next to the old family cabin. The sun had made its final descent in the western sky beyond the mountain ridge. Nighttime sounds were all around Liz, as well as the hungry mosquitoes that stirred, as she walked through the grass to the porch steps. Once inside Liz stretched and felt aches and pains in her muscles that she had not realized were there until that moment in time. She yawned as she headed towards the kitchen. As she turned on the kitchen light, she saw an envelope leaning against an empty water glass on the kitchen table. Liz paused in her step, then hesitantly walked over to the table. She had to wonder, was Peter trying to win her back, even though she had told him they were on hold until after Labor Day? Time would only tell.

Liz picked up the envelope and read a note from her mother. A sigh escaped from her pursed lips. Open mind. Open heart. Forgiveness. Her mother's words of warning raised Liz's anxiety to feeling like she was standing in the middle of a rodeo corral with a red flag, and a bull was standing at the opposite end of the pen with his head lowered and his hoof kicking up plumes of dust in the loose dirt. She drew in a breath and then stood a little straighter as if good posture was going to help her sinking feeling. Then Liz carefully opened the letter and began to read.

Dear Liz,

I'm sure I'm the last person you want to hear from and I hope that you will read my words before choosing to throw this away. Since you last ripped into me at yours and Peter's engagement party I've been in counseling. I have to tell you this has not been easy for me. During these sessions I've been finding out things about myself that I never wanted to acknowledge to myself, or admit to anyone else.

Devon and I are still going through with the divorce. We obviously have nothing to salvage in our fractured relationship. That's not my reason for writing to you. My therapist and I have been talking about our family and how I fit in as the youngest daughter. I don't mean for this to sound like whining, but you probably will think so. Anyway, here it goes. Do you have any idea how hard it was for me to be your younger sister? Ever since I was a little girl I never felt as if I could measure up to the bar that you and Caitlin set for the rest of us to follow. You are so beautiful and I don't just mean on the outside. You seem to radiate something that makes everyone want to be with you. You're like a magnet, a genuinely good magnet. While we were growing up, you and Caitlin never seemed to get into trouble like Sammie, J and I did. Mom and Dad would often refer to your goodness as something I should follow. There is more I can say about this, but for now as we both know, I rebelled. Boy did I rebel, and I lost a wonderful man and my sister in the process. I know this is probably not making fluid sense to you. I just have to say what I am feeling. I didn't want to be like you or Caitlin. Yet, at the same time I was jealous of you. Oh, Lizzie, what I did to you and Greg is beyond wrong. There is no excuse for my actions. I am so sorry for how much pain I brought into your life. Yes, I am dirt as you proclaimed. Lower than dirt. All I can do is hope that you will believe me that I will always regret everything I've done to you. Please forgive me for all of the pain I've caused you, especially with the loss of your child. I would have loved to be his or her aunt. Hopefully, if you'll forgive me, we can try to get to know each other as women—as sisters not in competition—but as sisters with family as our common ground and maybe someday as friends. If not friends, then perhaps as someone we can each tolerate for the sake of our family.

Be well, and good luck with your opening night. Yes, Mom and Dad have told me about your theater and being the Community Arts Director. I'm proud of you.

Jordan

Liz slumped down into the kitchen chair, released a sigh and reread her sister's words as tears slid down her cheeks. Family dynamics could be as beautiful as an Adirondack sunrise or sunset. Then, without warning they could turn and be as ugly as a major summer thunderstorm pummeling the mountains, or a blistering bone chilling winter nor'easter. Liz glanced down at the letter she had placed on the table. She was once again at a crossroad with her sister. She knew in her heart that how she handled the next step with Jordan would determine many years to come, if not the rest of their lives in the Callison family.

Liz got up from the chair, fixed herself a cup of herbal tea, picked up the letter and walked into the living room. She glanced at her watch and took a gamble that it was not too late to call her parents.

"Elizabeth," her mother's voice informed Liz that she had unintentionally worried them. "What's wrong?"

"Hey, Mom, sorry for calling so late. I'm okay. Honest. I know it's late and I guess I should have waited to call until tomorrow."

"Nonsense, Elizabeth. Besides your father needs to get up from sleeping in his recliner and head to bed." Liz couldn't help but giggle as she listened to the banter between her parents. "I've put my phone on speaker so your father can be included in our conversation. That is, unless you need for this to be strictly a mother-daughter conversation." Liz heard her mother gasp and giggle. She rolled her eyes while imagining what was happening. Not a good visual of her parents, nor one she should be witnessing.

"Hey, Lizzie J, are you ready for opening night?" Her father asked, then yawned. The noise she heard sounded as if he was stretching as well.

"You don't need to worry. We will be ready, Dad." She laughed at his response and commented.

"Who said I am worrying? I know firsthand all the work that's gone into getting that place in shape for this summer theater season. That's all."

Liz heard her mother sigh and then speak to her father. She smiled as she listened to them. Family.

"So, Elizabeth, now that your dad has totally spun the conversation in his direction, what is on your mind for you to call us this late in the evening?" Melissa gasped, then scolded, "James Callison, listen to what Liz needs to share with us. I mean it! Keep on and you will be on the couch!"

Now Liz could not help but laugh at her parents. After all of their years together, adult children and grandchildren to boot, sometimes they still acted like newlyweds! She cleared her throat.

"Well, Mom, Dad, I guess I have you to thank for the latest twist in my life." Silence. Liz giggled. "It's a good twist. I think. And I suppose I owe you both a thank you for meddling in Jordan's and my war."

"Oh?!" There was a collective gasp and releasing of air.

"Yes, as you both know, Jor sent me a letter."

Both Jim and Melissa immediately picked up on Elizabeth using her sister's childhood nickname. Interesting.

"And how do you feel about this?" Jim asked. He wished they were face to face while having this particular conversation so that he could read her expressions.

She sighed. "Well, Dad, my sister gave me some things to consider besides accepting her apology and forgiving her."

"Are you going to forgive Jordan?" Melissa quietly asked her.

"Mom, this morning I would have told you no. But now, as I said, Jordan's letter has given me a lot to think about."

"Elizabeth, you haven't answered your mother."

Liz couldn't help but smile, as she heard the tone in her father's voice. Yes, she had been evasive in her answer. "Let's just say that it may not take thirty years for Jordan and me to reconcile our differences."

She heard her father sigh, and say something to her mother. Her mother responded to him in a muffled voice than clearly said to her, "Liz, we won't pry any further tonight. You are right that the timing for you and your sister mending your ways is between you two, not us. Thank you for reading your sister's letter, and sharing your news with us."

"And I thank you, Mom," she yawned, "And, Dad, just so you know, I called to share this news with you and Mom before I told Aunt Amanda about Jordan's letter. As much as I love Aunt Amanda, I love you two more and wanted to share this with you. Thank you for everything that you both have done for me. I love you both to the moon and back."

"I love you too, Lizzie J." She heard her dad sniffle and clear his throat.

"Liz, you know I love you, and now, as your mother, I'm telling you it's time for you to get yourself quieted down for the night and to bed. After all, Director, you have a busy schedule with preparing for opening night."

"Yes, ma'am. Good night." Liz sighed as she ended the call. On one hand, she was exhausted. On the other hand, she was filled with joy and happiness. Life was looking up for Elizabeth.

The whole Great Sacandaga Community and surrounding towns were abuzz with excitement about the upcoming opening of the Community Arts Summer Theater. For this first year under

Liz's direction, there were only two full length productions. The first scheduled to open the season would be a musical *Bye Bye Birdie,* and to close out the season would be the drama, *Barefoot in the Park,* one of Liz's favorite plays by Neil Simon. In between the two productions would be a resident artist's craft fair, a two-week music camp for eastern Fulton County youth, and a jazz fest weekend. Coordinating everything had Liz going at full speed on minimal sleep, too much coffee and her family fully involved working behind the scene where needed.

While the final rehearsals and preparation were underway for opening night of *Bye Bye Birdie,* Elizabeth decided that she would call Jordan, rather than writing to her. Time was of the essence for what Liz hoped would happen. Liz slipped out past the mess hall to the path that led into the forest. She found a quiet place father past the roughhewed bench, sat down on the rock and placed her call. Jordan answered immediately. Shocked and delighted at the same time. The two sisters took the next step towards repairing their relationship.

"Are you sure, Lizzie?"

Liz could not help but softly smile as she heard her sister's uncertainty. "Yes, Jor I'm sure. I can't imagine having opening night without all of my family being here with me. Well, JJ can't be here, so I'm hoping to have all three of my sisters by my side."

"Well," Jordan hesitated. Liz quietly listened for her sister to say, "Okay, Lizzie. I'll put in for the time off and plan to be there."

With Jordan agreeing to come home, and stay with her at the family cabin Liz finally released a sigh of relief. Of course, she'd have to deal with her parent's disappointment that Jordan was not staying with them. She smiled as she thought of how short-lived their disappointment would be. Especially when they saw that their daughters truly were mending their broken fences.

The opening night of *Bye Bye Birdie* had arrived. The mid-summer Friday night was typically cool as the sun sank down behind the mountains. Volunteers were positioned in the parking lot to greet people, answer questions, direct them where to park, and then to the box office. Solar lights strategically placed along the path illuminated the way to the box office, and then along the aisles through the fully restored cement benches.

The Callison family gathered inside the house, then made their way to the bench that had a reserved sign on it. Callie Anne and Nicholas were bubbling over with excitement and both seeking their grandparent's undivided attention, while Caitlin and Jordan fussed over their sister. Sammie was far into her pregnancy and waddling as she walked. Her abdomen looked like she had a beach ball full inflated under her loose maternity blouse. She was tired and had not been feeling too well since early morning. But tonight, was her sister's special night and she was not about to miss it!

They all had nicely taken their seats, greeted the Jones family, the Johnson brothers and their dates when the house lights dimmed to inform them that the show would begin in ten minutes. Jordan found herself watching and listening to family, friends and people whom she didn't know all share their excitement about the theater being reopened after so many years of neglect. She felt pride as she listened and looked around her. Her sister had had a vision and the God given gifts, education and experience to make it happen. As the lights dimmed again to inform people to get to their seats because the show would begin in five minutes, she heard someone speak and slightly turned her head to sneak a peek and confirm her suspicions. There sat Peter Jones alongside his uncle, Phil Johnson. Jordan did not like what she overheard, and was deciding how she would address it with him when the lights dimmed and the orchestra began to play the overture.

By the time the curtain closed everyone was on their feet applauding, some whistled, while others yelled out in approval. After the second opening of the curtain Elizabeth emerged with a microphone in hand. She took center stage and began to thank the community for their support in making the night a success. Then, as she began to introduce the crew there was a blood curdling cry. Liz looked out into the house and focused on her family. Oh yes! The Callison family was in action and Liz knew what was happening.

"Well folks, it looks like my little sister has just upstaged me and my theater troupe by going into labor! I love you, Sammie." Liz beamed with pride, chuckled, then said, "Good night everyone." She turned to smile and give her troupe a thumbs up and exited stage right.

Everything after that moment was a blur for Liz. She had her responsibilities as the director, paused to text her mom or Caitlin about how Sammie was doing, and was totally oblivious to what Jordan was up to. Jordan was on a mission to address her annoyance with Peter Jones. She slipped away from the center aisle clogged up with slow moving people to the outer aisle, and caught up with Peter as he went past the box office. Good. Jordan preferred to have this conversation away from the majority of people, especially his parents and uncles.

"Peter," Jordan spoke loud enough to get his attention, but not too many other people's attention.

"Jordan." His voice revealed his surprise to find her standing there. "This is a surprise. I thought you and Liz were sworn enemies. Does she know that you are here?"

"She does." Jordan was not smiling. In fact, her expression suggested that messing with her would be dangerous. "I'm here because Lizzie invited me to join her for this celebration."

"Then she's obviously forgiven you for what you did."

"Yes, Peter, and now I'd like to discuss with you what I heard you say to your uncle before the show began." She drew in a breath to steady herself. Then she gave him an earful ending with saying, "I hope to God that she does not give you a second chance. Lizzie's a class act and she deserves someone better than you in her life. She needs someone who will trust her, love her, and appreciate her for the beautiful woman that she is."

Jordan did not realize that people had stopped to listen to their altercation. Peter had the sense to look fully chagrined, especially when he heard people talking among themselves and agreeing with Jordan and singing Liz's praises.

It was 3:29 am when Mary Elizabeth—for Samantha's grandmothers—and Daniel Mark—for Christopher's grandfathers, were born. Twins. Sammie and Chris had known, and kept the secret for the past three months, that they were having twins. Needless to say, everyone was bursting with joy and excitement. Jim and Melissa both fought back their tears as they cradled their newborn grandchildren in their arms. Of course, pictures were sent immediately to Amanda. Jim had to laugh when his phone rang at 4:47 am. He excused himself from the overflowing maternity room and quietly spoke into the phone, as he headed for the waiting room.

"So, what do you think of our newest additions to our family?" He asked as he sat and a yawn slipped from him.

"This is the nicest and only way an old great aunt enjoys being woken up at this ungodly hour of the morning." Amanda yawned, said something to Kevin that Jim couldn't quite make out. She told him what had been said, causing Jim to laugh. "Please give Sammie a hug for me, and sneak a kiss or two on those beautiful grand babies for me as well."

With all the excitement of his newest grandchildren being born on top of Jordan being home and reconciling with Lizzie, and Lizzie's opening night, he had forgotten that they were in Tucson, AZ with Kevin's family and involved in a family medical crisis. Jim couldn't help but smile. He had so much to be grateful for. God—The Great Spirit had given him and Amanda a second chance to be family, and they were doing it to the best of their ability. "No problem, Sis! I'll call you later and send more pictures as well." He chuckled at her response. "For now, you get some more sleep for both of us! Bye."

Liz and Jordan finally were able to pull Caitlin away from their sister long enough to share their idea with her. Caitlin listened, her brows scrunched as they always did when she was skeptical about something. Then she relaxed and began to nod as she shared her own ideas. Before Sammie's children were twelve hours old her sisters had organized the next six weeks of their lives to be ready to help her and Chris with the babies.

"But Jordan," an exhausted Samantha whined, "You can't take six weeks off from work to be up here with us." Then she turned to Liz, "And you have too much going on already with the Arts Center Programs and Theater. Plus, I'm sure Caitlin that you are busy getting ready for the new school year. No." She shook her head. "I can't expect you all to put your lives on hold just because I happened to surprise you all by having twins."

"Samantha," their mother's quiet, yet firm voice caused all four young women to immediately grow silent. Then the three sisters standing beside the bed turned to face their mother, as she took her place on the opposite side of the bed. "You need to listen to them. No buts." Melissa tilted her chin down. Her three girls standing by the bed silently linked fingers at their sides. "Having raised you four girls and your brother, I will tell you from experience that there is no shame in accepting your family's help. I also will be helping you during these next few weeks. Now, to put your mind at ease, I will coordinate with you regarding what you need from all of us and when we will be helping you."

"Okay," Samantha whispered just before she collapsed into a full-blown crying jag.

Callie and Nick were in heaven when the twins were born. But when their mom became busy helping their aunt and not spending her undivided summertime attention on them, the novelty soon wore off for little Nick, even though he and his sister were allowed to participate in the summer youth music camp. Jealousy was rearing its ugly head in the Callison family. On one day in particular, when Nick was feeling out of sorts, and wandered away from the group. He found himself in trouble with his aunt, when she found him with an open can of paint and a brush in his hand against the side of a cabin. Yes indeed, Aunt Elizabeth was furious with Nicholas. She didn't pay any attention to the crowd that gathered nearby to see her call him out for his actions. But Nicholas did. The little boy fought back his tears of embarrassment, and heartache of feeling unloved by his family. After receiving his punishment and everyone returning to their own business, he stormed off down a marked and groomed trail that leads into the forest. When Nick got to the old sign that said, *you are now entering state land....* he paid no attention and kept walking on the trail that had not been cared for in a very long time, and perhaps never by humans, as it looked like a deer path.

Two hours later, after searching everywhere within the property of the arts colony, Liz had still not found Nick. She returned to the mess hall to refill her bottle of water, pulled out her phone and made the first of two important calls. Caitlin reacted as Liz had expected. Shock. Anger. Of course, she was calling her husband Nicholas Senior and was on her way to the colony to search for her son. Liz's second call went to her dad.

"Yes, Dad. I've searched this place from top to bottom. Nick has disappeared. I need you to come and use your tracking skills to help me search."

"Of course, Lizzie. I'm on my way, and Lizzie J,"

"Yes, Dad?"

"You did the right thing reprimanding him as you did. We'll find Nick, and when we do that young man is going to hear from me as well."

Liz released a long, heavy sigh as she clicked off her phone and returned it to the back pocket of her jeans. She sniffled back her anxiety as she felt a smaller hand rest on her arm. Liz drew in a centering breath as she looked down at her niece, Callie Anne. Fear radiated from the child. Without a word Liz drew her into her arms and hugged her.

"Don't worry too much, Callie. I promise you that we'll find Nick. Your grandpa is on his way and he is one of the best trackers. If he can't find your brother, nobody can."

"Aunt Liz, remember last year when Grandma, Aunt Amanda and the twins and I went hiking and I fell?"

"I sure do."

"I know that it was Grandpa and Uncle Kevin who found us. But if Aunt Amanda hadn't been able to tell them how to go, we might have been up there for more than one night. Maybe we should call her and ask for her to come help?"

Elizabeth could not help but smile as her eyes filled with moisture. She gently smiled at Callie as she hugged her close. "Oh honey, Aunt Amanda is back in Baltimore from her trip to Arizona. It would take her too long to get here by car or plane. But I'm sure if she was closer," Liz sighed, "She'd be here in a minute to help us search for Nick." At that moment, Liz touched Callie's chin with her index finger and tilted it upward. "Right now, I need for you to say a prayer for Nick and for your grandpa to be able to find him. Your mom just pulled into the parking lot. Let's go greet her."

Forty-five minutes later, Jim appeared back at the mess hall where Caitlin, Nicholas, Callie Anne and Liz waited for any word about Nick. Liz handed her dad a fresh cold bottle of water in exchange for his empty bottle. It was then that he gave them all the news.

"It appears that Nick took it upon himself to either wander, or deliberately leave the colony and head out onto state land. He's following an old deer path up into the mountain."

"Then why aren't you going, Grandpa?" Callie asked just before she melted into tears, and was drawn into her father's protective arms.

"Because it's state land and even though I'm a good tracker, I know a state forest ranger who is one of the best, if not the best tracker in the area. John Runner will be here in about fifteen minutes. So, for now I'm going to rest and grab something to eat. Lizzie do you have any fruit?"

"We sure do. Dad, I'll fix and knapsack of snacks and water for you to take with you."

Liz had just returned to the mess hall porch when two vehicles pulled into the parking lot. The first one had official New York State identification on the doors. The second was Melissa Callison with Sammie and the twins. Liz's eyes grew larger with surprise as her gaze passed from the occupants of both vehicles. She should have known that her mom and sister would appear. But Liz had not been prepared for the state forest ranger.

John Runner took her breath away. Jet black hair neatly combed back, tanned skinned face and arms, a uniform filled with what she knew in her heart would be a solid toned muscular physique, drew her in like a whirlpool as he approached them with confident steps. When Jim stepped down the walkway to greet the new arrival, Liz finally remembered to breath. She watched and listened as Jim began the introductions.

"And this is my daughter Elizabeth. Liz is the director of the colony and the arts center in town. She's also the one whom my grandson is currently mad at and took to the mountain to sulk while licking his wounds."

John smiled at Liz as he extended his hand to greet her. Liz felt her heart beating faster, stronger, as she returned a smile and gently took his hand. "Ranger Runner, thank you for coming and helping us find Nick."

"Please call me, John." His eyes held hers as he said, "I wish we were meeting under different circumstances." Their fingers lingered together as he gazed at the other Callison's gathered there and added, "We'll find Nick, don't you worry. The woodland spirits will point the signs along the way. I know this because the Holy Spirit warned me this morning that I would be needed to find and guide someone home." John had released Liz's hand that still tingled from his touch. He looked at Jim, nodded and said. "It is time. Show me the way to the trail and we will find the child."

Liz silently watched them walking away from them. She was unaware that her mother had seen the subtle interaction between her and John. Melissa stepped away from Caitlin and Samantha, gently took Liz by the arm and led her down the steps away from their family.

"It's no fun to be seen as the bad guy. Is it?" Melissa quietly asked, as they stopped and sat down on a bench under the shade of a maple tree.

Liz released a deflated breath, then looked at her mother. "Oh, Mom, I feel awful having yelled at Nick as I did. But he knew better." She sighed as she looked at her mother with an unspoken plead for help.

"Yes, he did know better." Melissa shook her head, as a sad smile took shape on her lips. "He's also a child who now has to accept that he's not the youngest anymore. He's no longer the only grandson in our family. Jealousy can make the usually sweetest, kindest person stink to the high heavens!" Her smile had disappeared as her voice grew with disgust.

"Mom, when did you become so insightful about human nature?" Liz asked while she watched the art camp ending for the day, and members of the theater troupe gathering near the theater back entrance.

Melissa softly chuckled. It was healing balm for Liz's tattered nerves. "Shortly after your sister Samantha was born, you and Caitlin threatened mutiny for my paying too much attention to your baby sister and not doting on you two girls."

Liz laughed. "I don't remember that."

"Of course not. You were too little to remember. But I do. Goodness you girls were jealous. You both made me pay by turning your sights on your father for his attention."

"Really?" Liz was amazed by what she was hearing about herself. "So, is that when Dad and I became so close?"

"Yes, it is." Melissa gently smiled. "And as a postpartum mother dealing with three small children it was a difficult pill for me to swallow."

For a moment Liz was confused. She thought about what her mother had just said. "Oh, my goodness. Mom! First Caitlin and I were jealous of Sammie, and then you were jealous of Dad?" She saw the slight nod, the moisture in her mother's eyes. Liz reached over and gently squeezed her hand. "Oh, Mom, I hope that you eventually figured out that dad could never take your place in my heart. Caitlin…I don't know about."

By now Melissa had linked her fingers with Liz's, just like when Liz was a child and they would sit and talk. "It did take a while and by the time JJ made his appearance into our family, well, I was a pro at dealing with jealousy, especially when your dad would whine about my being too tired to spend quality time with him."

Liz laughed at the thought of how her parents could be upset with each other and in the end how love prevailed. She sighed as she released her hand from Melissa's. "Thanks, Mom. I needed you to help me make peace with myself for how I handled the situation with Nicholas." She stretched her legs out in front of her then back in sitting position. "Now, I had best go see how my arts camp and theater troupe are doing."

Jim and John stopped as they came to a fork on the trail in the woods. They both took a bottle of water from their knapsacks and drew in a long drink. It was John who spoke first. "Tell me about your daughter Elizabeth."

A hint of a smile grew in Jim's eyes as he looked into John's dark eyes. Without hesitation he gave John the rundown of family pecking order, Liz's surprise return to the north country a year ago and Liz once again being on the rebound. "Even though Peter is nine years younger than Lizzie, I had hoped that they would be happy together."

"Perhaps he was the one God chose to open her heart to love again, and to prepare her for meeting her true love that is yet to come."

"Perhaps." Jim said as he watched John turn his eyes to the ground. He took a few steps on the path to the right, then returned and took a few steps on the path to the left, he bent down and looked at the ground, the twigs, the leaves. John stood and said, "This is the way he went."

"And this is why I called you." Jim said with a smile of relief. "I'm good, but you have a true gift to see the most subtle of signs of disturbance on the earth."

"We haven't found him yet, my friend. So, don't puff me up with honor when I might fail you in the end."

A half hour later, after slowly making their way through brush then onto a precarious path along a cliff they found a whimpering heap of a little boy sitting on the dirt with his legs drawn up to his chest. His chin rested on his knees as he sniffled and continued to whimper. John quietly spoke to Jim and carefully changed places with him, so that Jim could go to Nick.

"Grand-pop!" Nick exclaimed, then melted into tears, as his grandfather opened his arms to him. Nick got to his feet and wrapped his arms around his waist. "You found me! Am I in trouble?"

"Yes, little one, I found you and we will discuss your fate when you are safely home with your parents. Here." Jim said as he swung the knapsack from his shoulder and withdrew a bottle of water for Nick. "Have a drink and then we'll follow John back down the mountain."

Applause erupted from the arts colony as family, artists in residence, and theater troupe members all greeted the weary rescuers and the once lost boy. Caitlin burst into tears as she ran with her husband to her son. Liz sniffled, and smiled as she watched them for a moment, then drew her eyes to the rescuers—to one in particular. She watched as John and her dad spoke as they rejoined everyone. There was something different about John Runner, and that something was drawing Liz to him, like a honeybee to clover.

"Ranger Runner," Liz spoke with politeness that she hoped would not betray her interest in the man whom she knew nothing about. "Thank you for coming to our rescue. In gratitude for your help, there will be two tickets for you for opening night of our last theater performance for the season. We will be doing Neil Simon's *Barefoot in the Park*. I hope that you will be able to join us."

"Well, thank you, Ms. Callison." His eyes held hers. Sparks seemed to fly between them like a summer meteor shower. "I'd be honored, if my schedule allows me to be here." He gave her a very slight nod, and a touch of a smile that made her breath catch.

Just as Liz was about to respond a member of her theater crew came up to her and interrupted. "Well, Ranger Runner, John, if you will excuse me, duty calls."

Liz was glad to have the distraction from the very sexy forest ranger still with her family there at the colony. Summer in the Adirondacks was suddenly sizzling and Liz was uncertain if she was ready for what she suspected might be happening. Could they be attracted to each other? Could there be something more between them than the physical interest? *Oh, God help!* Liz sighed out, as she walked through the side door and into the orchestra pit to deal with the latest stage issue.

CHAPTER 16

J im and Melissa arrived home thoroughly exhausted from the
day's events. As they entered their home through the garage
door, a welcoming aroma of food being cooked greeted them.
Jim drew in a deep breath savoring the combination of smells. His
stomach growled in response and anticipation of what was to come.
Melissa turned and gave him a look of *Really, Callison? You are so
predictable!* Then, she laughed.

"Oh, Jim, it looks like we had an intruder while we were gone,
and not someone we need for you, or your buddies on the force to
go searching for." Melissa continued to express her thoughts, as they
followed the pleasant aroma into the kitchen. They both spotted the
crock pot on the counter busily cooking the pot roast, potato, onion,
carrot, celery, and Jordan's favorite addition of mushrooms and fresh
herbs.

While Melissa was checking on the progress of their meal, Jim
spotted a plate next to the crock pot that was wrapped in aluminum
foil and a note lying beside it on the counter. Before he read the note,
his stomach grumbled again and curiosity led him to lift a corner of
the wrapping. Biscuits. Jim knew from first glance that they were

homemade too! Of course, he had to sample one to make sure that they were edible and delicious for Melissa to enjoy with dinner.

"Oh, Mellie," Jim said with a full mouth. He couldn't help it! They were good! Really good! "Jordan, did a—well here," he said as he gently pushed the rest of the biscuit to Mel's lips causing her to open her mouth. "Jordan, did an amazing job on the biscuits, and if they are any indication to what our meal is going to be like, well, we may just have to convince her to stay north and become our full time cook." He saw the rising brow and quickly added, "Not that I don't appreciate all that you do for me!" As his hands came up in surrender.

Melissa couldn't help but laugh with happiness and exhaustion as she stepped into Jim's embrace. "I know you appreciate everything that I do. I love you, Callison, right along with our wonderful children and grandchildren. Our family is going through more growing pains, and isn't it wonderful to see these blessings unfolding in the midst of their turmoil?"

"It sure is, Mellie, and yes, God—The Great Spirit—has blessed us. Now, let's sample this meal that Jordan lovingly has made for us."

Morning came with brilliant pink in the eastern sky. Liz had awakened from a restless night's sleep as soon as daylight peeked in through the eastern window. She quietly went about her morning routine trying to not awaken Jordan, dressed in a clean jeans, a short sleeve red gingham cotton shirt, and thong sandals on her bare feet. Then Liz grabbed her breakfast and made her way to the front door with a mug of hot coffee in her hand. She paused as she walked onto the porch to lower her sunglasses from positioned in her hair to her eyes to protect them from the sun's brightness. She took a sip of coffee from the old ceramic mug, swallowed, then drew in a cleansing breath. A new day was bursting forth with untouched beauty. Another family crisis that could have been tragic, had been resolved with the expertise of Forest Ranger John Runner, who had helped her father find Nicholas. Forest Ranger Runner, John. Liz sighed, as a tingling feeling swept through her like a refreshing warm gentle spring rain. His eyes, smile and physique—oh goodness! Liz was in trouble. Emotionally and physically, and she was glad that Jordan was inside the cabin sleeping in the bed that was used by their aunt and uncle when they visited. This allowed her the quiet time that she needed to further consider a couple of the reasons why she had tossed and turned for the majority of the night.

A smile came to Liz's lips as she thought of the joke that they were contemplating playing on their aunt and uncle. Of course, the joke would lay in waiting to greet Aunt Amanda and Uncle Kevin the next time they visited. It had been a few days ago, when Liz and Jordan had been discussing the stories that they had learned of their aunt's devious side, and the practical jokes that she had been said to pull on people. Their father being one of Aunt Amanda's prime targets. Liz smiled as she thought, *why should Aunt Amanda have all the fun playing pranks? What good is a bed if it can't be short sheet-ed at least once?* Liz knew in her heart that while it would be fun to play the joke on Aunt Amanda, well," Liz sighed, "Aunt Amanda was not one to forget, and 'if' being the key word, if they short sheet-ed the bed, well, Liz knew that sometime in the future when she least expected it, Aunt Amanda would remember and was sure to pay them back. Liz was not too sure that she wanted to be the recipient of one of Aunt Amanda's practical jokes. She released a long, slow breath, because she knew that Jordan's and her plan was not the primary reason for her restless night's sleep. Then Liz took another sip of coffee as her thoughts returned to and centered on John Runner. She liked the idea that he was a forest ranger. More than that, it was obvious to Liz that the man is of Native American heritage. She had to wonder, was he married? Oh, good grief! A sigh made its escape through her pursed lips. What was her overactive mind thinking? Her heart was still healing from her last relationship catastrophe with Peter.

The last thing she needed right now was a new man in her life. The sound of a squeaking floorboards from within informed Liz that her sister was in fact awake and up trolling around inside. Liz drew in a calming breath to steady her nerves and prepare herself for Jordan's appearance.

"Hey!" Jordan called out as she headed towards the door to join Elizabeth. "I thought I'd be up long before you. What time did you finally get in?"

"Morning." Liz yawned. "Around 1:00 am. I didn't get to sleep until around 3:00am."

"Lizzie, that's not good. You're working too hard and you need more sleep than that." Jordan said as she looked over her mug with concern, then took a sip of steaming hot coffee.

"I know. Nicholas' and my blow out derailed my day and after he was found,well, I just had a lot to do at the colony. Then, on my way home, I stopped at the arts center to take care of some final prep for the Arts Council Jazz Fest Weekend. Once I got home, I was still wired and thinking about some stuff."

"I know Nick gave us all a scare." Jordan quietly spoke while studying Liz's features. She knew better than to comment on the fatigue she saw in Liz. She also knew better than to ask Liz if she was eating proper meals. Yes, indeed. Liz would blow like a dormant volcano, if, Jordan pestered her too much. Still, Jordan was curious to know what was going on with her sister. So, she asked, "Were you thinking about Peter? Maybe wishing that he had been here waiting for you last night?" Jordan asked. They hadn't talked about Peter, since she had come to her sister's defense on opening night of the first show. So, she didn't know what Liz was feeling towards him, and at that moment, Jordan realized that she wasn't curious simply to be nosy. She truly cared about how Liz was feeling. As Jordan finished asking her questions Liz snorted, or, something close to it. Jordan wasn't sure what the noise was that came from her sister. Regardless, she was on high alert as she listened.

"No. Not Peter." Her voice was almost as quiet as the still early summer morning. "I had other things on my mind." She softly smiled at her sister, as she thought about how she had so much to be thankful for, especially with how God had helped them resolve their differences. "Peter Jones was here to greet me last year when I came home broken apart emotionally, and he was a healing balm I needed to help me recover from Greg's and my demise."

"No thanks to me." Jordan added with sadness in her voice.

They both were momentarily lost in remembering the events that had occurred in New York City, and then the brawl that they had occurred between them year before in their parent's upstairs hallway. So much had happened that had driven them apart, and now here they were rebuilding their relationship one day at a time.

Liz reached over and gently squeezed Jordan's hand as they both moved their feet to start the glider into slow motion. "Hey now, we've crossed that shaky old bridge! We are not going to fall off and back into the murky waters that drove us apart. We've talked about this. Greg was responsible for his own actions. Just like you were responsible for your actions, and I was responsible for my actions. How I responded and am responding to the situation. Now Peter is responsible for his own actions." She paused and drew in a breath, then took a sip of coffee.

Silence.

"You know, Jor, I'm really okay with how things have worked out between Peter and me. While we had fun together and enjoyed our physical relationship—well, until now, I hadn't wanted to admit to myself that our age difference was an issue for me. I'm truly at a different place in my life than where Peter is with his." Neither one spoke. Then Liz snorted and said, "Can you imagine what it would have been like for me to have had Summer's dad as my uncle?"

With that question the two Callison sisters burst into laughter and shared their thoughts on the subject of Stephen Johnson, their cousin Summer and then they grew serious, as they discussed the latest situation that they had created with their Aunt Amanda. Needless to say, the Callison sisters were feeling quite defensive of their aunt. Liz stretched as she glanced into her empty coffee mug. As much as she was enjoying spending the beginning of her day with Jordan, it was time for her to get to work.

"So, I guess I won't plan on seeing you too early tonight?" Jordan asked, as Liz returned to the porch with her purse and car keys.

"Unfortunately, you're probably right. Rehearsals are getting amped up and I have a few loose ends to pull together for the jazz fest this coming weekend, not to mention making plans for the fall arts center programs and fundraisers."

Jordan shook her head with awe as she watched and listened to Liz recite the rest of her plans for the day. Her sister made Jordan's busy day of conducting multiple autopsies at the Nassau County Morgue look like child's play. How did Liz keep everything straight in her mind and then deal with the added pressure of unforeseen glitches in her plans?

"Is there anything I can do to help you?"

"Not today, but I'll keep you in mind and maybe take you up on your offer to help me before you head home." Liz took a step, paused and smiled at Jordan as she said, "Yes, you can do me a favor. You can give those two new additions to our family a hug for me." She sighed. "The rate I'm going, those two will be as big as Callie and Nick before I get a chance to begin spoiling them."

Jordan returned a smile and laughed. "Oh please! You and I both know that after the summer theater closes you will find plenty of time to dote over them."

"I hope so!" Liz smiled brightly. "Later!" Then she bound down the steps to her car.

Jordan remained standing on the porch and watched Liz drive out of sight down the mountain. She thought about their great grandmother, Mary Freeman. Visiting their great grandmother had always been a high point in Jordan's day when she was growing up. There was always a hint of mischief in Gram's eyes. Jordan remembered the way that they sparkled. She found herself laughing, as she remembered how the family matriarch could look or speak and bring her father to a pause. Yes, Great Gram was the matriarch and she made sure that even Dad toed the line. Yet, regardless of what was happening in the life of the family, it was always apparent that Great Gram deeply loved and cared for all of them. How often had she stood in that exact spot, where Jordan now stood, and watch them leave? A breeze stirred. Jordan smiled. Family. Memories. It was a good feeling to know that peace once again reigned in the Callison family. Well, at least in Jordan's and her sibling's generation.

Liz moved through the day's commitments and dilemmas with confidence and an inner peace that she had not felt for a very long time. Of course, her family was at the top of her list for her feeling good. But it was more than that. Not only was she home, she was home with a purpose. Her life had a meaning, and since she had returned home, she had found inner peace that had been missing during all the years she had lived and work in New York City.

It was late afternoon, when Liz was sitting on a bench quietly conversing with a cast member about some unforeseen drama unfolding in the member's life, and she noticed Josh approaching them. He was walking with and conversing with a stranger. Liz watched them approaching her, then she sucked in a breath as she recognized the man who was walking with Josh. It had been a couple of weeks since Liz had met John Runner. Without a doubt, the forest ranger still had the same effect on Liz. Sizzle, sizzle, sizzle. It was like a slab of bacon slapped on a hot griddle. Oh, so hot! She quickly ended the conversation with the actress, drew in a calming breath and rose to greet them.

"Ranger Runner, John," she softly smiled and added, "It is a pleasure to see you again."

The woman who had been seated on the bench with Liz quietly excused herself and disappeared along with Josh. Of course, they were glancing back as they walked away and speculated about Liz's obvious pleased welcome of John's appearance at the colony. Neither Liz nor John seemed to be concerned about what others might be thinking, or, speculating about them at this point in their individual lives. For a moment neither one spoke. They simply gazed at each other and learned of each other with their eyes. Oh yes! There was heat—underlying sparks of fire and desire smoldering between them.

"Elizabeth, -" She liked the way he spoke her name. Liz had to remember to breathe as she listened to him say, "-I hope my being here unexpectedly is not an imposition on you. I didn't have your phone number." John stated while not taking his eyes off of her eyes, her facial features, as if memorizing them forever in his brain.

"You are not imposing." She swallowed, while suddenly feeling all flustered like a lovesick teen. *Oh, good grief!* She thought, then said, "What may I do for you?" Liz had to wonder if her voice sounded as breathless as she felt. *Ugh,* she moaned internally. *I'm pitiful!*

"First, I apologize for taking so long to return. You may, or, may not have heard that four hikers were lost up on the high peak not far from the fire tower in Speculator." His eyes tenderly held hers, as he watched her respond with a nod. He wasn't sure why it was important for him to share the cause for his absence with her. But, deep inside, he knew that it was. "I was a part of the search and rescue, and then after we got them to safety, well you obviously have experience with interruptions in your day's plans. My unexpected presence here today being one of them."

His eyes smiled at her. Oh man, he was good! Liz decided to add considerate to her growing mental list of attributes that made John Runner a man worthy of knowing. Yes indeed! She could visualize him sitting on the bank of a stream, or a lake or perhaps in a boat while fishing. He was using just the right size hook, right amount of line and perfect weight sinker while reeling her in to him. Liz returned a smile.

"John, thank you for being concerned about interrupting me, even though you aren't." He was. Liz silently prayed, asking for forgiveness for her lie. Her smile grew. "I guess I never thought about how often people must get lost, or how easy it is to become disoriented and lose your way in the forest. Nick sure did give us cause for worry. Our family owes you so much for helping my dad find Nick."

"You are welcome, Elizabeth." His eyes tenderly held hers. Deep concern resonated from him as he asked, "How is the young boy doing?" Liz's smile lessened as she shared with John the family consequences dished out by Cait and Nick for little Nick's bad behavior. John nodded. "That sounds reasonable for what he did. You should know that Nicholas could have met grave peril, if, he had continued on that particular trail."

"Oh?"

"Yes, after I was back in my office, I looked on some old maps of the area and noted that a mile further ahead of where he was, the path goes back into the forest. Then about a half mile further up the next ledge of the mountain the terrain changes again, and there is a sheer cliff with a one hundred foot drop into the stream on the ground below. Up in there the coy dogs, black bears and mountain lions are known to roam freely without much human contact. I shudder to think what might have happened, if he had encountered wildlife or fallen." Liz sucked in a breath and gasped as she listened. "Even though your nephew's wandering away caused your family alarm, he actually did both of us a favor."

"Oh?"

"Yes." He gave a slight nod, while his warm, dark brown eyes reminded Liz of a delicious creamy chocolate bar. "Because of his wandering onto state land we became aware of the old sign that is weather beaten and not readily noticeable for hikers. There needs to be a clear warning for the people who are visiting here at the arts colony of the potential and real danger out in the wilderness. With your permission, I would like to go through your land to remove the old sign from the state property line, and then replace it with the new sign that I have in my vehicle."

She had watched his eyes as he spoke. His concern for Nicholas and others to follow her nephew onto state land was apparent. Liz found herself wondering what the man, not the forest ranger, John Runner was like. She felt drawn to him like a moth to a warm light on a cool summer night.

"By all means you have my permission to be here. Please take your time, and do whatever you consider necessary to address the needs for our safety." She smiled and invited John to return to the mess hall for a cold drink or a cup of coffee when he completed his task.

To her surprise, he asked, "Would you care to join me? So, that you will know firsthand where the state land and trail begins, and then you can share the information with present and future visitors."

"I'd love to." She said without any hesitation, nodded and pointed as she added, "I'll meet you in front of the mess hall, after I let my assistant director know where he may find me, if he should need me before we return."

Liz went off in one direction, while the forest ranger went in the other direction. It didn't take long for John to gather the sign and equipment, and then meet up with Liz at the mess hall. His quiet manner was totally opposite from what Liz was used to in her male family members and friends. Liz was certain that under that quiet appearance was a strong man, someone worth getting better acquainted with. She was aware of the ease that John moved through the forest. It was as if he was a part of nature. As they walked together, Liz realized that there were things about him that reminded her of her father. Liz couldn't help but smile to herself. Attributes similar to her father were a good thing. A very good thing in Liz's eyes.

As they walked together Liz shared information and answered John's questions regarding her work. The conversation was not too personal, that is, until Liz said, "The day when we met, I sensed that you and my dad have known each other for a while."

"We have." A look of admiration came upon John's expression. His deep brown eyes seemed to warm like a cup of hot milk chocolate, as he shared part of his life story with Liz. "I was fresh out of the police academy when I met your dad. He's nearly 30 years my senior. I'm now forty-two, in case you were wondering," he added with a touch of laughter in his expression. *Oh,* Liz thought, *the man is smooth.* She carefully tucked way the obvious, but smooth information as she continued to listen. "Anyone who works in law enforcement in the area knows who Jim Callison is. The fact that he is retired makes no difference for us. He's still one of us and he is one of the best." Their conversation took a turn as Liz shared with John what it was like to find her grandfather's body at the colony, and how relieved she was to have her dad with her at that moment. "Elizabeth, you were blessed to have him present. That day he saw things you missed. That's how it always was with him. Everyone wanted to work with him. We all learned from him."

"I know, Dad is a good tracker, John. But you should know that he holds your tracking skills in higher esteem than his."

"That is very kind. He is too modest of his own gifts. He is a wise elder. I have often sought out his counsel professionally and even personally." He gave her a touch of a smile. "Your father taught me, and guided me to follow my heart. My passion. His mentoring eventually led me to change vocations and follow my heart's true passion to become a state forest ranger."

Liz didn't feel the need to hide her smile. "That sounds like Dad."

John returned a smile. Liz felt the invisible pull between them. It was like a path or a road that was leading her to him.

"Jim and I share a bond beyond our vocations."

"From my observations of you, how you've spoken of respecting Dad as an elder, I gather you are Mohawk."

"Yes. I am full blooded Mohawk. I like your watered-down father, as I like to tease him. I am known for my tracking skills, and that is why he contacted me to help him find your nephew."

It took Liz a moment to catch on to John's humor about her family heritage. Then, a giggle seemed to flow from her like a newly found spring of water bubbling forth from the earth. The man has a sense of humor and Liz not only like what she heard, she longed to discover more about him.

"So that makes me more diluted," her eyes danced with mischief, "and trust me, I don't have good tracking skills. So, don't look to me for help if someone gets lost." Her eyes shone with happiness as she teased.

He laughed. Liz felt it slide over her like a smooth piece of silk as he said, "Diluted or not, you're still one of us. In time we will tap into your other skills." John finished saying as they stopped at the tree that held the old sign. John shook his head. His eyes seemed to mourn for the way the tree had been treated by those who had driven the nails into the bark so long ago. Then after touching the tree he carefully removed the sign to keep from inflicting more damage to the scarred tree. Liz held on to the new sign, and waited as John drove the pole, he had brought that would hold the new signage into the ground. Their conversation, time spent working together filled Liz with a feeling of contentment, as well as anticipation. What had he meant when he said, *in time we will tap into your other skills.?* Liz found herself returning to that question, as she watched him wave and slowly pull out of the quiet parking lot.

While Liz was busy getting on with her life, Peter was also getting on with his life. He had to admit that his visit with his best friend James Callison Junior – Liz's younger brother–was exactly who he had needed to speak with to help him to begin to put his life into perspective. Peter was heading home, tired from his long overdue vacation to the coast of Massachusetts. Boston was a great city to visit, especially when you best friend and his girlfriend had an apartment within walking distance of the harbor. It had been good to be in a place where a memory of Elizabeth didn't assault him with every step he took. A yawn escaped from Peter, as he drove north on Route 30, and was glad that his dad's and uncle's business wasn't too far away. Having spent the past four days hanging out and having long heart to hearts with JJ had been the starting point of Peter's new direction. Now he needed to talk with his dad, and hoped that his mom hadn't taken it upon herself to visit the shop at that moment.

Peter was glad to see his dad's and uncle's pickups, as well as three unfamiliar SUVs were in the parking lot. *Good, no Mom*–Peter amended his thought and added, *even though I love her*. He took a minute to allow the engine to idle down from the hard-running trip. Stretched. Released a long, heavy sigh of fatigue, emotional and physical. Then, shutting of the engine, Peter emerged from his car. He glanced over at his dad's and uncles' pickups, allowed a smile to take shape on his lips as he contemplated the need for a new image, perhaps more of a hellion like his uncle had been in his younger years. Then, he thought about the consequences of his uncle's behavior. He shook his head. No. He might happen to respect Uncle Stephen, for the most part, but Peter knew if he emulated him – well – his mother would string him up for bear bait as sure as the sun rises in the east and sets in the west. His smile had grown to full size, by the time he turned the handle and opened the door to the shop.

"Hey, old men! The youngster's returned!" Peter couldn't help but laugh as he heard the comments from them as he shut the door.

"Wes, I thought you said he was going to be gone for four weeks?"

"I thought so too." Wes responded, his smile and tone of voice told Peter all he needed to know. His dad was happy to see him, and both his father and his uncle appeared to be in a good mood.

"Sorry to disappoint you both and return after four days. I happen to know of the trouble you two can get into when left to your own devises. So, I didn't trust leaving you two for any longer than four days." He smirked as he helped himself to a cup of coffee. "Am I going to die from drinking this liquid called coffee?"

Wesley shared a smile with him as he watched and listened to his son, noticing every nuance. There was something different about Peter's attitude. Even though things were currently a bit precarious between the Jones-Johnson family and the Callison family, Wesley couldn't help but feel that Peter's trip to see JJ had been exactly what his son had needed.

"I made this pot so you'll live, son." Wes laughed and jokingly commented to Stephen.

"Thanks Dad." He took a sip. "Ah," he closed his eyes as if in heaven. "I sure am glad you made the coffee and not Unc. The last thing I needed was to drink what he thinks is coffee and tastes like mud!" His smile filled the room.

Wes laughed at that comment. Then, he proceeded to tease his brother in law some more.

"You know, if I wanted instant heartburn, I could have simply made a phone call. I didn't need you two to gang up on me!" Stephen responded with a total lack of humor in his voice.

From there the insults, teasing, and laughter continued to fill the bait shop. Men being men enjoying one another company. Family.

"Unc, would you mind if I snag Dad away from here for a little while so we can talk?"

Stephen was about to tease Peter, then thought against it. He nodded. "Actually, the lawn does need to be mowed from the side of the building to the lake shore, and the weeds need to be trimmed down by the pavilion patio. That ought to keep me out of here for a while so you two can talk in private."

They both remained quiet, sipping their coffee, as they watched Stephen place his ball cap on his head, and walk toward the door. Then, Peter walked over and took the stool his uncle had vacated. He sighed.

"So, what's on your mind?"

"Well, Dad, I'm glad I went to see JJ. I think that I'm starting to understand how important your friendship is with Uncle Stephen. I mean beyond being related. I'm talking about how important you are to one another as good friends."

Wes smiled as he listened to his son. Peter was maturing. Maybe the devastating end to his relationship with Elizabeth had actually been a blessing for his son. Wes could only wait and see.

"While it's too late for this season, I'm contacting the ECHL mid-level professional ice hockey league to try out for a team for next season. I'm hoping from the inquires I've already made to try out and make the Adirondack Thunder's team." Wes nodded in agreement as he listened to Peter continue. "I'm hoping for the Thunder since they are based in Glens Falls. That way then I wouldn't be that far from you and Mom. Who knows, if I make the team, maybe you could even come watch me when we play in the Arena."

"Well, you certainly do have the skills and passion to play hockey." Wes smiled. "You've obviously given this some thought to not being too far from your mom and me."

"But?" Peter intently watched his father.

"But, is this a way for you to run from Liz while saving face?"

"It's funny that you should ask that because J and I spent some time talking about Liz and stuff." Wes listened to Peter continue. "Besides being close to you and Mom, a home cooked meal every now and then, there's more to my plan."

Wes raised a brow, "Oh?"

"Yeah, I did some inquiring and found that a couple of schools in the Glens Falls area are in need of an English teacher. While I was with J I went ahead and sent in my resume to the schools." He watched his father's eyes as he added, "Now, I'm waiting to see if any of the school districts are interested in what I have to offer them."

"Well, son, isn't it a bit late in the summer to be looking to change school districts, especially if you are considering trying out for a professional hockey team?"

"It might be, but didn't you and Mom teach me to be open to listen to God speak to me and guide me in my life?"

Wes couldn't help but smile at that. Then he chuckled as he shook his head. "Son, you just threw out the God card and that trumps an Ace any day. Remind me to not play cards with you, or at least against you."

Peter laughed as he saw the humor in what his dad had just said. "I have a feeling that the God card is the one that I need to lead off with when I broach this subject with Mom."

"That would be wise." Was added in agreement. Then their conversation returned to hockey, which the two men thoroughly enjoyed playing and watching.

Stephen shut off the lawn mower, pulled the cloth handkerchief from his back pocket, wiped his forehead of the sweat on his brow, returned it to his pocket and sighed. He needed a break from his work in the sun. Twisting the corner of his lip up, he thought, *serves*

you right, old man, using the push mower rather than the riding one.
Stephen knew exactly why he had used the push mower. He had
things to mull over in his mind. Walking helped him sort through
his troubled thoughts. Now he was ready to take a break under the
oak tree on the shore of the lake. He glanced at his watch, calculated
the time difference, and pulled his phone from his back pocket. He
selected the first number from his favorites and waited.

"Dad, this is a wonderful surprise." Summer's greeting was a
treat for Stephen. For thirty years, neither had known of the other
existence. Who would have ever guessed that Junior McGrath and
Shannon Greene's altercation with Amanda, on that fateful New
Year's Eve, would have led to uniting father and daughter? Since the
spring of 2010, when they met, Stephen and Summer had grown
close. Stephen had so much to be thankful for, and plenty to regret.
His latest demise with Amanda, and the feud between Summer and
her mother had driven him to make this call.

"And how is my princess?" They laughed as Summer regaled
him with her and Adam's latest canoe trip on the Colorado River.

"So, you found some white water that was too tough to navigate
through. I'm sure you two being swamped was something to see, and
that the water was as cold as you say." Stephen smiled as he listened
to Summer share what Adam had said. Then he laughed.

Their conversation meandered from one thing to another, like
following a footpath along a gently flowing stream in the mountains.
Then, it was time for Stephen to broach the reason for his call.

"Summer, have you given any more thought about working
on reconciling your differences with your mother?" Stephen pulled
his phone from his ear and still could clearly hear every word flowing from Summer's mouth. He smiled in spite of himself. At that
moment, there was no denying who his daughter got part of her temper from. Amanda! Heaven help him! He sighed. "Look Summer, I
know that you feel she overreacted and are hurt by her ultimatum.

Princess, since her words with you, and rather unfortunate conversation that probably ended any further relationship for me to have with Amanda, I've had plenty of time to think." He knew by the silence on his phone that he had her full attention. "Let me tell you a story."

Stephen told Summer about the conversation he had with Amanda in the spring of 2010 when they were on the state trail sitting together by the stream up in the mountain at the top of the falls. "Your mother's words have come back to haunt me. Let me finish. Before we started down the mountain, she warned me to not hurt you."

"Hurt me? Dad, you haven't done anything to hurt me. Mom's the one who hurt me."

He sighed out his pain. His heart felt like it was breaking. "Child, I can understand you feeling that way. Please let me finish." He heard her mumble and couldn't help but smile. "I have hurt you by poisoning your thoughts towards Amanda. Summer, that woman, your mother—loves you. Before you begin to argue the point, I ask you to listen to me. Do you realize that when your mother discovered that she was pregnant and thought you were Junior or Shannon's child, that she could have chosen to abort you? She kept you as a part of her, made a choice to welcome you into her life. Do you think it was easy for her to raise you while having a daily reminder of the hell that they put her through? Do you think it was easy for her to be a single parent? Of course, you haven't thought about any of that. I know I haven't thought enough about all that she's done in her life. Amanda is the strongest woman I've ever known. Junior and Shannon get blamed for a lot, and rightly so. But, princess, neither one of those two dirt bags broke her spirit either time they assaulted her. But I did."

"You?"

"Yes, Summer I did. First in '79 when I foolishly threw our love away, and this year when I told you and Belinda things that were neither one of your business. As a result of my actions I hurt you and your mother. Because of me, you two now have an estranged relationship. All I can hope for is that you will put your pride aside and reach out to her. You and your mother need each other." Stephen listened to Summer share her feelings about his request. "No. She won't make it easy for you. But I'm trusting you to do the right thing."

A few minutes later their conversation ended. Stephen stood in the shade of the tree, replaced the phone to his pocket, wiped his brow one more time, looked longingly at the lake wishing he had time for a swim, pulled the cord on the mower and continued on with his mowing. He had no idea that Wes and Peter had been watching him from the bait shop window.

It didn't take long for news of Peter's plans to spread between the Jones and Callison family. Liz felt a sense of relief when her younger brother called to check up on her after breaking up with Peter. In the back of her mind a demon or two had been playing with her, driving fear into her soul that JJ might be mad at her for her actions. But that was not the case. In actuality, Liz discovered that JJ had grown into a caring young man. Of course, he was a Callison through and through, and as opinionated as the rest of the family was about Liz and Peter's break up. Liz smiled as she listened to him. When had he become so wise? She couldn't help but wonder.

"Well, Lizzie, I am glad to hear that you are not filled with regret for breaking up with Peter. You know Pete is my best bud."

"Hmm. Am I hearing a but coming from you?"

J chuckled. Liz smiled. She had always loved to hear her brother laugh. It was a genuine sound that seemed to bring sunshine into the moment, even on the stormiest of winter's day. "While you two were together, I held my tongue because I knew that neither one of you would accept my opinion. Now I am free to say what I think." Liz responded, then listened as J continued, "Peter needs to get away from The Great Sac Community just like I needed to for my own reasons. Ever since we were kids Peter has always dreamed of playing professional hockey. Lizzie, Pete needs to try out for a team before he becomes too old and then ends up living with regrets of what might have been."

Liz certainly could understand J's point about needing to get away. After all, she had done the same thing when she was younger. Life's journey is about spreading one's wings. Finding one's way. Leaving the nest. Sometimes leaving the nest might mean physically moving far away, like her aunt, Amanda had when she moved to Baltimore. Or, it could be like going a short distance, as with her dad by going off, gaining his education and then returning to settle down in the community. Liz's time away had taught her valuable life lessons. Liz smiled, as she acknowledged to herself that the nest, she had been constructing with Peter was faulty. Not strong enough to protect and shelter her from future storms in life. Yes, Liz was home. Now, she was carefully constructing her own nest, one twig at a time. This new revelation was as beautiful as an Adirondack sunrise.

"J, you are absolutely right. Peter and I were better as friends. I hope at some point in the future we may return to friendship with new respect for each other. As of now, I have new opportunities before me. I am open to see where my life goes professionally and personally."

"Ah, Lizzie. That's my sister. I remember. The strong, confident, amazingly talented, annoying, opinionated, bossy..."

"Okay! Okay! I get the hint! I can be a trial for you to endure as my little brother. J, thanks for being equally annoying, opinionated, strong...I love you, you jerk."

"Back at you, Lizzie. I love you too, and I'm really glad you and I have had this chat. If you ever feel like taking a vaca', you are more than welcome to come to Boston and crash with us."

"Thanks. I might take you up on it this winter when things quiet down a bit. I have a quick question before we end this call. Are you coming home for the Labor Day Weekend celebration in town?" She waited and listened as Peter spoke in muffled voice, then back into the phone.

"As you probably heard, I don't know yet. I do have to tell you, Mom and Dad have been asking me the same thing. If we do get back, we'll shack up with them."

Liz found herself laughing. "I should have known that Mom and Dad would have already been inquiring about your plans. You've made a wise decision to take up their offer. Mom will love having you there to dote over, and Dad will be thrilled to have another male in the house as an ally against all of us females."

JJ snorted. "Right about Mom. Dad on the other hand, he enjoys strutting around like an old rooster with Mom and all you girls as his hen and chicks."

Liz broke into laughter that included snorting, as an image appeared in her mind. The laughter continued and tears soon followed. Her brother had drawn her a place where she could let go and simply be herself. JJ teased her some more, which only made it more difficult for Liz to regain her composure. When she finally did, they shared more comments and laughter about their family. Liz realized that it felt good to relax with someone other than Caitlin who simply allowed her to be herself. All too soon the call ended. Liz had to return to her responsibilities as director.

The sense of peace and happiness continued to reside in Liz as she went over to the amphitheater and quietly stood in the stage left wing watching practice. She felt a tickle on her shoulder, glanced over and saw nothing. She smiled as she whispered, "Hello resident spirit. Are you enjoying the play?" As she watched, she noticed a prop on a stage set piece slightly moved. She shook her head and smiled. No one else noticed. But Liz had, and that was all that mattered.

"Hey, Liz, I saw your lips move." Josh whispered in his stage voice. "Did the ghost tell you what it thinks? Does it have any devious plans for our rehearsal?"

Liz could understand that her friend was skeptical and not thrilled about the idea of lingering spirits in their presence. Since the serious conversation she had with them earlier in the summer, Liz was pleased with how well behaved that they had been. In fact, she enjoyed unlocking her office each morning to see what surprise that they had in store for her. They never did anything mean or destructive. Even now with the spirit playing with the prop, it was intended to simply be something for Liz's amusement.

"Great job!" Liz said as she stepped onto the stage at the end of the next scene. "I'd like for everyone to come down into the orchestra pit for a brief meeting." She noticed most everything being said in conversation around her, stage set up, discussions happening between lighting staff, and complaints between actors. For the past couple of hours clouds had been rolling in from the west. Now the sun was ducking in and out of the thick cumulonimbus clouds that had rolled into the area casting shadows on the stage. A breeze was kicking up as had been predicted in the early morning weather forecast.

Once everyone was assembled, Liz scanned her clipboard and began the late morning meeting. "I'm pleased to see how rehearsal for our final summer production is coming along. Tim, did you work out the glitch in the backdrop for the second act?"

"Yeah, Lenny, Torrie and I put our head together and we figured out what needs to happen. Now we just have to get the screen made." Liz listened and asked further questions regarding the stage design and set up. Then she turned to Andre for his input. Satisfied with what she heard, Liz made a notation, then checked it off on her list and moved on to the next topic. A rumble of thunder was heard off in the distance. "The storm is moving in and brings me to the most important topic for today. There has been a severe storm warning forecast for the area. If, we should have a tornado warning from the national weather service or local service and need to seek shelter, we will do like we did with the storm that hit us earlier this summer, and we all come here to the stage and go underneath to be safe. Any questions?" Liz asked, as she watched and listened to quiet comments being exchanged between members of the troupe. "Alright. Break time!" No one complained.

Liz had just reached the mess hall porch when the first rain-drops hit the roof. She stood on the porch and watched people scattered about scurrying for cover. The sky had an ominous darkness coming over it as the clouds churned above the valley. Rumbles of thunder grew louder and closer. Lightening was also drawing closer. The wind picked up. Liz remained on the porch tucked against the side of the building near the door. She felt safe where she was. Much to Liz's surprise a vehicle pulled into the visitors spot just as a clap of thunder shook the buildings. Liz immediately recognized the SUV, and had to wonder why John was there in weather not that was not even fit for fish in the Great Sacandaga Lake. She moved from her spot towards the entrance to the open porch.

"John!" She exclaimed, as he stepped onto the dry porch. "Whatever were you thinking to come here in this weather?"

His smile brought the sunshine back into her day. "I heard the forecast on my way through the area and decided to stop up and make sure that you are aware of the severe weather warning. We have a tornado warning as well." His grim expression combined with the concern in his eyes meant the world to her. He cared.

"Thank you." Liz felt totally surprised by his tenderness. The wind was beginning to drive the rain onto the edges of the porch. Lightening intensified. Thunder clapped. "We have our plan in place should we need to seek shelter from a tornado." John was pleased with her plan of action. He shared additional insight and was preparing to leave. The storm was nearly overhead. "John, do you think it is safe for you to be on the road? For now, please join me inside with the others who are in here." Liz couldn't imagine how she would forgive herself, if, he left and met peril. She released a sigh of relief when John accepted her invitation to stay, especially when a clap of thunder drove her into his arms for protection. As soon as Liz realized what she had done, she began to draw away from him. "I –" Liz couldn't find her voice. She realized that she was still encased in John's arms, safely held against his warm, strong, muscular chest.

"No apology, Elizabeth." He continued to hold her close. His voice a whisper against the backdrop of the storm. "I'm here to protect you." His eyes confirmed his spoken words as he gazed down at her. Liz swallowed. Unable to speak, she simply nodded.

Once inside John was introduced to many of the members of the theater troupe who were hunkered down in that location. He watched as Liz remained in her role as director. She quietly spoke with individuals who sought her out. Comforting them. Then she addressed the whole group. "Quiet conversation is acceptable. We just need to be able to hear and then pay attention to any weather alerts that are broadcast on the weather radio." Her tone of voice, her willingness to share some stories of her youth growing up in the mountains all seemed to help put the people at ease. John took notice of everything about Liz. He had enjoyed the feel of her in his arms a few minutes before when they were alone on the porch. He noticed everything about her as he watched her speaking with the people whom she was responsible for. Then, Liz disappeared through a side door and returned with an arm full of kindling. John hadn't expected to see that. He placed the empty water bottle in the recycling bin and headed towards her.

"Elizabeth, please either allow me to carry this armful of wood, or tell me where the wood is, and allow me to help you gather more wood for the fire."

"Thank you, John." Her eyes danced with happiness as she spoke. "Perhaps you'd be willing to build the fire while I bring in the wood." She extended her hand revealing a book of matches. His eyes held hers as a whisper of a smile touched his lips. With a slight nod, a gentle stroke of the tips of his fingers against the warm flesh of her palm, he removed the matches from her hold. The lightness of his touch sent an unseen streak of non-weather-related lightening soaring through her. She drew in a quick breath. His eyes, and touch of a smile at the corners of his mouth, indicated to her that he had noticed her response to him.

In no time at all the fire blazed in the large hearth. Someone began to strum their guitar, while a small group began to sing quietly. Another small group found long handled forks and roasted marshmallows. Liz and John sat together on the polished pine floor with their backs resting against the knotty pine wall, silently listening to the others and enjoying one another company. She knew that she would remember the exact moment when John slipped his hand over hers. Their arms touched. They simultaneously released sighs of contentment.

Before too long, the worst of the storm passed, leaving in its wake a steady rainstorm, tree limbs littered the ground. No one was in a hurry to leave the dry building. That included forest ranger John Runner, until his cell phone rang. Liz watched as he answered his phone and stood with ease. He walked towards the buildings entrance, stopped and continued his conversation. Liz sensed that their time together had come to an end, or at least the moment that they had been sharing. She slowly began to make her way towards the other side of the room to where John stood. Their eyes met. He nodded, as if he knew what she was thinking. She smiled and returned a nod.

"Elizabeth, I am needed to aid some people who lost their way while seeking shelter in the mountain during the storm."

"Of course. Be careful, John."

He eased her hand into his, gave it a slight squeeze. Then, released it. His eyes held hers. It was as if he was looking into the depths of her soul seeking to find her inner beauty.

"You be careful as well, beautiful storyteller, Elizabeth." Her brows drew together with questioning. He winked. "Sometime, remind me to tell you what that means." His eyes seemed to shine with mischievousness.

"I will," She said as they walked together out onto the porch. Liz stood there and watched John sprint through the rain to his vehicle. She returned his wave as he drove down the drive.

Liz continued to stand on the porch drawing in a deep breath of the rain drenched air. The scents of summer in the Adirondack Mountains mingled together and filled her senses. Laughter flowed from within the mess hall. She realized that the rainstorm had given them all a break that they had needed. *Thank you, God.* She breathed out. The sound of the door quietly opening and shutting did not take Liz from her thoughts. That is, until she was surrounded by her friends.

"So, do you want to let us in on exactly how close you and the delicious hunk are?" Natalie asked.

"I have a feeling that we're going to be seeing more of him." Andre added.

Liz couldn't help but smile when Blaine added his own impressions and curiosity about John. Her nosy, wonderful friends cared about her happiness and wellbeing, and it felt good. Really good!

"I told you that we'd be seeing more of him," Andre whispered to Liz on the Friday afternoon opening of the Jazz Fest Weekend. Liz knew things Andre didn't. Such as that John had been calling her every chance he got, since his work was keeping him further out into the county, not close by. So, Andre's words didn't immediately register.

Liz was amazed at what a hit the weekend was already turning out to be. The amphitheater house seats were sold out. All of the benches were full and people were paying to sit on blankets on the side hill that was known as the nosebleed section. She had been too busy addressing the need to open up the hillside for seating to notice who was arriving. Andre repeated his words and stopped her dead in her tracks. She looked in the direction where Andre was looking.

Her heart did a flip-flop as John walked towards her. Much to Liz's surprise, he held a bouquet of wildflowers in his hand; Queen Anne's Lace, Black Eyed Susan, and Chicory. As John approached Liz and her friends, he nodded in greeting them. Then he turned his gaze on Liz. It was as if everyone else evaporated away into space at that moment.

"These are beautiful! Thank you." Liz breathlessly said as she took the flowers. Flowers! The man had brought her flowers. More importantly, he had obviously picked the flowers before bringing them to her.

"I'm glad you like them." His eyes never left hers as he spoke.

"I probably should put these in water." Liz felt as if her heart was going to beat itself out of her chest. Flowers! She couldn't think straight.

"I'd be happy to walk with you, if you'd like." His smile. His eyes. Each tenderly held her.

Liz nodded, turned to speak with her friends gathered around them and then returned her gaze to John, only to find that he had not taken his eyes off of her. There was a twinkling of mischievousness in those dark chocolate eyes. Her heartbeat quickened as she drew in a breath. "I think there is a container in the mess hall that will work as a vase." Liz was finally able to say.

The wildflowers, or weeds, as some people would call them, were carefully arranged in the plastic two liter soda bottle that had been cut to make the top have a larger opening. Liz placed the arrangement on the small table nestled between two Adirondack chairs on the open porch. Then she stepped back to look at the scene she had created. The bright, wispy colors against the aged pine logs of the building looked like they should be on the cover of a magazine advertising Adirondack living.

Liz sighed, gazed up at him and said, "Oh, John, you surprising me by being here, and these flowers that you took the time to pick really made my day."

"I'm glad, Elizabeth." He took a hold of her hand and drew her close. "Dance with me." He said as he began to move to the beat of the music that drifted towards them from the amphitheater. Without hesitation, Liz followed his lead. They meld together as one fluidly moving together on the old, worn pine planks. Their footsteps were hardly heard as their bodies brushed against each other.

"Is this a private dance party?" A familiar voice asked, causing Liz and John's steps to falter and stop. They simultaneously looked towards the open doorway to see Jim and Melissa approaching them.

"Mom. Dad!" Liz breathlessly greeted them.

Melissa gently smiled as she noticed the flushed coloring of Liz's cheeks. She also saw the happiness that shone from her daughter's eyes. So, Jim's suspicions apparently were right about the young forest ranger. Now Melissa would have to make good on her part of the bet, because she had lost. Darn! Now that Jim would be declared the winner in their private bet, there would be no living with him for a few days.

"Mom, do you remember Ranger John Runner?" She turned her gaze to John as Melissa responded.

"Of course, I do. John it is good to see you again." Melissa continued to carefully watch their interaction. It was obvious that there was a mutual attraction between them. But Mel also realized that there was something different that she couldn't put her finger on. That something had not been present in the relationship that Liz had with Peter.

Melissa was still thinking about the scene, that she and Jim had stumbled upon that afternoon at the arts colony, as she climbed into bed. Jim had assured Mel that John is a good man. That should have eased her mind. But Melissa had her concerns for her child. She sighed, as Jim reached over and eased her into his arms. He didn't speak. He simply held her. This caused Mel to sigh again, then snuggle in closer to his chest. Jim's arms tightened protectively around her as she lay against him with her head resting near the juncture of his arm and chest.

"Do you want to talk about your concerns?" Jim quietly asked.

Melissa sighed. "It might help."

Silence.

"Mellie, as much as I'd like to sometimes be able to, I can't read your mind." He lightly stroked her arm as he quietly encouraged her, "Tell me what's wrong, sweetheart."

"I'm concerned that Lizzie is rushing into a new relationship before having time to fully heal from her broken relationship with Peter." She began to lazily move her finger in a circular motion in the mat of hair on Jim's chest. Then she added, "I just don't want to see Lizzie hurt, by rushing from one man to another before she's truly ready."

"Sweetheart, I also don't want to see Lizzie hurt. For now, let me help you take your mind off your worries." He moved his thumb and index finger to Mel's chin, tilting it just enough so that he could claim her lips with his.

Sometime later, Melissa yawned in contentment, as she lay in Jim's arms. Her fingers rested against his damp chest. Without a doubt, Jim had taken her mind off of her worries. As a lover, he never ceased to amaze her with how passionate and considerate that he was to her needs. She felt his lips gently touch her forehead. "I love you, my sweet Melissa. Our family will be okay. Get some rest."

"I love you too, Callison." And with that, Melissa closed her eyes to sleep and dream of the man who had long ago claimed her heart.

CHAPTER 17

A noise from out in the main area of the old cabin awakened Liz. She moaned as she pulled the pillow over her head to block out the noise. It didn't help. She grumbled. Then she threw the pillow and covers aside with an exaggerated huff before she sat up, yawned and stretched. As she did her tee shirt raised baring her midriff. Her pajama shorts were twisted from her restless sleep. She felt and looked like a mess! So, what?! It wasn't as if she had someone of importance in her life! Liz sleepily needed to edit that thought. There was someone with a lean, muscular body, the perfect height for her to meld against, ebony eyes, black hair with similar coarseness to hers. Liz sighed and smiled as she felt her body awakening to her thoughts. John Runner. Now he was the perfect way to begin her day, even if the man was only in her thoughts.

The noise that had awakened her was continuing, like the annoying dripping of a leaking water faucet. *Drip, drip, drip.* There was only one explanation. Her dear sister, Jordan. On the one hand, Liz was so grateful for the peace and reconciliation that they had found in their once estranged relationship. On the other hand, Jordan was her younger sister, and at that moment in time, Jordan was annoying her, and she was going to receive a piece of Liz's mind. She stood, sighed, rubbed her sleepy eyes and headed towards the door. As her hand touched the knob, she heard a voice. A very familiar voice.

"Caitlin, what are you doing here?" Liz asked as she stormed into the living room, stopped, and promptly glowered at her sisters, who were relaxing on the couch while sipping cups of steaming hot coffee.

"Well, good morning sleepy head." Caitlin smiled while taking in Liz's rumpled attire and hair. Her eyes shone with humor. Liz knew that look all too well. Something was up! Besides Caitlin finding humor in how she looked when she first greeting the day, Liz wasn't too sure she wanted to know what her sisters were up to. "Now that you finally decided to join us, we can get on with our plans for the day." Cait snickered knowing that Liz would not appreciate it. Oh well!

"Excuse me?" Liz was still not smiling. "I don't recall making plans to spend my one day off with either of you, especially this early in the day." She yawned and stretched, finding a few sore muscles in the process.

"Well, you are going to join us, so get the led out of your butt, get your coffee, a shower and then get dressed for the day. Casual will do. And don't bother to argue with me." Caitlin had that bossy older sister look and it didn't go over too well with Liz. Without even thinking she rolled her eyes as she tilted her chin down in response to Caitlin's dictatorial attitude. "And don't bother to act put out with me. I've had years of experience with you and I remember your routines all too well!" Cait added for effect. Jordan snickered, as she listened to her sisters bantering back and forth, like a couple of feisty hens clucking around a hen house. Goodness, they were funny when they got their feathers ruffled! Well, until they both glowered at her for laughing at them, while Caitlin clucked on at Liz. "Move along now! The days wasting and we have some fun things planned for us to do together. So just trust me and get dressed. You will want to be part of this."

Liz was skeptical, but there was something in Caitlin's expression that suggested, she had better trust her sister. She sighed. "I'll make my final decision about joining you two after I have my coffee."

"That's fine. Go get ready. I can't wait to see your face when you see what we have planned."

"Keep on being bossy with me Cait, and I'll skip the coffee and shower and go directly back to bed."

"You two stop!" Jordan yelled! That got their attention. They both looked at her with surprised expressions and listened. "At first I thought you two were funny. But not now! I had thought it would be nice to spend the day with my sisters before I head back home. Now, I'm not so sure! If you two want to act like bickering teenagers that's fine with me. I'll go on and have fun without the two of you. It won't be the first time, and it certainly won't be the last!"

Liz noticed something in Jordan's eyes. Sadness. Concern. Liz didn't quite know how to read her. "Sorry, Jor. I certainly don't want to ruin your plans." She gave her younger sister a weak smile, then added, "I'll go quickly get ready."

Both sisters watched Liz quietly turn, then disappear into her bedroom. Caitlin busied herself tidying up the kitchen, fixed a cup of coffee in a travel mug and handed it to Liz, as she stepped back into the living room fully dressed for the day. Caitlin smiled as she looked at Liz's attire: cotton tank top, faded cutoffs, thong sandals, her hair pulled back into a ponytail with sunglasses tucked in her hair on her head. She wore lip gloss and no other makeup.

"So where are we going," Liz asked as the three piled into Caitlin's SUV and headed down the mountain to the main road.

"It's a surprise." Was all Caitlin would say as they rode down the mountain to Route 30.

Liz knew that for the moment, it was best to simply surrender to her sisters. They had obviously taken great care in planning their surprise. She glanced out the window and realized it had been too long since she had been able to relax like this. Her mind began to drift back to work, and as it did, she reigned in her thoughts. She let work go and breathed in the day. It was beautiful. Summer in the Adirondacks, carefree, enjoying the moment with her sisters. At first Liz thought that they were going to their parents. Wrong. As they cruised on by the familiar old road, Liz glanced over at the speedometer. She softly smiled and slightly shook her head. Led foot Caitlin had taken that turn a bit faster than she would have. Suspicions formed in Liz's mind as Cait drove on. Then, Caitlin slowed down, and turned down the back-road heading towards Sammie and Chris's home. A smile took shape on Liz's lips, as she turned to look at Cait, and then back at Jordan. "Does Sammie know that we are invading her household?" Concern resonated from her voice.

"Oh, yeah! It was her idea for the four of us to get together before Jor goes home." Cait was smiling at their success in pulling off their surprise.

"At first, I wasn't too sure it was a good idea." Jordan added. "You know, having spent time with Sammie and the babies, I know how tired she is. Those two are only infants and goodness they already are a handful! Plus, I know how you feel about being surprised."

Liz was deeply touched by her sister's love and concern for her and Samantha. A sister's day together, and time with the twins. This had the potential to be a wonderful day for all of them, or, disaster. Time would only tell.

Sammie greeted them as she graciously opened and welcomed them into her home. After the initial hugs, they all tip toed into the master bedroom to peak into the two cradles at the beautiful bundles of joy, sleeping peacefully. It didn't take long for the Callison sisters to fall into sync. Cait and Jordan brought in the food that they had made, as well as, the goodies they had bought for their lunch, while Liz assisted Sammie with setting the table. Liz couldn't help but notice that Caitlin had taken the time to make sure that each sister's favorite picnic food was included in their lunch. Leave it to Cait to act like the '*mother hen*' loving and caring for them all.

The Callison sisters had nicely settled in on the living room furniture, quietly chatting, while sipping iced tea, when the little ones awakened. Liz held back allowing Jordan to accompany Caitlin with diaper detail. Sammie had disappeared into the kitchen to prepare formula for her children, then returned to the bedroom to find Caitlin and Jordan doting over the twins. Liz was nowhere to be found. Leaving the babies in the competent hands of their aunt's, Samantha went on a search for her missing sister. It didn't take long for her to be find Liz out in the back yard, kneeling by Sam's overgrown flower garden, gently pulling weeds. Sammie knelt down next to her and joined in pulling weeds.

"Lizzie, I've been covertly watching you." Her voice was quiet, filled with concern. "I have a feeling that you are acting in the role of your life, as my happy sister. Do you want to talk about how you are really feeling?"

"Not really, Samantha." She quietly responded, then sniffled as she kept her watery eyes focused on the weeds and flowers.

"I will respect that. Would it help you to hear me say, I'm sorry?" Sam whispered as she touched her sister's arm. That did it! Unwanted tears broke over her lids and tumbled down her cheeks, like water breaking over the Conklingville Dam. Liz stopped pulling weeds, pushed her sunglasses into her hair and wiped her eyes with a tissue, then returned the sunglasses to protect her eyes from the sunshine.

"Sammie, your twins, Mary Elizabeth and Daniel Mark, are beautiful." Liz sniffled as more tears tumbled. She drew in a calming breath. Then, without meeting her sister's watchful eyes said, "Those babies are precious miracles and you have every right to be happy."

"Yes, they are beautiful and I am happy. But, Lizzie, as much as I try, I can't imagine how hard it is for you to see me with two babies, when for whatever reason," Samantha drew in a breath to settle herself, then continued, "you were denied to have your child. Life is so unfair!"

Without another word, they clung to each other and wept for each other and for themselves. Liz sighed, then drew in a deep breath. This was real life. Not a scene on stage for Liz to direct. Their emotions, concern for each other, love, were all real.

"Sammie, unfair or not, life goes on for both of us. Yes, there are unexpected moments, like today, when I still grieve. Thank you, for caring in a way other haven't, or don't know how to. Well, besides Aunt Amanda and Mom." She gave Sammie a smile she didn't totally feel. Sighed and said, "We better go inside and save your kids from Caitlin totally spoiling them."

"More like Jordan. Caitlin, even though she means well, is too bossy and will keep them in line! Just look at how she took control of today?" Samantha smiled with a touch of playfulness in her eyes. "I used to think it was just a growing up thing when we were kids. But, watching Cait with us here today, it is obvious that she really does relish being the eldest sibling."

Liz couldn't help but laugh at Samantha's comments. There was humor and there was truth in her words. Caitlin, the eldest, did have a habit of expressing her opinions, whether her siblings wanted to hear them or not. Even so, Liz was also well aware of Cait's other traits that they all often overlooked. "A word of wisdom, my dear little sister: don't ever underestimate our older sister's love for us. Caitlin is someone you always want to have in your corner right along with Mom and Dad."

At that moment, the back door opened. Caitlin stuck her head out and called out, "There you two are! Sammie…" *Cluck, cluck, cluck!*

Liz and Samantha looked at each other, smiled, burst out with laughter as they linked arms and headed to the house, while Caitlin continued to express her thoughts to them.

The sun was setting over the western mountain ridge. Liz was sitting on the glider, gently rocking back and forth, not thinking of anything in particular, when she heard the sound of tires on the gravel drive. With darkness settling in, she didn't recognize the shape of the vehicle or the headlights when it came into view. A mystery. Liz had moved to the top of the steps and waited. As she stood there a wave of melancholy enveloped her. She sighed. Whomever was there was not Peter Jones. Peter Jones. It had been days, weeks since she had found herself second guessing her decision to break things off with him. John Runner had entered her life and Liz was enjoying exploring what his place was to be in her life.

A smile began to form as she listened to the quiet footsteps approaching her. Then the visitor took form. John. Liz drew in a quick breath. What did his presence mean? Was it coincidence that she had just been thinking of Peter and then John? She drew in a deeper breath. It had been a week since they had last seen each other. On that day, John had stopped in to see her at the Community Arts building, and they had discussed the fall program that they were putting together for the community on fire safety.

"Good evening," Liz's voice was clear in the still of the night cool summer night. The peepers and tree toads were beginning their evening songs, as if they had been waiting for Liz's permission to sing. A bat swooped low from the old barn towards the forest. She hardly noticed, as she felt her breath catch with anticipation as John approached the stairs.

"Good evening, Elizabeth." John was now standing in the shadows at the bottom of the steps looking up at her silhouette, as she stood with the porch light behind her. "I know that you were not expecting me to come over this evening. I should have called, but I -"

"John, you don't need to apologize. I've been a night owl since I was just a kid. Mom and Dad used to have quite a time getting me to settle down for the night." She softly laughed, then continued. "In a way it was natural for me to gravitate towards a profession that requires me to work in the evening. So, you need not worry about me being sleepy and heading to bed." She smiled invitingly at him, as she felt the energy being exchanged between them, drawing them together. "And, you're always welcome to come visit. In fact, you're right on time to sit with me, and watch the stars begin their night-time dance in the sky."

His footsteps were not heard as he came up the stairs. He didn't waste any time drawing her into his arms. Liz in turn raised her arms to his shoulders. Then, without a word, John lowered his lips to brush hers. Warmth. Tenderness. Everything Liz needed. Their lips meld deeper together. It was like coming home after a long, weary drive. John drew Liz closer to him so their bodies were touching. As if on cue, in the changing of a musical score, their kiss deepened with their sensual dance, as their lips parted and their tongues touched. They savored every moment of the fire growing between them, as night fell around them. The stars they had planned to watch together, appeared overhead without either of them noticing. The sky and nocturnal sounds of nature joined together, and provided the necessary backdrop for the scene that they were creating together.

Finally, they drew apart. Both were stunned and shaken by their mutual response. They drew in steadying breaths as their eyes shifted and gazed out into the darkness.

John sighed as his hand gently stroked Liz's jaw. His eyes once again held hers. "Elizabeth, as much as I was enjoying the moment between us, I have just about reached the point of no return." John's heart was racing, his body vibrated with desire as he drew in a slow breath, then continued, "As much as I'm enjoying having you in my arms, well, I don't want our first time to be -"

Liz gently placed her finger on his lips. She was well aware of what was happening between them. She too was feeling deep needs, unexpectedly bubbling up within her from the intimacy that they had just shared. They had a connection that she had never experienced with another man. Not Greg or Peter.

"John," her voice was soft, filled with emotion. "I also had nearly reached the point of no return. What we have between us is special, I appreciate the respect that you have shown me here tonight, and I look forward to seeing where the future takes us." Then, she softly chuckled.

"What is it?" He asked. Watching. Waiting for her to open up and share her world with him.

"I was just thinking about my family and how they have been known to arrive here at the worst time."

"Oh, like your parent's interrupting our private dancing at the jazz fest." He nodded in understanding as he gently tucked a stray piece of hair behind Liz's ear. The brushing of his fingertips against her scalp sent warmth vibrating through her.

"You have no idea!" Liz smiled as her eyes sparkled like the stars twinkling in the sky overhead. "The jazz fest with Mom and Dad was nothing compared to what my Aunt Amanda can be like."

"From what you've shared with me in our conversations about your family, your aunt sounds like she's quite a character."

Liz laughed as they slowly stood from the glider, and began to walk towards the stairs. "My aunt is indescribable. She is someone you have to experience."

"All jokes aside, knowing how important your aunt is in your life, I look forward to the day when we meet."

Liz stopped as they reached the top step. She turned to face him, looked up into his eyes, and asked, "Are you real? Or, am I asleep and dreaming? Have I conjured you up in my overactive mind?"

His fingers softly stroked her jaws, like the whisper of the wind, before gently holding them in his fingers. He tenderly held her eyes with his as he said, "I'm as real to you, as you are to me. The Great Spirit has drawn us from our rough places of sorrow to here on the flat plain. We have met to walk life's journey together, for how long? That is for The Great Spirit to know. We will take each day as it comes, and give thanks for what we have been given to take care of."

Liz laid in bed, reflecting on John's words that he had shared before leaving for the night. A hoot owl called out in the night from over in the woods. *Who, who, who, who!* There was a bit of a ruckus outside her bedroom window. Then, the most unpleasant aroma drifted in through the open screened window. A skunk had just sprayed. Phew! Oh! How it stunk! Liz coughed and gagged. Oh, it was awful! She sprang from her bed and closed the window, hoping she had been quick enough so that the pungent odor did not seep into her clothes and the cabin. She dropped back into her bed, drew her pillow over her face and moaned. Tentatively removing the pillow from her face, she drew in a cautious breath. Her worst fears were confirmed. The cabin would need to be aired out from the skunk passing nearby! Liz sighed, shook her head and grumbled as she went about opening all the windows, and opened Great Gram's old tattered book of handwritten remedies for different things. Skunks, Liz discovered, had two pages of different things to do to rid oneself, clothing, dogs, cats, even a horse, and the cabin of the stench that they left in their wake.

The sound of jazz music filled the cabin, and wonderful aromas of sausage, cinnamon and other spices suggested homemade coffee cake was in the oven. These were aiding in de-skunking the cabin. The smell of fresh brewed coffee filled Liz's senses, drawing her from sleep to wakefulness. She glanced at the bedside clock. 7:30a.m. She moaned, yawned and felt a pang of hunger. Great! After last night's adventure with the skunk, Liz was not in the mood to entertain family. Jordan had returned to Long Island the week before, so she couldn't imagine what her parent's or Caitlin were doing up at the cabin this early in the morning.

Liz emerged with hair rumpled, in a tee shirt and shorts that had absorbed the skunk odor, and bare feet. Needless to say, she was in desperate need of a shower, as she yawned and looked around the kitchen that was illuminated by the sunlight light casting in through the window.

"Aunt Amanda! Uncle Kevin!" She exclaimed in total surprise and confusion. "What are you two doing here this early in the day?" She glanced around the kitchen at what her aunt and uncle were busily preparing for breakfast. With the few hours of restless sleep that Liz had, she knew that they had not slept there last night. When had they arrived? Liz was so confused. So, she began to unravel her thoughts with the most obvious questions, while she rubbed her sleepy eyes. "When did you get here? What's all this?"

"Good morning." Amanda responded, as she wiped her hands and stepped over to hug Liz. She continued to speak as Liz moved from her to Kevin for a hug. "A little birdie ratted you out to me that, for too many mornings this summer you have not been eating a good healthy breakfast. So, we came to make you a good hearty breakfast to get you started for your busy day. From the unpleasant aroma that greeted us this morning, and open windows, I gather we arrived right on time to help you finish the unpleasant job of de-skunking this place." Amanda's eyes shimmered with delight. Liz was not smiling. There was no humor in the adventures that she had with the skunk that had passed by last night.

"It's not so bad, now that you've been cooking. Thank you." Liz still was not smiling as she helped herself to a cup of steaming hot coffee. She sighed with delight as the pleasant aroma filled her. "Now that I'm beginning to be human and coherent, do you mind telling me when you got here? Did you drive all night?"

At that moment, the timer rang indicating that the coffee cake was finished baking in the oven. Amanda busied herself as Kevin, who was leaning against the counter with a small bowl in his hand and whisk in the other busily scrambling the eggs that would go into the iron skillet, after the sausage was finished cooking responded to Liz. She sipped her coffee and listened.

"We left last night as soon as we both got home from work and loaded the car. Once we made it to Albany, with everyone else who was heading north, we decided to stay on the NYS Thruway over to Amsterdam and then up route 30, rather than going to Saratoga and over the local roads." Kevin yawned into his upper arm to contain some of his germs. Liz couldn't help but smile as he said, "Oh, excuse me!"

"You're fine, Uncle Kevin." Liz's eyes were beginning to soften to the idea of two of her favorite people invading her morning. She took a sip of coffee. Swallowed, as she gave thought to how they had traveled there. "Actually, you made a wise decision to go to Amsterdam. You should remember that, Aunt Amanda!" She did, and Liz laughed at her response. "Well, our side of the mountains is a little quieter, more peaceful. Certainly, more peaceful than last night. There was a sellout concert at SPAC— Saratoga Performing Arts Center. Plus, the city of Saratoga is still mobbed with people from the Traver's Day Race last weekend. Then of course, this weekend is the last weekend of racing for the season and there are plenty of people in the area. Summer in the Adirondacks. There's nothing better!"

"Oh, I do remember some summers worth forgetting." Amanda sighed, then added with a tender look in her eyes, "I'm glad your summer memories are turning out to be more pleasant. Well, except for the skunk!"

They all laughed. Amanda had become wound up from the lack of sleep and the caffeine she had consumed. Liz sipped her coffee as she listened to her aunt share a story about her, Liz's dad and their mutual friends summer adventures at Saratoga. She wasn't too surprised to hear that they stayed away from the track and attended concerts at SPAC. Liz also realized that there was a lot about her dad's youth that she had previously not been privileged to know about him. Interesting.

"So, I gather you stayed in a hotel somewhere between Albany and here?" Liz was feeling more awake as she sipped the coffee. She found herself beginning to smile as she listened to her aunt and uncle.

"With how late it was when we got off the thruway in Amsterdam, we decided to stay in a hotel for the night." Kevin said, then yawned again.

"Actually, you decided for us." Amanda clarified with a raised brow and spatula in her hand pointed accusingly at him.

"Well, we both were tired, and that would have been fine, if there hadn't been a group of motorcyclists who also decided to stay there, and did not pay attention to quiet hours. Then, there were a couple of long-distance transit haulers who were parked close to our room. We had just settled into bed when they started up their rigs. Well, words were exchanged between the motorcyclists and the truckers."

"Elizabeth, Kevin is making light of it! The noise of the various motors and the men's language was terrible!" Amanda added, as she returned her attention to the sausage, she was cooking in the frying pan over medium heat. Liz's stomach grumbled loud enough for Amanda to glance at her with a raised brow. Liz didn't respond. She took a sip of coffee instead. Amanda simply shook her head.

"Needless to say, neither one of us got much sleep last night, actually, early this morning. So, we got up, dressed, checked out, and headed here for much needed peace and quiet. We stopped at the Walmart on route 30 -"

"I know the one you mean, Uncle Kevin." Liz added, then softly laughed at her aunt's comment before Kevin added, "It was an adventure to shop early this morning with your aunt."

"Oh? Do tell, Uncle Kevin." Liz playfully encouraged. He did. Liz listened to their tired voices, and noticed the tender glances they shared as they conversed with her. As she listened, the conversation she had with John came back to mind. Even with the significant age differences between her and her aunt's generation, Liz was beginning to see some similarities in their relationships. Rough places. Pain. Suffering. Life leveling out. Peace. Happiness. Love. Liz sighed.

"Do you care to share with us where you disappeared to for a moment in that mind of yours?" Amanda quietly asked as she nudged Liz with her hip from where she stood in front of the sink, so that she could wash her hands. Liz smiled and shook her head, as Amanda grabbed the hand towel to dry her hands. Her eyes studied her niece. "I gather it was a very pleasant place. I'm glad." Liz nodded as Amanda continued, "It's good to see you happy. Now, grab some more coffee for yourself and go sit down for breakfast."

Liz couldn't help but laugh. Her eyes shone with happiness as she exclaimed, "Aunt Amanda, if I didn't know any better, the way you just spoke to me, I'd think Caitlin had taken her bossy lessons from you!"

"Trust me, even if I had been around here when you all were young, Caitlin, would not have needed any lessons from me." Amanda responded, then punctuated her thought with a roll of her eyes.

Laughter filled the cabin as Elizabeth and her aunt and uncle continued to discuss the joys and woes of the sibling pecking order.

Liz was intrigued as she listened to Kevin share his feelings towards his older brother, Kurt, who happens to be the eldest. She had met Kurt and his wife Madeline last year when she was visiting her aunt and uncle at their home in Baltimore, before coming home to the Great Sac Community. Liz had liked them and many other members of Kevin's family whom she has met, especially his granddaughters. They all had made her feel loved and included as part of their family, even though she wasn't.

It was shortly before 9:00 o'clock when they finally got up from the breakfast table. Amanda had just handed Liz the family skunk odor cleansing lotion that she had made, and shooed her out of the kitchen to get herself ready for her day, when the front door opened. A familiar voice called out a morning greeting, as Jim and Melissa entered. Of course, their arrival once again deterred Liz from her morning routine and plans. It was a good thing that she had already called and given Josh a heads up about the skunk, and her need to de-skunk herself before going to work at the arts colony. Finally, with her mother's gentle nudging, and the concoction her aunt had made in her hand, Liz disappeared into the bathroom to shower and wash her hair.

A short time later, Liz reemerged from the bedroom in the clean undergarments, cotton sleeveless top, and jeans her aunt had washed and hung out to dry earlier in the morning. The clothes smelled normal with no trace of the smell of a skunk. Of course, before Liz headed out the door, her dad seized the opportunity to tease her more about the previous night's misadventure. Both Amanda and Melissa came to Liz's defense, only to have Jim remind Amanda of her own unfortunate encounter with a skunk. It had been over forty years since Amanda had come face to face with a skunk. Fortunately, it wasn't rabid. But oh goodness! It sure did stink! Liz couldn't help but laugh as she listened to her dad and her aunt. Hearing them remembering the experience, remembering their grandmother, mother and great uncle, whom Liz had never known, helped her feel better about what had happened. Now she had one more thing to add to her list of things she shared with her aunt. The loss of a child and a skunk! What a combination?!

"Alright, Jim," Amanda's voice had a touch of warning, while her eyes shimmered with playfulness. "Teasing Amanda time is officially finished for today."

"Don't count on it, little sister." His dark eyes simmered with mischievousness as his lips turned upward. The downward tilt of her chin caused Jim to chuckle.

"You really are a pain," Amanda exhaled, shook her head and asked, "Why, don't you give Mel and me some peace and quiet, and go out back with Kevin and mark out the area that we have discussed for the addition?" Amanda suggested.

"Addition! What addition?" Liz asked. This was the first she had heard anything about it. She gazed between her family members, and realized that there was more to her aunt and uncle being there, than the summer theater's final weekend. Obviously, a whole lot more!

"We've been in conversation about the layout of the cabin for some time. Now that we have the loft open for guests, we are going to be making changes to gram's room to convert it into a larger master bedroom with a handicap accessible bathroom for when Kevin and I semi-retire here."

Liz's eyes sparkled with delight at the prospect of her aunt and uncle spending more time in the north country. "Oh wow! So, you're moving here? When?" Liz's face fully shone with happiness as she looked around the table at her family members gathered there.

"Liz, as your aunt said, the move will not be permanent," Kevin reiterated, then gazed and winked at Amanda, "But, we will certainly be here for longer periods of time, and considering that Amanda and I are getting older, we are planning ahead for our changing physical needs."

"Well, I approve of anything you want to do here, not that my input really matters." Liz smiled as her aunt and uncle responded. Then she grew serious as she looked at her father. "Dad, please do me a favor, and don't argue with Aunt Amanda and Uncle Kevin over what they want to do here."

Jim gave his daughter his look that said, *child, don't press your luck!* Then he said, "Lizzie J, I've already agreed to everything your aunt has said that she wants to do here. But you know, from your own experiences with your brother and sisters, that there is a limit to your patience with them. Well, there's also limit to my patience with her and her demands. So, I'm sorry to say that you're asking the impossible for me to not argue with your aunt." His sober expression did not reveal whether he was teasing or not. Liz raised a brow in concern. What if he was serious and did disagree with Aunt Amanda, causing her and Uncle Kevin to decide to not come north anymore?

Amanda rolled her eyes, shook her head and huffed. "Oh, stop teasing your daughter!" She cuffed his upper arm as she continued to chew at him, as only a younger sister was—or at least thought— she was entitled to do.

"Hey now, little sister, you had best watch your hands. I just might have to press charges against you for sibling abuse." Jim smiled as Amanda responded. She reminded him of a crow cawing as it took flight from a corn field. He chuckled while Amanda continued to sputter, and Melissa and Kevin commented on their observations of the Callison siblings.

Liz threw her hands up in surrender. "Oh, Dad! I should have known that you were teasing me! Thanks for sticking up for me, Aunt Amanda. At least I know you have my back!" Amanda commented, causing everyone to laugh. Liz rolled her eyes and shook her head in surrender. Everyone had always called Liz and Caitlin two peas in a pod. Well, she'd like to set them all straight because the two original peas were standing next to her. "See you all tonight." She then hugged each of her loved ones, bid them farewell and headed off to work.

"Jim, you really shouldn't have teased Liz like that this morning." Amanda quietly said to Jim as they sat out back under the shade of the maple tree, sipping sun made iced tea.

"I know I shouldn't have teased Lizzie like that. But you have to admit, her expression was priceless." Jim had a twinkle in his eyes. It was the one Amanda loved to see on him—it told her he was happy.

"One of these days our kids are going to retaliate against you for your teasing." Melissa added. "When they do, don't be surprised when I say, "I told you so!"

Amanda lazily smiled as the four of them conversed, laughed, and eased into companionable silence, until someone else found something of importance to say to them. The refreshing breeze up on the side of the mountain, the cool shade of the maple tree, quiet conversation was all conducive for Amanda to relax. As she sat with Kevin, Jim and Melissa she found it increasingly difficult for her to keep her eyes open. She yawned. The gentle touch of Kevin's hand on her forearm drew her fully awake.

"Sweetheart," his voice was quiet, filled with tender suggestion, "Since you worked a full day, then drove halfway here, added to not getting much sleep last night, perhaps you'd like to go in and rest on the bed."

Amanda yawned. "Oh, Kevin, you take such good care of me. I am tired, and think I will go in and take a nap." With that, she stood, apologized for leaving them, then slowly made her way along the old walkway to the back door leading into the kitchen.

Both Jim and Melissa noticed the way that she was moving with obvious stiffness on her right side. Mel and Amanda had gone hiking with their granddaughters last summer, so Mel was aware of some of Amanda's limitations—not so many that she would allow to hold her down. What Mel was seeing this summer, as Amanda walked away from her, it concerned her. So, Melissa, along with Jim commented to Kevin about the changes that they both were seeing in Amanda's limping. It was years ago. It was during Amanda and Jim's estrangement that Amanda had been in the near fatal motorcycle car accident. With how mangled her Harley was, how broken her body was, it was truly a miracle that she had lived. Kevin had been the assistant director of the Shock Trauma ER at that time, and had cared for Amanda when she was brought into the trauma bay on that hot mid-summer Saturday. At that time, they were strangers. Patient-doctor. Life moved on for both of them. Then, in 2009 their mutual friends had introduced them. It didn't take long for them to connect the pieces of their lives, their past encounter with one another. Kevin recognized that spirit that had amazed him so long ago, was still a vital part of Amanda. They fell in love and married. Now Kevin sat and quietly shared with Jim and Melissa his concerns on multiple levels from his extended family issues, to his greatest concerns, the physical changes that were happening with Amanda's body, and the impending surgery to address her aging hardware in her leg.

"So, Sis has been putting off her surgery because of your sister's battle with cancer, and wanting to come north to support Elizabeth and her summer theater program." Jim stated while shaking his head.

Kevin sighed. "That's right, Jim. Amanda was adamant with me and her surgeon about us going to Arizona to be with my sister Cora, and to help care for her family when Cora had her surgery. When we were out there, I noticed other changes with Amanda's mobility. These were things that she couldn't easily hide or attribute to doing something out of the ordinary in her day. You can be sure that we had words when I confronted her about her condition."

"I'm surprised it took you that long to notice." Melissa stated.

Both Kevin and Jim looked at her in surprise. Kevin asked for Melissa to elaborate on what she meant by her statement. She did, and unfortunately, it didn't help Kevin with his concerns and annoyance with his beloved wife. As the conversation was moving on to other topics of interest, Jim's cell phone rang.

"Hello," he answered in an even tone. Listened. Released a short breath and said, "Yes, Johnson, Manda and Kevin are here." Jim's eyes and Kevin's met. He rolled his eyes, as Kevin shook his head, Melissa mumbled under her breath, and together they listened to Jim's side of the conversation. "Neither of them has mentioned anything about Summer to me or Mel—to my knowledge." He added. "No. The last I knew, Sis and Summer were still not on speaking terms." Jim shook his head as he listened to Johnson sputter on about his sister, and watched Kevin and Melissa quietly conversing together. "Look," Jim sighed. "You have no one to blame, but yourself for this mess. What you did was wrong. You might be my friend, but Amanda is my sister, and this time, I am doing what is right. I'm standing by Amanda. That's right! Now, if, and when you decide to broach the subject of your stupidity with her, make sure you do it when I'm around. That's right. No. I won't be there to defend you. I want to be a witness to Amanda skinning you with her words."

Amanda had risen from her rest, and had come into the kitchen to get a cold drink of water from the faucet. With the door open, allowing the cool breeze to enter the kitchen, no one saw her from where she stood in the shadows. But Amanda had a perfect location to see and hear what was happening in the back yard. It didn't take long for her to figure out who Jim was speaking with, especially when he raised his voice. For a moment she had to wonder if, the skinning of Johnson was to follow her stringing him up for bear bait. She sighed and shook her head, as unanticipated moisture formed in her lids, and an unexpected tear slid down her cheek. She thought of their grandmother's words from so very long ago. Jim was proving to be the good man that gram had said he was. He had figured out what is most important in life. The love of family, and today Jim Callison was proving it. Amanda sniffled, then breathed out in a whisper, *"Thank you, Gram."*

CHAPTER 18

Cheers erupted as the sellout crowd stood to congratulate Liz, the cast and crew for their production of *Barefoot in the Park.* As the curtain opened for the final call, Elizabeth, dressed from head to toe in black, along with the stage and lighting crew, emerged to take her place on center stage. She bowed to the audience, then turned, applauded and bowed to her cast and crew, before partially turning again to the crowd and sweeping her arm towards her troupe. Yes. She was the director. However, without the people who stood on the stage with her, Liz knew that without them, their sweat, their drive and passion along with her for the performing arts, the Great Sacandaga Community would not have had a successful summer theater season. Tears of joy streamed down her cheeks as Josh, her assistant director, who in many ways was like a brother to Liz, handed her a bouquet of long-stemmed red roses. She didn't care if her tears looked silly, as the reality of all of the hard work of her past year set in. The accolades that she, and her theater troupe were receiving from the community on that star lit, cool, summer night in the lower Adirondack Mountains, meant more to Elizabeth than a phenomenal critics review in the arts section of the New York Times.

She was a success where it mattered most, in her hometown with her family and friends.

Liz was euphoric as she made her way down the side stairs into the orchestra pit to where her family and John were waiting for her. Hugs, tears and laughter flowed from the Callison women. Liz thought she saw her dad sniffle back his emotions, and perhaps a touch of moisture in his eyes. His expression caused Liz to lose control of her tears once again. Without a word, Jim drew his daughter into his arms. Like a 'big old proud papa bear,' he was ready to quietly whisper words for only Liz to hear. As Liz snuggled into her father's arms, she handed off her roses to the family member standing closest to her. Callie Anne promptly stood a bit taller when she took a hold of the roses for her aunt. Liz sniffled, drew in a calming breath and then released it. A few moments later, without a word spoken there was the parting of the Callison family and John emerged to stand in front of Liz. John reached out and tenderly took Liz's hand into his. He drew her fingers to his lips and gently kissed them. Liz didn't notice her sisters and mother's reaction to John's greeting. Nor, did she notice when her family quietly slipped away, or what the cast and crew were doing. At that moment, there was only Liz and John.

Then John drew Liz into his arms. His eyes held hers as he whispered, "I'm so proud of you. I'll kiss you for real when we're alone." She nodded. "Elizabeth, this production was amazing! People sitting around me were raving about the quality of your work, and they are already looking forward to next summer. So am I." His hands gently stroked her back-touching spots that Liz hadn't realized were aching. She moaned and seemed to melt under his touch. John continued to rub in that spot causing Liz to nearly purr like a content kitten.

"Thank you for everything, John. For being here with me. For telling me what others have said." Liz sighed, as she leaned against him. "I can't believe we did it! My theater friends, high school youth, community volunteers and my family, they all pulled together and did an outstanding job."

John lifted his fingers to her chin and gently tucked it between his thumb and index finger. Tilting her chin to gaze in her eyes, he responded. "You, Elizabeth Callison, were the director of this troupe. Remember, I've been here and seen firsthand how you are with every one of these people. You conduct yourself in a way that commands respect, without being obnoxious. You are genuine in living out your passion, and you alone are the reason that everyone else has shone so brightly. Broadway may boast of having Tony Award winning directors, but after tonight's finale, they hold nothing over the Great Sacandaga Community. We have you, sweetheart. You, Elizabeth Callison are our star!"

His words made Liz's head spin. She felt as if someone had filled her with helium and she would float on air, if, it wasn't for John holding her down on the ground. John's accolades, and his calling her sweetheart had touched her deep within. Liz leaned into him, as his arms slid back around her. "And I have you." Liz quietly added. "Will you join us at our afterglow party?"

"I'd love to." John released his hold on Liz, laced his fingers with hers as they started up the stairs. At the corner of the stage, they paused. "Guys and gals!" Liz called out, "Don't spend any more time than is necessary here tonight. We'll break this set down tomorrow. For now, we all have a party to attend."

John quietly watched and listened, as Liz spoke with her crew, then waited for them to make their way off the stage towards the mess hall to join the party. "If you hadn't stopped to talk with the crew, would they have come over to the party?" John asked, as he was absorbing her theater world, wanting to know the intricacies of putting on a production, at least the closing at this point in time.

"Eventually, they would have made their way over to join in the celebration." She sighed with contentment. "This has been a wonderful summer theater season. As crazy as it has been in bringing this theater back to life, the first production, all the little events during this summer and our final show I hate to see it all end. Yes, I have events planned for here in the fall, as well as our fall and winter events planned to take place at the community arts center, but it won't be the same. The theater is special."

John paused in his step. He drew Liz against him, with his fingers, he tenderly touched her chin, tilting it up so their eyes met in the moonlit night and solar lights on the pathway. Their eyes spoke as John's lips brushed against hers. Moist, warm heat sizzled between them. Then the sounds of the party getting underway drew them apart and back to the present.

Liz softly smiled, and quietly spoke, as if, to not disturb the mood or night around them. "If, this production had been on, or, off Broadway, and we were celebrating our show's success in a private club in the city, there would be copious amounts of alcohol." She laughed. "You can be sure someone has seen to it to bring something with a kick to it, even though I've told them our party will be alcohol free. But still, our afterglow party is different from what it would have been in the city. Back there besides the alcohol, someone may have brought illegal drugs to share with those inclined. Here, my troupe knows my feeling about drugs, and to my knowledge they are in agreement with me that there is no place for illegal drugs in this arts colony. In the city, the crew that you saw still working on the stage would have arrived at the party when many people were trashed -" Her voice trailed off.

"And you liked to be a part of that type of partying?" He asked with innocent curiosity, not accusatory.

"I understood the culture around me, and tended to stay with my select group of friends. We would usually make an appearance at the afterglow, size up what was happening and then head home. My choices of not actively participating in the culture, opened the door for my former boyfriend to stay behind and make plays on other single women. Then, as if that hadn't provided Greg with enough opportunities to cheat on me, when my sister Jordan came to see our show," Suddenly, Liz felt as if she was like a mountain stream thawed with the warmth of spring and rushing down the mountain impatiently seeking to join the larger streams and rivers. She fought back unwanted or expected tears, "Sadly, it was during a vulnerable point in Jordan's marriage that Greg seized his opportunity and committed adultery with her." Liz released a long, slow breath. "In retrospect, I am glad I had the ten years' worth of experiences in New York City. Of course, Jordan and I both could have done without our family drama. But those lessons—the good, the bad and all of them—prepared me to move on and spread my wings as the director here in the Great Sacandaga Community. This valley in the lower Adirondack Park is home. My home. The place where I hope to someday have a family of my own. Of course, now given my age and the fact that I am single, I am probably going to have to look into adoption. Maybe I can be content with foster care." She shrugged. "I guess for now, I have to wait and see what The Great Spirit—God—has planned for me. Maybe I'll have to be content with simply being a doting aunt."

For a brief moment they walked along in companionable silence, as both were lost in their own thoughts. John had listened closely to Liz's thoughts, her very intimate feelings about her life. He wondered how often she allowed herself to be this revealing of herself with others. As he was enjoying getting to know her, he knew in his heart that for Elizabeth to reveal this much of herself to him, she must truly trust him. He was glad. Trust was something that John did not take for granted. He knew all too well from his own experiences that without trust between the couple, a relationship would not work. They had nearly reached the porch of the mess hall when John paused, causing Liz to abruptly stop and begin to trip over her own feet. His hand gently took hold of her elbow to steady her. He continued to lightly hold her arm as he spoke with quietness, as if to not disturb the rhythm of the night sounds of the tree toads and Katy-Did. An owl hooted as he said, "Trust in the Lord with all your heart, and do not rely on your own insight. In all your ways acknowledge him, and he will make straight your paths."

"Proverbs 3:5 and 6." Liz breathed out. She felt a sense of warmth flow through her body. John had shared scripture, but not to be preachy as some people can be. Liz understood his words as his caring for her, as well as, his insight into what she had shared with him about her and Jordan's demise last year. He spoke with wisdom and deep spirituality that caused Liz to silently pray, thanking God for leading her to this man. A smile filled her heart and found its way to her lips as she thought, *I can't wait to see where this new path leads me to!*

Laughter. Teasing. Singing - on and deliberately off key. Liz sighed, re-positioned her sunglasses, as she walked towards the amphitheater on the cool early morning following the closing night of the summer theater season. The noise of screw guns reversing screws out of the set pieces and backdrops, pieces of lumber being neatly piled up on the side of the stage, raised voices clearly heard over the business of breaking down the set, waterproof containers stacked and ready to be filled with props, all this and more caused a bittersweet smile to creep onto Liz's face before she drew in a deep breath and then took a sip of coffee. She looked around at everyone and everything that was going on in the arts colony. Moisture was forming in the depths of her eyes. Now, under the guidance of Josh, her summer theater assistant director for only a few more short hours, everyone was busy attending to the task at hand. Even though there was a joyfulness with the cast and crew busily working together, Liz knew that there was also a sense of sadness lurking within them. Yes, her friends and colleagues who had worked for a mere pittance, would return to the stage on and off Broadway. They were already talking about their next auditions, and plans for the winter. But even though they were going on to different things, this was also goodbye to the stage that had been their home for a brief season in time. Liz understood their emotions as she too was dealing with the magnitude of what they had accomplished together. In less than a year, with numerous hiccups along the way—the discovery of her grandfather's remains being prominent—Liz had met her personal and professional goals even though many of the community arts association board had said that her vision was impossible. She paused at the rear of the theater house next to the last row of bleachers, sipped her coffee and watched her troupe work together. The moisture was increasing. "Oh, what the heck!" She said out loud, as she allowed the tears to fall. At that moment, Andre and Natasha noticed her from where they stood on the stage and they began doing improvisation. Then Blaine joined in and others. Liz was so overcome by her emotions that she sat down on the bleacher and watched. Speechless. Tears streamed down her cheeks. Sobs followed as Andrea said, "And so, dear Elizabeth, our friend and director, this is the end of our season, the first of many more to come. You are stuck with us because," he then turned his head from side to side to the others gathered on stage with him, and looked back at Liz with open arms as they all shouted, "We love you, darling!"

Liz was a mess! She cried, laughed, snorted and hiccupped, not necessarily in that order. But it didn't matter. Today was to be a very emotional day, and everyone else was right there with her emotionally. Family goodbyes, especially in the life of the theater, were never easy. Drawing in a centering breath, Liz stood and made her way to the stage. From then on to early afternoon when they took a break for lunch, Liz worked side by side with the cast and crew. Props and set pieces were categorized, plastic bins were labeled and put away on new sturdy shelves in the prop and set storage rooms under the stage.

Tarps and plastic were secured around backdrops, lumber was stored on the upper area above the stage, along with the portable lighting. After lunch it was time for everyone to return to their cabins and pack up the rest of their belongings and then leave.

Natasha found Liz in her small office in the back of the mess hall. She silently stood in the doorway watching Liz as she sat at her desk, dabbed her eyes, and sought to gain her composure. The light tapping of Natasha's knuckles on the door casing drew Liz's attention. She sniffled and looked up.

"Hey," she attempted to smile. Who was she kidding? Natasha would see right through her smile and know how sad she was, so Liz didn't even try to hide it. She stood and moved towards her friend. "So, does this mean that you and Andre are ready to head out?"

"Almost. We are waiting on Blaine and the others. I wanted a few minutes to be alone with you."

"I'm glad we have these few minutes to be together. You know, Natasha, I'm going to miss you and everyone else." Liz sighed, then blew her nose. She was an emotional mess! "I always did hate the end of a shows run. This summer is no different."

"I know exactly what you mean." Natasha went on to share memories with Liz, who in turn added some of her own. They laughed, sniffled, and shed a few more tears together, as they walked arm in arm towards the parking lot.

It was time for final farewells to begin. More hugs. More tears. More laughter, and to Liz's delight, everyone told her that they expected to receive a call from her during the winter to invite them back for next season. Yes, the Great Sacandaga Community Summer Stock Theater had been a success. The fact that her friends were willing to give up the money that they could make working in the city to work in a small community theater, meant the world to her. Andre, Natasha, Blaine, Anton and the others were lingering, while one more group of crew members was slowly pulling out of the parking lot, when a familiar SUV pulled in and came to a stop next to Liz's vehicle.

"Liz darling, Anton looked concerned. "Are we going to have more drama with your new man being jealous of us hugging you as we say goodbye?"

A sad smile tugged at Liz's lips, as she recalled the horrid scene with Peter, at the beginning of the summer theater season. "Thank you for your concern, Anton. I happen to believe that John is in a different place in his life, from where Peter was when he met all of you. In fact, I happen to know that John has enjoyed getting to know each of you." As Liz finished speaking, John emerged from his vehicle. He smiled and waved as he headed towards them. "See!" Her eyes remained focused on John as she commented to them, "You do realize that he came to see you all off. Don't you?"

"Hello, everyone!" John called out as he approached them.

Greetings were exchanged, as John eased next to Liz. His eyes held hers for a moment before he turned to the others. No one missed the warm connection between Liz and John. Her protective friends indicated their approval of John, with slight nods, smiles, a wink, and other positive subtle expressions, and Liz was glad. In fact, her heart was bubbling with happiness like a shaken bottle of a carbonated beverage about ready to burst. John's voice told her that he cared as he said, "Liz had told me that you all would probably be heading out by midafternoon. I see that, if, I had been any later, sadly, you would have left before I had gotten here to say goodbye."

Liz listened to the quiet dialogue exchanged between John and her friends. In a brief time of them all becoming acquainted, and she and John began to casually date, mutual friendship between John and her theater family was being established. There was no apparent jealousy. As she listened to them, her recent conversation with John came to mind. Liz felt her heart do a flip flop. The man trusted her. In that moment, Liz realized she trusted him as well, and she was falling in love with John. When had that happened? She couldn't be in love. It was too soon! Or, was it? Their relationship wasn't even serious— or was it? One thing Liz was sure of: she had questions and in time she would be finding answers.

Liz felt Natasha slip her hand around her arm. Their eyes met, silently conversing as Natasha addressed everyone. "Will you all excuse us for a moment? I need to have a final private word with our dear Elizabeth, before we leave."

John and the others watched as they stepped away, arms linked together. He knew from having visited Liz and the theater troupe that their friendships were strong. It was also apparent to John that, Liz was having a difficult time with her friends parting, and he was glad that he would be there to comfort her when they were gone. For now, he turned his attention to Andre, and the others, while remaining fully aware of Liz's presence close by. It touched his heart when those surrounding him warned him, "Our Elizabeth is a very special friend and colleague. Within the past two years we've seen two men break her heart. So far, since meeting you and spending time with you during this summer, we like what we see in you, Forest Ranger John. Elizabeth acts tough, but underneath her exterior is a caring, loving, gentle person. Treat her well, and we will not have cause to dislike you."

John had admired Liz's friends. Now, their loyalty to Liz had skyrocketed them to the top of his list as people whom he respected. His eyes and the slight turning of his lips upward revealed his earnest thoughts. "I agree that Elizabeth is all that you say and more. In the company of the wilderness and its spirits, and God as my witness, I assure you I am not like the men of her past." He nodded as his gaze wandered towards Liz. "I plan on taking very good care of Elizabeth Callison." Then John smiled fully. His dark eyes twinkled with unspoken knowledge, leaving them all to wonder what he was thinking.

When the last car door was closed, the last motor started, final goodbyes and waves as each vehicle slowly pulled out of the parking lot, John eased Liz into his arms. Without a word spoken between them John lowered his lips to hers. The sun shone bright in the sky sending its heat down upon them. Truth be told, the sun's heat was nothing compared to the heat sizzling between them. Liz was used to playing with the buttons on John's uniform shirt. Today he was casually dressed in a dark blue tee shirt, and well-worn jeans that hugged him in all the right places. She enjoyed gently touching him feeling his chest and abdominal muscles ripple underneath the cotton fabric against her fingers. She was lost in the moment, the sensations of John's fingers brushing her skin on her back where her blouse and jeans met. Then, without warning she felt a tug of her ponytail that stuck out from the back of her baseball cap on her head.

"Owe!" She gasped as she pulled away from John. Needless to say, their romantic moment was broken. Liz scowled as she turned from John. "That was not necessary!" She huffed.

"I didn't do anything!" John exclaimed. His eyes were wide with confusion, as he held up his hands in defense.

"Sorry, John. I wasn't yelling at you. It's our resident spirits." She sighed. "Later, I'll fill you in on everything thing these two mischievous spirits have been up to this spring and summer." Liz turned to face the parking lot that appeared to be empty. "But for now, you two—I should have known you both have been too quiet!" She stepped away from John. "Really! Pulling my hair? Now, isn't that a bit childish?"

John listened as Liz continued to converse with nothing that he could see. A lazy smile began to take form, as his drawn brow began to relax. John was wise enough to know that the spirits were real, and he was beginning to sense their presence in their midst. Interesting. And for whatever their reason, they had developed a relationship with Liz. "In the past, have they done anything to hurt you?" He asked.

"No. They simply like to tease me, and play jokes on me." She smiled at John, then turned her gaze in the area where she suspected that they might be lingering. "Spirits, thank you for leaving the theater troupe alone, as I requested. See. I held true to my promise, and they have left us until next spring when they will return. I'll be coming back out here to finish closing down the buildings for winter. Then, I too, will leave you in peace and quiet. But I do warn you that I may have others join me to do some of the work that remains to be done. If that happens, I expect you both to be gracious and on your best behavior."

John could not help but smile as he listened to Liz. His eyes twinkled with delight. Her understanding and acceptance of spirits being among them was a wonderful discovery. *Thank you, God—Great Spirit,* he breathed out. Just as Liz turned back to him, his cell phone rang. John answered. His eyes held hers as he listened and responded, then ended the call.

"So, I gather you need to go." Disappointment filled Liz's voice.

"I'm sorry. I was looking forward to a day off and spending the evening with you and your family. But I'm needed to assist with a fire that includes a possible search and rescue up in Hamilton County. Duty calls."

"I understand." She said as John once again drew her into his arms. "Do be careful."

John placed a tender kiss on her lips. "I will. After all, I have you to come home to."

Liz ran her tongue over her lips, yet again, as she slowed down to pull her vehicle onto her parent's front lawn. She could still feel and taste John's lips on hers. Well, her memory of them at least. Liz shut off the motor and remained sitting in the driver's seat. She needed a few moments to collect her thoughts before joining the annual Labor Day barbecue fully underway. Squeals of delight drew Liz from her thoughts. Looking out of the passenger side window she saw Callie Anne running towards her. In her wake was her brother Nicholas and a couple of other young boys, whom Liz did not know. She wasn't too concerned, and knew that before the night was over, she would be introduced or reintroduced to everyone who was attending the barbecue.

"Where's John?" Caitlin asked, as Elizabeth walked around the side of the house and into the backyard with Callie at her side.

Liz twisted her lips in what was known as the *Callison displeasure look!* —then she rolled her eyes. Her gaze moved from her sister to her niece. "See how she greeted me, Callie Anne? My own sister kicked me right to the curb. Sheesh!" Then, she gently elbowed her niece and added, "At least you were happy to see me!"

Caitlin opened, then closed her mouth as she looked at Liz. Her sister was not smiling. "Ought oh! Did something happen?"

"Well, yeah!" Liz's expression spoke to Caitlin as loud and clear as her words. "You skipped right over hello, Liz...and went right to 'where's John', and how do you think that made me feel? Kicked me right to the curb you did. My own sister. Tsk, tsk, tsk!" Liz was still serious as she turned her undivided attention to Callie. "I tell you, Callie Anne there was a time in my life when I could depend on your Mom." Liz sighed, while slowly shaking her head. Callie Anne gazed between her aunt and mother. The young girl was alarmed that something was dreadfully wrong between them, as she remained quiet and listened.

"Elizabeth Jeanne, you can be such a brat!" Caitlin exclaimed. "You're acting—teasing me, aren't you?" Caitlin's expression was priceless as she intently looked at Liz.

"So, was I believable?" Liz asked, as her whole face grew into a smile. Her eyes shone with such happiness that Caitlin burst into laughter and drew Liz into a hug.

"I'm so glad to see you so happy. But you know it wasn't nice to tease us like that." Cait quietly drew her daughter into her embrace to console her. Liz added her own words of comfort to assure Callie that she and her mom were not mad at each other.

"Is this a private conversation, or can my little ones and I join you all?" Sammie asked as she pushed her babies in the double carriage towards them. Callie quickly forgot her Aunt Liz for her new cousins and Aunt Sammie. Samantha graciously accepted Callie's offer to push the carriage so her aunts could relax with her mom.

"So, where's John?" Sammie asked, as she looked around not seeing him. Caitlin moaned. Liz snickered as they stood arm in arm, and gently put the sides of their heads together. Then they released a collective sigh. "Oh my!" Samantha gasped. "You two are so strange! It's like we're in a time warp and you've regressed to your teen years."

"What's that old saying?" Caitlin asked. "Some things -"

"Never change?" Liz asked.

"Well, that too! I was thinking somethings never die!"

"That's true, especially with that love that we share in our family."

Jim was standing away from his daughters, so he was unable to hear what they were saying to one another. He could, however, see their expression, their body language. At that moment, his cell phone rang. He answered it and stepped away from the group of friends he had been speaking with. "Hey, Jordan. This is a pleasant surprise." Jim listened to his daughter. He smiled and responded, as he slowly walked towards his other girls. "They are all here. Sure, I'll put my phone on speaker, so you all can hear each other." As he brought his family up to speed on who he was speaking with, he turned to Liz and innocently asked, "Where's John?"

Peals of laughter erupted from the three Callison sisters who were gathered in their parent's backyard. It didn't take long for Jordan to join in the laughter, and Jim to also find the humor. As Jim listened to his daughter's he had a feeling that the question, *Where's John?* was going to be asked on a more frequent and regular basis. Having spent time in the past working with John, in the present knowing the man's work ethic, as well as, his devotion to his extended family, and having seen John and Liz together on several occasions, Jim had some thoughts— good thoughts—about the younger man who was becoming an important part of Elizabeth's life.

"Elizabeth, Caitlin, Samantha, I hope you all are not going to fall into a new round of laughter when I ask my next question." Jim smiled at their responses, then asked, "Do any of you girls know where your aunt and uncle might be? I expected them to be here a couple of hours ago. They aren't responding to my text or calls either." Liz sighed. "Oh great!" Jim sighed. "I know that look. Where are they and what are they doing?"

Liz pulled a small envelope out from her back pocket of her jeans and handed it to her father. Jim took it and immediately recognized the handwriting. He closed his eyes, shook his head and released a slow breath. "They're not coming." He said while looking deep into Liz's eyes.

She felt a pang of sadness for her dad, knowing why they were not there. "No, Dad. They are not going to be here. Aunt Amanda asked me to give you this note that she wrote for you, telling you in her own words why they are not here."

Jim sighed, as he took the note and stepped away from the group of people that was gathered in his and Melissa's back yard. Standing alone by the flower garden, the same one that Caitlin had little Nick sit by on more than one occasion to think about some unacceptable act or behavior. Jim carefully removed the folded paper from the envelope. Quiet growling noises began to make their way from Jim's throat as he read.

"Something wrong?"

The question. The familiar voice. Both immediately caused Jim to feel the sparks of anger stirring within him. Fire was beginning to smolder within. Then, his expression turned from fire to homicidal, as he turned to glare at Stephen Johnson. The man who had been his best friend for too many years to count, was fortunate that Jim was physically able to control his temper.

"Something is always wrong when you are directly involved in my sister's life." Jim snarled as he stuffed the note into the envelope and then into his back pocket. Stephen immediately responded to Jim's statement about him and Amanda. Then Jim asked, "Take a look around my backyard. Do you see Amanda and Kevin here?"

"Well, no." Stephen said, as he glanced around and then looked at Jim, who was not smiling. The muscle on the top of Jim's cheek was twitching. His brows were drawn together. A very bad sign. A warning. Imminent danger lay ahead.

"My sister has informed me that they are on their way home." His expression grew more deadly, if that was even possible. "They chose to not attend Melissa's and my annual Labor Day barbecue, so that we could enjoy it with all of our friends. You being one of them. Manda was concerned that, if, you two were here together -" Jim drew in a breath to keep control of his emotions that were ready to blast like the release of his grandmother's old .16 gauge shotgun. Then he continued, "Mandy feared that she might verbally take you apart, and out of respect for Mel and me, she chose to avoid a possible feud with you and possibly rip apart your girlfriend." Jim watched Stephen, as he processed Jim's words. "No response, I see. I'm not surprised. Amanda has once again made a sacrifice, and you are the one who is reaping the benefit from her actions. You had better go enjoy yourself, because next year I don't plan on having a community event, if, it means my sister and brother in law will not be here."

Stephen sighed. "I'm sorry for messing things up with you and Amanda. If I had known how strongly she felt about not attending because of me and Belinda being here," Stephen sighed. His eyes were filled with deep sorrow. Pain, and something else Jim couldn't identify as he listened to Stephen speak. "Jim, if I had known how she felt, we would have not come here today. Jumpin' Bullfrogs! Things are so messed up between Calli and me." Jim smiled to himself, as he heard Stephen use his sister's nickname. It was the name Johnson had given Amanda many years ago and everyone else in their group of friends had adopted. His sister's nickname had also been Caitlin's inspiration for Callie Anne's name. As Jim listened to Stephen, he believed that even though right now things appeared to be rather bleak, there still was hope that someday those two stubborn souls would resolve their differences once and for all. For now, it was going to be a bumpy ride. "You know I could cope with this rift, if, it was just between Cal and me. But, Jim, that mule headed sister of yours -" Jim raised an eyebrow at Stephen's choice of words for Amanda, "You know I'm speaking the truth about how stubborn Amanda is!" Jim nodded with some reluctance. He could not deny that Amanda was stubborn. Truth be told, so was Johnson! "Amanda and Summer used to be so close and now—well, it tears me apart to see what has happened between them."

"And who's fault is that?" Jim pointedly asked. "Who opened his big mouth and once again betrayed my sister's trust. Don't place blame on my sister for her estrangement with your daughter. You are the source of the conflict. You are the one who hurt Amanda. Having said that, I suggest that you think for a moment about how your nephew Peter has hurt Elizabeth. Do you see any parallels between you and Peter? I sure do! Now, if you will excuse me? There are other guests for me to socialize with."

Melissa had been tip toeing around Jim's grumpy mood for a week since the annual barbecue. This morning was no different. Well, Melissa had finally reached her limit, and she was ready for things to get back to normal for a while. Too bad, if Jim didn't think that he was ready to clear the air! It was time for them to talk out the things that he had bottled up inside of him.

Crack! Thump! Crack! Thump!

The sound of Jim's ax blade slicing through the wood echoed in the valley on that clear, brisk fall morning. A soft smile touched Melissa's lips, as she headed out the back door armed with a steaming cup of coffee in her hands. Her eyes were on Jim, as he continued his task of splitting a cord of wood, he had picked up the day before, and later would be piled in the back of the garage with the other piles of wood for winter. She watched him lift the ax over his head and bring it down with precision splitting the wood with one swing. Tension rippled through his body.

Even though Jim was using this task as a stress release, he had noticed the movement when she first came outside. Not too much happened around Jim, that he wasn't aware of. Now, he glanced over as Mel stepped closer, drove the ax blade into the stump he was using for his chopping block, and graciously reached for the cup of coffee Mel was handing him.

"Ah, my sweet Melissa, thank you!" He took a sip, sighed in contentment as its heat warmed him from the inside out. "You must have read my mind, and knew that I needed this."

"I wish I could read your mind." She quietly said, as she sat down on the stump and took a hold of the ax handle. "Is splitting wood helping you sort out your concerns?"

With that question, seeing the sadness in Melissa's eyes, Jim sat on the other side of the stump, with one butt cheek on the stump and his other leg positioned to steady himself. His body touched Mel's as he reached over and gently took her hand into his. Their eyes met and conveyed their love that didn't need any words to make the other understand their feelings.

Jim sighed, then drew in another breath. Mel waited. Then, when Jim was ready, he told her everything that had been on his mind since his heated words with Stephen. Melissa quietly listened, and when he had finished speaking his mind, she tenderly smiled at him and said, "I'm glad that you stuck up for Amanda as you did! Jim, you're right about Johnson betraying Amanda. I don't understand him and why he feels that he has hurt Amanda in this way. Maybe we'll never understand how things are between them. But, as for you? You have proven to Amanda that she can trust you to be there for her. I'm pleased to see that since your *come to Jesus moment—Gentle Spirit's intervention*— you two have come so far in restoring your relationship with one another. Speaking of Amanda -" Now Mel's eyes grew full of concern. "Has she told you anything else about how she is doing?" Mel asked as Jim stood, held out his hand and assisted Melissa to her feet. She smiled tenderly. After all the years that they were together, Jim still remembered and did those special little things that made Melissa feel and know that she was loved and cared for. Theirs was a by gone era.

"You mean about her health? Her limp?"

"Yes." Melissa nodded. Her eyes shone with deep concern.

"Amanda hasn't—but Kevin has."

Melissa wasn't too surprised to hear that Amanda was being tight lipped about her physical condition. She could understand Amanda wanting some privacy about her life, that too many people knew too much about. She also had a feeling that Amanda was not saying too much because she didn't want them to worry, which only made them worry more! Just as Melissa was placing the cold cuts on the table for their sandwiches, Jim's cell phone rang.

"Speaking of the old devil," Jim said with a touch of laughter in his voice, as he picked up his phone from the table. "Hey, Sis. Perfect timing. We were just talking about you and wondering how you are doing."

Jim listened to Amanda regale him with what had been going on since she and Kevin had returned to Baltimore. Sometimes having your spouse as a physician was a very good thing, especially when he was the director of the trauma emergency room. Plus, it helped that Amanda's orthopedist and Kevin were colleagues and friends outside of work. As a result of his connections, the majority of their medical issues were addressed in a rather timely fashion.

"So, your surgery is scheduled for two weeks from now. Hold on a minute, Sis, Mel is saying something."

"Ask Amanda if she needs for us to come down?" Concern resonated from her as she added, "Then, when she say's no, tell her we're coming anyway!"

Jim allowed a smile to ease to his lips, as he relayed Mel's questions and statement to Amanda. Of course, Amanda had a response. Jim chuckled and continued to smile. It was his I knew this was going to happen—chuckle and smile. Then, he bowed out of the conversation and handed his phone to Melissa.

"So, looking at the calendar," Jim said, as he looked over his reading glasses at Mel, "We will have to reschedule a couple of our own appointments that conflict with us going to Maryland to be with Sis and Kevin."

"That's no problem, Jim. I've already changed your annual physical to the end of next month. Imaging has an opening so my mammogram will be done this next week. That leaves our dentist appointments. No big deal there for either of us, since they are routine cleanings." Mel informed Jim as she placed a piece of homemade blueberry pie in front of him.

Jim looked up at her with his brows drawn, a common expression when Jim was processing information in his mind. "Thanks for the pie. How did you reschedule our appointments without calling the doctor's office and imaging for your mammogram?"

Mel held up her phone as she cheerfully said, "I did it through the apps for each medical provider. It is so much easier than having to call and go through the hassle of the automated system and then being asked to hold and so forth."

"The marvels of modern technology." Jim said under his breath as he shook his head with wonder. Of course, his wife would know all about these application's features and use them. Jim, on the other hand, didn't get too excited about the latest technology that was supposed to make life easier. He enjoyed an excuse to go visit someone, or pick up the phone and hear their voice. As for doctor's appointments? Well, Jim would rather avoid them and contacting the office like the plague! Thankfully, his wife had no problem taking charge of that part of their lives. He took a bite of pie, savored the tart and sweet taste of the blueberries, that they had picked together last summer and now filled his mouth, chewed and swallowed. Then, while placing his fork on the plate, he said, "Mellie, we need to let the kids know what is going on."

"Have that covered, as well." Mel replied and smiled brightly at him before placing a bite of pie in her mouth.

"Of course, you do!" Jim's eyes smiled back at Melissa, as he too took another bite of pie. "Do you care to elaborate for me on how we are dealing with this?"

"We're calling a family meeting for our family members who are here in the north country. Then, we'll phone Jordan and JJ to bring them up to speed with what is happening." Jim saw something in Mel's eyes. He knew from experience that she was not finished with her thoughts. Sure enough! "I also think that we need to respect Amanda's privacy, and keep our knowledge of her surgery within our family."

"I agree." Then, Jim raised a questioning brow as he asked, "Has she told Summer what's going on?"

Mel recognized the concern in his eyes, as well as his love for his family. She reached over and gently placed her hand on his, as it rested on the table by his phone. Mel released a troubled breath. "No, Jim, and Amanda has firmly stated that she does not want Summer, or, Stephen and the rest of his family to know anything about her medical issues."

Jim slowly shook his head, as he gave Melissa's hand a gentle squeeze. "This is such a mess! I think Sis should tell Summer what is going on. But I know!" He sighed. "It's her decision to not tell her daughter. I also know there will be questions about why we are going to Baltimore. How do you propose we handle it?" Jim asked as he tucked his chin to his neck and watched Melissa's eyes turn bright with knowledge and she smiled with delight.

"Simple! We are going south for a vacation, and to celebrate our anniversary with Amanda and Kevin."

A slow smile tugged at Jim's lips, and his eyes began to light up with wonder. "Sweetheart, you are a genus." Then his brows drew close with concern. "Not a very romantic way for us to spend our anniversary though, is it?"

"Oh Callison, every day is a romance with you. Would you like for me to prove it?" Her smile, then slow lick of her lips with her tongue punctuated her question for Jim. He answered her by standing and holding out his hand to help her from her chair. Securing the locks on the doors, they quietly headed for the stairs and up to their room. Both knowing that love does get better with time, just like a rare aging wine.

CHAPTER 19

Liz sat at her desk in the community arts building and looked at the flowers that she had just received from the arts association board of directors. A smile crept onto her lips, as she breathed in the aroma of the burgundy and yellow chrysanthemums, and greens in the stunning autumn gold vase. The message on the card congratulating Liz on her successful first year of leadership was what had really hit home with her. She breathed out a sigh of contentment, as her smile grew. So much in her life had changed over the past year. Some of life's lessons had been rather difficult to experience, driving her to the inner depths of her soul in anguish reaching and searching, while Liz was not convinced that she had the stamina or courage to face down her demons. Still, there were other experiences that filled Liz with hope and optimism in what the future would unfold for her. Without a doubt, her work held the greatest joy. Well, her work, family, and oh yes, the amazing—every time she thinks of him makes her heart do a flip flop—Forest Ranger John Runner. A dreamy feeling swept over Liz as she sighed, while placing her chin in her hand. She closed her eyes, lost in her thoughts of the summer season that was now a good memory.

Every day, John was becoming more significant in Liz's life. Today, being no different. Earlier in the day, as she was stepping out the front door of the cabin and onto the porch, her phone had indicated that she had an incoming text from him. She paused and read the text, smiled and replied, before continuing on to her car and down the mountain to go to work. Something as simple as wishing Liz a good morning and his hopes for her day, meant the world to her. Liz knew that it was other little things that John did as well, such as sending her a *good night and sweet dreams* text. Or, him showing up at her door after spending a grueling day on foot, or in an all-terrain vehicle out in the forest, simply to let her know he cared about her, and for her to see for herself that he was alright. Liz giggled to herself. She had a sneaking suspicion that John actually showed up on her doorstep because he was the one who needed to see her. Either way, it didn't matter! Liz's heart was healing and melting with delight. As busy as they both were with their careers, and their family commitments, their relationship shouldn't be working, especially, since John is ten years her senior. Liz laughed as she thought about their ages. All she had done was reverse the age difference from one man to the other. Peter had been younger by nearly ten years and John had ten years on her. Hmm. Now that silly little fact intrigued Liz. Why? Why, had she chosen to have recent relationships with such tremendous age differences? Greg—the thought of him made Liz's stomach churn—he was only three years older than her.

A quiet knock on the office door drew Liz's attention back to the present. "Come in." She watched to see who was entering, and in need of her time. "John!" She exclaimed, then drew in a breath as a smiled eased onto her lips. She felt the heat rising in her cheeks and knew that the coloring of her cheeks was too. Oh well! Liz pushed back her chair, rose to her feet and eased around her desk to meet him. She felt his eye's openly surveying her clothing choice for the day, and then his eyes focused in on her face. His smile drew her in, as she too noticed everything about John's appearance from his head to his feet. They had yet to be totally intimate with each other, so Liz could only imagine what it would be like for them to be one with each other. Still, she knew enough about him romantically, and with their growing friendship, to take great pleasure in having John in her life. His uniform was still neatly pressed, only showing wrinkles in his pants from his sitting in his vehicle or on a chair. "So, how were the children at Northville Elementary School? Did you have a fun time with them?" Her warm chocolate eyes sparkled with unmasked happiness, as she slid into his embrace.

He drew her close, inhaling the scent of the vanilla body wash she had used that morning to bathe in, which lingered on her body. Then, there was the other scent of wood smoke on her clothing and something that was purely Elizabeth. Everything about Elizabeth drew John to her, like a moth seeking the warmth of a bright light on a cool summer night.

"Spending time with the children at Northville Elementary is always an adventure. Today was no different!" John' responded. His eyes tenderly held her along with his arms protectively enclosing her to him.

Liz was looking into his eyes, as she lightly stroked her fingers across his shirt towards his shoulders. Her eyes and smile indicated how much she was enjoying this moment standing there with his arms holding her close to him. As Liz studied John's expression, she noticed a hint of laughter in his eyes. She was becoming aware of his subtle signs of amusement, displeasure, annoyance among other emotions. It was obvious from the clues that he had given her, that something had happened. Liz mulled that over in her mind. She had her suspicion.

"Did you happen to see my sister? My nephew?"

A smile took form on John's lips. His eyes began to sparkle like drops of sunlit dew on the morning grass. Then he laughed and said, "Oh yes, I saw them!"

Liz paused with her stroking John's chest, while he continued to stroke her back. His smile, his eyes all made her all the more suspicious that something really embarrassing must have happened. "What did Nicholas do? Or, don't I want to know?"

"How about I tell you about my adventure with them over lunch?" Was all that John would say, as he promptly changed the subject to Liz's plans for fall programming, and patiently waited for her to get ready to join him for lunch.

Two hours later, Liz was back at the Great Sacandaga Community Arts Center breaking down tables that had been used in a recent senior citizen program and arts show, 65 & Over Hidden Talents Show. From the success of the event, the participants enthusiasm and community response, Liz went ahead and added the event on the roughly outlined calendar for next year. Her ultimate goal was to have something happening through the arts association on monthly, rather than a quarterly basis. She smiled to herself, as she thought about the success of her first-year programs, then she shook her head as she thought of the failures that would not be held again next year. Fortunately, her successes far outnumbered her failures. Throughout the first year as director, Liz had spent a considerable amount of time networking in the community, listening to people as they shared their ideas, their passions with her. In time, Elizabeth would meet and surpass her goal. After all, she was a Callison and when she and her family members put their minds to doing something—well, there would be no stopping them!

"And who do I get that determination from?" Liz asked herself and laughed. "Dad would say I get my pigheadedness, my unflappability from Aunt Amanda. Hmm."

Liz walked over to the chair where she had left her water bottle, picked it up and took a long, slow sip. She sat down, stretched her legs out, and pulled her phone from her back pocket. Then, Liz opened up her favorites in her contacts and dialed her aunt.

"Elizabeth, hello! How did you know that I was thinking of you?" Her aunt's voice, obvious pleasure in hearing from her filled Liz's heart with happiness.

"I was thinking of you, Aunt Amanda, and decided to take a chance that I am not interrupting you from your work. I'm not, am I?" Liz sincerely asked. She truly loved and treasured any moment that she spent with her aunt, via cell phone, or in person. The last thing that she wanted was to be an imposition in her aunt's busy life.

"Elizabeth Jeanne, you of all people should know that I would tell you, if I was unable to chat with you at this time."

Liz found herself laughing, as she listened to her aunt continue on about people's rude behavior and lack of phone etiquette. From there the conversation moved on to how the fall was shaping up for both of them. Liz was bubbling over with excitement for the fall season at the arts center.

"Yes, I am in the process of preparing the room where we had the show last year." Liz laughed at her aunt's response. "We, make that, I, deeply appreciated you and Uncle Kevin supporting our event. You might be interested in knowing, that I'm getting the room marked out for the first of hopefully many Great Sacandaga Community High School Fall Arts and Craft Shows. Yes. It's similar to their spring event. From the conversations that I've had with some of the high school art students, I know that they have a vision with how the room should be set up for their show. So, for now, I'm simply marking venue spaces. Yes. Ten by ten for most of our exhibitors."

Liz continued to elaborate on the plans for the event, then broke into a fit of laughter, as her aunt exclaimed, "The girl wants to bring in a live goat and leave it there for the duration? Granted, I think goat milk soap is a wonderful thing to make and have at the show. Of course, I want some and will send you money. But, Elizabeth! A live goat!"

Their discussion of the goat, and Amanda being needed to assist with something at her work, drew their conversation to an end. Liz was still smiling as she stood, returned her phone to her pocket, picked up her painter's tape used for marking spaces, the collapsible tape measure, and her water bottle. She headed to her office and as she entered through the door, she saw the poster for the Community Fall Fire Safety Meeting with the Great Sac Volunteer Fire Company and Forest Ranger John Runner. Scanning the poster that Liz knew by heart, the memory of her earlier conversation with John about her nephew came to mind. Without any question, Liz loved her family. But, sometimes little one's said things that they shouldn't say or repeat, and unfortunately her dear nephew Nick had not learned when to keep his mouth closed. Now, thanks to Nick, everyone in the elementary school knew that she and John were dating. So much for privacy! Then, Liz sighed and found herself smiling, as she imagined Caitlin's mortified expression when Nick had diarrhea of the mouth during the school assembly. No sooner had she finished her sigh, when her phone rang. She smiled as she drew her phone to her ear.

"Hey, Cait, I hear you all had a fun day at school." There was a hint of laughter in Liz's voice. Her smile grew as she heard Caitlin groan, then share her version of the school assembly. "Really, Caitlin, it isn't as bad as you think. John and I actually have been able to find the humor in it. Please cut your son some slack. He's excited about John being a part of my life, and Nick is only trying to carve out his place with the rest of our family. Your dear son is no different from how we all were when we were growing up. Think about it. Is Nick any worse than JJ was when we were kids?"

"Yes—I mean no! But—" Caitlin sighed.

"—No buts. Remember the time when JJ -" Liz shared her memory with Caitlin. As she did, Cait laughed and joined in with Liz reminiscing about their family. Before too long the two sisters were laughing so hard that Liz had to take out a tissue and wipe the tears from her eyes. Yes. Over the years the Callison siblings had their share of humorous and embarrassing moments. Liz realized as they chatted together that families, especially theirs, had a habit of becoming great sources of amusement.

"What's so funny?"

"Just our family, from Dad and Aunt Amanda to us and the next generation of Callison's." Liz sighed. "One thing is for sure. With all of us there is never a dull moment!"

"True, and since you began the subject of our family with Dad and Aunt Amanda, our generation needs to meet and make plans for Mom and Dad's surprise anniversary party, while they are out of the state with Aunt Amanda and Uncle Kevin."

"Okay. I'm free in the evening, but not for the next few weekends." Liz further explained her weekend plans to Caitlin both professionally and personally with John. Caitlin was ecstatic to hear how things were progressing for her sister in all areas of her life. Things were obviously heating up in their relationship for Liz to plan to go with John further north in the Adirondacks to Saranac Lake to meet his parents and his grandmother. Caitlin kept her thoughts to herself, as she wondered how long it would be before they decided to marry. She was secretly glad that Liz couldn't see her right them, as a smile graced her lips.

Jim and Melissa sat in the hospital waiting room with Kevin, along with Amanda and Kevin's friends Cassie and Andrew. Through the years, since Jim and Amanda's reconciliation in 2009-2010, they had come to know and appreciate the other couple's friendship with Amanda and Kevin. It had been four hours since Amanda had been taken into the O.R. Weariness was setting in as they waited. Then, finally the orthopedic surgeon entered the waiting room.

Jim stood to join Kevin in greeting the surgeon, who had paused to greet Andrew, who apparently was also a colleague and friend with the surgeon. He listened to the surgeon as he explained to Kevin what he had done to Amanda's right foot. On one hand, Jim was relieved to hear what had been done to relieve his sister's pain. However, on the other hand, alarm rang out through every fiber of Jim's body as he heard the surgeon say, "So, Kevin as you well know from having attended to Amanda when her foot was mangled in the accident in 1999, that it is truly a miracle that she has done so well, for so long with the plate, and screws holding her foot together. If anyone else had told me that they had gone ice skating a few years ago, I would have thought that they were lying. Knowing Amanda, and her inner strength—I'm not at all surprised! I'm also not surprised that she waited this long for us to address her current needs." Jim softly smiled, as he watched and listened to everyone speaking with the surgeon about Amanda. Yes. His sister was something special. Jim was recalling his memory of watching Amanda and Kevin skating out on the frozen lake in late December of 2009. He simply could not imagine her skating with—Jim's thoughts were interrupted as he heard the surgeon say, "We cut the mass out from the bone and sent it for biopsy. At this point, we don't think it is cancerous. But-"

A mass. A biopsy. Jim did not hear the rest of the conversation as his mind went back in time. It was 1971 all over again for him. Except, the woman in his memory was not his younger sister. She was his mother. Jim recalled the day, as if it was today. His mother had been sick and had finally gone to the doctor. Then she had begun to have tests, and stayed overnight in the hospital for a biopsy of her breast. Then came the further exploratory surgery. Her diagnosis, was metastatic breast cancer. Within the year she had died. It was a long, slow, cruel death for all of them. Jim was eighteen and

Amanda was sixteen. He felt moisture forming in the back of his eyes. He wouldn't allow himself to cry. The soft touch of Melissa's hand on his arm drew Jim from his thoughts. He looked down into her concerned, loving eyes. Without a word she told Jim just what he needed to know.

"Amanda is going to get through this, Jim. You need to remember that she's not your mother. Amanda has medical treatment options that your mom, and so many others never had. Now, we have to pray and hope that Amanda's prognosis will not be like your Mom's, and she will have earthly healing." Her quiet words were as soothing as a cool glass of water sliding down a parched throat on a scorching hot day.

Jim sighed and nodded. He drew in a slow centering breath. "Kevin, if you'd like, we'll wait outside of Amanda's room, so that you can have time alone to talk with her about her surgery and what was found."

It was Kevin's turn to sigh. He was exhausted and overwhelmed in a barren place where other people usually were: not him, the doctor. Today his world was spinning on its wobbly axis. "Jim—Mel, thank you for your offer. I'd like for you both to be with us," Kevin drew in a breath, then continued, "When Dennis—her surgeon—talks with Amanda about her surgery and the outcome."

"I agree with Kevin." Cassie quietly said, as she moved over to place a comforting hand on Kevin's arm for a brief reassuring moment. Her gaze passed between Jim and Melissa as she continued, "Amanda needs all of you to be with her, as she begins to process the possibilities of what may lie ahead for her, and for all of you."

"And what about you and Andrew?" Jim asked. "You are two of Sis's closest friends."

"That's right, Andrew and I are very close to Amanda and Kevin. For many years Amanda has been like our sister, and in the days ahead we will be here to do whatever is necessary to aid both

Amanda and Kevin with her recovery. Amanda will get through this. Even if the biopsy does come back as malignant, it will not defeat her. We all know that Amanda is a proven fighter and champion of overcoming life's adversities."

It was late evening when Jim and Melissa returned with Kevin to his and Amanda's apartment. All three of them were exhausted, as they stepped into the relaxing space Amanda and Kevin had created to be their home. Tomorrow Amanda would be discharged for home, in a hard cast that would be removed in 6 weeks. That is, unless the biopsy of the small mass that had been found on her bone during surgery, that previously had been thought to be a shadow on the plate in her foot, turned out to be malignant. For now, Jim and Melissa were going to stay for the remainder of the week and assist Kevin with Amanda's care, since she was non weight bearing on her right leg. If the biopsy indicated the need for surgery, chemotherapy or other cancer treatment, they would be there for Amanda and Kevin.

Little did Jim and Mel know that while they were busy helping Amanda and Kevin, and trying to remain positive, their five children were busy conspiring together. One or two of the children teaming up together was a normal occurrence in their family. But, all five together for a common purpose was trouble with a capital T! Unfortunately, Jim and Melissa were also unaware that Amanda, prior to her surgery, and while recovering from surgery, was in the thick of the planning with their children.

Laughter filled Samantha and Chris's home as the Callison sisters, spouses and one of the newest boyfriends occupied the couch and chairs. Caitlin and Nick had wisely left Callie and Nicholas with Nick's parents, so that they could relax, talk freely with the other adults, and not have to worry about their children inadvertently saying something to their grandparents, that the older couple was not privileged to know at this point. Jordan and her new boyfriend Thomas had driven up from Long Island, and were staying with Liz, who was house sitting for their parents. So far, Liz, Cait and Sam approved of Jordan's new boyfriend. He was proving to be able to handle Cait and Liz's interrogation and teasing. Liz laughed to herself, as she watched and listened to Caitlin speak to Thomas. At that moment, her sister reminded Liz of their dad with her serious expression and tone of voice. *Oh, good grief!* Liz thought. *It will be a miracle if Caitlin doesn't fully intimidate the poor man and send him running back to Long Island!*

"What struck you so funny?" Cait whispered to Liz.

Liz turned and looked at Caitlin in utter surprise. "How did you know I was laughing to myself?"

"Oh please," Caitlin rolled her eyes for effect. "As if, you didn't know I would read your body language. Geesh, Lizzie!"

Liz sighed, smiled and shook her head. Caitlin was right. She did know her too well! At that moment, Liz had to admit to herself that she wouldn't want it to be any other way. Liz was glancing at Jordan who sat snuggled up against Thomas and was thinking, *annoying little sisters aren't too bad either!* when Samantha joined them.

"Where's John?" Sammie asked, as she gazed around the living room with a well-worn cloth diaper, that had once graced hers, or perhaps one of her sibling behinds, and now served as a spit up towel for liquefied burps. Cait's eyes sparkled with that *older sister, I'm a mother too* look that Sammie had come to recognize on her. At first Sam had thought it was sweet. Now, she had to wonder, if, perhaps her sister was envious of her? For now, she'd tuck that thought away to contemplate over during one of her many long nights of little sleep, as she cared for her babies.

"Where's John?" Liz quietly repeated to not awaken Mary and Daniel because if the twins joined them, their family meeting would be adjourned for sure. Her expression was devoid of emotion as she responded. "You know, it's nice that you all accept John as my boyfriend, but really now-" Liz paused for dramatic effect. It worked. "Your obsession with him is a bit disconcerting. Just kick me to the curb, why don't you? Who cares about Liz being here as long as John's with her!"

For a moment, no one spoke, then everyone burst into muffled laughter. Having sleeping babies in the house was proving to be a chore, especially with Liz, providing the dramatic and comic relief for all of them. Once Jordan got JJ on face time, and everyone said their hellos, family decisions were quickly made—with Caitlin leading the group as usual and Liz recording their decisions, while making notations regarding who was responsible for what.

"Some things never change." JJ said as his sisters seemed to be winding down with their thoughts regarding how the party for their parents should go.

"What things?" They all simultaneously asked him.

With four sets of older sister's eyes watching his every move, JJ had to be careful with what he said and how he said it. The last thing he needed or wanted was for one, or all of them to be mad at him. He drew in a hesitant breath and rapidly said as he exhaled, "Cait is still the boss of us, and Lizzie is once again her side kick! The chief and the enforcer reign again!" His expression was priceless! Liz burst into laughter right along with everyone else. Sometimes there was no denying the truth, especially when it applied to their family. As the elder sisters, Caitlin and Elizabeth were a force to be reckoned with!

Liz slowed down her car, put on the directional and pulled into the parking lot of the bait shop. She had purposely stayed away from there since her and Peter's demise over the summer. Anxiety was consuming her. With how she felt, Liz had to wonder if her aunt's panic disorder was anything like what she was experiencing at that moment. She knew in her heart, that Amanda's panic disorder was worse than what she was feeling.

Earlier in the day Liz had made the phone call to Becky Jones that she had been dreading, and had intentionally put off making for some time. Then came the Callison children's plans for their parent's surprise party, and Liz reluctantly said that she would talk with Wes and Stephen about using the bait shop pavilion for the party. Finding courage, she had called and asked for Becky to meet her at the bait shop. She was glad, and equally uneasy to see that Becky's car was parked next to Wesley's pickup. Liz pulled in next to Stephen's pickup and stopped. She turned off the motor and sat for a few moments to collect her thoughts before meeting with the Jones' and Stephen Johnson. Drawing in a centering breath, Liz, slowly released it and opened the car door. She straightened her shoulders with more confidence, than she felt at that moment, as she stepped towards the bait shop door. The familiar jingle of the bells on the door were the first to greet Liz as she entered the building.

"Hello!" Liz called out, as she shut the door to keep the cool fall air outside. Her heart pounded in her chest. So many thoughts swept through her, as she stepped towards the counter. Awkward silence greeted her. Then Becky stepped around the counter and met Liz.

"Good afternoon, Liz. It's so good to see you! I've been meaning to stop over to the arts center to congratulate you on a very successful summer with the theater." Becky's smile began to ease Liz's turbulent emotions. Why, had she opened her big mouth and offered to talk with them for her siblings? Liz scolded herself, knowing fully well exactly why she was there, and what she needed to do.

"Thank you, Becky. I appreciate your kind words. Hopefully next summer's theater season will be even better!" Liz softly smiled. "For now, I have another mission to accomplish, and it hopefully will involve all of you as well."

"You've got my attention!" Wes called out. For a moment, sadness consumed him, as he watched Liz and Becky walk towards the counter. He noticed subtle differences with how Liz carried herself, since he had last seen her in the bait shop with Peter before breaking off their engagement. Confidence. Happiness. Wes drew in a breath as he looked more intently at Liz. He had heard community gossip about a forest ranger being seen in Liz's company. Yes, Wes was curious. But he was also smart enough to keep his questions to himself at this point in time. He listened to Liz present the Callison children's plan to surprise their parents. A smile touched his lips. "Of course, we will help you all with your surprise for your parents." Wes said without first conferring with Stephen about the use of the pavilion.

"Wonderful!" Liz exclaimed. Her face shone with delight, as she regaled them with what her and her siblings envisioned for the surprise party. "Thank you, Wes, Becky. It really means a lot for me and my family. Especially, for me with everything that happened, or, should I say, didn't happen with Peter and me. I'm sure my breaking off the engagement with Peter has not been easy for you both to accept. Your friendship with Mom and Dad is important to me. The last thing I want is for you both to have problems with my parents because of me."

Becky immediately responded and hugged Elizabeth so tightly around her waist, that she was nearly unable to breath. It also helped Liz to relax when Wes reinforced what Becky said regarding their family friendship. Phew! Liz felt as if a weight had been lifted from her shoulders, by knowing that things were going to be okay between her parents and their friends. The pavilion was reserved for the party, and Liz was ready to leave. She had taken a step towards the door when Stephen spoke to her.

"Hold on a minute, Elizabeth." She should have known it was only a matter of time before he had something to say, and she was fairly certain what the topic of discussion would be for him. "So, where exactly did your folks go on their vacation with Amanda and Kevin? When do you expect them to be getting home?"

Liz's expression did not reveal how she felt about his tone of voice, or his all too revealing eyes. The poor man had really gotten himself into hot water this time with her parents, and her aunt. Oh well, that was his problem! "Mom and Dad are spending another week with Aunt Amanda and Uncle Kevin." She drew in a breath, smiled and said, "We're really glad that they are taking this time to have well deserved fun away from here. Plus, their absence has made it perfect for us to get everything planned before they get home. So, on that note, I'm off to take care of the next thing on my list." She bid another farewell to Becky and Wes, then turned her gaze back to Stephen. "Oh! Before I forget, we would like for you to make a toast for Mom and Dad."

"Me?" Stephen asked. Considering how strained things had been between their families, Stephen was surprised by the request.

"Well, yes!" Liz looked at him as if to say, *that's the dumbest question I've ever heard, or been asked!* Then, she said, "Well, you were Dad's best man, after all!"

Stephen nodded. "Well, yes I was. I'd be honored to make a toast for your parents." He watched Liz leave, listened to Wes and Becky talking about Liz stopping in and how good it was to see her. Stephen felt the fine hairs on his neck bothering him. That was not a good sign. He had a feeling that even though Liz had answered his questions about her parents, something was going on. It was that unknown something that involved the Callison siblings that bothered him.

CHAPTER 20

Autumn was in full swing in the Adirondacks. Hardwood trees were responding to the cool nights, light frost, followed by warm days and bursting forth with vivid splashes of color. Anyone living in the north country knew that this was a season of change, preparation for what was to come. Changes were not only happening with the seasons, but also with people's lives, especially among the Callison family and their friends. On this crisp fall Saturday night, a year since Liz's return to the north country, she was curled up on the couch lying with the back of her body tucked against John. His arms tenderly encased and held Liz against him. A fire blazed in the hearth, making the space warm and cozy in the old family cabin. Liz and John had an old worn throw blanket tucked around them for added warmth. The television was on low so that the college football game did not wake John from his slumber. Liz knew that it had been a tough week for him as a forest ranger, especially when a hiker, who was unfamiliar with New York State bow hunting seasons, had not dressed appropriately to identify himself as a human being, and not as a deer wandering through the woods. The young man in his late twenty's, while innocently hiking on a state trail, had wandered off that trail and onto a path leading deep into the back country where bow hunters were waiting for a passing deer, and he was struck with a near fatal arrow. John had been involved with assisting a fellow ranger from up in Hamilton County with the rescue of the injured hiker, and the arrest of the hunter. There had been other little things that occurred on a daily basis, that had added up to form a strenuous tiring week for John. Now, John's steady, deep breathing as he slept informed Liz of just how tired he was. It felt right for Liz to have his arms protectively around her, and the warmth of his body against her. At that moment, she couldn't imagine any place that she'd rather be than lying there in John's arms. A sigh of contentment eased through her lips. Liz knew that this contentment that she was feeling was real. She had fallen in love with John. When had it happened? Liz honestly didn't know, especially since they had not known each other for very long. Was it the little things he said, or, did that had drawn her to him? Liz couldn't answer her own questions. She smiled softly. One thing she did know, was that it was many little things that added up to her being in love.

"I love you too." John quietly whispered in her ear. His breath against her hair sent warmth down through her entire body. Liz hadn't realized that John had awakened from his slumber. She snuggled in closer to John, as if that was possible with how close they already were lying together on the couch.

"Did I do something to awaken you?" She quietly asked him, then added, "How did you know what I was thinking?" Liz was truly amazed at how often they seemed to know what the other was thinking, or needed. The bond that was being formed between them was stronger than anything she had experienced in past relationships, including her most recent relationship with Peter.

"I was dreaming of you—" John lazily, gently, like the brushing of a feather against her warm skin, rubbed her arm as he proceeded to tell Liz what she was doing in his dream. She sighed in contentment and amazement as she listened to him say, "No woman has ever made me feel like how you make me feel. I feel your love even without you saying the words, whether I'm awake or asleep."

"I feel the same way, John." Liz sighed, as she leaned back against him, while his arms drew tighter around her. Warmth flooded over her like a fluffy down comforter covering her from the cold of winter.

John had awakened with a heightened need for physical release. So far, out of respect for Liz, knowing her past, he did not want to rush her into a physical relationship with him, that he wasn't sure she was ready for. Yes, they enjoyed kissing, touching, being intimate to a point of nearly no return. In every intimate moment, John had always managed to control his needs. But, tonight, the way she was pressed against him, the gentle, innocent rubbing of their bodies, he ached. Elizabeth was about to send him over the edge of his restraint.

"My precious, Elizabeth, as much as I'm enjoying lying here with you, we better get up for now." His fingers with feather lightness traced her jaw. Liz drew in a quick breath. She understood the desire that John was fighting. "One day we will lay together. Not yet, my precious storyteller. Not yet. The Great Spirit will tell us when the time is right for us."

Liz was restless and couldn't sleep. Her earlier conversation with John, and the way their bodies were responding to each other's touch, his obvious arousal, all kept replaying in her mind. She looked over at the bedside clock and grumbled. "Two in the morning and here I am awake and all alone. Tossing and turning. Oh, yes! I know what I am missing and longing for. I'm a thirty something, sexually frustrated woman!" She huffed to the empty dark room. "Well, John Runner, I sincerely hope The Great Spirit—God gives you the go ahead before too long!" Liz turned on the bedside light, threw back the covers, and got out of bed. She pulled on her warm house coat and slid her feet into her puffy brown dog slippers with droopy ears – a present from Callie Anne and Nicholas stood, yawned and headed for the bedroom door. After a stop in the bathroom, Liz went on into the kitchen to make a cup of tea.

The first light of day was peaking in the east window when Liz flopped back on her bed and drew the covers over her. Her eyes closed. Then, her phone rang, awakening her from her sound sleep. Liz glanced at the clock, as she reached for her phone. Noon! She gasped in disbelief that she has slept for so long.

"Hey, Cait!" She yawned, stretched and made an ungodly sound.

"Hey, yourself! You missed church, so, I'm calling to check on you and make sure you are okay. From the sounds of it you were asleep. Alone? Or, did I interrupt something?"

"Ugh! Don't start!" Liz was fighting to hold her eyelids open. She sighed. "I'm alone for your information. Not that it is any of your business." Liz added with a sting of annoyance in her voice. Silence. "And stop smiling!"

"Who said I'm smiling?" Caitlin asked with innocence, while beaming brightly and glad that Liz could not see her grinning from ear to ear. "I called because you told Callie that you'd be attending church with us today. Callie was concerned, since she was singing with the junior choir, and she had expected her aunt to be there to gush over her after church."

"Oh great!" Liz moaned. "I meant to be there. It's just that I had a rough night' sleep and…"

Caitlin listened to Liz explain what had happened, what she was wrestling with during the night when she should have been sleeping. Hearing Liz's reason was acceptable on an adult level, and as a sister. On the other hand, Caitlin was also a mother, and her child's expectations had not been met, crushed in fact, that Aunt Liz had not been there in the congregation with the rest of the Callison family to support her. "So, how do you plan on making this up to Callie

Anne?" Cait's voice indicated that whatever Liz came up with as a peace offering with Callie it had better be good. Really good, or else!

By now Liz was sitting up at the side of the bed with her bare feet resting on the bottom rung. Her flannel nightgown fell around her legs. She shivered from the coolness of the air in the room, rubbed her eyes with her free hand, and yawned. "Cait, I'm really sorry, and I'll make this up to Cal. When is her next day off from school?"

"Columbus Day weekend. Why?" Her voice was progressing from bristly toward not as irritated, but you're still not off the hook yet.

Liz rolled her eyes and shook her head, while knowing fully well that Caitlin was royally peeved with her, and frankly Liz didn't blame her sister. She loved her nieces and nephews, and the last thing that Liz wanted was for there to be a rift between them, of course, Samantha's twins were too young to be annoyed with her. Give them a year or two and they would be right along with Caitlin's kids! At this particular moment Liz knew that she needed to mend her tattered relationship with Callie.

"Well, maybe Callie would like to sleep over here at the cabin with me, and then go to work with me on that Monday, and be my assistant for the day. She could help me with getting ready for a couple of events at the arts center. Plus, I need to do a couple of more things out at the arts colony before winter sets in."

"That just might get you out of the doghouse with Callie."

"Oh no! I hear that tone of yours. The unspoken but!" Cait laughed. Liz scowled at that. "Since you are on a roll informing me of how I've messed up with your kids, go ahead and tell me how else I've failed as their aunt."

"Nicholas is not going to like being left out." Caitlin pointed out with that annoying motherly, *I'm the elder sister and I know what I'm talking about* tone of voice.

"Well, your son can sulk until he's one hundred for all I care! You can even tell him I said that. Because of his behavior last summer when he was in my care at the arts colony, he has lost any special privileges with me for a long time. A very long time!" Liz's voice had risen about twenty decibels. How dare her sister through the '*but he's my baby son*' card at her.

Cait sighed. Neither sister spoke. Then, Cait said, "Lizzie, I don't blame you for still being upset with Nick. But, do you think you could cut him a little slack? After all, it is because of him that you and John are now together."

"Unbelievable!" Liz exclaimed, as her bare feet patted towards the bedroom door, leaving her floppy slippers next to the bed for her to wear later. "My life keeps coming back to centering on John, even when I don't plan for it to be."

"And that my dear sister is a good thing. A very good thing which I full approve of. Now go get, some coffee. Get the grumpiness out of you. Shower. Get dressed and then get your butt over here so we can hang out together for the rest of the afternoon."

"Aye, aye, pain in my butt!" Liz snorted.

"I love you too! Sammie and Jordan both will do face time with us, so we can firm up our plans for the party. JJ has already said he will agree with what we think is best. All we have to do is tell him how much money he has to kick in."

"We should tell him the total cost, and make him think that's his part to pay." Liz snickered. She was becoming fully awake, anticipating the coffee that was dripping into her cup from the one cup machine she had recently treated herself to, and feeling her mood improving by the minute.

Caitlin gasped and exclaimed. "Lizzie! That sounds like something Aunt Amanda would say!"

Liz snorted as she thought of their aunt. "Yes, it does. Doesn't it? Perhaps later when we're all gathered together at your house, we should call Aunt Amanda. I think she'd appreciate our calling her."

Caitlin laughed, snorted, then responded. Liz couldn't help but laugh, as well. She was still smiling as she stepped into the shower. By now her thoughts had moved on to other things, like what she was going to do later that evening after spending time with her siblings.

Jim and Melissa had slowly eased into their day, as they continued to recover from the long drive north. Having spent the past two and a half weeks in Baltimore, it was good to be home. While driving north, they had freely exchanged their views on city life and country life. Both of them agreed that Amanda and Kevin could keep the city for all they cared. The Adirondack's would always be home for them! Their home no longer smelled uninhabited. The smell of morning coffee, and cooked breakfast lingered in the air, along with the soup Mel had heated for their lunch, popcorn and wood smoke.

They were relaxing in their recliners in front of the television watching a Sunday afternoon football game. The fire blazed in the fireplace making the room warm and cozy. A bowl of popcorn sat on the table between their recliners along with their drinks. Jim took a sip of flavored sparkling water, and smiled to himself, as he thought about this healthy change in his life. In years past, he would have been drinking beer while watching the game. Some time he still might. But, not today. Now, thanks to spending time with Amanda and Kevin through the years and recently, he was drinking flavored water. Jim could imagine what some of his friends would have to say, if, they ever found out about this change in his lifestyle.

Melissa's phone indicated that she had received a text from Amanda. It was perfect timing to draw their attention from the pitiful game that they were watching. Once again, the quarterback threw an interception. They both had been deeply touched by Amanda's heartfelt message regarding her and Kevin's appreciation for their love and support, during and immediately after her surgery. Jim had laughed when Amanda assured them that she was behaving herself. He knew fully well from having grown up with Amanda, and now having been with his sister as she was recovering from her surgery, as well as the weeks of rehabilitation that lay ahead for her when her hard cast was removed, that his younger sister's ability to behave was going to be tested to the limits of her universe. Heaven help Kevin keep his sanity with her! Then the sound of the ringing of the doorbell drew Jim's and Melissa's attention from the television and their conversation about Amanda.

Jim got up from his chair and went into the living room. As he approached the door, he glanced out the window. Oh boy! Jim drew in a long, slow breath. He turned the knob, plastered a smile onto his lips and opened the door. "Johnson! This is a surprise. Come on in!"

"Callison, good to see you. I took a chance that I might find you here. When did you and Mel get in?" Stephen asked, as he closed the door behind him. He made himself to home, taking off his coat and hanging it on the hook by the door. Wiping his feet on the door mat, he followed Jim into the living room. By now Melissa had appeared and stepped over to greet Stephen. She gave him a hug, as a normal friendly greeting. But Stephen noticed something in her greeting, and there was something in Jim's eyes that made him suspicious. It was that same feeling he had experienced a couple of weeks ago when he was speaking with Elizabeth on the day, she had stopped into the bait shop.

"We got in yesterday morning around 2:00 o'clock." Jim responded as they all made their way into the kitchen, where Melissa busied herself making coffee for them all. Quiet conversation about this and that took place between them all, while Mel fixed the coffee and brought over the container of cookies that Caitlin and Callie

Anne had made for them, as a welcome home present, along with Nicholas' home-made welcome home sign.

"I saw Liz shortly after you left on your vacation. She implied that you were staying it in Baltimore for the duration and not heading on down to the Carolina's or Florida. I didn't realize there was that much to do in Baltimore at this time of year." His gaze lazily passed between Jim and Melissa.

Jim wasn't fooled by the other man's demeanor. He had been attentively listening, watching Stephen as he spoke. He knew his friend was fishing, hoping to snag what he was looking for without being too obvious. Unfortunately, Stephen had used the wrong lure, and Jim didn't bite. An eyebrow rose as his chin tilted down, and he responded, "We had no desire to go further south. Mandy and Kevin living in Baltimore makes it quite convenient for going on day trips into the capital, northern Virginia, and the state of Maryland, even West Virginia, which we've done in the past. They have a spacious apartment and enjoy sharing their space with us. I think if we told them we were staying in a hotel, my sister would probably try to drop me from one of the bridges into the harbor." His expression dared Johnson to make a sarcastic remark.

Johnson wisely didn't take the bait. But he did laugh. "I could picture Amanda giving it her best shot to dump you over the rail of a bridge." Jim chuckled, and exchanged a brief, almost nonexistent glance with Mel. Stephen knew that they had just communicated on a level that no one else was privileged to share. He chose to ignore it for the time being and stated. "Maybe one of these days I'll suggest to Belinda that we take a vacation south, and since you know the area, you can give us some suggestions about what we might like to do." Now Stephen watched the more overt glancing, the unspoken communication between them. Oh yes! He knew without a doubt that the Callison family had secrets, and for some reason, they were not saying anything even to their closest of friends.

"I'm sure when and if you and Belinda decide to go to Baltimore, that we can give you some good suggestions. But, that's not what you really want to know. Is it?" Jim didn't wait for a response. His eyes told Stephen he would be smart to remain quiet and listen. "Sis, had vacation time to use up before the end of the year." Jim offered freely. "So, it was perfect for us to visit them, especially, now that it's not too hot and muggy down there. Plus, on the weekends Kevin and I were able to get in a few rounds of golf."

Stephen could accept both statements from Jim at face value. But they had been friends for too long. They knew each other too well. "I noticed the weather was supposed to have been nice while you were with them. That's good. It must have been nice for you to play golf with Kevin. Did you happen to go down to D.C. and see the monuments? How did you spend your days with Amanda?"

"Why the third degree, Johnson?" Jim asked. "Is there a problem with the fact that we went to visit our family?"

"No, Jim. There isn't a problem, unless, something is wrong with Mandy and for some reason you are not telling me, or Summer what's going on."

"Why does something have to be wrong?" Jim kept his tone even. His eyes revealed nothing about what he was thinking.

Stephen sighed. His gaze passed between them. The tiny hairs were still sticking up on the back of his neck, and Stephen had a very bad feeling. "Jim, I hope nothing is wrong with Amanda and Kevin. If, there is something going on with Amanda that Summer should know about," Stephen drew in a breath. He didn't know if he would be able to handle it, if something was wrong with the woman who had stolen his heart and never given it back. "Please. Try to reason with your sister and get her to contact Summer and tell her what's going on. Summer loves her mother, and she is beside herself not knowing how to bridge the cavern that now separates them."

Melissa tenderly placed her hand on Jim's forearm as it rested on the table. Her smile told him, *'I got this!'* Then, she spoke directly to Stephen. She held an even non-confrontational tone in her voice as she spoke. "Stephen, Summer, right along with the rest of us knows how to bridge the abyss that you and her created with Amanda. All Summer needs to do is put aside her pride, purchase a plane ticket, go to Baltimore and face her mother."

"Yeah, well-"

"No, yeah, well, about it!" The calm that Melissa had previously held was gone. She huffed in disgust. "Amanda is not going to beg Summer for her love. If, -" Mel held up her hand and shook her head. "Let me finish! If, Summer wants her mother's love badly enough, she knows where to go and what to do to find it!"

Stephen shifted his gaze to Jim, and unsurprisingly found his friend silently nodding in agreement with Melissa. He knew in his heart that Melissa had spoken the truth. The Callison's are a proud, loving family who will do anything for anyone. Many times, in their lives they have been walked on for their kindness towards other people. Still, they won't extend unkindness towards those who have hurt them. They simply move on and allow what is to simply be what is. Stephen Johnson knew that firsthand from his shared past with Amanda. He sighed as his gaze passed once more between Jim and Melissa. They both were silently watching him. "The next time you speak with Mandy, let her know I was asking of her. I also am respecting her wishes and not going to contact her." He released a frustrated breath. "As for Summer, I'll share your recommendation with her." He pushed the chair back from the table. "I better be going."

Jim and Mel stood in the living room next to the front window. They silently watched Stephen slowly drive his pickup out of their driveway and onto the road. Without a word Jim drew Mel into his arms, knowing that they both needed to hold on to each other, as they processed what had transpired with Johnson.

John was wet and cold from the downpour that he had been caught in while having to fix the flat tire on his SUV. Fortunately, the flat had occurred while at the office in Northville and not out on some gravel road off up in the mountains. There had recently been a number of vehicles vandalized in the area from Northville south to Mayfield. So, in the back of John's mind he had to wonder if, the flat tire had some help from a human in losing its air. With the tire in the back of his vehicle, to be taken to the local garage to be checked for the cause, John shivered as he slid onto the front seat behind the steering wheel, and turned the key in the ignition. A blast of heat soon filled the small space around him. As John sat in his vehicle, he pulled out his phone and placed a quick call to the garage. Five minutes later he was once again out in the rain, still soaked, and pulling the flat tire from the rear of his SUV. His wet clothes clung to him as he walked towards the door. The temperature was dropping, causing steam to come from his mouth as he breathed out. Stepping in through the side door by the overhead door John was greeted and relieved of the tire he carried. He waited and fifteen minutes later had his answer. Sabotage. There was a puncture mark—two to be exact—on the side of the tire. John and the mechanic both agreed that someone had probably used an ice pick to make the puncture in the tire. He knew that something the size of an ice pick would be easy enough to conceal and do the dirty deed. Before leaving the garage, John made a call to the Northville police department to report what had happened. Now, as he headed back outside to his vehicle to head home, he was wet, cold straight through to his bones and downright mad. Someone for some unknown reason had acted out against him. This troubled John, who sought to live a peaceful life with others. So, he had to wonder about the possibilities surrounding the flat tire. Was it random? Was it intentional because of who he was? Was his race a factor? Jon shivered from the wet cold clothes that the wore, and at the thought that the punctured tire could be a hate crime.

Then, his thoughts turned to his plans for the evening. It was time to head home, take a shower, and change into warm, dry clothes.

Liz was not a fan of driving in the rain, especially on the local roads in the area. It didn't matter what road she was traveling on, because as sure as she knew she was Jim Callison's daughter, the memory of her first accident, even though she hadn't hurt more than her pride, always came back to mind. Wet leaves were littered on the side of the road, water lay in wait on the surface, bidding her to go fast enough to hydroplane, just like on that dreary wet day during her teen years when she ended up in the ditch. A sigh of relief escaped from Liz's lips as she slowed, turned on her directional and turned right to head over the bridge into the village of Northville. At the corner she turned north onto Main Street. She slowly went past the Five & Dime, and other stores along the street were closed or closing for the day. With a smile, and a wave to the owner of the Adirondack Country Store, Liz continued on north out of the village. In a matter of minutes, she turned left onto the old road that would take her to John's cabin.

Liz enjoyed the drive up into the side of the mountain where John's cabin was nestled in among the tall white pines. In many ways the drive was similar to driving on the road to her family's cabin. A smile graced her lips as she thought, *Great gram would approve of John. Yes, she would. I can hear her sharing her uncensored views on his character, his maturity, his wit, of course the fact that he is a Mohawk—well, for that Gram would say I could do no better.* "I could do no better." Liz breathed out to the music playing in her car. Charlie might be singing that he has a golden ticket, but Liz—her heart did a flip flop, her breath caught—Liz knew in her heart that she has a golden man. Her golden man. Oh, she was wise enough to admit that he does have his flaws, just like the other men of her past. But his goodness far outshone his idiosyncrasies, and that mattered to Liz.

She drew in a breath, released it and allowed a full smile to appear on her face as she slowed down, turned into the driveway and parked next to John's SUV. Pulling the hood of her raincoat over her head, Liz grabbed her purse and the bags with her contribution for their dinner, opened the door, then sprinted to the porch.

As Liz got to the top step the front door opened. John welcomed her inside as he gently kissed her. Then he took the bag that held the rest of their meal, so Liz could remove her wet coat and rubber boots from her feet.

"So, I hope the biscuits and the pumpkin pie that I bought from the bakery will go with dinner." She sniffed the air. Deep, rich, aromas of venison, potatoes, and fall vegetables filled the air around them.

"That will be fine. Thank you." With one hand lightly touching Liz's back, he nudged her towards the small, but well organized and functional eat in kitchen.

"So, what would you like for me to do to help?" Her eyes sparkled with happiness, as she breathed in the smells of the food cooking in the slow cooker, and the oven. "John, earlier today you told me that you were making dinner in the slow cooker. What's in the oven? Or is it a secret?" Her smile, her eyes, everything about Elizabeth lovingly was melting John's heart, like butter in a pan over a low flame. He smiled, reached over and opened the oven door, so Liz could see what was inside. Acorn squash was baking.

John reached over onto the counter and picked up a long-handled fork. "We need to check these and see how near done they are."

The squash needed more time, which was fine with them. There was more to do before the rest of the dinner guests arrived. Quiet conversation flowed between them as they set the table for four. They were surprised to discover that they both were a little nervous about Liz's parents joining them for dinner at his cabin. In the past her parents had been with them on Callison turf, in the Great

Sac Community, or at the arts center or colony. For Jim and Melissa to be invited to John's domain was a monumental step in Liz and John's relationship.

"So, John, I hear you had a bit of a problem today." Jim's comment caught both Liz and John off guard. Melissa as well. His expression, the closeness of his brows, that Liz recognized as his deep concern look. The darker appearance of his eyes, intense with concern, and the tone that he had used implies an underlying statement, *tell me what happened today.*

"John, are you alright?" Melissa asked. Concern had immediately replaced her previously relaxed expression.

John had told Liz about his flat tire before her parent's had arrived. They both had decided it would be best to not say anything about it in front of her parents, especially since it appeared that someone had intentionally punctured the tire. Their eyes met, as if to ask the other, how did he find out? She knew from growing up in the Callison household that when her dad began a sentence with, 'So,' and your name, you needed to answer him truthfully the first time, or else. Liz gave John a reassuring smile and a slight nod that everything would be okay. He slightly nodded, then turned his gaze to the older woman who was carefully watching their interaction. Concern was in her eyes, the way she held her body.

"Melissa, Jim, I am fine. I just got soaked having to change a flat tire. It's no big deal." John hoped his tone did not lead them to conclude that he had not been totally truthful with them.

Jim had taken a sip of coffee, and was placing the mug on the table as John spoke to them. His eyes observed everything about John, the words he chose to use when he spoke, his tone, the way he was holding himself as he sat across from them. The man was lying and that did not bode well with Jim.

"Would you care to change your story? Or, are you going to hold on to your statement that the flat tire is not a big deal, so Melissa won't worry?"

"Geesh, Dad! You're retired and John's not a criminal, so stop acting like a cop! Please." Liz added, not feeling too comfortable with where the conversation was heading.

"Jim? John?" Mel asked as her gaze passed between them, then on Liz, before her gaze settled back on Jim. "What's going on, Callison, and don't even think of giving me the brush off. I've been your wife for to many years, and if something has happened that I should be aware of, then you had best spill it right now."

Oh boy! Liz knew that tone of voice her mother used when she meant every word that she was saying. Neither Liz nor John spoke. They watched.

"John, you might be able to use, 'It's no big deal,' with others, but not in our family. That's like a bull fighter waving a red flag at an old ornery bull who's just itching for a fight. I only happen to know what happened because I stopped at the garage ten minutes after you left to schedule an oil change for my pickup. The fact that Lara and Ken from the local police department were still there talking with Smittie, well, they told me what happened to you." At that moment, Jim turned his gaze towards Liz, who was watching him like a hawk. Heaven help him, if, he said something against John, because she was perched in her chair, as if ready to swoop in to protect him from peril. "Young lady, until this issue with vandalism gets resolved, you too had best pay attention to your surroundings, and who happens to be near your vehicle."

Liz saw the concern in his eyes. It touched her deep within. Jim Callison was not only concerned for his daughter's wellbeing, but also for John. "Yes, Dad. I'll be careful." At that moment, Liz slid her hand over to gently grasp John's hand. Her eyes met his as she added, "We'll be careful. Right?"

His eyes held hers, as he gave her a firm nod of reassurance. Both Jim and Melissa watched the silent interaction taking place across the table from them. They approved of what they saw. Liz and John had a maturity in their relationship that had been missing in her relationship with Peter. Oh, they had approved of Peter Jones, mostly because they knew his parents and extended family, and had watched him grow up with their son. Now, as they watched Liz and John together as a couple, they realized that Liz had been right in breaking off her relationship with Peter when she did. John was simply a more suitable partner for Elizabeth. They clicked as a couple. Both Jim and Melissa knew it will be interesting for them to watch and see how this relationship continues to progress.

The arts center was abuzz with activity. The members of the Great Sac Community High School senior class and select members of the drama club, were congregated in the main room to meet with Liz about their idea for a winter event. Liz had been both honored and concerned when Kellie and Amber had initially presented their idea to her. Now, seeing their enthusiasm, as they grabbed refreshments and began to take a seat around the tables, Liz knew that she had been right in making her decision. Their idea was fresh and certainly going to be out of many people's comfort zones. But the arts are often that way, often taking people from their comfort, the familiar, to experience life in a new way. Liz, knew that from first-hand experience having worked within the theater.

"Liz, do you think Mr. Jones is going to be mad at us for coming to you with our idea, instead of going to him and asking for permission to use the school?" Brittney asked.

Liz, had gotten to know Brittney during the summer, when the young woman volunteered at the colony and worked in the box office. Her question was a legitimate one, and deserved an honest answer, which Liz intended to give her.

"Well, Brittney, I wouldn't be a bit surprised to hear that he is hurt, when it comes to his attention that we are doing this Senior Extravaganza without his assistance. After all, he is your class adviser as well as drama club adviser and hockey assistant coach. Mr. Jones is one of your teachers that goes above and beyond the classroom. Even teachers who are willing to go further than other faculty members, sometimes need to let things go and allow others to take the lead."

"And you do it better than everyone else!" Kellie, senior class president, added as she came over to stand next to Liz. "I think we are ready to begin."

Liz couldn't help but smile. In the past year she had come to have an affinity towards Kellie. She was a special person, who would keep a special place in Liz's heart after she graduated and went out to concur the world.

"Alright then, let's get this show on the road!" They shared a nod in agreement, then Liz addressed the teens assembled with them.

An hour later the building was filled with laughter, excitement from all of the teens, then the outside door opened. They all drew in and released a collective gasp. Liz's eyes darted from the apprehensive students to their intruder. She moved defensively from where she stood to take her place between the students and the intruder. Neither her body language, nor her voice revealed how she was feeling.

"Good afternoon, Mr. Jones. Is there something I may do for you? Or, can whatever you need wait until we are finished with our meeting?" Liz recognized Peter's expression. He was sporting for a fight. Well, it was not going to happen in front of the young people who were watching them. Anticipating. She remained calm, while informing everyone, especially Peter, that she is in charge of her turf.

"I'm the senior class adviser and drama club adviser. Therefore, this meeting should be happening at the school. Or, is it here because you think you are the only creative person in the community, and that the arts can only happen with your leadership?"

Liz did not immediately respond. Instead, she turned to the students and addressed them. "Ladies and gentlemen, I apologize for this interruption in our planning meeting. Please, take a brief break, grab some refreshments and I will be with you momentarily. After I speak privately with Mr. Jones." The students responded in support of Liz, taking Peter very much by surprise. Then, she turned and took a step towards him. "Mr. Jones, if you will follow me, we will step over to my office to continue this conversation. Privately."

Her expression dared Peter to challenge her. Without waiting for Peter to respond, Liz turned and walked away from him and the students, who were silently watching them. They made it as far as the door to Liz's office when she stopped, turned and glared at Peter. Her voice was quiet so that he had to listen intently to hear her. "How dare you walk in here and start accusing me of taking over your school authority with these teens!" Her eyebrows drew close, as her eyes smoldered with the warning signs of impending fire. "In case you have for some unknown reason forgotten, let me remind you, this room that you are now standing in is the Community Arts Center."

Peter shifted his weight from one leg to the other, and drew in a breath as Liz continued with her finger pointed towards him. He recognized all the tell-tale signs. Elizabeth Callison was enraged with anger, and at any moment, knowing her, she was going to erupt like an old dormant volcano.

"And I, Peter, not you, me," she pointed to herself for effect, and it worked, along with her drawn eyebrows. "Elizabeth Callison, I am the director of the Great Sacandaga Community Arts Association. That includes the arts center which we are now standing in, as well as the summer arts colony. I'm sure you remember the events that took place this past summer at the arts colony. Regardless, of what you choose to remember, remember this." Her voice remained even, with unseen fire burning beneath the surface. "As long as I am the director, I do not need your permission. Or anyone else, for that matter, to meet with the teens from our community and hear their creative ideas surrounding things that they are interested in doing for fun and enjoyment."

"You got that right! Go, Ms. Callison! Great theater whisper!" Select teens said, as the group applauded her. Liz felt the heat rise in her cheeks and knew without a doubt that she had turned multiple shades of red. Oh well! She turned and addressed the students, then turned back to Peter. His glare almost intimidated her. Almost, being the key word. Liz was like an old-fashioned pressure cooker on top of a hot stove. She was ready to fully blow, if, he said one more stupid thing! Heaven help Peter, if he did!

"Elizabeth, since you are on a roll, you might as well finish your tirade by telling me what this meeting is about. I warn you that I am close to going to the community arts board with a formal complaint against you."

That did it! Liz had reached her boiling point. How dare he threaten her that he would go to the board with this! Peter was being ridiculous, and as their teacher, he was not setting a good example for them. But obviously he didn't care. Well, Liz did, and it was time to finish this ghastly scene before it got any further out of hand. This was not the example that she wanted to set for the students in their midst, as their mentor and friend.

"Peter, you really need to work on that ego of yours." That stung, as planned! "For your information, the majority of the youth sitting here with me have given up their time, not because they have to but, because they want to assist me with planning something that will hopefully be fun for our community." Quiet comments from the teens were heard supporting her. A smile shone within Liz as she continued.

"Yes. This event involves the senior class of our high school. Big deal! These teens have a life beyond the school grounds. For your information, what we are planning to do also involves the senior citizens of our community." She saw the look in his eyes. A light bulb went on in his brain and he was beginning to understand how deeply he had misjudged her actions. Good! "Peter, I'm not encroaching on your little drama club at the high school." Liz heard the whispers among the teens. She knew that she was not setting a good example, but right now it was like she was sucked up into a tornado that had begun as a small rope and was growing to become a wedge tornado, leaving nothing but sheer destruction in its wake. Her eyes flamed with rage. She beckoned for him to open his mouth, and say something else to feed her anger. He didn't.

"Speaking of the drama club, on the day in which I learned that I had been chosen to be the director of the arts center and summer theater, I spoke with some of these teens sitting here in this room. Perhaps you also will recall that day, since you were standing in the school parking lot with me when these teens and I first met. That afternoon, I listened to these amazing talented young people. I saw and heard their passion for the arts. Besides answering their questions about my work on and off of Broadway, I shared some of my ideas with them for multi-generational events that might take place here at the center as well as events just for them."

"I remember!"

"Me too!"

Liz smiled softly, as she listened to the teens come to her defense. She also noticed Peter's expression. Times like this reminded both of them of what they had shared. It also brought to light how difficult it may be to move on from a relationship, and have to deal with each other in different social settings.

"I am about ready to rest my case with you. As I already said, we are, that is, I am, not encroaching on your domain. This is a community arts event that happens to have been conceived by the creative minds of these young people gathered here. So, stop acting like a two-year-old who is mad because he had his toy taken away from him. Your temper tantrum time is over. You have thoroughly embarrassed me in front of my committee. In the future, if, you have a concern or issue with me, call and request a private meeting with me. Now, if you will excuse me, the committee and I have work to do."

Peter's gaze moved past Liz to the students who were quietly watching their interaction. He knew that by tomorrow morning, long before the first bell rang in the school, everyone would know of his and Liz's altercation. Peter sighed. "Everyone, I owe you an apology for my misunderstanding what was happening here, stepping out of bounds and interrupting your meeting. See you all tomorrow." He turned back to meet Liz's gaze. She remained quiet. Watching. Peter saw the slight movement in her eyes. The subtle signs. He had deeply hurt her, once again. "Liz, Elizabeth, I am deeply sorry for once again hurting you. I'm sure whatever you and the kids are planning will be great. I'll be going now. Take care."

Liz nodded. She was unable to find her voice. Actually, she was afraid of what else might come out of her mouth, if, she was to open it again. She remained facing the door, watching Peter as he walked away from them, dejected. So much had happened between them. Sadness sought to consume her, but Liz knew she had to reign it in, and not reveal to the teens how deeply Peter's presence had affected her. After all, the show—life—must go on!

CHAPTER 21

Liz was still zinging with annoyance, from her altercation with Peter, when she left the community arts center to head home for the evening. As she began her drive, going towards Route 30 to head north to the old road leading up to Gram's cabin, she pulled up her phone in her car menu and dialed her aunt.

"Well, good almost but not quite evening, Elizabeth!" Liz smiled at her aunt's greeting. She sighed, and felt the tension already beginning to lift from her, as she listened to Amanda. "How did you know that I was thinking of you?" Amanda innocently asked without a clue as to what had transpired over an hour ago at the community arts building.

"Hey, Aunt Amanda," Liz released a longer, slower sigh.

"Oh boy! I know that particular sigh. Who did what? Was it my brother? Or, don't I want to know?" Amanda asked with that tone that welcomed Liz to unload her frustrations. For the next few minutes she listened to Liz recap the afternoon highs and lows. Peter Jones was certainly the lowest point for Liz. She commented, sighed with disgust, inserted *tsk, tsk, tsk* countless times, as well as making some other noises, that Liz knew how to interpret. Too bad she couldn't see her aunt's facial expressions. She was sure they were also very telling. "Well, Peter Jones certainly is turning out to be a disappointment! But, then again, he is part Johnson, and given his uncle's track record, as well as the influence the man has had on Peter, I must say, I'm not totally surprised by Peter's behavior. A part of me is glad that Reverend and Mrs. Johnson have both passed away, so that they are not here to see how their family is acting towards others."

"Oh?" Liz needed to hear more about what her aunt thought of the situation regarding the Johnson family.

Amanda sighed. Liz quietly waited for her aunt to continue, as she drove on, slowed and cautiously drove past a couple of does and fawns standing at the edge of the woods by the road.

"This whole mess reminds me of the message our pastor preached last Sunday." She chuckled at Liz's response, then continued. "Yes, Kevin agreed to my request and helped me get ready and go to church. Thank goodness we have a handicapped entrance, and I was able to get in the building with Kevin's assistance. At any rate, what I want to share with you is this. You might want to read in the book of James, specifically the verse about the fire that the tongue sets ablaze. That's what the message was on, how the tongue is so destructive and is something we cannot tame. With it, we bless God and then we go and curse, and hurt people. We forget that we are created in God's image and we are all of sacred worth. Yet, as humans, we think nothing of ripping others apart, as if they don't matter. Sadly, Elizabeth, I, myself, am equally guilty. I usually try to cut others some slack for their behavior, but, given my history and current situation with the Johnson family, it is far too easy for me to judge, and say hateful things against Stephen. Then, there's my heartache over my own daughter, Summer, and now Peter is added to the mix. Sometimes, in my humanness I fail to recognize, or even acknowledge that I have sinned and fallen short of God's glory, particularly when it comes to the Johnson's. My tongue gets started and look out—it's an uncontrollable wildfire!"

Silence.

"Sorry, Liz, I didn't mean to go off on a tangent like that. As you can see, I have many unresolved issues with the Johnson family."

"Aunt Amanda," her voice was filled with quiet softness. "This is why I love you and respect you so much. You speak from your heart, and you gave me plenty to think about. Thank you for being confident enough with who you are to allow me to see your strength and your flaws. I think that makes you a beautiful person."

There was a sniffle sound, then a sigh. "Elizabeth, I love you too, and know that you are special to me as well!"

By the time Liz had turned up the old road and had driven up the side of the mountain past six deer and a number of squirrels who appeared to want to play - *dodge the tires* - with her, and then over the one lane bridge that takes her over the creek, she paused for a flock of turkeys. Then she came around the final bend in the road, then slowed and pulled onto the gravel drive leading to the cabin, she was feeling better. Once again, Aunt Amanda had come to the rescue. Liz smiled, as she stopped her car next to the old barn and put the transmission into park. She turned off the ignition and sighed, as she thought, *Aunt Amanda is awesome! Mom and Dad are going to be surprised big time!*

Jim had been feeling off, since he had gotten up that morning. His body ached, not his normal mid 60's aches. It seemed that no matter what he did, he couldn't get warm. Melissa had noticed his grumpy disposition, his sudden obsession with keeping the fire blazing in the fireplace, making the whole house hotter than the Florida Keys! As Jim sat at the kitchen table, after completing the noon meal, Mel got up from her seat to bring dessert over from the counter. She reached over and placed the back of her warm hand against Jim's forehead and then his cheek. She sighed.

"Callison, you don't have a fever. So, I don't know what's crept into you! I suggest that after we finish lunch that you go lay down and take a nap. Maybe that will help you shake off whatever is going on in you before we go out tonight."

"Tonight—ugh! I don't see how I'm going to feel up to going to this Art Association Appreciation Dinner that Liz has planned. Is she really planning on giving me an award for my volunteerism?"

Melissa softly smiled. "Yes, she is, and Callison, I have to agree with Lizzie. You have gone above and beyond with helping her, not only at the arts center with little things, mostly for what you did at the old arts colony. I'm sure part of the award is because of you were with her when your dad's body was discovered."

"I guess so." Jim gave her a grin. "That child of ours sure is something!"

"Yes, she is. I have a feeling this is one way for Lizzie to tell you and the community how much she loves you!" Mel placed a plate of chocolate peanut butter swirl brownies on the table, returned to the counter and filled two mugs of coffee, then joined Jim at the table.

The afternoon nap Jim took in his recliner, along with the Tylenol that Mel had given him, had done wonders to help Jim feel better. He got up from his nap feeling refreshed, no longer in pain or cold. He knew better than to complain about how hot it was in their house!

Time was of the essence, so Jim hurried upstairs to take a quick shower, then leave the bathroom free for Melissa. Jim changed into casual dark blue pants, a light blue oxford shirt, a multi-color pull-over sweater to wear to the community event. He had just finished sliding into his brown leather shoes, when Melissa emerged from the bathroom. After thirty-five plus years of being together, including when they dated, the woman still took his breath away when he looked at her. Jim remembered the day that they met, like it was yesterday. Melissa was a hostess in her parent's eatery in Mayfield. He had finished working at the marina, and had decided to stop in for an early dinner, at the Mayfield Eatery, not his usual stomping ground. Their eyes met. They smiled at each other and as the saying goes, *the rest is history!* Jim lazily smiled like a cat that had just caught a delectable dinner to feast on, as he watched Mel's eyes look him over from his head to his feet.

"Do I pass your inspection?" He asked playfully.

"Oh yes!" There was a breathlessness, a wistfulness, in her voice, a hunger, desire that after thirty five years continued to grow stronger for her as well. "Already, I can see how tonight will be. I'm going to have to keep a close eye on you, Callison. I just know that I'm going to have to ward off the other women. No doubt, they will be throwing themselves at you."

"Possessive, are you?" His brow lifted. There was playfulness in his eyes and the corners of his mouth.

"You better believe I'm staking my claim. You are mine!" Her coy smile about did Jim under. She licked her lips, then added, "Till death and only death parts us!" With that said, the subject was officially closed. Melissa turned and walked over to the closet where she began to take out clothes and toss them onto the bed. Jim remained seated on his side of the bed and watched. Memories took shape in his mind. He laughed. Melissa looked up from the two outfits she was debating between wearing to the special dinner party. "What struck you, Jim?"

"Oh, I was remembering back to the winter when Mandy returned, and we were preparing to go to see her at her and Kevin's friend's cabin. That day you also had a difficult time figuring out what you wanted to wear when you met Sis for the first time, if, my mind serves me well."

"Shish, Jim! You and Amanda have memories like elephants! And your timing for remembering things never ceases to amaze me!"

Melissa rolled her eyes, as a grin took shape on her lips. She shook her head with amusement.

Jim stood, walked around to where Melissa stood by the bed, gently took the dress from her hand, placed it on the bed, then drew her into his arms. "Yes, I do have a decent memory. Most importantly, I remember all the reasons why I love you." He gently brushed his lips over hers, "And now, I'm going downstairs, so you can get ready without my distracting you."

The early November night was already dipping down into the mid-twenties. The wind rolling in from the west through the lower Adirondack's and the Mohawk valley had a bite to it, ushering in the new frontal system. Snow, unfortunately, was in the forecast for Sunday. Regardless, of what the weather brought to the community, there was a party planned for that Saturday night. It was sure to be a memorable community event.

Elizabeth decided to take a brief break from the final preparations, much to Caitlin's chagrin. It wasn't like Liz hadn't done a blessed thing to help with organizing the party! It had been a couple of weeks since she had seen Samantha and the twins. So, Liz claimed a few minutes to be with Sammie and hold Mary for a few minutes, before getting back to final preparation for the night's festivities. From where the Callison sisters stood, they had an optimal view of the people gathered thus far. Much to their delight, JJ had been able to get home, and had remained hidden from his parents by spending the weekend crashed and Cait and Nick's home in Northville. That wasn't what drew Liz's attention. She was pleased with how JJ, Chris and Nick were including both John and Thomas in their conversation.

Sammie sighed, as she removed the bottle from Danny's mouth, drew him to her shoulder and patted his back. The burp that came from her infant son caused everyone to stop what they were saying, or, doing and cast their eyes on Sammie and her son. Laughter and comments from the men followed.

A gentle hand on Samantha's son and another hand on her opposite shoulder eased her displeasure.

"Don't let them bother you." Caitlin quietly commanded. "It's a man thing!" With that said, the three sisters drew Samantha into their fold for their own solidarity, and they engaged in their own private sister laughter.

Family. Liz sighed, as her turn with holding one of the babes had come to an end. She handed off Mary to Jordan, then went off with Cait to attend to greeting guests who were beginning to arrive for the party. As Liz and Cait made their way to the door, both John and Nick Senior joined them. Liz felt John slide his hand over hers and lace their fingers. Then, she felt a gentle squeeze. She looked up into his dark brown eyes, that with the subdued lighting in the pavilion, looked black as coal, and felt her heart do a flip-flop.

Liz and John along with Jordan and Thomas stationed themselves by the door to welcome the guests to the party. Becky and Wesley Jones, as owners of the property, had helped with setting up the pavilion for the party. Then, during the late afternoon they had disappeared to go home and get ready for the evening's celebration. Now they were back. Liz breathed a sigh of relief, when she saw that Peter was not with them. Then, much to her disappointment, Becky whispered to her that Peter would be arriving later, along with Stephen Johnson and his girlfriend Belinda. Liz thanked Becky, then turned to quietly share her troubling news with John. He drew her into his arms, and away from the newly arrived guests.

"Elizabeth, sweetheart, remember our conversation that we had after your confrontation with Peter?" His fingers gently stroked her back, easing the tension that sought to strangle her.

Liz tightened her arms that were around John's waist. She laid her head against his chest and sighed. Tilting her head up towards his chin, she quietly said, "Yes, I remember, and thank you, John for being here with me."

"There is no place, I'd rather be."

A soft eclectic mix of music played, since there were infants in the room and loud damaging noise was a factor for their delicate hearing. The plan was for the professional photographer, who was there taking candid pictures of the guests, to take formal pictures of Jim and Melissa, and their family soon after their arrival. Then, the twins would go home with Chris' parents to Sammie and Christopher's home, so that they would be free to party with their family and friends.

The moment that everyone had been waiting for finally happened. The five Callison children, their spouses, significant others, and the four grandchildren all gathered by the entrance. Everyone else, from Stephen Johnson, Jim's best man, and Nora, Melissa's cousin and maid of honor, and friends stood behind them. Then, the door opened. Everyone yelled, "Surprise!"

Surprise wasn't the word for it! Jim and Melissa simultaneously gasped, their eyes widened as their gazes passed from their children to their friends, then back to their children and grandchildren. Their fingers had found each other, and laced together, as tears welled up in both sets of shocked eyes. This obviously was not a party involving the arts center, as they had been led to believe. Jim sniffled back his emotions, as best he could, while Melissa waved the white flag of defeat and allowed her tears to freely tumble down her cheeks. So much for the makeup that she had carefully applied before leaving their home! At least she didn't have on mascara that would leave streaks on her tear reddened cheeks. Callie Anne and little Nick managed to get their hugs, while Mary and Danny decided to let everyone know that they did not appreciate the noise. Leave it to Mel to rotate from guest of honor to doting grandmother, and break away from Jim to check on and console the little ones. Of course, each of the Callison sisters had responses to their mother's actions. Mel simply smiled, as Jim placed his hand on the small of her back and got in on checking on the little ones.

Stephen Johnson, experienced a multitude of unexpected emotions, as he watched Jim and Melissa with their family at their celebration of thirty five years of marriage. He glanced over at Belinda, his current girlfriend, as she quietly conversed with Becky. Then, his gaze returned to Jim and Melissa. A tug of grief that seemed to spring up like an unwanted weed in the middle of a pristine garden, sought to consume him. Jim was his oldest, dearest friend, after his brother, Phil. On this night, if life had been different for him and Amanda—Stephen momentarily closed his eyes to force back what he was feeling—he would have been standing there not only as Jim's friend, but also as his brother in law. Life obviously had not gone as they had imagined.

Still, Stephen had a job to do, as the best man who had stood at Jim's side thirty five years ago. He stepped up to the microphone, and encouraging everyone to find a seat, and a glass of sparkling cider. He ushered Jim and Melissa to the special head table that was prepared for them, and their small wedding party and their partners. Then, Stephen proved to everyone that he was the right person to give the toast. His words were filled with humor, kindness, respect and admiration for their loving marriage and family that they certainly could be proud of. The dinner, much to Jim and Mel's surprise, along with everything else, was a catered affair. Jazz music softly played in the background while they ate.

As Jim and Melissa sat with their wedding party, they shared memories of their lives together through the years. The Callison children had placed a note by a bottle of French champagne—explaining that they were expecting them to chill and enjoy together later in the comfort of their home. From the table where they sat, Jim and

Mel were able to see their children, grandchildren and their friends, who were sharing their special night with them. They leaned close so that their shoulders were touching, and quietly spoke to one another about how the evening would be perfect, if, Amanda and Kevin had been able to join them. But they both understood that the trip would have been difficult for Amanda, even though she was eight weeks out from her surgery. The hard cast was off of her foot, and she was walking with a boot on her right foot, and alternating between crutches or a cane, depending on her threshold of pain. Still, their family members absence was felt by them. "Honestly, Mellie," Jim quietly said, "Amanda not being here is like how it was when we married. At least now we know where she is and why she's not here."

Jim's grief did not linger for too long. Especially when the DJ announced that it was time for the first dance of the evening. Jim and Melissa stood. Jim protectively placed his hand on the small of Melissa's back and guided her to the small dance area. As the familiar old music began, they were amazed to hear that their children had taken the time to make sure that their song was played for them. Even though they had been married in the early1980's their song would always be from the 70's. *How Deep Is Your Love* by the Bee Gee's belted out from the speakers, as Jim and Melissa moved across the floor in perfect harmony with each other and the music. Everyone had their eyes on Jim and Mel, so they were unaware of things that the Callison children were orchestrating out of their sight.

The music stopped, the dance came to an end and everyone clapped, as Jim and Melissa turned towards their family and friends. It was then, that they saw the ultimate surprise their children had prepared for them. There, leaning on crutches, in a dark blue long sleeve dress with a high waist and swing skirt, a low heel navy blue shoe on her left foot, and a clunky black boot on her right foot stood Amanda biting her lips to not break out into laughter. Kevin did grin, as he stood protectively at her side, looking dapper in his burgundy dress shirt, black sports coat, black slacks and black dress shoes. As if on cue, Jim and Melissa's mouths dropped open. They both were unable to speak, and that didn't happen too often for either of them! Fortunately, Caitlin, appeared to have her emotions under control. With microphone in hand, she stepped into the empty space between her parents and her aunt and uncle.

"Mom, Dad, now that Aunt Amanda and Uncle Kevin have finally made it here, well, we have a few confessions to make to you." Her eyes shimmered with joy.

"A few!" Jim finally found his voice. He shook his head in disbelief at all the surprises his family had come up with for them.

"Well, yes." Caitlin confessed with laughter in her voice.

"And your mother and I expect to hear your confession in a minute." Jim said with a smile, as he led Melissa over to where Amanda and Kevin stood. Without a word, one of the Callison children took Amanda's crutches, as Jim engulfed her into his arms for a hug.

"Perfect, Dad!" Caitlin exclaimed as her smile grew. "You saved me from having to tell you what to do!"

Jim, continued to hold on to Amanda, as he drew his attention back to Caitlin. His eyes held a touch of mischief, although the rest of his expression suggested that he could be serious. "Child, I'd be careful with throwing your weight around, thinking you are entitled to tell your mother and me what to do."

Amanda whispered to Jim, causing him to shake his head. Then, he threw his hands up in mock surrender and laughed.

"Thank you, Aunt Amanda, for whatever you said to Dad." Jordan spoke up.

Amanda commented causing everyone who heard her to laugh as well. More comments and laughter followed. Then, Caitlin regained everyone's attention and said to her parent's, "Since, Grandma Callison had died and obviously was not at your and Mom's wedding reception to dance with you, we asked, -" by now Jim was looking down at his sister. Everyone watching them could see Jim physically swallowing his emotions. Amanda's eyes twinkled with delight. She slightly nodded and softly smiled.

"-Sis, I was there for your surgery. I know what you've been through. You can't be serious?" Jim was asking, while in his mind he knew that with his sister, this far out from major surgery, wearing a boot to protect her foot, was not going allow her surgery to impede her from dancing. She might not be able to do intricate steps required in fast dances, but Jim was certain that she sure could and would slow dance! Heaven help the person who tried to stop Amanda!

"I'm here, aren't I?" She raised a playful brow along with her lips. "Later we'll tell you what we went through to get here! But, for now, you owe me a dance for Mom, and the one I didn't get to share with you on your wedding day!"

"Okay. Now that we have you two set for the dance," Caitlin turned her attention to her mother. "Mom, we didn't forget about you. So, since Grandpa isn't able to be with us, because of having Alzheimer's, and unable to do the father-daughter dance with you, we had to be creative."

"We all didn't want you to be left out. You know, thinking we loved Dad more than you, or anything like that!" JJ said.

Cait turned to pointed gaze at JJ. "J, I got this!"

"Gee, Caitie, you don't need to get snippy! I was just trying to help and move you along. The rate you're going we'll be here until midnight before you finish with your explanation."

Amanda was fully amused to watch her nieces and nephew in full force with Jim and Melissa. Her quiet words to JJ didn't go unnoticed by Caitlin.

"Thanks, Aunt Amanda. As I was saying, Mom, after minimal discussion, because it was a *no brain-er*, and Aunt Amanda shared her words of wisdom with us, we asked Uncle Kevin to do the honors and dance with you."

416

That did it! Melissa looked lovingly at Amanda and Kevin, then burst into another round of tears. Their scheming wonderful loving children and their accomplices had thought of everything. The night could not have been any more perfect!

Sammie and Chris left shortly after Jim and Mel had finished their dances, and everyone else filled the dance floor. The rest of the Callison children and their mates eased into the night of celebration and were either sitting conversing together, or were on the dance floor. Liz and John had finished dancing and had helped themselves to a cold drink, when Amanda drew their attention, and they took a seat next to her.

"John, I'm glad to finally meet you and have this opportunity to chat with you." Amanda said with an even revealing tone, and a smile. Liz was watching and listening to her aunt. For some reason, she felt as if she needed to be on high alert. Perhaps, it was because of her past experiences with Aunt Amanda when she was dating Peter.

"The feeling is mutual, Amanda. Elizabeth, holds you in high regard. I value her judgment." John politely responded.

Amanda's expression was even. But there was something in those dark brown eyes of hers, that informed them that she was sizing him up, and by the end of the night would have formed her opinion of John Runner, good or bad. John's eyes grew wide with surprise, as Amanda spoke to him in Iroquois. Liz was dumbfounded by this, and watched John, as his lips formed a slight smile. Then, he responded to Amanda in the language of their people. One full blooded Mohawk and one of mixed heritage sat together on the common ground of their language. What they shared was important for both of them.

Jim and Mel, along with Kevin, who had gone off to get cold drinks for Amanda and himself, had arrived in time to hear Amanda. Their gazes were fixed on Amanda and John. Liz attempted to cut into their conversation, when Jim cautioned her to remain quiet. Something innately told Jim to trust Amanda's lead, and allow this conversation to continue on its path. Jim watched John as he responded to Amanda, turn his gaze to Liz, smile, then return his gaze to Amanda. Ah! So, their conversation involved Elizabeth. Jim felt himself smiling within and allowed others to see how he was feeling as he outwardly smiled.

"Dad, what's funny? Do you understand their conversation?" Liz wanted to know. Her gaze darted between her family and John like a ping pong ball bouncing out of control.

"No. But, I do know that you need to trust your aunt. One thing I am certain of, and that is, that when the time is right, we all will know what they shard together here tonight." Jim said no more. He turned his gaze to his sister and John. Oh, yes! Amanda was on a mission.

Liz yawned, as she slowly moved about in the cabin. It was noon on Sunday, following her parent's anniversary party, and she felt as tired as she used to be after working a show on Broadway. Last night's party was more than enough reason for her to be this tired. Unfortunately, it was what happened after the party ended, that had caused Liz to have minimal sleep. She yawned, paused and stretched, then slowly made her way to the kitchen to make a pot of coffee. She then would take a good hot shower, and get dressed for the remainder of the day. Just as Liz had turned on the coffee maker, and turned to head back into the bedroom to prepare to take her shower, her cell phone rang. She immediately recognized the ring tone. John. Well, he could leave her a message on her voice mail. Right now, she was not in any mood to talk with him. Liz didn't appreciate how John and her aunt had spoken to one another in Iroquois in front of them. To her it was downright rude! Plus, when she asked for them to interpret what they had said for the rest of them, neither John, nor her aunt would share with them and tell them what they had said to each other. By the time John had walked Liz to the door of the cabin her mood was turning very dark with sparks of anger, that was nearly ready to become a fully engulfed flaming fire of anger. So, she had not invited John to come in for a little while, and promptly sent him home with a rather bland kiss.

Liz was still mumbling to herself when she got out of the shower and dried off. She needed to do something, anything, but talk with John or her family. What she needed to do was to burn off some of her emotions, her wounded ego, anger. Liz sighed, as she looked out the window of her bedroom as she zipped up her faded blue jeans. The clouds were thick. Easing into her wool sweater, Liz walked over to the window and looked outside. She really needed to go for a walk. A hike up into the mountain would be even better. Gathering her wool socks and insulated hiking boots, Liz headed out to the living room of the cabin, flopped down on the couch and began to put on her socks. By the time she had finished lacing her last boot, Liz had made her decision. She fixed a thermos of coffee, grabbed an apple, a bottle of water, and her cell phone before heading to the coat rack. Sliding into her winter coat, Liz grabbed her knapsack with her snacks, threw her driver's license and some tissues in it as well, then made her way to the door. Keys! How did she plan on going anywhere without her keys? Liz grabbed them and her gloves. Then she was ready to head out.

As Liz headed down the road, she realized that she had not listened to John's message. Her heart hurt, and Liz knew why. John and Aunt Amanda conversing wasn't the problem. The problem was that Liz felt scared. John's reluctance to honestly answer her had caused Liz to have flash backs to Greg and his dishonesty with her. Because of Liz's stormy mood that matched the impending weather, she needed to walk out her frustration, her anger, and whatever else she was feeling.

Liz cut over back roads, and was not surprised to find the parking lot at Goodman Park was empty, except for her. She was glad that the state park had a decent well marked state trail that led up to the falls. She needed time alone with her thoughts. Looking up at the sky that seemed to be ready to open and dump its snowflakes at any moment, Liz parked next to the registration box where she would sign in, so in case anything unforeseen was to happen, her family would know where to look for her. Her family. Liz sighed as she pulled the key from the ignition, opened the door, grabbed her knapsack, and her thermos. Yes, her family needed to know where she was, so, as Liz stood, she called Caitlin's house—not her parent's for obvious reasons. She was glad that Callie Anne answered the landline, and even more glad to hear that Caitlin was not home. Especially, to not give her the third degree for heading up the mountain with an impending storm marching towards them.

Stephen had spent the morning mulling over the party that the Callison children had thrown for their parents. His mood had not improved as the day progressed, and was as stormy as the sky outside his window! The last thing he had expected to have happen at Jim and Melissa's party was for Amanda and Kevin appear. But they had. That would have been fine, if things were different between him and Amanda. He sighed, with a sound that resembled a deflating tire when the last of its air passes, and it collapses to total flatness. Hours removed from the party, it still irked him that every time he attempted to speak with Amanda, she blatantly ignored him. The darn maddening woman had her avoidance moves down pat, either by talking with someone else, and promised to give him a few moments later in the evening—which never happened—or, she was sitting and all snuggled up close to Kevin. Granted, the man is her husband, but come on! She lives with the man for goodness sake, and should have been able to separate herself from him for at least a minute or two!

Stephen drew in a breath. He shook his head in disgust with himself. That woman truly tested his sanity! Stephen drew in another deep breath as he acknowledged to himself that, eventually he might be able to come to terms with Amanda's silent treatment, as part of their tumultuous relationship. But, seeing Amanda obviously recovering from some type of medical procedure on her foot— well, that just knotted his stomach with a sense of helplessness. Something was going on in Amanda's life, and he had not been privileged to know anything about it. As he spoke with his family, Becky and Phil, it became apparent to him that they also were not privileged to know of Amanda's health issues. Still recovering from that shock, Stephen was certain that Summer was also in the dark about her mother's health. Well, Stephen decided as he put on his winter coat and pulled his truck keys from his pocket, today he would find out where Amanda was hiding within the Callison family and get his answers from her.

When Stephen slowly pulled into Jim and Melissa's driveway, he was disappointed to find that the driveway was empty of any extra vehicles. *Well, then she must be at the cabin.* Stephen thought. At that moment, as if on cue, he saw the garage door slowly rise. Jim was standing inside by the driver's side of his pickup. The sound of Stephen's pick up, drew Jim's attention and he glanced outside to see Stephen bring his truck to a stop in front of him. Jim quickly surmised why his friend was there. Time would only tell if he was right! Without hesitation, Jim came outside and waited for Stephen to emerge from is pickup.

"Hey, Johnson! What's up?" Jim asked as Stephen stepped towards him. His eyes drew in everything about Stephen from his clothing to his facial expression, and the way he carried himself. *Great!* Jim thought. He knew that classic Johnson look and attitude.

"I'm looking for your sister, and hoping get honest answers to my questions from her. Since she obviously isn't here," Stephen was not smiling, in fact, his expression was as ominous as a summer storm pummeling the mountains valley with rain, thunder, lightning and wind, while threatening to kick up a tornado as an exclamation point to the storm. "I gather she's up at your family cabin."

Jim momentarily closed his eyes, shook his head and sighed. "You gather wrong."

Stephen did not attempt to hide his surprise from Jim. "So, where is she?"

Jim shivered as the damp cold air shot through him. He knew by the look on Stephen's face that the man was about as ugly as an old black bear with a brier stuck in its paw. The conversation that they needed to have was too involved for them to stand outside in the cold and discuss. "You better come on in, so we can attempt to sort out you and Mandy, as if, that's remotely possible -" Jim rolled his eyes as he added, "- over coffee."

Melissa appeared in the doorway of the kitchen from the hall, as Jim and Stephen stepped in through the kitchen door. Her eyes momentarily met Jim's. She released a breath anticipating where their conversation would probably go with Stephen. "Stephen, welcome. This is an unexpected surprise." Melissa smiled warmly at him. "Thank you again, for your kind words last night."

"Your welcome, Melissa." He gave her a little nod, then slid out of his coat, and placed it on the back of the chair, which was the chair he usually sat in when he congregated with them around their kitchen table.

"Mellie, I was going to put on a pot of coffee for us have while we talk with Johnson and sort out some things." Jim had moved over to the counter and was already getting out the coffee and filter as he spoke.

"Jim, why don't you go ahead and sit down with Stephen?" She asked, then nodded towards the coffee maker as she added, "While I tend to things over here. I might even be able to find some apple pie for us to have with our coffee." She laughed at Stephen's response.

Knowing where the conversation was probably going to end up, her apple pie would be just the right thing to sweeten the answers that Stephen had undoubtedly come there looking for.

Jim took his seat next to Stephen. "You're looking a little haggard this afternoon. Did you and Belinda go out drinking after you left the party last night?"

"He -" Stephen cleared his throat. Then sighed. "Ah, moose muffins! No. We didn't go out drinking. I have your sister to thank for how I look and feel today!" Jim had to bite back a smile as his gaze scrutinized Stephen's pained look. "Don't even think about laughing at me, Callison." Stephen snarled, as Melissa slid a small plate with a large piece of apple pie on it in front of him. His eyes glanced down at the pie, then back up at Melissa, as she handed him a fork. "Thank you, Mel. So, Jim, do you mind telling me where Amanda and Kevin are hiding?"

"You'll probably find it hard to believe me when I tell you that they're not hiding from you, or, anyone else for that matter."

"You're right, Jim." Stephen said as he returned his fork to his plate. His expression held no humor when he replied. "It looks to me like they are."

Jim had his fork loaded with a perfect bite of apples with a flaky bottom crust and crumb topping, and was about to place it in his mouth. The saliva in his mouth was forming in anticipation for the flavors that would touch his taste buds. He sighed, as he lowered the loaded fork to his plate. "Johnson, I know Mandy avoided you last night. And I know why." He shot Stephen a warning look. "Stop with the grumbling! For goodness sake, listen to me, and then you will have your answers." Stephen grew quiet and gave Jim a curt nod. At that moment, there were plenty that Jim would have liked to say. However, he chose to hold his tongue and say instead, "Before they left here to go to Albany to catch their flight back to Baltimore, Manda gave Mellie and me permission to share what's happened with you, or anyone else who thinks that they are entitled to know about her business."

"They went home already?" Stephen was totally confused by this piece of information.

"Yeah, my annoying, all too generous, loving sister who is still recovering from major surgery, and Kevin wedged out enough time in their lives to get a flight north, drive here for part of the party, catch a few hours of sleep, then head back home for the rest of their weekend commitments."

For a moment, no one spoke, as Jim's words settled in on Stephen like a cool, damp blanket, and he was feeling very uncomfortable.

Melissa quietly placed her hand on Jim's forearm, as it lay on the table next to his plate. "I just got a text from Amanda." Both Jim and Stephen quietly waited for Mel to continue. "Amanda said the flight was on time and uneventful. They arrived at Danielle's and Janelle's dance recital just before the curtain went up. Needless to say, everyone is happy, and Amanda is planning on going home and collapsing."

"Well, I'm glad to hear that they made it on time. Those two girls mean the world to both Mandy and Kevin, and they would have been disappointed to have missed one moment of the recital."

"I agree, and I certainly don't blame them. Having spent time hiking with Amanda and the girls last summer, and our impromptu camp out, I saw the deep bond that has been forged between Amanda and her step granddaughters." Mel softly smiled while observing Stephen's reaction to their conversation. Interesting.

"So, you're saying that Amanda and Kevin left early today, so that they could get back to Baltimore in time to see his grandchildren participate in a dance recital?"

"That's right, Johnson. They returned to see their granddaughters in their recital. They happen to take their family commitments very seriously." Jim replied as he lowered his coffee mug to the table.

"In fact, on Friday night, Mandy and Kevin were at one of Kevin's brother's sixty fifth birthday bash. Then yesterday morning they were at the twins' school for their indoor track meet. Unfortunately, there was a delay in one of the events, so Mandy and Kevin missed their scheduled flight that would have gotten them into Albany, and then here for the dinner. Because of the delay they had to catch a later flight up here to be with Mellie and me. Now, I happen think that is more than decent of them. You and I both know that they could have stayed in Baltimore and attended all the events with Kevin's side of their family and left it that. But they didn't do that. Amanda, told us that she had made a promise to our children before the Baltimore events had made their way to the calendar. My sister and brother in law did their best to be where they needed to be for those whom they love."

"Stephen," Melissa quietly broke in, "It is pretty amazing that Amanda and Kevin made the trip north simply to spend a few precious hours with us. Rather selfless, if you ask me." Silence. "We have so much to be thankful for."

"They're quite the saints with their sacrifices for their families." Stephen's voice dripped with sarcasm. His gaze passed between Jim and Melissa. He saw raw emotion in their eyes. He swallowed then asked, "Will you tell me what's going on with Amanda and her foot?" Maybe now he'd get an answer to his questions about her health. He could only hope!

Jim nodded. "Back eight weeks ago, when you were asking me about our vacation, I couldn't share what was going on with Manda."

"Couldn't or wouldn't?" Stephen challenged.

"Both!" Jim replied. He sighed. "We went down to be with Amanda and Kevin while Sis had her foot surgery, and then to help her and Kevin out during the first week, or so, after she was home from the hospital."

Stephen felt the small hairs on the back of his neck standing up. He was unsure of how to read Jim's expression. "There's more. Isn't there?" He swallowed back his turbulent emotions. Afraid, that whatever Jim was going to say would change his life forever.

"Manda had been experiencing pain in her foot, the same one that was severely damaged in the motorcycle accident she had years ago. The surgeon had x rays taken, a cat scan done and in doing so, he found a shadow by the plate. Surgery was scheduled to remove the plate and replace the old one, or fuse bones, whatever was to be optimal for Mandy, after the surgeon had a clear view of the inside of her foot." Jim drew in a breath, then took a sip of coffee.

At that moment, Melissa picked up their family story for him. "When Amanda was in the OR her surgeon found a tumor between her bones and the plate. The tumor was the cause of the shadow on the film images, and the reason for her tremendous pain when she walked."

Stephen was speechless. His world was crashing in around him.

Jim saw the bewildered look in his eyes, fully understanding Johnson's concern, as he said, "They did a biopsy for cancer. Needless to say, we all were on pins and needles for a while." Jim slightly shook his head, as if to help himself process what all had happened. Their emotional hills and valleys. Their memories and anguish of their mother, whom they had loved so dearly. His expression softened as he continued. "One of the reasons that Sis and Kevin made sure they got up here for the party was," Jim smiled and shook his head, as the memory of last night soared through his mind. "So that they could tell us in person their news regarding the results of the biopsy."

"Jim, just tell me. Does Mandy have bone cancer?" Stephen asked, while anticipating what Jim would tell him. He too had shared memories with Jim and Amanda of their mother. He had loved Mrs. Callison and had thought of her as his adopted mom. Now, Stephen felt as if his life was spinning out of control.

"No! Mandy does not have cancer." He paused. Released a heavy sigh. Ran his fingers through his hair as if needing to find something to do with all his unused energy. "Mom dying from cancer was more than enough for our family." Jim sighed with relief. "We can thank God for answered prayers. Mandy is going to be okay. Well, after her foot totally heals from her surgery."

Relief washed over Stephen, like spring rush with the thawing of the mountain streams. Now he knew what had been going on with Amanda. Now he knew why Jim and Melissa had been so secretive about their so-called vacation with Amanda and Kevin. His gaze met Jim's. There he saw everything that defined who Jim Callison was as a man. A good man, who loved his family for all he was worth. Amanda's words came back to haunt Stephen. She was right. Jim had proven himself to her. Stephen knew that he was in need of time alone with God to talk, and more importantly to listen, to hear how he was supposed to mend Amanda's and his tattered relationship. He drew in a calming breath, then quietly said with the utmost of sincerity, "Well, Jim, Mel, I'm glad to hear that Amanda is going to be alright."

"Thank you, Stephen. We also are extremely relieved, and looking forward too many more years together as family." Melissa said, as she stood next to Stephen and gently placed her hand on his arm. She held the coffee pot in her other hand, and without asking poured more hot coffee into his cup. Then she filled Jim's and her cup before cutting another slice of pie for each of them.

The air was changing, wind was picking up from the northwest, and there was a bite to it. Liz paused, looked up at the clouds, heavy laden with precipitation, and ready to tumble to the ground as snow. She uncapped her bottle of water, took a long sip, closed it and returned the bottle to her sack. "This is stupid!" Liz informed nature that surrounded her. She was half way up the trail to the falls.

Glancing up at the sky, then up the deserted trail, Liz sighed and continued on her way. Walking usually helped Liz sort out her thoughts. Not today. In fact, the walk was leaving her more confused. It was as if she was caught in a whirlpool and couldn't get out. The more she fought and struggled for clarity, the more confused she became. She walked on.

The rushing sound of water informed Liz that she was close to the stream and the water falls. It grew louder as she came around the bend. Just as she reached the edge of the water, she felt and saw the first snow flake. Then another. Liz shook her head as she looked down at her attire. "Not smart!" She scolded herself.

Liz was shocked to see how fast the storm moved in. Blew in! One minute she watched the first flake fall and now it was nearly impossible to see the trail, or the water. This was bad! Stupid! Liz lectured herself for being so irresponsible. Now she had a situation that could have severe, or even deadly consequences. Why was she there in that situation? Because she allowed her temper to guide her by the words she had exchanged with John after the party.

Between the wind and the snow, Liz could not see in front of her. It was useless to try and find the trail leading down the mountain. Think. She had to act fast to survive being on the mountain in severe weather, without adequate supplies or clothing for protection. Drawing in a centering breath that she used when working in the theater, Liz quieted her spirit. She emptied herself and prayed. Stillness surrounded her. A sense of peace came over her. At that moment, Liz remembered the old trappers lean to that was not far from the trail. Now the question was, could she find it in this storm? Would the structure still be standing and safe? Or, had the state taken it down? Time would only tell, and was of the essence. Liz trudged towards the woods.

In among the shelter of the pines, hemlocks and hardwoods, the temperature didn't seem as bad. The wind was not as powerful and the snow was slowed as it became tangled in the evergreen branches. Liz prayed for all she was worth as she walked along, unsure if she was going in the right direction. Then, in total surprise, she saw the outline of the lean-to fireplace. She shivered as she made her way to the lean to. Relief set upon her, as she found shelter in the three-sided structure. Still, her life was in peril. She only had an apple, some coffee, and a little water left. She did not have on winter clothing to protect herself from the cold. She was wet, and she had no fire to keep warm by.

Elizabeth was cold right straight through to her bones, and couldn't stop her teeth from chattering, as she looked around the sparse shelter. Fortunately, the snow and some of the bitter cold wind was blocked from having a direct hit on her. Light was quickly diminishing with the storm and the lateness of the day. Liz glanced at her watch. She sighed as the bleak reality of her situation set in. It would be dark soon. She still would be alone, and because of her response towards John and her aunt's private conversation, she would probably freeze to death.

Liz had to do something to keep her wits about herself and to keep alive. She scuffed her feet in the dirt, as she looked around the barren shelter. It was then that she saw a small wooden box with a latch positioned on the ground in the far-left corner. At first, she had missed it. Of course! Liz chided herself. She rolled her eyes as she thought, *me and my temper sure has gotten me into a bloody awful mess this time! Think, Elizabeth! What would Dad and Aunt Amanda do in a situation like this?* She laughed at herself, then said out loud to the emptiness around her, "They would have had sense enough to stay home and not be here! Duh!" She shivered. Somehow, she had to keep warm. A fire would be nice. Of course, she didn't have matches, or anything else to assist her in starting a fire, even if she could go out into the woods and find any downed dry tree limbs. Liz released a heavy sigh. She shook her head with disgust at herself. Sighed and said to herself, "Alright, enough with the self-pity. You got yourself into this mess, now do something. Anything!" It was then that Liz decided that before she was plunged into total darkness, she might as well investigate and see what was in the wooden box. So, she walked over to the box, squatted down and tentatively opened the latch. Goodness only knows what was going to greet her! With Liz's life experiences during the past year, anything was possible!

Much to Liz's surprise, she found minimal emergency supplies. There were simple instructions folded neatly inside a waterproof container that also contained a piece of flint and a striker. Plus, there was dry paper for her to use in starting a fire. A fire! Liz felt a tear form and trickle down her cheek. She sniffled and sighed. There was hope in the midst of this storm that was rapidly intensifying. Liz quickly returned everything to the wooden box to keep it dry. Then she stood and hurried out into the cold to hopefully find some dry, or nearly dry wood that she could use to build a fire to keep warm by for even a little while. Blowing snow fell all around her, making it difficult for Liz to walk and see. She didn't go too far, while grabbing as much wood as she could possibly carry, and headed back to her shelter. Liz was exhausted as she dropped the wood inside the shelter overhang. She leaned against the inner wall to catch her breath and rest, while planning out her next strategy. The large fireplace needed to be prepared for her to build her fire. That meant Liz would have to go back out into the elements, lay her fire, start it, and hope that it would remain lit. If, her fire stayed lit, then she would worry about whether the dead pine branch she had found, and drug back to the lean to, would provide her with enough different sized pieces of wood to make a small fire. She hoped, as she wearily trudged out to the stone fireplace.

CHAPTER 22

J im and Melissa were standing inside by their front door with Stephen, as he was preparing to leave, when they heard the sound of a vehicle door slamming shut. Jim opened the front door, looked out and saw John making a mad dash towards the front door through the rapidly falling snowflakes.

"Jim, have you seen or heard from Elizabeth?" John called out. The urgency in John's voice, along with the quickness in his step, immediately kicked Jim into high alert.

"No, John. I figured you and Lizzie were hunkered down together, and that's why we hadn't heard from her today." Jim felt the calm he had been experiencing five minutes before John's arrival evaporate into the cold snowy air, as he looked into his troubled eyes. "Oh boy! I knew this quiet day was too good to be true! Come on in and tell Melissa and me -" Jim heard Melissa's anxious voice from behind him, quietly spoke to her, then turned his head back to face John. "-Tell us. What's going on?"

John didn't remove his winter coat, as he remained standing inside the front door of the house, just far enough for the door to be closed behind him. Upon hearing the urgency in both Jim and John's voices, Stephen Johnson changed his plans and didn't leave, as he had originally planned to do. He sensed that something was wrong, and well, despite the ongoing saga he had with Amanda, Jim was his best friend and so he was ready to help, if need be. It didn't take long for John to retell the condensed version of the story, of what had been said between Liz and him after the party, nor Liz's coolness when they parted at the cabin door. Stephen shook his head and interjected a comment about the situation. Unfortunately, Jim and Melissa had to agree with Stephen's observations. Elizabeth's response was mimicking her aunt in too many ways. Concern ran rampant between them, as they listened to John continue to share his feelings with them. John had been trying to put himself in Liz's place, and now he could understand some of the reason why Elizabeth was miffed with him. But, for her to not answer her phone, for her to not be at the cabin when he arrived, and now the storm settling in on them, well, John was worried. No! The man was a mess! Needless to say, now that Jim and Melissa were aware of what had transpired, and Elizabeth was apparently pulling an Amanda—well, they also were deeply worried.

Stephen had removed his coat and had disappeared into the kitchen. His mind was racing as fast as a car doing the final laps at the Daytona 500. This day was crashing in around him, as too many memories came racing forward in his mind. Elizabeth—Amanda! Two different women with two different situations. But they both had many similar traits, and had their own shares of pain and suffering in their lives. He sighed. Then, he quietly prayed for his friends and John, who seemed to really care for Elizabeth. Elizabeth. Not so long ago that spunky, vibrant young woman was going to become his niece. Now, because of Peter's behavior, who unfortunately reminded Johnson of himself in too many ways, Elizabeth had moved on to find happiness with another man. Yup! Peter had ripped the page right out of the old Johnson playbook and memorized the lines too well, leading to his demise. Lost in thought, Stephen made himself right to home in Jim and Melissa's kitchen and prepared another pot of coffee, that he figured they were going to need, or at least appreciate in the hours to come.

While Stephen was busy in the kitchen, both Jim and Melissa were busy on their phones calling their children, to see if Elizabeth was with one of them. All of a sudden Melissa gasped and exclaimed. "Oh no!"

John, Jim, and Stephen, who had just returned to the living room, all focused their attention on her and listened.

"Are you sure? When did Callie Anne take Liz's call? Oh, heaven forbid!" Mel's eyes were wide with horror. Melissa drew in a ragged raw breath, then calmly said, "Caitlin, please, don't yell at Callie. She only did as her aunt said, after all." Mel sighed, as she listened to Caitlin speak, hearing the concern in her daughter's voice, and with good reason to be concerned. "Yes, we all are worried. John is right here. Yes. He came looking for your sister, shortly after it had begun to snow. Right. Cait, I'll call you back, after we get him on his way to find her. Yes. I love you too." Melissa released a sigh, drew in a calming breath, ended the call, replaced her phone to the back pocket of her jeans, and slid into Jim's arms in one fluid motion. "John, right now I'm really glad that you are a forest ranger." With that said, the first of many tears to follow silently fell.

"Me too! Now, please tell me where Elizabeth told Callie Anne she was going?" His serious expression did not reveal how deeply troubled his spirit was, as he waited for Melissa to respond to him.

"Apparently Liz called Cait's house a while ago, as in three hours ago, and told Callie that she was at Goodman Park."

Jim and Johnson's eyes met. The two old friends didn't need to utter a word between them. They stood there together in solidarity, while knowing where their thoughts had gone. Goodman Park was a huge area of wilderness. On a bright sunny day in the middle of the summer it could be dangerous, depending on where you chose to go hiking. Add snow, wind and freezing temperatures to the mix and trouble was brewing up mighty fast. Right now, with the intensity of the storm building, not knowing exactly where Liz was, if, she was still up there, or, if she had come out of the mountain, and someplace in peril time was of the essence to find her.

"Well, I must say, that I'm grateful that Liz had sense enough to call and tell Callie where she was going. That gives me hope by knowing where to begin my search and perhaps rescue." John sighed, as his gaze scanned the three older people, two of whom he deeply cared for, and with good reason. "Right now, I'm very glad I'm a forest ranger and have valuable resources at my disposal. I'll let you know when I find her." John assured them, as he headed out the door into the storm.

The wet and heavy snow that was coming down at a steady pace covered a very thin layer of ice, coating the frozen ground. All of these factors added together made driving on the twisty country roads, extremely dangerous. John was amazed to see how quickly the storm had settled in the region. He hoped within his heart that Liz had signed in and out of the park before the storm hit, and that she was someplace warm working through her anger towards him. Time would only tell. John had a bad, ominous feeling as he drove on. Already with the intensity of the storm, anything could have happened to Liz. He didn't want to think about the what if's, as he pulled into the parking lot. Through the snow falling around his vehicle, the windshield wipers frantically pushing the snow from his windshield, John saw Liz's car parked next to the registration box at the beginning of the path leading up the mountain. John felt a mixed sense of relief and urgency, as he saw that snow that was blanketing her car. Liz had been there for quite a while, and obviously was not sitting in her vehicle. He sighed, then prayed to The Great Spirit—God—for guidance in finding the woman that he loves. Before getting out his SUV into the elements, John called Jim and Melissa to let him know where he was. Then, he got out of his SUV, went to the back and got his winter backpack, snowshoes, as well as his search and rescue equipment. Ready to make his ascent up the mountain, John walked over to the registration box, dropped it open and immediately found Liz's name, time of arrival, as well as her destination. Concern rose within John, as he signed in under her, and then closed the box. He pulled out his radio and contacted a fellow ranger, working at the Northville ranger's station to let him know where he was, and that he was about to begin conducting a search and rescue. Yes, John knew that it was unwise for him to be going out in what was deteriorating into near blizzard conditions, putting his life in danger. Yes. He knew that he should wait until the storm had passed. However, this was no ordinary search and rescue. This was Elizabeth, the woman he loved and her life that was in peril. John knew in his heart that he had to do whatever was necessary, and within his power to find her. So, he drew in a breath, then took his first step towards the trail leading up into the mountain, where he hoped and expected to find Liz.

John continued to pray to God—The Great Spirit, as he meticulously made his way up the mountain. As a forest ranger, a person familiar with winter weather in the north country, he was dressed in water resistant insulated gear, as well as boots, and prepared for this weather. Still, he shivered. The snow and wind were relentless. Any footprints that might have been in the rapidly falling snow to indicate Liz's presence had long since been obscured. So, John relied on his hearing, listening to the wind. Listening for other sounds, any sound, hopefully human. Hopefully Liz's voice. Nothing. Nothing but the storm telling him that for the time being, the forces of nature was in control of the situation.

After about a half a mile into the hike, the depth of the snow was too much for him to trudge through. John was feeling winded from the hard work required to take a simple step. He took out his thermos and took a sip of water to wet his parched throat. Then he strapped his snowshoes onto his feet, took another long sip of water from his thermos, then began to move along the trail at a better pace on top of the snow. As he walked on, carefully keeping track of the path leading upward in the mountain, it was as if The Great Spirit was guiding him on. Then, about a mile up the trail he was guided to stop and listen to nature speak to him. So, John paused, while not really knowing why. He stood for a moment with nature in control of the situation around him. Then, he noticed it. John drew in a breath. Was nature giving him a sign? Direction? He drew in another deep breath. Yes. There was a faint, very faint smell of smoke. John knew that smoke was an indicator of fire. Now he had his first sign of hope. Hope, that Liz had been resourceful and able to make a fire to keep warm, and that he was not smelling smoke from someone's home.

As John came to the clearing by the top of the falls, he stopped to rest, pulled out his thermos and took a sip of water. He stood quietly, listening to the sounds of nature. He drew in another deep breath and allowed a slow smile to ease to his previously taunt lips. There is was again. Smoke from a fire that was battling the elements to burn was in the air, and now it was stronger. John quickly processed this, and determined the direction the smoke was coming from. He allowed his body to feel a sense of anticipation, an adrenaline rush, as he headed off in the direction towards the old trappers lean to, where he hoped to find Elizabeth. John called out, only to have his voice swallowed up with the wind.

The increasingly stronger pungent odor, of dried and wet wood attempting to burn in the snowstorm, drew John on towards the lean to. Then, like a foghorn guiding ships through the perils of a storm he heard a noise. Elizabeth. John felt his breath catch. Liz was crying. His heart clutched with tightness as he heard her mournful sound. He called out, and still was not heard by Elizabeth, as once again the wind sucked away his words. John moved on swiftly with the ease of his snowshoes through the snow laden pines and came toward the lean to. He called her name against the howling wind, but he still was not heard by Liz. The first thing he noticed, as he came around the side of the enclosure, was Liz's meager fire that struggled to burn its brave battle against the wind and snow. A smile tugged at his lips, while silently giving Liz credit for trying. In a few minutes he would tend to resurrecting the fire. But, first, John had to get out of his snowshoes and get under the protection of the partial cover and to Elizabeth. It was then that he got his first glimpse of her. She was sitting on the ground with her forehead resting on her knees. Her arms were hugging her legs close to her body, while attempting to stay warm. John knew that he would never forget this sight of brokenness for as long as he lived.

"Elizabeth."

The sound of John's quiet voice drew her from her distress. She looked up and gasped.

"Yes, Elizabeth, sweetheart." His voice remained quiet, filled with love and concern as he approached her. "I'm here, now, and you are going to be okay." John was now kneeling down next to Elizabeth and drawing her into his arms. "Oh, Liz! I was afraid I wouldn't find you in time."

"You're really here!" Tears continued to tumble down her cheeks.

"Yes, Liz, I'm here. The Great Spirit told me to keep going, to follow the signs and led me to you." His soft word and his gentle touch, lightly brushing her hair back from her face, his hands moving over her jacket sent much needed warmth through her, as he said, "I won't let anything happen to you."

Liz was still softly crying, while attempting to gain control of her tattered emotions, as she blurted out, "John, oh John, you came for me!" Then, she collapsed her weight against him, and cried her heart out.

John held her tightly against his strong body, to provide her with much needed warmth, as he whispered words of reassurance to her. When it was obvious that Liz's tears had about run its course, for that moment at least, and sat upright, John withdrew a few tissues from his inner pocket and began to dab her cheeks, while Liz attempted to blow her nose with her icy cold fingers. Liz began to apologize to him, for doing something so stupid as to take a walk up into the mountain, when she knew a storm was approaching. John's gaze held her tear ridden eyes with tenderness and understanding. He knew that this certainly was not the time to lecture Liz, about the unwise choices that she had made. There were more pressing issues to attend to. Time was of the essence. So, John unzipped and reached into his backpack. Then he pulled out another thermos that he had brought with him. The whole time he quietly spoke words of reassurance to Liz. She answered his questions and gave appropriate responses to his comments. Little did Liz know that he was observing her for hypothermia. He'd check for signs of frostbite in a little while. Right now, he needed to help her to begin to get warm. John unscrewed the cap, poured some steaming hot water into the aluminum cup, and handed it to Liz.

"Here sweetheart, sip this hot water." He gently placed her hat back on her head and over her cold pink ears. John recognized the signs, and tucked away that information in his mind to keep track of for frostbite. "While you sip this water, I am going to see what I can do to rustle up a nice hot fire for us to spend the night by and hopefully keep warm."

"The night? Oh, John!" Liz sighed. "Not only was I careless about myself, now I've put you in peril as well! Oh, why did I do something this dumb?"

He drew her against him, tenderly hugging her, as she collapsed into another round of tears. Given the circumstances, everything that she had already been through, he decided that she had a right to cry. Then, John lightly kissed her hair on the top of her head. "We'll talk all of this all out, in a while. For now," John said, as he stood, looked down at Liz, as her gaze turned upward, meeting his tender gaze. "You finish sipping that hot water, and then help yourself to more, while I see about getting this fire blazing hot for us."

John held true to his word. He quietly chatted with Liz, while he added more wood to her small fire. He told Liz about how proud he was of her using her head to come to the shelter. Plus, she had found the flint and striker and had done her best to build a fire. He assured her that other people in her position would not have known what to do, and they would have given up. But she hadn't. She was a strong woman, the type of woman that John admired, and wanted to have in his life. A few minutes later John disappeared out into the darkening forest to gather more wood. It seemed to Liz that he was gone for a long time. When John returned five minutes later, she saw that one arm was loaded with various sized pieces of wood, which he dropped along the side of the lean to under the protection of the roof. Then, Liz saw what else he had. Good grief! It looked like he had a half of a tree, at his side, or close to it! It made John smile to hear her exclamations, and her giggles at the wood that he had retrieved for them. Then, after placing a kiss filled with love and promise on her lips, he set about reconstructing the fire. In no time at all, the embers from Liz's fire heated the fresh, dry kindling John had added and a new, hotter, fire began to burn. Slowly and methodically John added one or two pieces of wood at a time, and before Liz knew it, the whole lean to was filled up with light and warmth.

While Liz sat close to the entrance of the lean to and the fire, discovering that she was feeling considerably warmer, John remained busy setting up camp for the night. She was amazed to see what John had packed in his backpack. Warm, dry wool socks were now on her feet. Her cheeks felt flushed with color, as she recalled her surprise a few moments ago. John had removed a large zip lock bag from a large side pocket of his backpack, opened it and pulled out insulated microfiber pants, that were now on her legs. Before stepping into the dry pants and wool socks, John had insisted on checking Liz's legs and feet for the first signs of frostbite. Liz had removed the wet jeans and socks from her body and placed them near the fire, where they would hopefully dry out by morning. It felt good for Liz to move around, and not be quite as cold as she had been before John had appeared on the scene. Right now, Liz knew in her heart that there was no one else who she would have wanted to be there with her in that moment.

John silently prayed, thanking the Great One for all the blessings they had already received. He was pleased with how things were taking shape in their emergency camp for the night. The fire was crackling hot in the large fireplace. But John knew that there was more to do to ensure that they would make it safely through the night. Reluctantly, he told Liz that he had to go back out into the elements. They both turned their gazes and looked out at the snow that was coming down with a vengeance, and the wind that was whipping on the side of the mountain with angry blasts. Darkness was beating down on them, ready to suck away the last light of the day. John drew Liz into his arms. Then, he tenderly brushed his lips over hers.

"Elizabeth, I need to gather more branches, and I have to walk to the creek and bring back water for us to drink."

"John, I didn't think this water was safe for us to drink." She responded, then yawned, while her fingers played lazily with the zipper of his jacket.

"Not right now, it isn't. But it will be." John said, as he knelt down to his backpack and unzipped the one small compartment on the side. Reaching into the backpack he pulled out and showed her the two straws with filters, that would enable them to drink the water from the creek and not get sick. He stood and handed them to Liz, who continued to be amazed to see what John had with him. She was certain that Mary Poppins couldn't hold a candlestick to what John Runner could do! "When I get back, I have more surprises for you.

For now, rest. We have a long night ahead of us." He kissed her then said, "I promise to not be too long."

Liz was surprised that she had fallen asleep, as she awakened to the gentle touch of John's fingers brushing her hair from her cheek. Her body felt achy from the hardness under her. The air around her was warm and chilly at the same time, an interesting combination. She yawned and stretched, as she looked over to find John quietly watching her. Liz shook off her momentary disorientation, quickly remembering where she was, and what had happened to cause her to be on the cold ground. The lean to was fully illuminated be the fire that raged in the fireplace. Beyond the stone, darkness had made its final descent, the snow continued to fall and the wind blew. The fire crackled and sizzled as snow melted from its intense heat.

"How long was I asleep for?" She asked, while fumbling to find her watch tucked under her coat sleeve on her wrist, feeling totally disoriented with time and sore from laying on the hard ground.

"About an hour. Your body needed the rest, and since you were warming up by the fire before fatigue over took you, I let you sleep." He sat down next to her, and drew her protectively close to him. "When I first found you, I was concerned about frostbite and hypothermia. But, when I had you change into dry pants, and socks I was able to see the color of your skin on your extremities. That along with the clarity of conversation we had, I was able to put my fear of hypothermia and severe frostbite aside. So, I let you sleep. You look better."

Liz glanced around their shelter noticing all that John had done while she slept. The man was amazing. "John, you have large fresh green branches in here. Are you planning to burn them as well?"

"No." His eyes smiled, as he explained his intentions to Liz. "These branches are for you to lay on, so that tonight when you sleep, you are off of the cold ground." He reached alongside of himself and unfolded a thin blanket. He placed it around Liz's shoulders for added warmth. "It would be better if I had a blanket for each of us. But all that matters is for you to be warm throughout this night."

Liz was surprised to find that the thin blanket was warmer than she expected. "John, you've done so much for me." She felt more tears forming, unexpected emotions. "I don't expect for you to give me your blanket, and possibly catch your death of cold on account of me."

"Elizabeth, you will be sleeping, and will need the added warmth, while I tend to the fire to keep us warm through the night."

"But John -" Her words were silenced, as his finger gently touched her lips. His tender gaze held her captive.

"You need not worry. I will rest, then fully sleep when we are safely down from this mountain. For now, would you like to have dinner?"

"Dinner?" Liz's eyes grew wide with surprise as she gazed at him, and watched John prepare their food for them to eat.

The fire crackled and blazed with warmth, as they sat nestled together. They both were pleasantly full from the ready to eat meals that John had brought with him, and the hot cocoa he had made for them to drink. Hot cocoa! Liz was still surprised by that pleasant surprise. For a while neither one spoke, as they were lost in their own thoughts. It was John who finally broke the silence between them.

His hand gently ran up and down her arm as he asked, "Elizabeth, are you ready to tell me why you didn't return my call from earlier today?" He knew better to push her. So, John sat holding her close while looking at the fire. Quietly, patiently waiting. It didn't take long until he heard Liz sigh.

"Well," her voice was little more than a whisper. "I was hurt that you and Aunt Amanda had left me out of your conversation." She drew in a breath and then forged on with what was on her heart. John quietly listened, allowing Liz to unburden herself.

"Oh, my precious sweetheart!" John's voice was filled with surprise, perhaps regret. He tenderly took her hand and laced their fingers. "Liz, I ask you to believe me when I say that I never meant to hurt you. I have a feeling that your aunt would also be upset to know," he paused to draw in a breath and protectively placed his other hand over their locked fingers. "That our conversation caused you such distress to send up here in the midst of this storm. Elizabeth, I had planned to tell you what we had discussed, after we go north to visit my parents, and for you to meet my grandmother. But now I see the error in my thinking." John's gaze held hers, as he sighed. "So, let me tell you about your aunt's and my conversation. Perhaps, then you will feel better, and hopefully feeling less hurt by our actions." His gaze tenderly held hers, as he lifted their interlocked hands to his lips, and then gently kissed her knuckles.

"Your aunt, as matriarch of your family—in the Iroquois tradition—specifically asked me what my intentions are towards you." He saw the surprise, as it settled in Liz's ebony eyes, while she processed his words. "Liz, I need for you to understand that our conversation was important to both of us. Your aunt loves you, and she was very clear in communicating her expectations to me and, perhaps more importantly, of me. I definitely respect her, and I do not want for her to have a cause to dislike me." John's serious expression, and the conviction in his voice caused Liz to giggle and respond. The love she saw in John's eyes warmed her more than the fire that burned in the open hearth. "So, out of respect for her and my love for you, -" a hint of a smile formed at the edge of his lips, as he watched Liz draw in a breath. "-Tonight, in the comfort of your family's warm cabin, in front of the fireplace, I was going to share this and more with you."

"Oh, and I royally messed it up for us!" Liz's body was consumed by regret. Her eyes shimmered with wetness.

John immediately recognized that look, and gently touched the edge of her eyes with the pad of this thumb. "Please don't cry,

Elizabeth. Yes, your desire to go for a hike in near blizzard conditions, did change the location where we are having this conversation. But, sweetheart, look around you. We're together and we still have a blazing fire to warm us." His smile, the mischief in his eyes caused Liz to sigh, and find her own smile.

"I love you, John. I'm so sorry." She sighed, then added, "For everything."

"I love you too, Elizabeth. Sweetheart, you do not need to be sorry. I will simply change the sequence of my plans, that's all."

"The sequence of your plans?" Liz saw something unrecognizable in his eyes. They were so dark, intense. Yet, there was a warmth, a fire of their own burning with passion. Desire? Then she recognized it. Love. Intense love that she had never witnessed before in John, or any other person for that matter.

"Mm-hmm!" His eyes seemed to sparkle like summer sunlight casting down on the early morning dew blanketing the grass. His voice was tender, as he explained his previous intentions to her. "Liz, I had wanted for us to go up north to visit my family, so that you could meet many of them, and for us to receive their blessing before I ask you, -" Liz felt her heart do a flip flop, as she was held captive by his gaze. She drew in a breath. "Elizabeth, you are more beautiful than sunrise over the Great Sacandaga Lake, or any lake in the Adirondack Mountains, for that matter." He held her hands tenderly in his, gently squeezing them with his fingers as he said, "You are my first thought in the morning when I awaken, and my last thought as I close my eyes to sleep. In these few short months of walking into each other lives, you have become my best friend. I can't imagine life without you, or loving another woman as much as I love you. Will you do me the honor, and marry me? Please, be my wife, my partner to journey through the rest of our lives together?"

"Oh, John! Yes!" That was all Liz was able to say. She was a mess, and didn't even attempt to hold back the tears. John drew her to him. Kissing away her tears, then touching her warm moist lips with his lips. They tasted the salt of her tears, as they sealed their commitment to one another.

A short while later, John eased Liz from his arms. He rose to his feet, went and stirred the fire, before placing more wood on the fire. Then, once again John took his place at her side, drawing her into his arms.

"John, I love you, and I really am sorry about messing up your plans in how you wanted to propose to me."

"Elizabeth, tonight is a perfect example of how life does not always go as we plan. What's important is that we love each other and we will be married."

Liz held his gaze and searched him for further knowledge. She saw something unrecognizable in his eyes. "John, I can tell that you intended to do something important. Please. Tell me."

He nodded, while holding her gaze in return. When he finished, Liz sat quietly for a moment. Then she released a long, slow breath. She studied the fire as she spoke. "Some time ago, Aunt Amanda and I had a conversation in which she shared her thoughts on a passage of scripture pertaining to the tongue being like fire. The words that I spoke against you last night, and my actions today have hurt you, John. You are honorable, good, loving man and I, in my" she sighed, "I guess, my selfishness, I ruined your intentions of seeking your family's blessing, as well as my family's before proposing to me."

"Elizabeth, you simply needed for me to change my plans to accommodate your needs." His eyes began to twinkle. "But," Liz was on high alert as she listened, "Just because I compromised on the way I proposed to you doesn't mean I will compromise on everything with you in the future."

"Oh?" Liz watched, waited for him to further explain himself.

With a stone-cold expression John responded. "That's right. I will not allow you to ravage my body until after we are officially married by a minister."

Silence. Liz processed what John had just said and burst into laughter.

"You're serious, aren't you?"

"Yes, I am. I love and respect you, Elizabeth. I guess you could say I'm a throwback to a lost time. I know that neither of us are virgins. But just the same, it is very important to me that our relationship is consummated on our wedding night and not before. Yes, being stranded up here in the side of the mountain in the middle of a snowstorm is quite romantic. But tonight, is not the right night for us to give ourselves to one another in that way. Hopefully, you are not going to get another invisible brier stuck in your fanny over this, and understand my intentions."

Liz felt the tension within her body. Her longing. Her unfulfilled needs as John held her close. Still, there was a pure intimacy, a bonding in that moment that they were sharing. It was almost sacred. In the stillness Liz reflected on the words that John had just spoken to her, and she remembered the night, when John had whispered to her that they would wait until they married to be as one with each other. Once again, he was reiterating his intentions.

"Oh, John! You never cease to amaze me with your consideration, your sense of values. No man has ever treated me as you do, and I'm actually glad."

"Oh?" His gloved hand gently stroked her arm as he questioned her.

"Yes, because now I know how blessed I am, that the Great Spirit—God—has brought us together. I do love you." She sighed with contentment, leaned up and softly brushed her lips on his cheek, before nestling in against him in the safety of his arms.

Liz awakened to find herself wrapped in the blanket on the pine branches, that had been used to make a bed for her. She yawned, as she wiped the sleep from her eyes, stretched, finding muscle aches and pains, and looked out toward the fireplace. The sky had turned light, although the sun was obscured by lingering clouds. Fortunately, the snow had stopped falling sometime during the night, and the wind had died down. The fire danced in the fireplace, making the lean to quite pleasant. Liz realized that she was warm enough to unzip her jacket a little bit, so she wasn't too warm. She did not see John. Liz shook her head as if to get rid of the cobwebs in her mind. Where was John?

As if, on cue, he appeared from around the right side of the lean to. "Good morning, sleepyhead. Time to rise and shine." His smile made her heart zing with happiness.

"Good morning. What time is it anyway?" She asked, then promptly yawned, while fumbling with her jacket sleeve to find her watch on her arm.

"7:00. It's later than I had hoped for us to be breaking camp. So, we need to get a move on. I've been over to the creek and got water for breakfast." He smiled as he saw the look of amazement come into Liz's eyes. He chuckled. "I know of your morning needs, sweetheart. The water is in an aluminum thermos in the fire heating. There will be enough water for us to each have a bowl of instant oatmeal and a cup of black coffee before we head down the mountain."

"Coffee?" Liz had untangled herself from the blanket, and was on her feet moving towards John, who was stepping towards her. "Oh, John, you know me too well and made my morning!"

From that moment on, they were as busy as ants going in and out of their colony. First order of business for John was for him to radio in once again to the ranger's station. He advised the ranger on duty that they were breaking camp, and the he gave his estimated time of arrival in the parking lot. Liz had tried to reach her parents on her cell phone, but still had no reception. She felt awful for the worry she was sure to have caused them. A sigh of relief escaped from Liz, as John told her that he had asked for the other ranger to contact Jim and Melissa and let them know that he was bringing Liz home.

Liz drew in deep cleansing breaths. Life was wonderful. Well, minus the twelve inches of snow that they had to trudge through to get to the parking lot over a mile away. Still, Liz felt happy, content, as she cleaned up the minimal utensils and dishes that they had used for eating, while John carefully returned everything to its rightful place in his backpack. She was grateful to find that her blue jeans were dry enough to put on over the thermal leggings, that John said she could keep. The added warmth would be greatly appreciated, as they made their way down the mountain. Together they put out the fire, and placed the unused pieces of wood in the far interior corner of the lean to for the next occupants. They took one more look around to ensure that they left as little of a trace of their presence as possible, and then they began their slow decent from the mountain.

Jim and Melissa arrived at the Goodman Park parking lot with plenty of time for Jim to lower the plow on his truck, and clear a big enough area for their truck, as well as plow out the area around Liz and John's vehicles. Then, with Melissa's help they cleared the snow from John's SUV and Liz's car. Burr. It was downright cold up in that side of the mountain. Chilled through to their bones, they got back in Jim's pickup started the engine and turned on the heat full blast.

"Look, Mellie, there they are!" Jim exclaimed, as he leaned over and soundly kiss Melissa, who was sitting on the passenger side. "Come on, Mellie!" Jim's heart was racing with relief, as he opened his side door, was standing outside and closing the door in one fluid motion. Melissa got out of her side of the pickup and joined Jim by his side of the pickup. Jim drew her against him with his one arm, while looking at his watch on his other wrist. He released a sigh of relief. "They made good time getting back down here."

"What time is it?" Melissa quietly asked, while keeping her gaze fixed on the path and the glimpses of Elizabeth and John that she saw, as they passed through brief clearings along the trail, while coming towards them.

"It's 2:30pm. Knowing how much snow that there probably is up in the mountain, I honestly didn't think that they would be here before three or four o'clock."

Melissa felt a wave of relief washing over her. So, of course, tears were to follow!

"Oh, Mellie!" Jim sighed out, as he pulled his cloth handkerchief from his back jeans pocket, and handed it to her. Then, as she dabbed her eyes, he drew her to back against him.

She wiped her nose, and softly chuckled. "I know. I'm a mess!"

"And with good reason, sweetheart."

They remained standing by the registration sign in box, quietly conversing about this and that, to fill the time, as they waited for Liz and John to exit the forest. Somewhere close by a blue jay was calling out. Its call seemed to echo off the mountainside. Then a male cardinal whistled for his mate, as if to not be outdone by the male blue jay.

Silence. Then, they heard the most beautiful sound.

"Mom, Dad!"

Without further prompting, Jim and Melissa released a collective sigh of relief. They waved and called out in return to Liz and John, as they trudged through the snow towards them. Jim and Melissa stood together, silently watching, praying while knowing that their family had literally come through another storm. But, as they watched Liz and John come closer to them, they both sensed that the emotional storm that Liz and John had endured together had changed their lives forever.

John quietly watched as Jim and Melissa embraced Elizabeth. He noticed the little things, the important things that were being shared within a family—soon to be his family. John liked the way that felt and sounded to himself: his family. A touch of a smile edged onto his lips, as he watched Jim discretely brush away a tear from the edge of his eye. If, anyone had told John at the beginning of the year that he would meet, date, and fall in love with one of Jim's daughters, he would have said that they were crazy. But, fall in love he definitely had. A smile tugged at his heart. As they all stood together in the freezing cold, John remembered back to when he had been a state police officer riding on patrol with Jim. During that time, he had envied Jim, as he spoke with such unabashed love for his family. Now, years later by the guidance and grace of God, John was becoming a part of Liz's family, and his mentor and friend would soon be his father in law. John smiled as he felt Jim's strong gloved hand grasp his shoulder, and clear his throat. Then Jim spoke with honesty from within his heart.

"John, you will never know how Mellie and I felt yesterday afternoon, when we listened to you share your feelings with us, then watched you go out into the storm determined to find Elizabeth." John watched Jim as he spoke, paused, reigned in his emotions, that threaten to breach Jim's emotional dam. "Obviously God heard and answered our prayers for you and Lizzie." Jim's gaze wandered from John to Liz, who was standing next to John. "I can't tell you how relieved we were when Forest Ranger Asinski called us this morning. John, you put your life in peril to save Elizabeth." Jim sniffled. "We can never adequately show our appreciation to you for what you've done."

John tenderly squeezed Liz's hand. "Well, Jim, Melissa, I know of a very simple way for you to show your appreciation."

"Oh?" They asked in unison, while two set of questioning eyes moved their gazes between Liz and John.

Liz couldn't help but smile at her parents' expressions. She giggled with anticipation of what she assumed John was going to say to them.

"I asked Liz to marry me, and I'd like for you to accept me into your family."

Jim let out a whoop of joy that appeared to wake up every bird in the area surrounding the parking lot. The sounds of blue jays, cardinals, chickadees, mourning doves, and countless others filled the air, as many took flight. Melissa, wasn't quite as showy with her joy. She simply allowed her tears to openly fall, as she drew Liz into her arms, and quietly spoke to her. Jim nodded at John, then drew him into a hug, as he welcomed him into the family.

Hours later, in the Mayfield Community Hospital ER after being thoroughly checked for frostbite and hypothermia, which neither Liz nor John had any signs of, they were released and sent home. John had tenderly kissed her goodbye, as they stood together in the parking lot, and headed back to his cabin to get some much-needed sleep. Then, after giving another round of hugs and reassurance to her parent's that she was capable of driving back to the cabin by herself, Liz headed home. The last things she remembered before shutting her eyes and falling asleep in the warmth of her bed were, John's phone call telling her that he had made it home safely and that he loved her.

Liz yawned and stretched, as made her way to the bathroom. She smiled. Happy thoughts floated through her achy body. Then, an unexpected laugh escaped from her, as she thought about where she was forty eight hours ago. John had been with her up in the old lean to on the mountain in the near blizzard conditions. When Liz needed to relieve her bladder, and had gone out away from the shelter, her fanny had gotten down right cold! Goodness only knows how happy she was, during her ER visit that she didn't have to show her butt for frostbite inspection!

Liz was on her way out to the kitchen when her phone rang. She smiled, as she pulled her phone from the pocket of her fuzzy warm housecoat.

"Hello, John." A yawn and stretch followed, then Liz asked, "How are you doing today? Are you at work?"

"I took the day off." His voice was quieter that Liz expected. Then he sneezed.

"Bless you, John." She Listened and immediately was concerned. "John, you sound like you caught cold while we were up in the lean to."

"I think I might have. I've taken some cold medicine, and am having a bowl of chicken soup." He sighed and coughed. "I feel lousy, Liz. So, I'm not going anywhere today, except to necessary rooms and furniture here in my cabin."

"I understand, John. You go rest and I'll call you later."

Liz clutched the phone to her. John had caught cold all on account of her. She sighed, then thought about her options. Coffee. Shower. Clothes. Action. All of a sudden Liz felt energized. She had things to do. Places to go and important people to see.

After John spoke with Liz, he had changed into clean sweat pants and a sweat shirt, as well as clean wool socks. Then, he had fallen asleep on the couch, covered with a quilt that his grandmother had made for him many years ago. He had been dreaming, until the loud rapping on his front door awakened him from a very pleasant dream. He yawned, shook the sleep from his brain. Bad idea! His head was filled with congestion, and now it oozed with pain. "I'm coming!" He croaked like an old bullfrog nestled in marsh by the lake, as he made his way to the door. "Elizabeth!" He promptly coughed, as an added exclamation point while opening the door. "I don't think it is a wise idea for you to come in here."

Liz couldn't help but smile, as she eased John back from the door, closed it, then leaned over and brushed her warm lips against his unshaven bristly cheek. "If, I end up sick, then you can take care of me." She placed her basket on the floor beside her, slipped out of her winter jacket, and out of her wet boots. Then, Liz leaned over and brushed her lips against John's cheek, this time to confirm, if, he had a fever. "Hmm. You are very warm. Have you taken your temperature?" Liz asked, as she began to usher John back to the couch.

"No. I think I'm just chilled from being out in the cold for an extended period of time. I just need some rest."

"Uh-huh! Liz was not smiling, as she tucked the quilt in around him. "Do you have a thermometer?" Liz asked, as she stepped over to the doorway to retrieve the basket that she had brought with her.

"In the medicine cabinet." John mumbled, as his eyes drifted close.

The next time John opened his eyes the cabin was dark, except for the glow of the fire blazing in the fireplace and the small reading lamp by the overstuffed chair. He slowly turned his head, and focused his eyes on the chair. A smile brushed his lips as he recalled images of the past hours. How many hours? He did not know. What he did know was, that Elizabeth had been there with him. She had been lovingly taking care of him. Actually, John recalled battling with Liz at one point. Over what? He didn't recall. Even if he did remember, it wouldn't matter because he was sure that with how he was still feeling, Elizabeth had won!

A feeling of calm, peace rested over John. First, he had cared for Liz in her hour of need up on the side of the mountain, and now she was caring for him in his time of need. John sighed, and smiled, as he saw a shadow, then felt a gentle hand, and saw Liz's tender loving smile.

Two weeks later, life was back to normal for Liz and John. Well, in their work life, that is. On the personal, relationship side of life, they were just about over the moon with happiness, if that was physically possible. News of their engagement had spread through their families and the community with less fanfare that Liz's previous engagement to Peter. Liz was glad. She needed for things to be more peaceful, allowing the ebbs and flows of wedding plans to take place without much drama. As if that would ever happen! Liz hoped. Especially, now as she sat at her desk in the arts center busily working on final preparation for the senior extravaganza, that was scheduled for the following weekend. Liz heard the door of the building open and close. She was not expecting anyone in particular. At that moment, she realized that she probably should have locked the outside door. But then, that would have defeated the open-door policy she wanted, and envisioned for the arts center to be a vital part of the Great Sac Community.

"Caitlin!" She exclaimed when her sister stepped around the free-standing senior class mural that was to be part of the senior extravaganza. "What are you doing here?" It was then that Liz glanced up at the wall clock. "Oh my gosh! The last time I looked at the clock it was 11:30. I guess I forgot lunch. When did it get to be so late?"

Caitlin couldn't help but laugh, as she shook her head and responded. "Oh, Lizzie! Being engrossed in things of interest, your passion, and loosing track of time will never change with you. I'm glad," she added, while slipping out of her coat, and casually laying it on the long empty table. "So, am I interrupting you from something vitally important? Or, do you have time to take a break?"

"Of course, you are interrupting," Liz broke into her happiest of smiles. "And I'm glad because now we can talk about some of my wedding ideas, without Mom's lovingly input, or Sammie's meddling."

"Wow!" Was all Caitlin could say as she read over Liz's detailed plans for the reception that would be held at the arts colony mess hall. "This is going to be amazing! I'm curious about this symbol you have here next to head table?" Cait watched the soft knowing smile appear on Liz's face, along with the silence. "Okay, I won't ask—for now!"

"Wise decision, Caitie Did!" Liz bit her lips together, as she watched Cait's classic response to the nickname from their childhood.

Laughter filled the empty space around them, as Liz and Cait shared the moment, reminiscing and then returning to the present. "Elizabeth, in all honesty, I know I've already cried and shared my feeling with you. But I feel as though I need to tell you once again. Thank you. Being your sister is a joy in its own right. Having you ask me, over our other sisters, to stand by your side when you marry John, -" Oh yes, the tears were flowing for both of them. "-Well, it means the world to me." Caitlin blew her nose. "Oh, good grief! Look at me! I'm already a mess and we're months away from your wedding. I just know that I'm going to be a blubbering idiot, and totally embarrass you on your wedding day!"

"Cait, I won't mind if you cry." Liz sniffled, as she reached over to hug her close against her. "All I want is for you to be there with me as my matron of honor. My sister. The other pea in my pod."

Neither of the Callison sisters had realized that their dad had quietly slipped into the building, while they were talking and crying together. He had remained standing out of their sight, unnoticed and listened to part of their conversation. Then, without a word, he silently slipped back out of the building, allowing his *two peas in a pod* to have their special moment together uninterrupted by him.

Liz could hardly contain her sense of pride, as she stood watching the Great Sac High School senior class pull together the finishing touches for the Senior Extravaganza. The anticipation Liz was feeling was similar to the feeling she used to get in years past while working in the theater, and last summer at the arts colony. A smile graced her lips as she listened to Kellie, the class president praising the other committee members for all of their hard work. Yes. They all had worked hard to make this event a success. But then Liz already knew of their work ethic.

"Guys and gals," Liz drew their attention. "I am also proud of you. We have three hours before the doors open." She couldn't help but smile, as she heard some of the quiet comments being passed among the group. "Yes. Time moves quickly and will go even faster after Forest Ranger Runner arrives with the pizza for our dinner. Now, when he does get here," she paused and shook her head, sighed and raised her voice. "Listen up!" Silence. "Thank you. Now, as I was saying, we all will have things to complete after we eat, to ensure that we are ready for when our imaginary curtain to goes up this evening. Kellie do you have any announcements that you need to make at this time?"

"I don't think so, Liz. The check list you created with me has worked really well."

"Okay then," She smiled as the door opened and John entered. "Pizza's here. Time to eat."

John could not believe how quickly the teens swarmed around him and dug into the pizza. Liz laughed, as she listened to John share his amazement with her, as they each ate a slice of cheese pizza, and watched the teens polish off the rest of the eight pizza pies. She wiped her mouth, released a sigh of contentment, and stood to clear the area of used paper plates and recycling, when the door opened. A hush fell over the teens, as they watched a strikingly tall, blond hair woman with a mid-calf leather coat, matching gloves, leather hand-bag and leather boots sticking out from under her dark pants entered the center.

"Regina!" Liz exclaimed, tears took shape in her eyes, as she turned to John and breathed out, "Oh, honey she made it. Come with me, so I can introduce you to each other."

With that John allowed himself to be swept across the room by Liz to greet their guest he had heard so much about. The joy he saw in Liz would be hard to miss. He was glad that her special night's art center program, and side plans were going as she had hoped and planned.

"You made it! Oh, this is wonderful." By now the two women had bridged the gap between them and hugged, as Liz continued to welcome her. Then Liz drew away from her friend, while easing her hand into John's. There was a slight rise in the corner of his mouth, as he felt Liz possessively take a hold of him. It felt good for him to know that his woman—his mate—the love of his life, was staking her claim for everyone to see. "Regina, I'd like, -" her gaze moved to John as the softest, sweetest smile touched her lips and her eyes. "It's my pleasure to introduce you to John Runner, my fiancé."

Regina, had been discretely watching the subtle interaction between her friend, and the new man in her life. Oh yes! Elizabeth had clearly stated her position and staked her claim. The non-verbal, yet thoroughly visible *Hands Off! No Trespassing!* sign had been posted for Regina and any other woman to see. She extended her hand, which John politely took a hold of, then immediately released. "John, it is a pleasure to finally meet you. Liz has told me that you are a forest ranger, and that she's recently provided you with some rescue adventures." Her smile was laced with unspoken mischief and humor.

John's gaze passed between Liz and her friend. He hadn't missed that the color had changed on Liz's cheeks. Oh, yes! Her friend had intentionally, or inadvertently, betrayed Liz's confidence in her. "I agree with you, Regina. It is fortunate that I am a forest ranger, since

Liz and other members of the Callison family appear to frequently be in need of my help."

Regina's gaze passed between them. She was intrigued by their silent communication. They had stories between them, that she was itching to hear about.

"Yes, well, now is not the time for us to pull the Callison skeleton's out of the closet." Liz's face was flushed. "You both have stories about me and I really would appreciate if, neither of you shared them while we are here." John quietly leaned over and brushed a kiss on Liz's flushed cheek, then winked at Regina.

"I agree with you, Liz. Now is not the time for us to further explore this interesting topic. So, how about you introduce me to your aspiring artist?"

Liz released her hold on John's hand and stepped away to speak with Kellie. She knew she didn't have to worry, or feel threatened in any way while leaving John and Regina together. A smile tugged at her lips. Liz realized that what she was feeling was trust, respect, love and other emotions towards both John and Regina. Having known Regina since their freshman year at Syracuse University until Regina had sadly needed to return to New York City to run her father's, Nico Sullivani's, Art Gallery, due to a family emergency. Then, eventually, she would complete her studies at Columbia University. Liz knew she could trust her friend to be respectful and not make passes towards John. After all, Regina had been one of Liz's friends whom she had turned to when Greg had cheated on her with Jordan.

"Regina, Kellie, it is my pleasure to finally be able introduce you both to each other." She glanced at her watch. Smiled, as she listened to them greet each other. "We do have enough time before the doors open so, Kellie, perhaps you'd like to show Regina some of your work that we currently have on display."

John, placed a protective hand at the small of Liz's back, as they watched and listened to Regina and Kellie head over towards Kellie's oil paintings and watercolors. He was well aware of the other activities happening around them. His smile grew, as pride swelled within him. Elizabeth, with her creative direction had made the evening's events happen. Seizing the moment, John leaned over and brushed his lips over her soft, moist warm lips. He felt her lips immediately respond.

"Excuse me! Hey, man, this isn't Making Out City!" Other unwanted comments followed, along with some whistling.

Liz felt the color rise in her cheeks. She simply shook her head and smiled at the teens, who had become a special part of her life through the drama club at the high school, and the summer stock theater. Liz sighed. "John, we've been busted." She glanced around observing what everyone else was doing, or not doing. "Derick, Aiden, how are you guys coming along with the final lighting and sound checks?"

"Good boss! As if you need to worry about your tech crew!" Their expressions were quite priceless. They knew just how much teasing would be tolerated before they were disrespectful. Crossing that fine line was not an option for either teen.

Liz slowly shook her head, then breathed out, "Modesty is obviously not an issue for either of you. Why do I feel as though I've helped create a couple of techies with major egos?"

The other students responded for both of the teens. "Oh Please! They had huge egos before you ever came back here. You simply provided them with the outlet to further annoy the rest of us!"

Laughter filled the room. Even John, who was feeling more comfortable with the teens, each time they were together, joined in with the fun light bantering that was taking place. By 6:30pm the senior citizens who were participating in the evening had begun to arrive to get settled in for the show. John stepped back, grabbed some refreshments and claimed one of the two tables that had been reserved for him and the Callison party of twelve. From that moment on, it was a ruckus with getting last minute things done before 7:00 pm when the doors opened for their paying guests. John watched Liz, as she interacted with the two different age groups of people. At some point she had pulled her hair up into a ponytail, and now had her familiar cap on her head, a pencil behind her ear, and a clipboard in her hand. No person, question or need was beyond her ability to attend to. Jim and Melissa's arrival with their friends, as well as Liz's family drew John's attention from Liz.

At exactly 8:00 pm Aiden cued up the opening music for the night. Liz, who had at some point removed her cap from her head, combed out her hair to fall onto her shoulders, and added a touch of lipstick to her lips, took her place on the stage area to welcome everyone, while Derick used the baby spot light with precision. Then, Liz turned over the evening to Kellie, who was to be the mistress of ceremony for the show. Music from vocal to instrumental spanning the decades, comedy, magic tricks, poetry reading, as well as improvisational drama from the high school senior class to the talents of community members from age 60 and above entertained the community for two hours. By the end of the night they all had proved that everyone regardless of their age had something entertaining to share with the community. As the show came to an end, Liz once again took over the directing. She invited all of the participants to come up on the stage for a final bow. Then, with microphone in hand, she made two important announcements. Both, involved two of her favorite teens.

"Amber, please step forward." She turned and met the young woman's nervous gaze, smiled and nodded. Amber took a hesitant step, then drew in a breath and walked over to where Liz was standing.

"Wait!" Derick exclaimed as he headed towards the lighting.

"Derick, we don't need it!" Liz called out into the microphone. The mic squealed. Many people gasped while placing their hand over their ears. "Sorry everyone! Sometimes I forget that I have a big mouth and don't need this thing." People laughed. Unfortunately, too many people agreed with her. Liz smiled, as she glanced down at the microphone and shrugged. It was then that Liz pulled a large envelope from under the papers on her clipboard, as she spoke directly to Amber. "Amber, tonight you took a risk, and allowed us all to hear your beautiful poetry." People spontaneously clapped. Liz smiled at the audience. "Yes. Amber does deserve our accolades. Her-" Liz returned her gaze to meet Amber's nervous eyes. "Your talent needs to continue to grow and blossom, and touch other people as much as you have touched us. So, as the director of the Great Sacandaga Community Arts Association, it is my pleasure to inform you that you are this year's Arts Scholarship recipient. Tonight, you are receiving your award to have to frame and include in your resume. Upon your graduation, you will receive your monetary award as well."

The seniors applauded, along with the crowd who had risen to their feet with their ovation for her. Amber was a mess! Tears flowed as she hugged Liz, who was also teary eyed with pride for the young woman who had come so far, since the previous spring. On many different levels, the evening's senior extravaganza had once again proven what Liz was always affirming. The arts are a necessary and vital part of life!

Jim, Melissa and John knew that just because the show had come to an end, that didn't mean that Elizabeth was ready to leave. Like magic, Liz's hair was back in a ponytail and the cap was on her head. They also noticed that her high heels had been replaced with sneakers. As people slowly began to leave, pausing to view artwork on display, she had work to do tonight to break down the room and return it to order, before preparing it for the next event. Liz's parents and John had offered to help Liz, but she graciously turned them down, sighting that she had teenagers who were responsible for helping her with tearing down the room, especially if they wanted her to provide them with a good reference in the future.

"Liz, who is that woman with Kellie?" Melissa quietly asked. Liz smiled as she turned to glance in the direction where her mother was looking.

"Oh, Mom, have you forgotten my friend Regina Sullivani! Oh! Of, course you probably have, since you haven't seen her in years."

"Regina Sullivani." Melissa was drawing upon her memory of all her children's countless friends through the years. "I seem to be drawing a blank."

Liz quickly brought her mother up to speed on her friend. "Regina is spending the weekend with me. Later I'll reintroduce you to her." A quiet voice drew Liz's attention from her mother to Amber, who was standing by her. "Yes, Amber, how may I help you?"

"I want to thank you for the award. It really means the world to me." Amber's eyes shone with happiness as she added, "I, um, I think I'm in shock because Mr. Jones just spoke to me, and he has asked me to be his assistant director for our spring play."

Liz made a gasping noise as she smiled and drew her into a hug. "Oh, Amber I am so happy for you. Assistant director is an important position, and you are the perfect person for the job."

"You think I'm perfect?" Liz saw the insecurity in her body language, and it was confirmed when Amber added, "I thought Kellie would get it."

"This is going to be your time to shine. Don't worry about Kellie. She has other things going on in her life that need her attention."

"You mean your friend who's here and spending time with her?"

Liz responded and spent a few more minutes with Amber, who then disappeared into the crowd that was still mingling. She spoke to more people, then once again found herself with John and her parents. Of course, she continued to have one eye on what the senior class was up to with breaking down the room.

"Lizzie, since you already said you don't need the portable lights for your next event, I'll take them back up to the colony whenever you're ready to get them out of here."

"Thanks, Dad. Since the rest of this weekend is going to be busy, let's aim for Monday, weather permitting."

"Sounds good."

John was getting a good taste of what it is like to be Liz's other half. Waiting. Watching. He looked around at the people who were still there, drew in a deep breath and exhaled a sense of pride. Elizabeth has so many gifts and the community was blessed because of her presence in their midst. Then he noticed that Peter Jones was still there. Interesting. John instinctively went on high alert. He watched. Unknowingly, a slight smile formed at the corner of his mouth.

"Care to let me in on what is funny?" Liz whispered in his ear as she came along side of him. He inconspicuously slid his arm around her waist.

"I'm just observing." His eyes did not reveal any more than his words.

"I know who you've been interested in watching. What do you think?" Liz's eyes were bursting with mischief.

John tilted his head as he glanced down at Liz. His brow came up with questioning. His lips barely moved as he asked, "I thought I heard that he was planning on heading over towards Glens Falls?" Liz shook her head. John raised a brow, partly wondering how she knew the details of Peter Jones' plans for his life after Liz. "Interesting. Is he taking the bait you set out for him?"

Liz's smile grew like a cat that had just made the ultimate catch, by killing the old rabbit and was bringing its feast home in its mouth. "Oh, yes, the man is hooked for sure! Regina is perfect for Peter."

"What makes them perfect for each other?"

"Besides owning an art gallery, Regina, has her masters in writing, as well as her bachelor in visual art both degrees are from

Columbia. The visual art degree not only tapped into another creative dimension of Regina's mind, it also has helped her with running the gallery. Now, seeing the two of them together, I honestly don't know why I didn't guide them towards one another before I ever dated Peter."

John returned his gaze from Liz to Peter and Regina, then back to capture Liz's eyes in his gaze. Smoldering heat shone from his eyes, and he quietly said with a touch of a smile, "You're quite the match maker."

"Time will tell." Liz watched, as Regina and Peter began to walk towards them. "Maybe sooner than we think." She said under her breath.

ACT 3

*Two roads diverged in a wood,
and I took the one less traveled by,
and that made all the difference.*
Robert Frost

CHAPTER 23

The winter holidays came with a flurry, along with multiple days and nights of snowstorms. Snow in the north country was to be expected at this time of year, especially in the Great Sacandaga Lake region. For Jim and Melissa, this was a special year that they would surely remember for many years to come. All five of their children, spouses, grandchildren and their single children's mate were seated with them in the family pew at the Great Sacandaga Community Church for the Christmas Eve Service. Yes, it was a jubilant time.

Jim and Melissa beamed with joy, as friends welcomed their children and fussed over the grandchildren. Caitlin and Samantha shared private sister smiles, as they listened to the older women of the church compliment them on their beautiful children. Upon removing her coat and warming her cold hands, Melissa had managed to snag one of the twins from Caitlin, who had swooped in as doting aunt, as soon as Sammie and Chris walked through the front doors of the church. Oh yes! Grandma was claiming matriarch bragging rights and she was not going to be out maneuvered by Aunt Cait. A hint of a smile touched Jim's lips, as he watched and listened to all the conversations taking place around him. Even though Jim was smiling, he had lived through enough holidays in his life to know enough to expect the unexpected.

Once again Jim's gaze passed over his family: Caitlin and Nick, along with their children, who were getting on each other's nerves. Jim laughed to himself as he remembered a number of years when it had been him, the middle child bickering with his older brother Samuel and his younger sister Amanda, as the excitement and fatigue of the night were settling in with them. James Jr and Elise had arrived from Boston mid evening shortly before Jordan and Thomas had arrived from down state on Long Island, and were conversing with Nick and Chris. So that left Elizabeth and John as the only two of the Callison family offspring who were missing. Earlier in the evening when Melissa had spoken with Elizabeth, they were busy with last minute Christmas precipitation, and she had promised that they would meet the family at church. Jim glanced at his watch. He sighed as he glanced around at his family, then at the doorway filled with more people. Still, no Liz or John in sight. Jim didn't know why, but he was beginning to get an uneasy feeling deep in his gut. Past experience had taught Jim to take note of that feeling. His mind was on high alert. Then, much to Jim's relief he spotted Elizabeth and John as they came in through the door. Jim's smile grew as he watched them approach the family, greeting people along the way. Still, in the back of his mind there was something that made Jim suspicious about what his most unpredictable daughter and her fiancé had been up to. Time would only tell whether there was any validity to his suspicions!

Three hours later, Jim and Melissa were snuggled up together in their bed. The moon appeared to be playing hide and seek, as the clouds passed over it in the night sky. It was now early Christmas morning. JJ and Elise were staying with them, while Jordan and Thomas had opted for staying up at the cabin with Liz. In years past,

Jim and Mel had gone over to Caitlin's to have breakfast with her and her family and see what gifts their grandchildren had received. Not this year! Everything was different. Now that Sammie and Chris had the twins, they too wanted Jim and Mel to visit. So, after finding out what all of the other children had planned for the holidays, Jim and Mel decided that this year, they would remain at their home with their unmarried children. Then, later on in the evening the whole family, minus Amanda and Kevin, would gather together at the family home for the Callison family Christmas. Jim gently stroked Mel's arm. He breathed out a sigh of contentment, as they lay together in the darkness. This year, as with so many other years, there were many reasons for Jim and his family to give thanks.

"I love you, Jim." Melissa's voice was barely above a whisper. Jim thought it sounded almost angelic.

"And I love you, my sweet Melissa." He continued to lazily, softly rub Mel's arm. "I thought you were asleep. Did I awaken you?"

Mel moved her body, so that she was facing Jim. He sighed with contentment, as he moved his arms protectively around her back, and felt her warm body touch his.

"No. I was lost in my own thoughts. Replaying in my mind what it felt like to have our whole family worship with us on this sacred night. Oh, Jim, we are so blessed. We have so much to be grateful for."

"Yes, we do, Mellie. Tonight, was special indeed. I hope our children realize how special it was for all of us. It seems like just yesterday when our children were the young ones, filled with excitement and mischief when they were Callie Anne and Nick's ages, or as small as Mary and Daniel." Melissa quietly responded. Jim softly chuckled in the quiet of the night. "At one point during the service I found myself thinking of my mother."

"Oh?" Melissa questioned as her fingers gently brushed over the graying mat of hair on Jim's chest.

"It actually caught me unaware. Usually when the choir sings my thoughts go to Mom. Not so much tonight." Jim grew quiet. Melissa instinctively knew that Jim needed a moment, and so she quietly waited for him to find his words. "I seemed to feel her presence when Sammie and Chris were quieting their fussy little ones. Then, when the children quieted down, it was as if, Mom had never been there. It's funny how different situations can bring family members to mind."

"Yes, it is. I know from everything that happened this past year at the arts colony, and what your family, and now Elizabeth believes about spirits, that tonight was special for you. I'm glad that you felt your mother's presence." With that Melissa gently moved her hand further down over Jim's body. Then she moved her leg.

"Mellie, sweetheart, my memory of Mom was nice, but holding you -"

"Callison, shut up and kiss me!" Jim quietly chuckled, and did just that! Sometime later with Mel nestled back in his arms, he drifted off to sleep. *Not a creature was stirring, not even a mouse.*

Noise. Laughter. Food and beverages were placed on the table for easy access when someone was hungry or thirsty. A fire burned in the hearth in the family room in the Callison household. Oh, it was wonderful pandemonium. As the pile of torn wrapping paper strewn from unwrapped gifts increased on the family room floor, and unanticipated surprise and gratitude was exclaimed, Jim and Melissa turned their attention towards JJ who had the latest in technology in his hands. Their questioning gazes turned to each other. Surprise. Needless to say, their expressions were priceless when they heard Amanda and Kevin wish everyone a "Merry Christmas." Then they saw them in the device that JJ had with him.

"Geese, Sis, Kevin, this is almost as good as if you two were actually here with us."

"I'm missing you all as well. So am I!" Amanda and Kevin snuggled in together on their couch said together. Jim chuckled, while Melissa greeted her in laws. Then Amanda added with a note of sadness in her voice, "We really do wish that circumstances were different for us this year. But being able to help surprise you and Mel for your anniversary, and pay the consequences in days and weeks ahead with a setback in my recovery, well, I'd do it again in a heartbeat."

"And that's why we're here in Baltimore and not up there with all of you!" Kevin added. "Did any of you get coal for Christmas?"

All of the Callison children and grandchildren regaled Kevin on how wonderful they had all been, and some of the exceptional gifts that they had received. It was Callie Anne who asked, "Uncle Kevin, did you get coal in your stocking?"

Jim wasn't sure if he'd ever stop laughing, as he listened to Kevin share his near miss on receiving of a few months' worth of coal from Amanda. Oh yes! Jim could picture it, as he imagined Amanda in her fury when her health, their work schedules, and Kevin's family interrupted how his sister had wanted to spend the holidays. It didn't help when Amanda had found out that her and Kevin's special friends Cassie and Andrew were going to be vacationing at their cabin at the Great Sacandaga Lake for Christmas and New Year's. Oh yes! Jim could imagine the way she probably pouted and made Kevin's life miserable. Family. Jim gazed around the room at all of them. He listened and joined in with the laughter. Then, all too soon it was time to say goodbye to Amanda and Kevin.

Winter lingered on with snow, freezing temperatures, then fluctuating warm and cold. Of course, that wreaked havoc with snow thawing, and ice forming with colder night temperatures. Then flu season hit the north country with a vengeance. Liz was dressed in a warm sweater, jeans, wool socks and her insulated work boots. That morning upon arriving at the arts center, Liz had turned the heat up to 68 degrees. It normally was comfortable for work. Not today. Liz was still shivering and had begun to sneeze. Actually, she had been feeling off since the last round of storms moved through the area. It probably hadn't helped her by having been over to Caitlin's home, to care for her sister and her family when they were all down with the flu. She gasped, as she looked up from her last sneeze, ready to blow her nose and found John standing in the doorway to her office.

"Hi!" Liz was able to say before another sneeze blew out of her mouth. Fortunately, she had enough time to lower her face into her sleeve to catch most of her germs. "I think I caught Caitlin's and her family's flu. You might want to stay away."

"Beautiful, I'll take my chances." John did not appear to be phased in the least, by the prospect of getting too close to Liz and catching whatever sickness that she might have. He entered her office, and placed a brown paper bag on top of Liz's desk in front of her. Then, he removed his winter coat and placed it over the back of the chair that was positioned in front of her desk. With quick, efficient steps he moved around the desk and gently placed his hand on Liz's forehead. He sighed. Leaning down, he softly kissed her cheek.

"Sweetheart, I think you might have a fever." John quietly opened the bag and removed two round containers. Both happened to contain hot chicken noodle soup. "I think that after we finish eating our lunch, you had better call it a short day, and go home to rest."

"I think you might be right." Liz quietly agreed, then ate a spoonful of soup.

John watched Liz as she ate her soup. The fact that she readily agreed with him told John just how sick she must actually be. Much to their surprise, Jim arrived when that they were getting ready for Liz to lock up the building, and for John to follow her home before returning to work. John was cradling Liz against him, and had been rethinking the situation. He was concerned by how quickly

Liz's health was deteriorating and hadn't wanted for her to be driving alone.

Jim's gaze passed between them. He shook his head. "Looks like I got here in the nick of time. It's a good thing I had my flu shot! I kept telling all of you to get one. Stubborn kids! You should have listened to me and your mother." He sighed, and held out his hand for Liz's keys to her car. "Elizabeth, do I need to stop at the market on the way to the cabin and get you anything?"

Liz sniffled. "Oh, yes please! Ginger ale. Tissues." She sniffled and coughed.

He lovingly nodded as he looked at his daughter being propped up by John. "Lizzie J, I know the drill. You and John head on up the mountain. I'll stop at the grocery store and pick up the usual for a cold or flu."

Liz did not protest. It felt really good to be cared for by John, and know that her dad was going to stop at the store for her. She sighed. This late winter bug was really kicking her hard.

Morning came and Liz was feeling better. She laid in bed, stretched and simply enjoyed the moment. Her body didn't ache, or show any lingering signs of the flu. Two long weeks of feeling like death warmed over, one trip to urgent care and a regular visit to her physician, along with multiple prescription drugs, as well as bed rest, and her mother's TLC. Then, Liz's aunt called and informed Liz that she was to use specific home remedies, if, she wanted to return to land of the living any time soon! Liz graciously accepted the old-fashioned mustard plaster that her mother made according to Amanda's recipe. It was wet on her skin, and then it warmed her congested chest. Liz couldn't believe how effective it was, as well as, the remedies for the congested head and sore throat. Never again would Liz laugh at her aunt's suggestions, because their grandmother's home remedies worked! Nor, would she ignore getting a flu shot, because her dad had really enjoyed saying, 'I told you so'!

Now, Liz was finally ready to face the world again. An hour later, showered and dressed for the day, Liz was snuggled in one of the oversized chairs positioned near the front window and not too far from the warmth of the fireplace. The hot coffee and toast with strawberry jam actually tasted good. She had just finished wrapping an afghan around her feet and body when her phone rang.

"Good morning, Aunt Amanda." Liz coughed, listened to her aunt and responded. "Oh, I am much better, thank you." Amanda asked more questions, and listened to Liz's saga of her battle with the flu. They laughed, then Amanda shared more words of wisdom.

"Well, Elizabeth, now that you are on the road to recovery, you had better create a to-do-list for fumigating the cabin of your germs, so visitors do not become sick from you."

Liz recognized a very familiar tone in her aunt's voice. She could picture her no nonsense expression. Liz smiled at the thought. "Does this mean that you and Uncle Kevin are heading north before too long?" Liz asked with hopefulness in her voice. She wiped her nose as she listened to her aunt regale her with the current events happening in their lives in Baltimore.

"Wow! You do have a lot going on. So, it looks like you won't be up until around Valentine's Day, or maybe even Presidents Day Weekend." Liz pouted as she listened to her aunt elaborate on work and family commitments.

"We honestly are working on freeing up our time, so we can make it north before too long. After all, we need to get up there with the key to the old chest of Mom's. We need to see if her wedding gown is salvageable for you to incorporate into the wedding gown you are having made for you to wear. Right now, we're looking at a couple of weekends in February, or possibly the first weekend in March."

"Oh good!" Well, it would have been good, if, that exclamation from Liz hadn't driven her into a coughing jag.

"On second thought, Elizabeth, you still sound horrible! We might have to amend our plans, and wait to come north until Memorial Day weekend!"

Silence fell between them, as Liz attended to her immediate needs. She hated being sick. Then her aunt quietly encouraged her to end the call and go rest. Liz had to agree with her. She was exhausted from their brief phone conversation. Heaven help her, if she had even thought she was ready to return to work, as she snuggled in the chair and fell asleep.

John felt as if, the weight of the world was off of his shoulders, as he read Liz's text. He responded to her text, then placed a phone call to Paul's Pizza Pit and ordered their meal. Liz's recent bout with the flu had deeply troubled John. He was used to being in charge, making a difference, solving problems. When Liz got sick, John felt helpless in not being able to make her sickness go away for her. A smile brushed his lips, as he bundled up in his winter coat before heading out of the office for the night. Shutting off the light, he closed the door behind him, and headed out to his SUV parked next to the ranger's office. A quick check of his four tires revealed that they were all properly inflated. That was a sigh of relief, even though the vehicle vandal was still on the loose, and appeared to have moved south to Amsterdam to commit their acts of vandalism.

The ride home with a large pizza pie loaded with John and Liz's favorite toppings, a large garden salad, chicken wings and garlic knots, made John's stomach grumble, and his mouth water. As he pulled into his drive, he saw Liz's car in the spot that was now hers, and would continue to be after they married. By the time John had shut off the motor, pulled the key from the ignition, and opened the door, Liz was standing next to his vehicle. Her smile shone bright in the late afternoon sky while a blue jay called out, as if to welcome them home. John took one step forward and drew Liz into his embrace. She smelled of raspberry, vanilla, and a hint of wood smoke. His gaze held hers as his lips eased onto hers with tenderness. His tongue gently touched, Liz's lips beckoning her to allow him entrance, to share his deepening passion with her. She moaned. John felt her lips slightly part, inviting him to continue on with his sensual journey, while their bodies constrained by their clothing were responding to their heightened needs.

"Elizabeth, if we don't stop right now, I will break the promise that I made to you and to myself." John said breathlessly, as he pulled himself back from her. He released a strained breath as he fought back and downed his arousal. His hand raised to her cheek, lightly brushing back her hair from her jaw. "We had better get our meal inside before it's completely cold. At least this is one hunger we can satisfy."

Once inside the cabin, Liz immediately kicked off her boots, slid out of her coat, hung it on the hook next to John's, then headed for the kitchen. By now, she was familiar with the way John had the kitchen set up and gathered plates and utensils, carried them over and set the table. A smile brushed her lips as she thought about the day when John had told her that she could make changes to the kitchen, if there was a better way for it to be organized. John had started a fire in the hearth, and selected jazz music to play in the background. Before sitting down in his chair at the table, John lit the candle on the table. Then Liz carried the bottle of chilled red wine and corkscrew over to John for him to open, while she got out their wine glasses from the cupboard. Both agreed that the intimate setting that they had created in the privacy of the cabin was far better than being out in an Italian restaurant.

"So, earlier today I spoke with my friend Cookie." Liz said, after taking a sip of wine.

John swallowed his bite of pizza, then asked, "And who is she again?" He watched her eyes as she spoke. Her passion for the theater arts and her friends shone through her. Well, of course it did! The theater had been and still is a significant part of her life. He was proud of Liz and her accomplishments thus far in her life: Broadway and now the director of the Great Sacandaga Lake Community Arts Center. To think, now he too was a part of her story. At times, it was more than John could fathom. What has he done in his life, to deserve such a beautiful gift of love that he experienced with Elizabeth?

For years John had grieved over his loss when their family home had burned down, and only John and his parents made it out of the early morning fire. Smoke. Raging angry flames. Screams as his youngest sister died while being burned alive. John drew in a breath as the memory once again scorched his mind. When the fire was finally fully extinguished, the charred remains of John's older and younger siblings had been found, a total of three lives lost. The grief that consumed him and his parents had been overwhelming. For years, John had wrestled with…why? Why had he been spared and his siblings had died? For years he could not find any possible answers to his questions. Perhaps, the tragedy in his life had been a guiding force to lead him into his professional life. Perhaps, it had been a part of the path that would eventually lead him to the beautiful woman who was sharing his life, this meal with him. His smile gave a glimpse into the depth of his love for Elizabeth, as he listened to her speak.

Liz took a sip of wine, then found herself smiling, as she gazed at John. He was amazing in the way that he accepted her friends, whom she still had contact with in the theater district in New York City. Every once in a while, like in this moment, John mixed up the names of Liz's friends—who they were and what they did professionally. However, he always sought clarity, because if these people were important to Liz, then he sought be as respectful of her, as she was to him with his forest ranger colleagues. More than that, John had met many people whom Liz had worked with over the summer, and he knew from his own experience that they were good people. Otherwise, they would not be a part of Liz's life. So, therefore, Cookie had to be another good person.

"Cookie does costume design." She paused, then took a small sip of wine. "I wish I had pictures of her work, so that I could show you some of her amazing creations. I believe that she's one of the best, if, not the best in the business. Cookie has a rare gift, and she's been nominated for a couple of Tony's in recent years." Liz paused, took a bite of pizza, chewed and swallowed. "In my opinion, she should have won!"

"I can see by your expression and the conviction in your voice that Cookie is special to you." John couldn't help but smile, as he gazed at Liz. "So, what exactly is she going to be designing for you?" He ran through his mind the upcoming arts center events that Liz had told him were planned for the next four months. There was nothing that he knew of that would require a costume designer. Hmm. Plus, John knew that Liz had not made any final decisions about this year's summer theater productions. So, his mind was drawing a blank.

Liz's smile grew as she said, "Next month, Cookie, is going to come up and spend a weekend, so that she can help me design my wedding gown, and also the dresses that my sisters will be wearing. Time permitting, we will go over to Gloversville to the sewing shop to look at material, as well."

John listened, as Liz continued on regaling him with her excitement about their wedding plans and Cookie's assistance. He continued to eat his meal, nodding at the appropriate times, while Liz sparkled and bubbled with excitement, like a glass of fine champagne. John knew, without a doubt, that under Liz's direction, their wedding would be quite the production.

The parking lot of the J & J Bait and Tackle Shop was filled with an assortment of makes and models of pickup trucks and SUVs. Jim eased into a spot next to Stephen's pickup. He took his time getting out of his truck and collecting his ice fishing gear. Before heading out onto the ice to his shack for one of the last times this season, before dismantling it, Jim headed inside the bait shop for some minnows to use as bait. The first thing Jim noticed when he opened the door and stepped inside was the music that his friends had playing in the sound system. Classic Rock and Roll. Jim smiled. No country music. Well, that meant that Wes had gotten to work before Stephen, and he had selected the music that they would listen to during the day. Then, Jim heard their voices. Oh great! Jim rolled his eyes, pursed his lips and exhaled. At that moment, Wes happened to see Jim approaching them, from where they stood next to the ice fishing supplies, one aisle over from the main walkway through the shop.

"Morning, Jim." Wes greeted him, as he walked down to meet up with Jim at the end of the two parallel aisles. "You planning on fishing today?"

"Yeah, that's my plan. Looks like it's going to be another warm day."

"You're right about that. Ice is getting thinner. Looks like you and everyone else picked the right day to chance it one more time out there."

"Only one more day?" Jim knew that the weather had been rapidly improving temperature wise, but he had thought that there was a thick enough layer of ice on the lake to last for a few more weeks of fishing."

"One more, if you want to drive your truck out there. Even walking in some spots is getting dangerous" Stephen added to the conversation.

"Hmm." Jim removed his hat from his head and ran his fingers through his hair, then replaced his hat on his head. "I guess it's a good thing I planned on fishing today, and will certainly pay attention to my surroundings. Thin ice is nothing to play with."

Jim had just gotten in the house from ice fishing, with his meager catch of the day: four fish. That was it! Wes and Stephen had been right about the condition of the lake. The season was rapidly coming to an end with the ice thawing, making fishing more dangerous. But winter wasn't over just yet. The air still had a raw bite to it, and Jim was chilled through to his bones. He sighed, as he lowered the gutted, scaled fish into the sink, turned on the cold water and rinsed each one. Laying the fish on the clean counter top on the opposite side from where he had worked, Jim patted each fish dry, pulled a plate from the cupboard, and placed the fish on it. Then Jim cleaned the fish guts and scales off of the counter, before Melissa came in and saw what he had done. It was at that moment, that his phone rang. Pulling his phone from his hip pocket, Jim answered it before the 3rd ring.

"Hey, little sister! What's up?"

Amanda chuckled, "Well, hey to you too! My goodness, you certainly are in a good mood! Maybe I should be asking you the same question of what's up?" Amanda listened to Jim's response. "Okay. Fair enough. I was calling to let you and Melissa know that Kevin and I are coming north. So, this is your chance to run away before we get there!" Amanda laughed at Jim's response. "I'm glad to hear that we are always welcome to visit and stay with you." She sighed.

"That's not good! Who did what?" Jim knew that with the intensity of his sister's sigh that anything was possible. Jim didn't have to wait for Amanda to respond. She took off like a startled bird taking flight with a fury.

"That yellow bellied sap sucker of a man—well, he can go out on the lake, drill a hole in the ice and jump in! Maybe if he freezes some intricate parts of his body, he'll start using his brain. His real brain! The one that I know used to be quite intelligent!"

"Ah, Sis, dare I ask what Johnson did this time to ruffle up your anger?" Jim asked with his brows scrunched together in anticipation for what she was going to say. He even held his breath as if that would help. Then, he released a sigh, as Amanda with a slightly calmer tone enlightened Jim about her latest dilemma with Stephen. "Well, that's just great! Now you two have me smack dab in the middle of this."

"No, you're not!" Amanda huffed.

"Oh, yes I am, my dear little sister."

"Explain."

Jim lifted his phone from his ear and looked at it, as if, he could see his sister's expression. He shook his head. Then, he put his phone on speaker and calmly spoke into his phone, while silently praying for wisdom. Jim could tell that Amanda was doing deep breathing while listening to him. Good. "So, Sis, even though I love you, and am leaning towards your side, as a father I also am able to understand Johnson's position with regards to Summer. The bottom line, is, that he loves his daughter, as I love all four of my daughters. Somehow the two of you have to figure out how to get along and not have this tug of war between you both for Summer's love."

Silence.

"That's just it, Jim. There isn't a tug of war, as you put it. I dropped my end of the imaginary rope months ago. I gave in and conceded defeat." Jim felt a stab of pain in his heart, as he listened to the pain in his sister's voice. "Johnson won. He always has been a tough competitor regardless of what he is doing. He has to win, no matter the cost! So, I really am not too surprised that Summer has chosen him and Belinda." Amanda sighed. Jim silently waited for her to continue. "But, Jim, what I don't understand is, -" he heard her draw in a breath. "-That somewhere along the way, Johnson has forgotten that I wished him well, and I am moving on. Or at least trying to."

It was Jim's turn to sigh. He honestly didn't know who to feel sorrier for? "Do you want me to try to talk with Johnson for you?"

She made a ghastly sound. "Why bother? You and I both know that you can talk until you are blue in the face, and he won't listen. That's always been one of Stephen's problems in life. He thinks he knows everything and won't listen to reason." Jim did that quirky Callison thing with the corner of his mouth, as he listened to her grumble and then continue. "Jim, I'm truly sorry that even when I honestly try not to have it happen, you always manage to end up in the middle of Stephen's and my differences."

"I'm used to it." There was sadness in his voice.

Amanda sighed. Her voice was quiet as she said, "But, you shouldn't have to be. This division between Johnson and me is old, and I'm worn out from it. As much as I try not to allow it to happen, Johnson is a strain on my marriage. Can you explain for me why, if Johnson is so happy with Belinda, why does he seem to enjoy irritating me so much?"

"In all honesty, I'm worn out from your two as well. But having said that, you and Kevin continue to come up here as often as you like. We, as in you and me, we are not going to allow Stephen to sabotage your marriage to Kevin, so that you are once again single and unhappy along with Johnson." Jim heard Amanda sniffle. "Manda, I won't stand back and watch Stephen destroy you and Kevin's happiness." Jim found a touch of a smile as he listened to Amanda express her gratitude. Then, he drew the conversation to a place that he knew would make her smile. "I know Lizzie is excited about you and Kevin coming up here, and you unlocking Mom's old cedar chest. Actually, this may surprise you, but I too am interested in seeing some of

Mom's old treasures for you and me to share with each other and our family."

Their conversation continued with them focusing in on just that: their family and Liz's upcoming wedding. Jim had just said goodbye and returned his phone to his hip pocket, when Melissa entered the kitchen through the garage door. After the conversation Jim had just concluded with Amanda, his wife was the perfect distraction to help improve his mood.

John was still smiling from his most recent conversation with Liz as he slowed his pickup and pulled into Jim and Melissa's driveway. The elder Callison's home was one of Liz's requested stops for him to make before driving up to her family's cabin. There, in the solitude of the truck cab, he recalled how years ago, when he had served in the state police force with Jim, how Jim had told him about Melissa's *honey, to do list* that he was expected to complete before coming home that night.

Even though John wasn't married to Liz, she had called him with her honey do list for him to do before going up to the cabin. John allowed a chuckle to ease from himself, as he parked in their driveway. He remembered that first time, so long ago when he had come to their home. Both Elizabeth and her sister Caitlin were off in college. Samantha was a high school senior, while Jordan and James Junior, the younger children were active with junior and senior high school activities. Melissa had graciously welcomed John into their home. One of the things John had admired about Jim and Melissa was how they both spoke to each other, and of their children. The pictures that were on display and continue to be displayed in their home for everyone to see, captured special moments. John remembered seeing one picture in particular, that was taken of Liz and Cait after their high school softball team had won their game. Their unruly hair, sweat streaked faces, radiant smiles and dirty uniforms, as they stood with their arms around each other, and ball gloves dangling from their hands, perfectly captured their joyous moment. Way back then, when John only knew of Elizabeth from the family pictures, and Jim and Melissa's description of her personality and exploits, he knew that she would be a treasure for some lucky man to have in his life. Never in his wildest imagination had John thought that someday he might be that luck man.

He pressed the doorbell and waited for less than a minute before the door opened. Melissa smiled as she greeted John and invited him inside, then closed the door behind him. John unzipped his coat, but did not remove it, since he wasn't staying too long.

"Liz, called to ask me about borrowing this picture, and then she said that you'd be stopping by to pick it up for her." Melissa continued to smile, but this one was a tad different, especially when she glanced down at the framed picture she had picked up and held in her hands. John easily saw that it was a group picture from Jim and Melissa's wedding.

"Yes, she wants it for this weekend when her friend Cookie is here to help her design her gown, and her sister's gowns for the wedding."

A rumble of laughter drew John and Mel's attention to the living room doorway, as Jim stepped in from the kitchen where he had been working on the fresh fish dinner he was making for Melissa.

"Welcome to the honey do club!" Jim's eyes smiled with mischief, as he spoke and was finishing drying his hands on a cloth towel.

John chuckled. "All those years ago, I thought you were kidding!"

Jim laughed. Well, that is, until Melissa gave him a look that suggested he had best be careful, and lightly cuffed him on his upper arm.

"Hey, now, Mellie! I wasn't saying anything against you."

"Ah-huh!" She shook her head and rolled her eyes. "I know all about this list that we as women are supposed to create for you men to complete. Poor me! My wife has asked me to do *blah, blah, blah*! You all whine to each other. Woe is me!"

Both men wisely remained silent, and looked properly chagrined.

Jim tenderly gazed at Melissa, as he said, "Honestly, Mellie, we are never vindictive when we share stories about how blessed we all are to have loving wives."

John found himself enjoying watching his soon to be in laws. He understood that there was a lesson to be learned in watching them. After all, they had made it to thirty five years together as a married couple.

"Ah-huh!"

"Mellie, you know I love you and -" She raised her eyebrow, only to have Jim turn his gaze to John and ask, "Do you see that look?" He didn't wait for a response as he added, "You watch Elizabeth, because she gets that same look that her mother has right now."

Ten minutes later, John was laughing all over again as he drove up the mountain to Liz's family cabin. The picture that she had requested laid on the passenger seat, and two plastic bags on the passenger side floor board held items that Liz had requested he pick up from the store on the way up the mountain. "Jim sure called that one right! Yup! I'm being fully initiated into the honey do list club, and loving every minute of it, just like Jim." John said out loud. "Thank you, Great Spirit for bringing such an amazing, loving family into my life."

When John pulled into the driveway at the cabin, he saw Liz's aunt's SUV parked next to her car. He pulled his pickup behind Liz's car, shut off the motor, got out of his truck, walked around to the passenger side and opened the door. By the time he gathered the two bags in one of his hands and the picture cradled in his other hand and arm against his body, Liz was standing on the porch. Right away he noticed that Liz had omitted putting on a coat before coming outside to greet him.

"Oh, wonderful! You brought the picture for me. Thank you." Liz's excitement in her voice, and her joy was contagious. John couldn't help but smile, as he made his way to the porch steps. He seemed to do a lot of smiling these days, and he had Elizabeth to thank for it.

"You are very welcome." John said as he came up the steps, stopped in front of her, leaned in and brushed his lips over hers. Mm. She tasted of peppermint and chocolate. "Let me guess. Your aunt brought you peppermint candy?"

Liz giggled. "Yup, and I saved you some!"

"Well, thank you," John held open the screen door open, while Liz opened the old wooden door, for them to enter into the cabin.

Kevin came to his feet to welcome and shake John's hand, while Amanda remained on the couch with her right foot elevated. After John greeted Kevin, he bent down and kissed Amanda on her cheek. His manners deeply touched Amanda. She responded by quietly speaking in Iroquois. John laughed.

"Oh, great!" Liz exclaimed. "Here we go again, Uncle Kevin!" She threw her hands up in the air in surrender. "Will you two please speak in English?"

They both smiled at her. Then, Amanda softly responded, "I simply welcomed, John. That is all."

Liz gave her aunt a very familiar look of disbelief.

"Elizabeth Jeanne, don't even think about getting an attitude with me, or, John for that matter!" While her tone of voice was rather even, nonthreatening, her eyes spoke volumes. "If Gram was still with us, you had better believe that she would have had plenty more to say to both of you." Amanda sighed, as her gaze moved from Liz to the space around them in the interior of the cabin. "Mom, too, for that matter." She sniffled as family memories flooded her.

Liz and John quietly watched as Kevin, who had retaken his place next to Amanda on the couch, gently eased her into his arms. With closed eyes, Amanda leaned her head onto Kevin's chest. Then, she drew in a breath and sat up next to Kevin. Liz noticed her aunt's hand, as it rested on Kevin's leg. Her fingers seemed to be involuntarily moving, then they stilled, as Kevin laced his fingers with Amanda's and gently squeezed them. Liz heard her aunt release a breath, then draw in another intentional breath. She watched, and was amazed to see the depth of love between them, and how her uncle had quietly known exactly what was needed to help her aunt navigate through what appeared to be a mild panic attack.

Liz realized that she probably had over reacted to her aunt's greeting of John, when she should have been glad that John was welcomed and accepted by everyone in her family. She regretted that her words and actions had contributed to her aunt's latest panic attack. Fortunately, with Kevin's quiet intervention, Amanda was coming down from the visible signs of the attack. Liz, continued to quietly observe her aunt, and uncle. Then, she was struck by John's tenderness towards her aunt. He instinctively seemed to know how to assist Amanda, and helped to draw her into a calm place with his quiet humming. It was a familiar tune that Liz recalled hearing her father hum, as well as her great grandmother. His compassion caused moisture to form in Liz's eyes.

Liz had excused herself to the kitchen to prepare a plate of homemade cookies and hot chocolate for all of them. As she put the water on the stove to boil, she reflected on everything that had transpired in the past three hours. There had been ebbs and flows, like the tide in the Hudson River coming in and going out. The men in both her and her aunt's lives had cared, protected, loved, and in Liz's mind, they were the image of the ultimate male, very similar to her dad. Liz sighed with that realization.

"That was quite a sigh." The tender voice behind her caused Liz to smile as she turned. "I'm sorry, if I scared you with my mild panic attack."

"Oh, Aunt Amanda, you do not need to apologize." She took a step toward her aunt to close the space between them. Then, she allowed herself to be drawn into a hug as she spoke. "I actually was sighing as I was thinking about John and Uncle Kevin."

This statement had Amanda curious. A smile graced her lips, for she too had been thinking about how the men had responded to her panic.

"Did you come to any conclusions that you'd be willing to share with me?" Amanda quietly asked, as they drew apart from their hug. She then stepped over to the stove to turn off the flame under the kettle that that begun to boil with the water in it.

"I did." There was a mixture of joy and sadness in Liz's eyes as she spoke. "I was also considering the differences between them and Peter Jones."

"Oh?" Amanda's surprised expression would have been funny in a different context. Not, with where this discussion was going.

"Peter was a good person for me to begin to relax with while I was finding myself. He was a friend. I hope someday we can once again be friends."

"Don't use Johnson and me as a template for friendship after the love has soured." Amanda was not smiling. Sadness radiated from her as her gaze remained steadfast on Liz.

"I certainly have taken notes and crossed out that page from my play book." Liz instinctively knew that she needed to reassure her aunt that she would be okay.

"Phew!" Amanda released a breath through pursed lips.

"Peter is a good man. But he's not John. The man that I need as my partner in life. Just like Stephen is not Uncle Kevin, who you need as your partner in life. Plus, I observed special things when John was caring for you. What I saw, well, I think it was because of our shared heritage, and Peter would never have been able to care for you and me in the way that John did."

"And Kevin," Amanda added, as she drew Liz into her embrace. "We are very fortunate, truly blessed women to be loved and cherished by extraordinary men."

Kevin and John were standing together out of sight of the doorway, but able to hear the last part of the conversation taking place between aunt and niece. Their eyes met. No spoken words were necessary. They both turned and quietly returned to the living room. Kevin took the opportunity to gaze out the large window into the dark valley below. A sprinkling of lights in homes, cars on the local roads, reminded Kevin of fireflies that would someday return and light up the summer sky. John, busied himself by stoking the fire that gently burned in the fireplace. Pop. Sizzle. Bursts of flame as newly placed logs ignited.

Morning came with a mixture of smiles, enthusiasm, yawns, scowls and some things, well, it's best if they are not even mentioned. Amanda was up before Liz or Kevin, shuffling around the kitchen in her slip-on slippers, flannel nightgown and warm housecoat. The first order of the day, after her morning trip to the bathroom—coffee! With the coffee brewing in the old percolator, Amanda softly smiled as memories soared through her mind. She turned, quietly walked over and looked out the backdoor window. It was early enough in the day that the deer were out back in the old grasses peeking out of the diminishing snow, along with the wild turkeys looking for anything to eat to satisfy their hunger.

As God, the Great Spirit, cares for his creation, so too the Great one cares for me and my loved ones. Thank you. She breathed out, then turned, gasped in surprise to find Liz quietly standing in the opposite doorway leading from the kitchen into the living room of the cabin.

"Sorry, to startle you, Aunt Amanda." Liz's warm smile was filled with regret and a twist of mischief.

"M mm-humph!" Amanda's eyes spoke other words as she said, "And good morning to you too!" She sighed and shook her head. "You certainly are my brother's daughter! So, are you ready to have a quiet cup of coffee with me, before I head for the shower?"

By now Amanda was standing in front of the stove, turning off the flame under the percolator. She stepped over to the cabinet and removed two coffee mugs from the shelf and place them on the counter.

"Coffee will be great." Liz responded as she opened the refrigerator door and pulled out the container of half and half for them to add to their coffee.

It seemed as though everything happened at once for Elizabeth. John arrived, ready to take Kevin with him over to Jim and Melissa's where they would spend time together. While Liz and Amanda stood on the porch saying goodbye to the men in their respective lives, an unfamiliar vehicle slowly eased into the yard. The horn beeped. Liz squealed with delight. Then, she seemed to fly like a startled bird, all a flutter making her way down the front steps and straight through the snow to greet the new arrival.

"Cookie! Oh. My gosh! You made it!"

Liz was so engrossed in the moment, that she didn't hear the quiet laughter that was happening by her loved ones, from where they stood on the porch. She drew her weary friend into her arms, as she continued to welcome her. With initial excitement out of the way, they gathered Cookies overnight bag, as well as all of her art supplies that she would need to begin her wedding designs.

As the two dear friends, bubbling over with excitement, began to make their way towards the cabin, more vehicles appeared in the yard. Of course, this changed their plans. They remained by the vehicles and waited to greet the new arrivals. Melissa emerged from her vehicle, with a surprise for Liz. Jordan had managed to get home for the weekend. They both hugged Liz, met Cookie, waved at their family up on the porch, and remained by the side of her new SUV, patiently waiting to assist Sammie with the twins. By the time Caitlin and Callie arrived, Amanda, Kevin and John were also standing in the driveway. Then, as if on cue, the men excused themselves, they got into John's SUV and headed down the mountain together.

"Elizabeth, have you been up in the loft in the past few months?" Amanda asked, as she made her way into the living room from the bedroom. She had the cabin key ring with its assortment of Gram's old keys in one hand, and her special key to her mom's cedar chest in the other. All of the women assumed that Amanda had brought the keys with her from Baltimore, when in actuality, she had hidden them in the bedroom for safe keeping, and had just retrieved them.

Liz yawned unexpectedly. "Oh, excuse me! Um. Let's see, I know I was up there this past fall." She scrunched her lips, while being deep in thought. "I was up there looking for old Christmas ornaments from when you and dad were kids to use on the tree."

"Did you find any ornaments?" Amanda asked with skepticism in her expression and tone of voice. Liz responded. Then, her eyes twinkled with mischief, "What about bats?" Amanda asked, as a smile graced her lips, as she watched and waited for Liz to respond.

"Oh, Aunt Amanda!" She huffed, then exclaimed, "You had to go there! Didn't you?"

"Just checking." Amanda innocently shrugged. "Remember, Kevin and I, as well as Cookie, are staying here this evening. The last thing that any of us want is to be awakened by a bat flying over our heads!"

Amanda and Liz were the first to climb the narrow worn polished pine stairs, and stood on the narrow balcony overlooking the living room of the cabin. As they were making their way up the steps, they, along with Melissa's help from having also been there, regaled Cookie with the story of Liz's unfortunate encounter with the family of bats.

Cookie joined in with the laughter and added, "Goodness, Elizabeth, you went from theater rats to log cabin bats! At least you're coming up in the world!"

Cookie's humor was openly greeted and accepted by all of the Callison women. The sound of laughter seemed to shake the rafters of the cabin. Well, the twins, who had been sleeping until that moment in time, expressed their displeasure at the noise. Sammie sighed, and regretfully turned from following the others up into the loft. Her regret was short lived, as she looked into the teary eyes of her two little angels.

CHAPTER 24

Days turned into weeks. Spring finally decided it was time to make its grand appearance in the north country. No more nights dipping down to the single digits. Days filled with sunshine climbed steadily upward into the 50's and 60's. The Sacandaga River, as if on cue, flooded over in two different locations, as the high snow pack that had blanketed the southern Adirondack's was melting, bidding its farewell until next winter. Canada geese flying high in the sky heading further north, honked as they passed by, while summertime birds were slowly returning, singing songs that, as a general rule, lifted people's spirits.

Over the winter, John had been promoted from lieutenant to captain of the Northville Office. Of course, Liz and her family celebrated this accomplishment with John. Both John and Liz's professional lives were going quite nicely for both of them. They each had their own identities on a professional level, affirming each other's calling to their respective vocations. Their deepest joy came in knowing that in a few short months, they would be married.

Unfortunately, on this day John was not thinking about his relationship with Elizabeth. He was not feeling all warm and fuzzy. These days, with the change of seasons, people had spring fever. John was frustrated, because people were getting out on the trails, and unfortunately, they were doing what he considered to be downright stupid things. Not only were they putting their own lives at risk, often times his and other forest ranger's lives were in peril as well. Up on a trail near the Hamilton County line, in John's district, a pair of hikers had decided to go off of the designated trail. In doing so, they had managed to get into an area where the snow pack had begun to melt during the day, froze at night, then thawed again and was slippery. The hikers did not have cleats on their hiking boots, so they slipped and had fallen down the rock ledge onto the small shoreline by the creek swollen with snow melt. John had answered the call, using his ATV, rather than a snowmobile to get up into the side of the mountain for the rescue. Upon his arrival, and assessment of the situation, John saw that he had to call up to Hamilton County for the lieutenants to come help him. Besides that, he needed for the Great Sac Community ambulance to be standing by to transfer the injured woman to the local hospital, once they got her transported out of the woods.

Liz was busy working on finishing up the calendar of events for the spring at the arts center. The previous spring events that had been successful, were once again scheduled to happen. A soft smile graced her lips, as she thought about the senior class members who had been a part of the fall winter events. Kellie, one of her favorite budding artists would be participating with only one piece, since the majority of the young woman's artwork was now on display and being sold at Regina's gallery in New York City, Manhattan. The phone on her desk rang, interrupting Liz from her thoughts.

"Hello, Great Sac Community Arts Center, Elizabeth Callison speaking. How may I help you?" She said with a pleasant voice, then waited for her caller to respond.

"Let me thank you for your wisdom." A pause. "For knowing what we both needed and for your match making."

Liz gasped. Shocked by the sound of the familiar voice. Then, she couldn't help but smile and chuckle. Relief swept over her. "You're welcome, Peter. I'm glad to hear that things are working out for you and Regina. I know that she too is happy with you being in her life."

"Lizzie, please answer me honestly," He paused. Silence. "Did you know that Regina's brother Austin plays professional hockey, and that he is a team member of the New York Rangers?"

"Yes. I did." Liz sighed. "Austin is a great guy. Not my type, but great none the less! So, have you met his team mates?"

"I have, as a matter of fact, and I even was invited to join them on the ice in one of their practices." Liz quietly listened to Peter share his excitement over the experience with her. Then he added, "Elizabeth, I also see your hand in this."

"Peter, all I did was introduce you to Regina. You and her have done the rest. From what she's shared with me, and from what you are telling me today, I'm glad to know that things are working out for the two of you."

Their conversation continued on for a few minutes longer. The strain that had been present a few months before, was now removed. They had found a common place where they could work together as two professionals in the community, two old friends, whose parents continued to have close ties between them.

Liz was still feeling elated from the phone conversation that she had with Peter, as she returned to her work. She was busy preparing the large room of the art center for the 2nd annual high school senior class art show, when the main door opened. She paused from her work to see who was coming in. "Dad!" She exclaimed as the smile grew on her face.

"Hey, Lizzie J!" His own smile greeted her before he slightly turned to close the door behind him.

"So, what brings you here this-" She glanced at her watch. "-Afternoon! Oh great! Another day of forgetting about lunch."

"Lizzie." He gave her that familiar look, chastising her for not eating. Liz assured him that she had not suddenly developed an eating disorder, or that she was afraid of not being able to fit into her wedding gown. She simply had been busy and lost track of time! Then, as a feeling of relief washed over him, his expression softened. "How about I take you to lunch?"

"That would be nice. But, Dad, haven't you eaten lunch with Mom?" With those questions asked, Liz finally saw something in her father's eyes. "Is something wrong, Dad?"

"Yes and no!" He sighed while gazing at her. Then the corner of his mouth rose, as he watched her scrunch her brows at him as he continued. "Your mother is working today, and she had to respond to a rescue call up near the county line." Liz remained quiet. "There was an accident."

"Anyone seriously hurt?" Liz knew from the many accidents that her mom responded to as a part of the community rescue squad, that some accidents were horrific.

"Lizzie, your mom is up near the county line, helping John and the Hamilton County forest rangers with a rescue." Jim noticed the concern that flashed through Liz's eyes as he spoke. "John is okay. From what your mom told me, he's not too happy with the careless hikers."

"Oh boy! John's going to be in need of some TLC tonight after this tough day." Liz sighed.

Jim quietly observed his daughter. Oh yes! Jim knew that look, all too well. He wondered if Liz knew how transparent her love for John was when she spoke of him. Unlike with Liz's previous relationship with Peter, Jim saw maturity, peacefulness in his daughter.

"Well, I guess I'll have to cross that bridge when I get to it." Her smile shone bright. "In the meantime, how about we go get that lunch that you suggested. Are you treating me, or is lunch Dutch treat?" She added, with mischief in her expression.

Jim slowly drove his pickup truck down the gravel road leading into the arts colony. His eyes, like Liz's were taking in the scene before him. The winter had been hard and clean up at the colony was going to become a priority, if, Liz and John were serious about having their wedding reception at the colony mess hall. Liz took a sip of water, then returned the cap to the bottle. She sighed.

"I'm glad we had lunch before we came over here. I was up before the last storm checking on whether the melting snow was leaking into the basement storage room area of the amphitheater."

"How did you make out with the winter that we had?" Jim slowly progressed down the road, observing everything that needed to be done to prepare the area for a new theater season.

"Well, I'm really glad that I drove everyone nuts last fall when I demanded that items be placed in the plastic bins and properly marked. Now, even with the moisture that seeped into the rooms, our props are going to be fine for us to use. Thank goodness." Liz sighed. "As you can see, Dad, there are a lot of limbs that fell during the wind storm. We obviously have to get them cleaned up. I do hope that falling limbs have not damaged any of the artist in residence cabins, or the mess hall."

By now, Jim was parking in the drive alongside of the mess hall and was looking in the same direction as Elizabeth. A big old oak tree had succumbed to the strain of winter and toppled over with some of its branches on the porch roof. Liz gasped.

"Now, Lizzie," his voice was calm and quieting, "It might not be as bad as it seems." With his hand on the truck door Jim added, "Let's go see what we have to do to clean up this mess." He held out his hand, "Keys please, Miz Director." His eyes twinkled as he teased.

"I'll get the ladder and climb up onto the roof to see if there was any damage up there."

Liz watched her father, as he quietly ascended on the ladder to the roof of the mess hall, looking for any damage from the tree. None. Liz was relieved. Once again, her dad had been there during a crisis, only to calm her tattered nerves. After close inspection, it was decided that removal and cleaning up of the fallen tree would be fairly easy. A smile touched her heart, as she envisioned the teens responses when she recruited them to assist her with tree clean up. They were in for another taste of reality. The glitter and glitz of the theater's opening night didn't simply happen. It took a lot of work. Sometimes that work included manual labor of cleaning up the grounds. Well, it did in a low budget community organization, and with a thrifty Ebenezer director like Elizabeth Callison.

John stopped at the arts center to see Liz after his visit to the Mayfield senior center. It had surprised him to discover that a couple of older women, older as in his mother's age, had apparently found him attractive and openly flirted with him. Younger women that were somewhere around Liz's age, he knew how to gently let down. But those old cougars at the senior center, well, just thinking about it, John could still feel the heat of the woman's hand on his behind, when she had quietly spoken to him. Totally flustered, John was momentarily speechless. Then, he had recovered and was very glad that he could inform the women that he was engaged and off limits, especially to them. Unfortunately, that information did not appear to phase them in the least. They still flirted.

Liz sat in the chair behind her desk, wiping the tears from her eyes as she listened to John. His expression was priceless. "Oh, John, honey, I see that the women made you very uncomfortable. Do you want me to go over there and yell at them?" She was struggling to not laugh.

John was not smiling. He honestly looked mortified by what had happened. "Elizabeth, I can usually handle your teasing. But right now, you are not helping the situation any!"

Liz got up from her chair and walked around her desk to ease onto John's lap, and placed a gentle kiss on his lips. "I'm sorry. Maybe this will help to ease your mind." Her gaze held his eyes with such tenderness that John was lost in them. Then her lips returned to his as she quietly said, "Let me help you feel better."

As Liz's hands gently moved across his chest, John drew in a breath and broke their kiss. He pulled back, while easing Liz's hands into his, clutching them against his chest. His voice conveyed the depth of his feelings. "My love, we have to stop, before we go too far." His weight shifted under her in the chair and Liz immediately knew exactly what he was implying with his words.

She sighed, agreed, and rose from his lap. Liz returned to her chair behind her desk, knowing that John was right. With how they both were feeling, right now they needed for her desk to be a very visible barrier between them.

Liz was still feeling the unfulfilled ache from John's visit, as she was driving over to Northville to work with Caitlin on finalizing the guest list, then ordering the invitations. Much to her surprise, she had an incoming call. She smiled and answered. "Hello, Aunt Amanda."

"Hello, Elizabeth. How's life in the north country?"

"Which part of life are you inquiring about?" There was a tease in Liz's voice.

"Well, of course I want to hear about your wedding plans. But first, tell me about the snow! Did you all get dumped on with more snow, or was it rain?"

Liz slowed for a school bus that was turning off of Route 30 and onto a back road. Then, she increased her speed once again, as she responded. "Rain isn't the word for what we got! I swear, even the ducks and geese were saying 'enough already!' before it was over. The river, creeks and lake are really high!"

"That sound about normal for the lower Adirondack's and Great Sacandaga Lake area during this time of year. Any problems with water up by the cabin?"

"No, but I did notice that the water from the creek had risen and pushed from the banks onto the field."

Amanda sighed. "Yeah, it does that when it's a significantly wet spring. Be careful."

Liz chuckled. "Gee! You sound like Dad!"

"Guilty as charged!" Amanda joined in with the laughter. "Okay, so tell me about your wedding preparations."

"Well, right now, I'm on my way over to Caitlin's, so that we can work on the invitation list, finalizing who's on and who's off." She snorted at her aunt's response. "Well, yes, part of it is because of the cost, and the other part is who we truly want to share our special day with us."

"That is understandable. So, it looks like I chose the right moment to call you and discuss my concern with you."

Liz drew in a breath. "This sounds ominous."

"It might be." Amanda's voice was quieter than normal. Liz listened carefully as she shared her thoughts. "Liz, I've been thinking about our family. Our ups and downs. Everything that makes us family."

"Aunt Amanda-" Liz's tone revealed her discomfort.

"Liz, please hear me out. My thoughts will probably surprise you, because they involve your cousin, my daughter." Liz began to respond, only to grow quiet and listen. "I appreciate your loyalty in how you stuck up for me last year at the cemetery." She softly chuckled at Liz's response. "Well, yes, we certainly are Callison's through and through." Amanda sighed. "Look, Liz, what I'm trying to say is, years from now, I don't want for you to have regrets for not inviting Summer to your wedding, all because she and I are at odds with each other. So please, for your and Summer's sake, please consider inviting her to your wedding."

It was Liz's turn to sigh. And she was surprised to find herself in front of Caitlin's house. "Aunt Amanda, I've reached my destination, and I will consider your request. Before I hang up, may I ask you a question?"

"Sure." Amanda quietly responded.

"Do Mom and Dad know about your request?"

"No, Liz, only Kevin knows how I feel, and he agrees with me."

Liz found herself half smiling. "For some reason I'm not surprised to hear that Uncle Kevin agrees. My love to you both."

"Our love to you as well. Have fun with Cait."

Caitlin was standing in her doorway on the closed in front porch, watching Liz as she approached her home. Liz's expression sent up the warning signs in Cait. Something was going on with her sister, and time would only tell.

It was two months before the wedding and the beginning of the community summer arts programs, including the summer theater season. Liz was ecstatic! All of her theater friends who had participated in the opening summer season were returning. Plus, Andre and Natasha had recruited a few more people, who were donating their time and considering the summer as a long overdue vacation out of the city. Tears unexpectedly tumbled down her cheeks. That seemed to be a frequent occurrence these days. She sniffled, as memories of the senior class's recent surprise took center stage in her mind. Those wonderful teens had made her a gift of appreciation for all that she had done for them, and it now graced her small office. Liz wiped her eyes of their moisture, then blew her nose. She knew that her emotions were only partly over the top because of her professional life.

The previous weekend Liz and John had taken time from their hectic lives, and had gone north to Saranac Lake to visit John's family. His parents once again welcomed her into their home, their lives. Liz couldn't help but wonder, if, she was in some small way helping to fill the void in John's parent's lives from the daughters they lost in the deadly fire so long ago. Then, there were John's extended family members, his aunts and uncles and his cousins. Each of them in their own ways had also made her feel welcome, as if she had always been a part of their family. A part of her wished that she could invite John's cousin Layla to stand with her on their wedding day. But Liz already had all of her sisters standing with her. Their dresses were being created by Cookie, and well, that was just what she wanted. Liz stretched, rotated her shoulders as she glanced at her watch. The weekend was rapidly descending upon her. She would be lucky to find one quiet moment to herself before Monday morning, and her return to work. The sound of the outer door of the arts center opening drew Liz from her desk to see who had entered. There were no familiar voices. No voices at all. Liz felt the hairs on the back of her arms standing. Then Liz caught sight of who had entered the center, and she squealed with delight.

"Jor, you're here already! What time did you leave the city?" She beamed with happiness, as she exclaimed. Both sisters laughed and talked over each other, as they often had in years past. Then her gaze shifted. Her smile grew—if that was even possible—as she moved from hugging her sister to her aunt and uncle. "Aunt Amanda, Uncle Kevin, I knew Jor was coming home. But you two—I can't believe it! This weekend just keeps getting better and better!" The volume of her voice had increased, indicating that she did not require amplification to be heard. Of course, her aunt pointed out that fact to all of them!

Kevin quietly observed the gaiety of the Callison women, his wife being the ringleader. Amanda had managed to get her jacket off, carelessly thrown it on the table, then drawn both of her nieces into her embrace. A gentle smile tugged at his lips as he watched their interactions, and recalled how not so very long ago, Elizabeth and Jordan had been estranged from one another. Elizabeth had spent time with him and Amanda during her darkest days. Then, a while later Jordan had managed to appear at their home in Baltimore. Amanda had lovingly cared for both of her nieces when they had turned to her for help, guidance. A high-pitched noise like laughter, and then more hugs. Family. At that moment, Kevin could not imagine his life without any of these women in it.

Melissa had her cell phone propped up in the window sill over the kitchen sink, on speaker to allow her hands to freely work, as she conversed with Caitlin while working on preparing dinner for the houseful of people whom she expected to descend upon her within the next three hours. Laughter, joy and perhaps a touch of sadness filled her heart, as she listened to Caitlin give a detailed account for the final preparations for the surprise bridal shower she had planned for her sister. In one sense Mel was happy that Elizabeth had worked through all of the bumps, bruises and wounds that had led her home. Now her child was truly happy, with a happiness that runs deep, not superficial to be swept away with the next strong wind of adversity. She knew in her heart that John Runner was a good man. Perhaps that was why Melissa felt that twinge of sadness. Her job as Mom was changing yet again in one of her children's lives. Elizabeth was reaching a pivotal time in her life.

"So, Mom, tomorrow morning we'll have Jor call Lizzie to tell her that we can't begin our work until 11:00 am, because Dad is in our way doing a home repair. Here's where I need your help."

Mel was smiling, while her hands moved about from one place to another. The large pot of water was now boiling on the back burner of the stove, and lasagna noodles were being added to cook. A large iron skillet was on the other back burner with last fall's venison burger gently browning. She felt the tears slipping down her cheeks, as she chopped up the onion to be added to the venison. Sometimes cooking was a great way to hide what a person was truly feeling. Joy. Sadness.

"Before you get to my help—have you mentioned any of this plan to your father?"

"Well, no, Mom! This is where you come into the scheme." Caitlin giggled. Melissa had heard that particular gleeful laughter from her eldest daughter from the time she was a toddler. Another memory. Time to cut more onion to hide her tears from herself.

"I see! I suppose it shouldn't be too hard to think of something that is believable. But Caitlin you need to remember, I'm not an actress. Your sister might see right through anything that we come up with."

"Oh, Mom, you don't give yourself enough credit. Where do you think we all learned our sneakiness from?"

Mel couldn't help but smile as she said, "And for all these years I thought you all learned your deviousness from your father! Imagine that!"

Caitlin laughed, responded and drew more laughter, as well as a few more tears from Melissa. The conversation ended, with both women needing to attend to work in their individual homes, while knowing that they would be together in a couple of hours for a family dinner. Two pans of lasagna were prepared and placed in the hot oven to cook. Now Melissa had time to sit down for a few minutes, sip a cup of tea, then move on to the next task before everyone arrived. Much to Melissa's dismay, her few minutes of quietness didn't last for too long. Her cell phone rang. Then, just as the conversation was ending, Jim walked back into the kitchen. Her smile increased as he drew closer to her.

Jim paused in mid-step. "Mellie," there was hesitation in his voice. "I know that look of yours. What are you planning? And why do I have a feeling that I'm not going to like it?"

By now the smile had reached Melissa's eyes. "Oh, Callison, if I was a betting woman, I'd say that once you hear the plan, you'll love it."

Jim raised a brow as he responded. "It smells good in here. Any coffee?"

Cookie, had also arrived for the weekend and was welcomed into Jim and Melissa's home like one of the family. She laughed and conversed with everyone as they all dined together. Since Melissa had prepared the dinner, and the women had work to do, well, it was obvious to all of the Callison women what the men would be doing. Sure enough! Under the watchful eyes of Melissa and Amanda, Jim, Kevin and all of the younger men, were on clean up detail. Just before the two women disappeared from the kitchen, they advised them all to do a good job that would meet their satisfaction.

Jim immediately stepped over to Melissa and whispered in her ear. Mel felt the color rising in her cheeks as she laughed.

"Callison, you had better behave." Mel's soft warning was filled with love and smiles.

"Later, my love." Jim's response was filled with promise. Of course, the men had been listening and seized the opportunity to tease him. Perhaps what surprised Melissa most was that Kevin was the main instigator. Amanda was no help. She simply shook her head and disappeared with Callie Anne to find the younger women who were already upstairs.

Caitlin had once again eased into the role of the eldest sister, and the matron of honor as she helped Jordan and Sammie, get into their gowns. A warm, sentimental feeling swept over her as she helped her sisters. It seemed right that Liz had chosen their old bedroom for where Cookie was to do her alterations on their gowns for the wedding. Oohs and ah flowed from everyone's lips as Jordan and Samantha stepped into the light green mid-calf dresses. Cookie inspected her work as it hung on each of Liz's sisters.

Callie Anne was at a tender age of being a young girl dreaming of growing up and someday marrying like her mom and her aunts. She sat perched on the dresser out of the way, taking it all in. "They sure do look beautiful," she whispered to her grandmother, who had just stepped through the door with one of Samantha's babies against her shoulder.

"Oh wow!" Amanda quietly breathed out, as she caught her first glimpse of Jordan and Samantha. The little one she held against her shoulder began to stir. Without even a thought, Amanda gently patted her great nieces back, "Your Mommy looks beautiful, Mary. I'll try to be quiet and not waken you again." She softly kissed Mary's head and drew in the pleasant smell of the baby. It was like heaven. Then, an unexpected tear formed in Amanda's eye.

John had just finished his call with Elizabeth, when he heard the sound of a vehicle in his driveway. He glanced out of the front window of his cabin, and saw Jim and Kevin emerging from Jim's pickup. Nick and Chris had also been invited to hang out with them, and had mentioned that they might possibly stop over for a while as well. By the time the two older men had made their way onto the porch, John was opening the door. He greeted them with words and a smile while noticing their attire, laid back casual, Jim in his standard late winter attire of thermal shirt under a flannel shirt, jeans and his work boots, that were quickly removed after hanging his coat on the hook by the door. Kevin shed his jacket and revealed that he had chosen to wear a dark green pullover sweater with his jeans and hiking boots. There was a relaxed feeling, rapport between the three men. Laughter soon followed, as Jim enlightened John with what was happening in his home when they had left and what he imagined was happening at that moment.

"Seriously, the noise of all of the women of my family, including my sister, along with their friends—son you have no idea of what you are missing!" Jim shook his head and sighed.

"Jim, remember I spent Christmas with your family at your home."

"Trust me, John. All of our family together was nothing compared to what the noise volume that is in my home right now!"

Kevin agreed with Jim and added, "As a concerned great uncle, I jokingly pulled out and used my invisible physician's card by suggesting to Samantha that she allow us to bring her twins with us, so that the noise of all the women talking and laughing at the shower wouldn't hurt their ears."

Jim chuckled, then rumbled into a roar of laughter, as he added, "For a moment, when Sammie looked at Kevin, -" Jim was shaking his head, as the memory of his daughter's murderous expression played out in his mind. "Well, John, you've been around Liz's sisters to know that Samantha along with Caitlin are usually my two most rational daughters." The younger man nodded, and his brows raised as he listened intently to Jim. "Not today! This morning, I honestly thought my daughter was seriously contemplating committing a homicide."

The three men chuckled and commented, then John said, "From what Liz told me about the physical fight she had with Jordan in your home—the one when you handcuffed her—I have to agree with you that Cait and Sammie probably are the most rational out of your daughters. But, with what I know of how wild female animals protect their young, I don't imagine Samantha was behaving much differently from them in her situation."

Jim had that smile he was known for, when something struck him funny, as he said, "She was acting like a mean old mama bear!

Fortunately, we're both still alive to tell about it, and the babies—well—" Jim got that doting grandfather look that he was now known for having, when speaking about any of his grandchildren and then said, "- I'm sure that by now the children are being doted over by their grandmother, great aunt, and any other woman who is fortunate to get their hands on either child, or both."

As much as the three men loved the women in their lives, sometimes, as with today, it was nice to have time away from them to kick back and simply be a man. That was just what they did, as they each settled in for a quiet day of eating bowls of chili made with venison burger, assorted junk food, and cold beer, while watching various sporting events on ESPN and other sports channels on John's large flat screen television. By midafternoon all three men's cell phones rang simultaneously. They each laughed and commented. Their respective women were summoning them.

The Callison family home was abuzz with noise, as guests began to leave from the bridal shower. Amanda had disappeared out onto the back porch for privacy when she spoke with Kevin. After all, Becky Jones was there—which was no problem for Amanda—the problem was that fact that she had brought Belinda with her. The woman made the small hairs all over Amanda's body stand in high alert. Especially when she gloated like a fat cat that had just scored the most delectable rat, when Liz opened the gift that Belinda had brought, and the card on the gift said that it was from Belinda and Summer. Summer! Amanda's estranged daughter had the gall to go in on a gift for Elizabeth with Belinda. The gift wouldn't be a problem, if it hadn't been for the motives behind how it was given. Amanda had developed a rather sour taste in her mouth towards the woman, and for her family's sake, she was holding her tongue from saying what she felt. She was coming through the kitchen into the hall in time to hear Elizabeth expressing her concerns to Melissa.

"Mom, I swear if Dad and Uncle Kevin got John drunk, they will not be too happy when I finish sharing my thoughts with them." Elizabeth huffed. Her brows were drawing close together as she spoke.

All of the Callison women wisely bit their lower lips to keep from laughing. Of course, the few stragglers who hadn't left the shower laughed, only to be glowered at by Elizabeth. Amanda and Melissa made eye contact. The laughter and words that they hid from their lips, eased into and filled their eyes. Of course, Liz happened to glance at them at that particular moment and saw their expressions.

"Ugh!" She huffed. "It's not funny, Mom, Aunt Amanda! You two are supposed to be on my side. Aren't you?"

Melissa cleared her throat, then sighed, as she drew Liz into her embrace. She understood, as only a mother can, all of the emotions that were raging through Elizabeth like water tumbling over one of the waterfalls up in the mountains. "My dear child, you need to relax. Stop and think about what you are saying. You, know right along with the rest of us that no one is drunk."

"That's right, Liz. Kevin told me that today he drank two beers. That is nothing to be concerned about, especially since the alcohol was consumed while they all were eating John's chili. Apparently, your dad, Kevin, Chris and Nick, all thought it was a tad hot! After that, Kevin told me that he and your dad turned to water to continue to attempt to extinguish the fire within their bodies. Kevin said that he was scorched from his mouth to his stomach."

Liz's eyes had widened. "Oh, Aunt Amanda, I've had John's chili—oh my! I'm so sorry for Uncle Kevin. Dad and the guys." Liz drew quiet. She sighed, then gazed at her aunt with concern in her eyes. "But still, they all need to be careful with how much they drink and then drive."

Melissa tenderly gazed at her child as she once again drew her close to her. "Life changes for us when we have someone special to love. Doesn't it, Liz?"

"It sure does!" Both Caitlin and Samantha contributed, as they rallied around their sister, gently placing their hand on her shoulders.

The Callison women had been so engrossed in rallying around Liz in her distress, that the had momentarily forgotten about the women who remained in Melissa and Jim's living room. That is until they heard a raspy familiar voice.

"You are absolutely correct, Melissa." Becky paused. She drew in a short breath. Her chest was tightening, forcing her to use her rescue inhaler. Then she gingerly added, while not distressing her lungs any further, "I can't imagine what my life would be like without having Wesley in it."

Both Amanda and Melissa agreed with Becky, and affirmed Wes's good qualities. He was a man of faith, who quietly went about life, not tooting his own horn. He simply loved his family and friends, while seeking to do good for others, regardless of who they were, or their life circumstance.

Belinda had also been quietly listening and watching the women's interactions. Of course, she was not going to be outdone by any of them. She tilted her chin up as if that was going to make her any taller, while she said with a smug attitude, "Yes I agree, Becky. You and I are the fortunate ones. I simply don't know what I'd ever do without Stephen." Then, the woman simply couldn't leave well enough alone. Oh no! Then, she had the audacity to look down her nose at Amanda and add, "Well, Amanda, with the obnoxious display of fake lovey dove affection between you and your family," she slightly raised her nostril, as if to punctuate her point, "It's a good thing that I'm now a significant motherly figure in Summer's life."

There was a simultaneous gasp from the onlookers. Not from Amanda. Oh no! Fire, exploded in her charcoal black eyes, turning them to molten hot volcano red. Not good! Those who knew Amanda— really knew Amanda—had sense enough to keep quiet. They watched with baited breath. The telltale signs were there.

Amanda clenched her hands at her side, while her eyebrows drew threateningly close. It was an ominous sight. Then, Amanda made an equally dangerous sounding noise in her throat, as she took a step towards Belinda. Amanda appeared oblivious to everyone else in the room. Like a hawk ready to swoop on its kill Amanda stepped closer. Her eyes beckoned the other woman to speak. For once Belinda had sense enough to keep her mouth shut!

"Motherly figure to Stephen's and my daughter! We'll get back to my daughter and your influence over her in a minute."

Belinda began to speak, only to be warned by Becky to close her mouth. Becky nodded to Amanda to continue. Her eyes said some other reassuring things to her friends as well. Amanda understood and nodded at Becky.

"Let's begin with your assumption about the authenticity of the love you've seen shared between my family members and me. I know darn well that you will be running back to tell Johnson everything that you observed here today, and don't try to deny it. Then, the two of you will get on the phone and report to Summer what you saw, or think you saw." Her fiery eyes remained fixed on Belinda, who wisely chose to keep her mouth shut. "You do not know me as a person. The only impression you have of me is through what Johnson and Summer have told you about me. You don't know what my brother and I have gone through to regain the relationship that we now have between us. You do not know how deeply I love and care for my family. I am blessed beyond measure for the loving relationship I have with my nieces and my nephew. They all want me to be a part of their lives, as well as their offspring's lives. Yet, you appear to feel as, if, you have a right to judge me by what you see on the surface between us. Did it ever cross your mind that my nieces genuinely appreciate me, and that they enjoy having me in their lives? Did it ever cross your mind that they may lovingly be attempting to partially fill in a hole that is now in my life?"

Amanda held up her hand to silence Belinda, as she began to respond. She continued. "A hole that has been dug by you and Stephen. Actually, the hole was started by Johnson saying things about him and me —our past—that are none, and I repeat, none of your business. Oh, I understand perfectly well that you love the man. I once did too! You conveniently forget, or, perhaps you were never told that Stephen and I have known each other since he was nine years old and I was seven years old, when his family moved here and his father became our community pastor. Trust me, I can tell you stories about Stephen Johnson that would make you gasp in horror, and I could tell you stories about his love making that— well, that was then." Amanda wet her lips. She sighed. "Back to my daughter and the hole you and Johnson have dug. You see, as motherly as you may try to be for Summer, the simple fact is I gave birth to Summer. I raised her on my own, without Johnson or any other man to help me. She will always be my daughter. However, this hole, this chasm that has been made in our relationship will only be refilled, if—and that is a might big word right now—if, Summer chooses to realize how deeply her actions have affected not only me but her as well." Amanda flexed her clenched fists. Becky and Melissa drew in breaths filled with anticipation. "Until then, I will remain surrounded by my loving family. Now Belinda, I have one final word to say to you. I suggest that you listen to every word I say." Once again, Belinda wisely chose to remain quiet, as Amanda drew in a calming breath, began to relax her clenched fists, and stated, "If, I ever catch wind that you have said one ill word against my brother, James Callison, or any member of his family," the intensity of her piercing eyes put everyone on high alert once again. "Belinda, take heed. I will be your worst nightmare come true. That is not a threat. That is my solemn promise. I take care of my family!"

Belinda finally began to find her voice, weak as it was. But that was short lived, as Melissa silenced her. "Belinda, as Amanda has informed you, the Johnson family and our family became friends when Jim and Amanda met Stephen, Becky, and Phil many years ago. Jim and Stephen have been best friends for a very long time. Today you have been a guest in my husband's and my home primarily because you are Stephen's current girlfriend. As Johnson's girlfriend you have also been invited to be a guest at my daughter's wedding. That invitation still stands. However, as of today, due to your rude behavior extended towards my family, primarily my sister in law, you are no longer welcome in my home. It is time for you to leave." With that said, Melissa turned physically to face Becky. She sighed. "Becky, I'm sorry that Johnson's girlfriend is the cause for you having to leave so soon today. Please be assured that you and Wesley are always welcome in our home."

While the Callison family was unwinding from the earlier festivities of the day, relaxing, enjoying being family, Becky Johnson Jones was on a roll. As Becky drove Belinda and her back to her house for Belinda to get her car, Becky chewed her out. Upon reaching the house, Becky remained in her car. She had someplace to go, and she warned Belinda to go home and for once keep her mouth shut.

Becky was still fuming as she pulled her car into the parking lot of the bait shop. She hoped that Belinda had taken her warning, and not called her brother. The force of her opening the door, the jingle of the bells indicated her mood before she opened her mouth.

"Hello, sweetheart," Wesley cautiously greeted his wife from where he stood by Stephen on the opposite side of the room. He instinctively knew that something had happened to sour Becky's earlier good mood, as she had looked forwards to spending the day at Melissa's with the Callison women. "This is a pleasant surprise," Wes added, as he made his way down the aisle to greet her.

Becky stepped into his embrace, gave Wes a light kiss, void of any passion, quietly spoke to him, then marched towards her brother.

Johnson had been texting on his phone. He looked up as he heard Becky's purposeful steps approaching him. His gaze passed over her. He instinctively drew in a breath. His sister had a hauntingly familiar look in her eyes.

"Hey, Beck, I had thought Belinda would be with you. In her text she says that she is not feeling well. Did she tell you that she had a headache?"

"Headache? The woman is claiming a headache after what she did?" Becky was standing so close to her brother that he could almost feel her heart beating. Stephen took a step back, only to have Becky match it and step forward. Wesley, was right behind Becky to intervene, if necessary, but neither one noticed him.

"I gather something happened that Belinda is not telling me," Stephen was on high alert as he spoke. "And I gather you're here to fill me in on what occurred while you both were at the shower."

Becky was scowling with the fierceness of a hungry bear just waking up from its long winter's sleep. "Oh, I'm going to fill you in alright! And brother, you are not going to like it. But, too bad! You need to hear what I have to say."

"Alright, Then, go ahead and speak your mind. But I warn you I will probably have something to say in return that you will not like to hear as well."

"Only a stupid man will respond to what I have to say. Wes, you need to take heed to a few things that I'm going to say as well." And with that said, Becky began to lace into her brother. "As of this moment in time, my dear eldest brother you and your girlfriend are not welcome to set foot in my home under any, and I mean any circumstances. Once again, you have wounded one of my oldest, most cherished friends. Back in 1979 you, my jerk of a big brother and Jim devastated Amanda, abandoning her when she needed you both at the most critical time in her life. I thought all these years later that you had finally wised up. But, oh no! Not my brother. Now you have your long-lost daughter Summer to fill the place that Jim once held as your ally against Amanda." Neither man spoke. Wise decision. Becky had a full head of steam like an old locomotive chugging up a hill. She was puffing for all she was worth. "Amanda deserves better from the people who are supposed to love her. Stephen Johnson, I am ashamed to acknowledge you as my brother."

"Becky, -" Wes interjected only to be silenced.

Becky's index finger was now 1/8 of an inch from Stephen's chest. "You were brought up in the same family that Phil and I were. You sat in church with us listening to Dad preach the word, and you were taught the same values by Mom and Dad. As an adult you claim to be a Christian. *Tsk, tsk, tsk!* What a joke you are! Christian my fanny! I don't see love in your actions towards Amanda or Summer for that matter. Since Belinda has entered your life you've been flirting with darkness, my dear brother. I'll be the first to say that I've fallen short of God's glory by the sins I've committed. But you are quick to judge others, acting like you are so righteous, so free from sin. Get a grip! Change your life before it's too late!" Becky didn't wait for Stephen to respond. Really, at that moment, he was so shocked by his sister's words that he could not find his voice. She turned to Wesley to speak and as she did, she plummeted into a full-blown asthma attack.

The Callison family drama was short lived for the day, as Jim and Melissa's home continued to seem to burst at the seams with people. Callie Anne was thrilled to be given the job of babysitting the twins and her younger brother. Of course, they were only in the family room, away from the noise of the adults that filled the living room along with the mounds of opened and well inspected shower gifts.

Jim sat back in his favorite chair as the big chief of the family, he noticed the quiet, subtle interaction between Amanda and Kevin. As Jim watched them, the hairs on the back of his neck began to stand at attention. He raised a speculative brow and cleared his throat, drawing everyone's attention to him.

"Sis, Kevin, is there something going on that we should know about?" Jim knew that with his sister, and what he had heard about happening during the shower, anything was possible.

Amanda's eyes danced with excitement as she spoke. "Actually, Jim, your question is a terrific transition into a subject that Kevin and I would like to bring up with everyone."

"Oh no!" Jim moaned as his gaze remained focused on Amanda and Kevin. Even Kevin looked suspicious. Jim was worried, especially when Kevin spoke before Amanda.

"Elizabeth, John how are the honeymoon plans coming along?" Kevin innocently asked.

Jim felt that old cop instinct kick in. That question was packed with unspoken information.

The two simultaneously sighed.

"Well, not as we had hoped or had planned." Liz responded. John picked up their response to Kevin's question, providing details about the demise of their honeymoon location, as what they resigned themselves to as an alternative. Disappointment filled their faces, as Liz said, "But maybe it's for the best, since we are marrying right before my busy summer theater season begins."

"And fire season and summer hiker season will be under way for me." John added.

"Hmm." Amanda twisted her lips as she did when she was deep in thought.

"Oh no!" Jim sighed.

Amanda's gaze shifted to Jim. "What do you mean, oh no?" She innocently asked.

"That—hmm— of yours was loaded." His gaze held his sister's. "Alright, Sis, you and Kevin had best spill whatever it is that you two are scheming."

"Rob us of the fun, why don't you?" Amanda feigned annoyance.

Everyone joined in with teasing and laughing.

"Actually, Elizabeth, John," Kevin withdrew an envelope from his hip pocket, and handed it to them as he spoke. "Amanda and I were aware of your situation. So, we talked with my brother's and came up with a solution."

Everyone watched and waited for Liz and John to open the card. They simultaneously gasped. Shock. Disbelief. They looked at each other. Tears were finding their way to Liz's eye lids and freely tumbling down her cheeks. It was John who recovered first.

"Amanda, Kevin, this is a very generous wedding present. Thank you from the bottom of our hearts." His grin filled his entire face. "Wow! A real honeymoon! Wow!" With that John was on his feet and moving over to shake Kevin's hand and kiss Amanda, who was wiping away her own tears.

Liz had managed to reign in her tears, and had also found her way over to her aunt and uncle, who were now standing and hugging her, then once again embracing John.

"Excuse me!" Melissa's voice drew their attention to her, as she watched them from where she sat in her chair next to Jim. "Do you mind letting us in on this wedding secret?"

"Oh Mom, Dad, everyone," Liz's body vibrated with excitement as she exclaimed, "We're going to the Bahamas!"

By now everyone was caught up in the excitement of the moment. They listened, as Kevin and Amanda explained how the honeymoon would work. Jim was truly amazed at his sister and brother in law's kindness: a week stay at the Wentzel family home on the Grand Island of the Bahamas. The housekeeper would prepare breakfast for them, then the rest of the day they were on their own. The family car would also be available for them to use during their stay on the island. They had thought of a very generous gift. Perhaps what struck Jim the most was when Kevin shared his brother's response to Liz and John's honeymoon dilemma. He had forgotten that Liz had met Kevin's family during one of her visits to Baltimore, when her life was in chaos. How fortunate for their family! How bless Elizabeth was that Kevin's siblings had claimed her as an adopted niece.

It wasn't long after the last wedding gift of the honeymoon, and the excitement that followed that the women made their way upstairs for Liz and Caitlin's fitting of their gowns. Once again Melissa and Amanda, as well as Sammie and Jordan joined them. The younger men disappeared into the family room, to see if they could convince Callie and Nick to let them watch a baseball game. Jim and Kevin were content to dote over the twins.

"Oh, Cait, that dark green color and the design of the dress is perfect for you!" Liz said approvingly. "Cookie, you are the best! Wow!"

Then, it was time for Elizabeth to step into the dress that Cookie had created specifically for her. Tears filled every one of the Callison women's eyes, as Cookie carefully buttoned the back of Liz's gown. Amanda sniffled as she noticed every detail of the dress, finding pieces of her mother's wedding gown sewn into the dress. Then Cookie surprised them all, as she removed the head piece from a box that she had place on the dresser. That did it! Amanda gave in and broke down and cried as she saw what Cookie had done to repair her mother's veil. Elizabeth was going to be stunning on her wedding day!

Jim wisely chose to allow the dust to settle from the explosive weekend that they had all endured. Amanda had profusely apologized to both Jim and Melissa for her behavior after the shower before she and Kevin left to return home. Both of them had assured her that she had been within her right to express her feelings towards Belinda. Even Melissa, who usually didn't say too much to anyone, or about anyone had her issues with his best friend's girlfriend. Belinda. Jim sighed, as he mulled the name, the woman over in his mind. He didn't like the fact that one person was causing such tension within his family. Something kept tugging at the back of Jim's mind. It was reminiscent of his days of working as a state police officer out on patrol, then as a BCI officer. He had a feeling that both Amanda and Melissa were keeping something, one little significant piece of information from him. But what? That was the question. Well, perhaps Belinda had shared the whole story with Johnson. Jim hoped so, as he slowed his pickup truck, turned on the directional, then eased into the drive of the bait and tackle shop.

The warm spring weather seemed to be drawing people out of the woodwork, even on a weekday. The yard was littered with pickups and SUV's of spring fishermen. Jim, sighed, and rotated his shoulders as he opened the driver's side door and eased from behind the steering wheel. It was time to have a conversation that he wasn't entirely sure that he wanted to, or, should be having.

"Hey, Jim, good to see you!" Wesley called out as he entered the shop and closed the door behind him.

"Wes, it's good to see you too! How's Becky doing since her asthma attack that she had at the shower?" Jim saw the change in Wesley's eyes. "Is she alright?"

Wesley nodded as he sighed. "Well, Jim, after her mild attack at your house, she came over here, lit into Stephen, then had a major attack. Fortunately, that was the only one. But if this is any indication, it's going to be a long summer of breathing issues. So, thanks for asking, for caring."

"You're welcome, Wes. Why shouldn't I care? Becky and you are good friends, and you both mean the world to Mellie and me." Jim had removed his cap from his head and placed it on the counter. He pushed up the sleeve of his thermal shirt that peaked out from under the turned-up sleeves of his flannel shirt that he wore over his insulated top.

Wes was about to respond when the door leading down to the pavilion opened and Johnson emerged. "Hey, Jim!" His smile appeared genuine. "I thought I heard a familiar voice up here." By now Johnson had closed the door and was walking over to the counter where Jim and Wesley stood together.

"Stephen." Jim didn't actually smile in return, but he didn't scowl either. "I'm hoping that you have a few minutes, so we can have a private conversation."

"As in discussing your sister?" Stephen clenched his jaw and released it. His eyes locked defensively with Jim's non-telling gaze. Jim's nod said everything. Johnson sighed. He picked up his cap from the shelf behind the counter where it lay next to his keys. Stephen turned to Wes, "Can you manage?"

"I can and will." Wes's gaze passed between them, then he pointedly said, "It's more than enough with the women feuding with some of us. You two work this out between you."

The breeze by the shore of the lake was crisp, and easily offset by the warmth of the sun shining down on Jim and Stephen, as they sat together on the old log. For a few minutes neither man spoke. They allowed the gentle lapping of waves hitting the shore to calm their thoughts, their words.

Stephen sighed. "Callison, my life is a mess." Jim instinctively knew what was needed at that moment, and so, he remained quiet. "Are you aware that Amanda has threatened Belinda?"

Jim had not anticipated that question. "I've heard about Melissa banning you and Belinda from our home. I also know of some of what Amanda said to Belinda in her defense. But, threaten—what do you mean she threatened her?"

Jim listened, as Stephen told him what Belinda had told him. He had all he could do to not laugh, as he visualized his sister standing her ground while defending her family. Goodness, he loves her! He rubbed the small bristles that were beginning to appear on his chin. "Well, it sounds to me like my sister was justified in what she told Belinda. You might want to be thankful that she kept her hands to herself." Jim shook his head, as his memory of seeing Junior and Shannon after their altercation with Amanda on New Year's Eve 2009 flashed through his mind.

Stephen shifted his jaw, a clear sign he was agitated, and then he drew in a long deep breath. "I guess you're right. Belinda would not have stood a chance against her. As it is, I've been doing a lot of thinking about what Amanda said to Belinda. Actually, Becky gave me her unabridged version, which was a tad different from Belinda's side of it." Stephen sighed. "You already know that Melissa has banned me and Belinda from your home." Jim remained quiet as he nodded. "Well, Becky has joined forces. The women are standing in solidarity banning me from their homes. My own sister!" Stephen, paused and drew in a breath. "Actually, Jim, she spoke truth that I needed to hear. You know we say a lot about Amanda and her sharp tongue." Jim responded, then Stephen continued, "Let me forewarn you that Becky has an invisible stiletto on her tongue. Sharp isn't the word for it! My sister sliced me open and in doing so," Stephen sighed. "In doing so, I've needed to take a long hard look at my life, and the man that I've become."

"And what have you found?" Jim quietly asked, as he continued to watch the small waves make their way to the shore in front of them.

"I don't like the man whom I've become. My mouthy, opinionated sister is right. My life has turned dark. I need to seek forgiveness from too many people for my actions, not only recently, but for a number of years past."

Silence.

The gentle lapping of waves against the shore was the calming music that they both needed at that moment.

"Well, that sounds promising. I suggest you start at the top with God. From there, progress to your daughter and my sister. After you make amends with those three, -" Jim cracked a touch of a smile. His eyes took on a hint of mischievousness. "-The rest of us will be a piece of cake."

Stephen sighed. "Callison, I hate it when you're right."

"No, you don't!" Jim stretched and stood. "Well, I better be heading home to see if Mellie needs for me to help, or relieve her in caring for Mary and Danny."

Stephen stood. He extended his hand for Jim to shake. "You're a good friend. Thank you for your honesty. I hope you don't mind walking back by yourself. I need to spend some time here by the lake by myself."

Jim nodded, turned and walked away from the lake to the parking lot. It was a beautiful day in the lower Adirondack's.

CHAPTER 25

There is an old wise saying about time moving faster with age. Liz wasn't too sure that it was supposed to apply to her age. But, with everything that she had going on in her life, time was racing on like three-year-old horses, in the *Run for the Roses* at the Kentucky Derby! The current conundrum Liz was facing, was that she didn't know if she was supposed to be the jockey holding on to the reigns for dear life, or, the poor horse running as if its life depended on it! She sighed. On the personal level, the wedding was looming closer. Thank you notes had been written and sent for all the beautiful gifts that she and John had received. Liz smiled as she remembered her mother's expression, when she asked if the gifts could be stored upstairs in her and Caitlin's old bedroom until after the wedding. The tear that had formed in her mom's eye, well…Liz knew she had asked the right question of her mother.

Caitlin was once again proving to be Liz's other pea in her pod. Every day of the work week, during Cait's lunch hour, she faithfully called Liz to check in on her. Without fail, Caitlin listened, laughed with her, made suggestions, agreed with final decisions and provided reassurance that only an older sister can provide. Today was no different. Liz wiped her eyes and sighed, as she ended Caitlin's faithful daily call. Once again Caitlin had come through with the exact words Liz needed to hear. Now, with her sister supporting her near decision, it was time to talk with John. After receiving his input, then Liz would make her final decision.

Fortunately, when Liz and John met for dinner her fears proved to have been for nothing. John wholeheartedly agreed with her, for he too had been concerned about how tight it was going to be, to fit all of their guests into the old community church where they planned on having the ceremony. Liz listened to his suggestions and without further hesitation, she picked up her phone an placed a call to their pastor. Fortunately, he had just finished his dinner and was on his way to a meeting over at the church. He listened to Liz and John's quandary. Asked the important questions that they responded to. Then, he made a suggested that they pray together, seek God's direction and let him know what they decided.

"Liz, sweetheart, the Holy Spirit—Great Spirit—will guide us, as the pastor said. You know this is no worse than when you were up in the mountain during the blizzard. We both prayed and look what happened." His finger gently traced her jaw line. He didn't wait for Liz to respond. "I think we already have the answer that's right in front of us."

"Yes, we do."

John lowered his hand onto Liz's cupping his hand around hers. "First, tell me the total number of people we have invited, and then how many confirmed guests we up to at this point?" He asked, before taking a bite of the trout fillet, he had cooked over the wood fire.

"Well, our combined family and close friends adds up to one hundred and fifty people. Then, there are our work colleagues that we have invited and with them our total is three hundred and fifty invited guests. The maximum number our family church sanctuary will hold is two hundred and fifty people. Of course, part of the reason for that is because we have the choir loft and the pastor is at the pulpit." Liz sighed, then took a sip of water. "Right now, Cait and I have received responses from three hundred people, who have said yes, that they plan to attend our wedding. Now, you see why I am panicked!?"

Fortunately, John had swallowed his sip of water, when Liz told him how many people had responded that they intend to attend their wedding. He coughed with his surprise, and released a breath as his gaze held hers. His smile that formed on his lips eased Liz's tension.

"Elizabeth, my love, this is our special day, our celebration, of our love for one another. I understand that it is important to you that we be married in your family church. I do know that my church, the United Methodist Church in Northville, would accommodate our needs." He noticed her expression, and gently squeezed her hand. "I also know you and Caitlin already discussed the church, since she and her family are members there along with me. So, I'm not suggesting that we ask our pastor to perform the ceremony."

"You're not?" Elizabeth gazed at him with the look of *a deer paralyzed in the bright headlights of an oncoming vehicle.*

"No, I'm not. I think your pastor has reminded us that we already have the direction that we need. God will bless our union whether we are in your home church, or in his grand cathedral of his creation. Liz, think about it! The amphitheater will hold everyone that we have invited, unless of course it rains. Heaven forbid!" He sighed. "That is the perfect location for our ceremony." His eyes held hers with such tenderness, it took Liz's breath away. "Sweetheart, I know you wanted to be married in the family church. But honestly Liz, if you think about it, the colony is perfect in meeting all of our needs."

"Oh, John, you're right! Being in God's—the Great Spirit's— creation when we say our vows to one another will be perfect." She picked up her pen that was laying on the pad of paper by her place and scribbled a note. "So, for everyone who has said yes that they are coming, they need more than a social media notification about the change in plans." She sighed. "I guess we'll have to send each person a note regarding the change of location for our ceremony."

"Elizabeth, we'll make this happen. I promise you! Later I'll call my parents and tell them of our change in plans, and ask for them to tell the rest of our family. Then, they won't be so surprised when they receive our notice of the change."

"Oh, John thank you." Liz sighed. "Caitlin is going to kill me with this change."

He chuckled. "No, she won't. Cait loves you and wants our day to be as special for us, as hers was when she married Nick."

For a while, their conversation eased on to other topics as they ate more fish, fire baked potatoes, and toss salad, then as usual their conversation returned to discussing their wedding plans. By the end of the meal, Liz knew that on the following day she would be calling the local tent company, for the cost of one large enough for them to use in place of the mess hall. The tent needed to accommodate them for eating and dancing under. The tent would also serve as a backup in case God had other plans for the day, and they got rained out from using the amphitheater.

Melissa didn't usually stop in at the arts center to see Elizabeth at work. That was Jim's specialty. Interrupting. Meddling. But her daughter's scattered message earlier in the day, had Melissa more than a tad concerned. Over a year ago, Melissa had heard scattered words from her daughter in the weeks before, and as she moved home. So, Mel had good reason to be on high alert. She sat in her vehicle for a few minutes to collect herself. Then, she opened the door and stepped out into the bright warm sunshine. Some birds in a nearby tree sang out, as if, to welcome her, as she walked towards the arts center door.

Liz was quietly working at one of the large tables in the main room of the art center when Melissa entered through the door. A gust of wind took the door from her hand, and it banged against the building, as if to announce her entrance. The contrast of the room lit by electric lighting compared to the sunshine outdoors caused Melissa to pause and allow her eyes to adjust.

"Hi Mom! This is a nice surprise." Liz had stood and was making her way over to greet her mother. "What brings you here on this beautiful spring day?"

Melissa scanned and interpreted her child quicker than any medical imaging machine working at maximum speed. Elizabeth was in a good mood. That fact alone eased Melissa's mind considerably. Still, her daughter's career path, and personality caused Mel to still be suspicious, that something was a muck in Liz's life. Time would only tell.

"Well, since the shower it seems as though we haven't had a moment to talk. I see that you are deeply engrossed in your work,"

"Mom, I never realized how much work went into planning a wedding. It really has sucked up a considerable amount of my time. Fortunately, I know how to bracket personal and professional time." Liz smiled warmly. "Actually, Mom, you came at the perfect time. I just finished with this preparation for our summer theater season and I'm now ready to take a break. Tell me what you think?" With that said, Liz slid the sheet of paper across the table for Melissa to see. The older woman sat down and picked up the paper. Her eyes scanned the rough draft of the summer notice. Melissa knew it was rough by the little doodles, side notes, written along the edges of the page.

"Oh, my goodness!" Mel's eyes had grown as large as her smile, by the time she gazed up at Liz. "This is quite an undertaking for your second season!"

Liz returned a smile. Her bright, *I got this* smile, that her family knew all too well. Then, Liz responded. "In all honesty, Mom, if I didn't have the cast and crew that has committed their summer to me, then no. I definitely would not be doing these plays this summer. Andre and Natasha, as well as Blaine and Annie, among others, have recruited friends to come spend the summer with us."

Melissa was intently watching Liz as she spoke. "Are these people professionals who are expecting to be paid?"

Liz was beaming. Her eyes danced with happiness as she spoke. "Oh, they are professionals. Tony award nominated and some winning professionals, and they are the most generous people that I am honored to call my friends. Mom, some of these artists that will be in residence this summer are not accepting a salary. They are taking a vacation from Broadway, and the city to spend the summer up here in the country, relaxing."

"How are they relaxing, if they will be working?" Melissa honestly did not understand her daughter's friends, colleagues. "Working for nothing is unheard of in today's world!" Melissa added, with a touch of confusion in her voice.

Liz giggled. "You're right. It is unheard of and that is what sets my friends part from others. For them, and for me, the theater isn't a job. Mom, it's our life."

Melissa tenderly held her daughter's gaze. Yes. She had to admit, the theater is Elizabeth's life, professionally. Liz is as passionate for the arts, as she is for her family and John who takes center stage in Liz's life, *as he should*, Melissa thought to herself.

"So, with all of your theater colleagues coming to work here this summer, are you going to be casting extras from the community?"

Liz's eyes sparkled as her smile grew. Her face radiated with joy as she spoke. "Of course! Summer theater could not survive, or thrive for that matter, without the community's involvement. Mom, members of the high school drama club, and some other students who are interested in working the box office, and on publicity have already been in contact with me about volunteering at the arts community for the summer. Plus, I've had a few of our local business owners already contacted me to hash out summer work schedules for their employees."

"Oh wow!" Melissa truly was surprised to hear of the rapport her daughter now had with business owners. "I obviously knew that last summer was a success. But I never dreamed it had taken off like this." Melissa lovingly held Elizabeth's gaze. Then she sniffled unexpectedly before asking, "Have I told you lately that I'm very proud of your accomplishments?"

That did it! Liz sniffled, then drew in a calming breath. "Thanks, Mom! Your and dad's support means the world to me." She drew in another breath. She was close to crying tears of joy on multiple levels. If she did, well, Liz knew it would be a gosh awful mess! "Mom, I do have some things to share with you about the wedding, and I need your help."

Melissa intently looked into her daughter's eyes. They didn't appear distressed in any way to cause alarm. Still, this was Elizabeth that Melissa was conversing with. Her most unpredictable daughter.

"And what, might I ask, do you need my help with?"

"Well, we need to contact family and friends, and tell them that there is a change in venue for John's and my wedding ceremony." Liz's expression stated that she was serious. Mel could handle that, but it was the other part of Liz's expression that troubled her.

"So, you are not going to get married at our family church. And where might I ask are you intending to get married?"

"At the arts colony amphitheater." Liz responded with a tone and expression that informed her mother that the answer was an obvious one. Plus, it shouldn't have surprised Melissa, especially when Liz told her how many people were planning on attending the wedding.

Mel paused from speaking, thought about what Liz had just told her for a moment. Then, a slow smile took shape on her lips.

"Elizabeth, I agree, and I'm glad that you and John spoke with our pastor before talking with anyone else. So, give me a list and I'll do my part to help make this wedding be everything that you have imagined for it to be."

Later that night, Jim sat at the kitchen table, pleasantly full, or so he implied, from the dinner that Melissa had prepared for them. Just because she felt the need to cut back on her caloric intake didn't mean that Jim wanted to do the same. Unbeknownst to Melissa, Jim had been busy working on a project for John, a surprise for Elizabeth, and he was hungrier than he normally was these days. While Jim knew that Mel was terrific at keeping secrets, this one was far too great to share with even the love of his life. He'd deal with the consequences when the time came. Melissa placed a hot cup of freshly made decaffeinated coffee on the table in front of Jim, then took her place once again.

Jim stretched, took a sip of coffee, then sighed. "Good coffee, Mellie, even if it is decaf." Jim rolled his eyes.

Melissa shook her head, then added her own sigh to the mood that seemed to have settled over them. The bottom line was that they both were tired. "So, Jim, do you want to call Amanda? Or, should I?"

He cleared his throat. Darn spring pollen had never before been an issue until this year for some reason. He sniffled, withdrew his cloth handkerchief from his back pocket and wiped his drippy nose. Then he sighed. "Yeah, I'll call her." He said, as he pulled his phone out of his hip pocket.

Melissa quietly spoke as he opened his phone and pulled up Amanda's name in his contacts. He dialed, listened. His brows drew close as he glanced up at the wall clock. Voicemail. Jim sighed, then left his message. He clicked off his phone, as an ominous feeling began lurking within him.

An hour later, Jim's cell phone rang. Melissa muted the baseball game that they were watching on the large screen television, as Jim answered his phone on the third ring. She prepared to listen to Jim's side of the conversation and attempt to piece together what Amanda might be saying. More often than not, that was easier said than done.

"Hey, Sis, thanks for calling me back." Jim changed from reclined position in his chair to sitting up straight. Yeah, I have to share some news with you about the wedding." He chuckled at Amanda's response. "Rest assured, they are still very much in love. Yes." He chuckled at Amanda's response. Then continued, "This wedding is going to happen. John Runner is a good man, an ideal march for Elizabeth's personality. At any rate, my reason for calling is to let you and Kevin know that we've had to change the location where the wedding ceremony will take place."

Jim continued to share what he knew with Amanda. He answered her questions and laughed with her. As they conversed, that ominous feeling returned especially when they paused, so that Amanda could speak with Kevin. Jim turned to Melissa and quietly spoke.

"Mellie, something is wrong down south. I can hear it in Sis's voice." Jim's breathing as well as his eyes revealed his concern. He heard Amanda sigh. Then her words to Kevin. His heart began to sink.

"Jim, I guess you heard what Kevin shared with me."

Jim listened and heard Amanda sniffle. He wished that they were together, so that he could give her a hug. "Yeah, Sis, I did." Jim released a long, slow mournful breath. "How long do you all have?" His words were quiet to fit the change in their mood.

"How long for what?" Melissa watched. Her whole body was on high alert.

Jim reached over and took Melissa's hand into his. He gently squeezed it, and seemed to hold on as if for dear life!

"Okay, Amanda." He sighed. "Listen, you tell Kevin that our thoughts and prayers are with all of you. We understand. You keep us posted." He listened. Sniffled back his emotions. "I love you too, Sis."

Jim clicked off his phone. Once again, he took out his handkerchief and wiped his nose. Melissa quietly waited for Jim to regain his composure, as she slid her hand over on top of his forearm, as it rested on the table.

Her voice was quiet, filled with concerns she asked, "What's going on?"

Jim drew in a long, slow breath. He needed a moment to allow all the new information that he had received to settle. "Amanda and Kevin are pleased to hear about how everything is coming together for Elizabeth's wedding. Knowing our Elizabeth, as well as they do, they think it is perfect to have both the wedding and the reception at the arts colony. In fact, Amanda doesn't understand why Liz didn't decide to do that from the onset of planning her wedding." He released a sigh.

Mel saw and immediately recognized the telltale signs that Jim was withholding something important from her. "Jim, stop hemming and hawing. Just tell me. What is wrong?"

Jim's expression, the tear that managed to escape from the corner of his eye, caused Melissa to draw in a breath of impending doom. "Jim, tell me."

"Sis, told me that they are torn apart and that under the circumstances," Jim sighed while fighting for composure. "They might not make the wedding."

"What?" Melissa could not believe what she was hearing. "Jim, they're our family! They have to be here with us! Liz will be devastated. She can't wait for Amanda to see what Cookie did with your mom's wedding gown incorporating it into Elizabeth's gown."

"Mellie, while we are in the throes of wedding plans, new beginnings, joy and love," Jim's eyes conveyed troubled motions as he gazed at Mel. His jaws were tightly clenched. Then, he breathed out through his nostrils. Oh yes. Jim was reigning in his emotions. Then he spoke. His voice was quiet. Mournful. "Kevin has just returned from another trip to Tucson to see his sister." Jim had moved his arm and was now holding Mel's hand in his.

"What?" Mel's face filled with terror, as she began to interpret the meaning of Jim's words.

"Amanda told me that Kevin was out to Arizona to be with Cora and her family, as they discussed and processed all of the information that they had about her prognosis." Jim swallowed. Drew in a breath. Sniffled. "It's not good, Mellie. Kevin's a mess, from what Manda shared with me."

Silence fell between them, as Mel began to process Jim's words. "Jim, the last I had heard, everyone was elated that Cora was in remission following her round of chemo. How much time does Kevin's sister have?"

"She's now under hospice care in her home. Amanda said that at Cora's request, Kevin and his brothers fly out every weekend to be with the family."

A tear slid from Melissa's eye, as she processed what Jim had just shared with her. "Hospice care." She breathed out, knowing what that meant. "Why didn't they tell us sooner, how serious this is for them?"

Jim's moist eyes tenderly held Melissa's equally moist eyes, as he spoke. "Apparently, Manda and Kev were under obligation to not tell us everything that was going on with his sister. Cora Beth is a very private person and well," he drew in a calming breath. "She had been on a liver transplant list and hopeful. That is, until they found out that the cancer has metastasized and is aggressively claiming her brain." Jim drew in a breath. Then, he slowly released it. He didn't speak. His heart was breaking for his sister and brother in law. He sniffled and once again held Mel's gaze in his. "Amanda has assured me that they will do everything in their power to be here, if it is possible. For now, we have to keep this to ourselves. You heard me promise Manda, that we will not say anything to diminish Liz's joy."

"I know what Amanda wants, and I understand why. But, Jim, in all honesty, I think we should tell Lizzie, so she is prepared for the reality that her aunt and uncle may not be here to share her wedding day with us."

Jim was quiet. Then he slowly began to nod his head. "You're right. We better plan to tell her this news together."

Liz bracketed the news her parents had given her. Aunt Amanda had also talked with her, and Liz knew life—just like the show, had to go on—as she pulled into the parking spot designated for her at the arts colony. She softly smiled as she recalled how this had all came about. Last summer, on more than one occasion, Liz had to park in the overflow parking lot. Parking there in the morning had not been an issue. The problem arose late at night, before the new lights had been installed. It was a warm, full moonlit night. Unfortunately, Liz was leaving to go home at the same time a bear decided to take an evening stroll through the colony, and check out the dumpster for anything that might be edible. Liz screamed with fright, while feeling totally foolish. She had grown up in the mountains, for heaven's sake! She knew that black bears roamed around the area day and night. So really, she should have been prepared. That one experience with the bear, who fortunately was even more scared that Liz, was more than enough for Liz to insist on a special parking space close to the buildings. She smiled as she recalled her reasoning. Her cousin Summer was the naturalist, the conservationist, and she could frolic with the bears. Not Elizabeth. She might have grown up in the mountains, and returned to them to settle down and work, but she also wanted to feel and be safe.

The noise of hammers, saws, laughter, voices filled the morning air, as Liz walked towards the amphitheater. Soon the crew would be working on the set for the first of three summer productions for this new theater season. For now, they had another event to get ready for: the wedding.

"Good morning, Liz!" Natasha called out as she approached the amphitheater from the opposite direction of Liz. Liz turned her head to see her friend walking towards her with a cup of coffee in her hand. Her smile grew as Natasha began to sing out in a clear soprano voice the lyrics of a song from a familiar Rogers and Hammerstein musical. Liz laughed, as they came towards each other.

"Yes, Tash, it is a beautiful morning. Any morning here in the Adirondack's is beautiful." Liz's eyes, her smile, her whole body shone with happiness as she spoke.

"So, says the woman in love!" Natasha teased. They linked arms as they walked on together. "I'm so happy for you and John." She sighed. "With how shaky last summer began for all of us, being a part of the demise of your last," she paused. "Well, your real life is far more beautiful than the greatest Tony award winning theater production could ever hope to be."

Liz sighed in contentment. Her eyes shone with joy as she spoke. "Tony award, you say?" They giggled together as good friends who understood one another, as well as they do, could only share in that moment. Liz began improvising, causing Natasha to laugh, then add her own improvisation.

The crew quieted down, as the two women walked onto the stage. Liz smiled as her gaze passed over them. Then, she stopped and returned her gaze on the men standing by Andre. Josh was there, as expected since he is her assistant director. But, John? Her fiancé? What in the world was he doing there?

"John!" Liz gasped. She shook her head, as if to clear it from invisible cobwebs. Her gaze passed from John to the curiously amused onlookers. "Okay, everyone take five!" She stepped over to stand in front of John, who continued to stand with Andre, Josh, and Blaine, as if he was supposed to be there. Liz was fully aware of her friend's silent interaction. "Obviously, you three do not think I'm including you in the take five." Her slight tilt of her chin took the humor from their eyes as they watched her. It was John, who wisely spoke up for all of them standing in Liz's presence on the stage.

"Sweetheart, apparently you've forgotten that the high school science class is coming here today, to use the trail to go out on state land and do part of their earth science lab. I'm here to guide them, so that they don't get lost."

"Mm-hmm." She shook her head, while intently studying his eyes. "The students and you were not due to arrive until 12:30 this afternoon. It's 8:30 in the morning."

John allowed a lazy smile to begin to take form on his lips. "You're right. I'm using this morning to help with the construction of the arch and how you want-"

"-The set design, or in our case, the altar for our wedding ceremony." Liz raised her hand to gently rest on his chest. His hand cupped her hand while holding it against him. Their gazes held one another in captivity. At that moment, it was as if, well, as if no one else existed, but the two of them.

"I want our wedding day to be one of the most memorable of the rest of our life together." His breathing was erratic. Liz could feel his body touching hers. Intimately. The warmth of the sun shining down on them was nothing compared to the love and lust that radiated between them.

"Oh, John," Liz breathed out. Then, all of a sudden Liz realized where they were. Her cheeks turned rosy red, as she cleared her throat and stepped back from John. "I do believe our five minutes are done for now." She drew in a breath as her gaze moved from her amused fiancé to her equally amused friends and colleagues. "And that, ladies and gentlemen, is how you do a love scene."

Silence. Then, everyone on the stage erupted with laughter, before returning to their work. John winked at Liz. His gaze and hint of a smile held the promise that their love scene was a long way from being finished.

By the end of the day, Liz was exhausted. She had been off working under the stage with her crew sorting through the costumes and set pieces, determining what was going to be needed for this season's productions. With her clipboard in hand, her pencil tucked behind her ear, and her ball cap on her head, with her ponytail pulled through the back of it, she made her way up the stairs into the later afternoon sunlight. She stopped dead in her tracks, as she looked out into the theater house. The science field trip the students had been on with John, somehow managed to turn into another field trip, as they quietly sat on the bleachers with him and observed the stage crew working on the finishing touches for their wedding. Liz drew in a breath as she silently watched John interact with the students.

"You have quite a good man in your life."

The quiet voice made Liz jump and gasp. Then she slowly turned her gaze to look Blaine directly in his eyes.

"Yes, he is a very good man, Blaine." Liz sighed. "You are one friend who knows of my past, and certainly can make an accurate judgment call."

"I'm not judging. Just saying I'm glad to see you so happy." He winked, and gave her his classic smile, then added, "And it's about time!"

Liz drew in a breath as she scanned the theater house and stage area. Then after another quiet word with Blaine, she made her way up the side aisle to greet John and the students. By the time Liz made her way back to them John and the science teacher had risen to meet her. The conversation that ensued, led Liz to invite the students to join her on stage for another science lesson. Some of the students were amazed to discover how much science and math goes into the theater. Others were ready to call it a day and not enthused by the new science lesson.

John lingered after the students left, pleased that Liz had suggested he stay and then go out for dinner with her, Natasha and Andre. They all rode in John's SUV down to Mayfield to the diner. Having forgotten that it was senior citizen Tuesday, the place was swamped with people. While they were being seated in the back section that had recently been added on to the building, Liz saw her aunt's nemesis and his girlfriend walk in, followed by Becky and Wesley, who were being shown to the same section where Liz and John were with their friends.

"Oh, great!" She moaned. "And this had been such a nice day!" She added with great distaste in her quietly spoken voice.

John immediately noticed her distress, as Stephen and Belinda stepped forward and greeted them. He slid his arm protectively around her, as the introductions began. He didn't appreciate the tone of voice and attitude Belinda was expressing towards Liz and their friends. Yes, the two-theater people may have begun as Liz's friends, but they were now his friends as well, and John was feeling rather protective of everyone with him. He turned his gaze from Belinda to Stephen. His voice held a touch of a threat in it as he spoke.

Stephen stood a little straighter as he responded. "The DEC— Department of Environmental Protection—shouldn't have any cause for concern with our bait and tackle shop. Isn't that right, Wes?"

Stephen quietly asked his brother in law, who had become engaged in the conversation.

Wes' gaze passed between the men and Elizabeth. He noticed more than either of the other two men realized. It made him smile to himself as he saw how John was protecting Elizabeth from his brother in law. Wes cleared his throat, then spoke. "Johnson, right now the DEC is the least of your worries. You clearly are in hot water with a New York State Forest Ranger, and I wish you good luck." His gaze returned to Liz, who was nodding in agreement. Wes shook his head, as he added, "That mouth of yours is like a screen door not latched tightly and keeps slapping open and shut by a gust of wind. Annoying as he, -" Wes didn't finish his statement. Rather, he shook his head, then took Becky by the hand and led her to their table where the hostess stood waiting for them.

Liz was glad that the rest of the evening was basically uneventful for them. Her friends returned to their cabin at the arts colony for the night, while she and John headed home to their respective cabins. Her heart fluttered, as she thought about everything that was to happen in a matter of days. They would be married. There would be no more going home alone for the night.

She wasn't too surprised when her parents arrived at the arts colony by mid-morning the next day. Nor, was she surprised to see them pushing the double baby stroller with two sleeping cherubs, Mary and Danny. An unexpected tug of sadness swept over her like a sudden gust of wind. Grief. Liz didn't understand how after all this time, the loss of her child could still catch her unaware. Without realizing it, her hand gently rested on her stomach. She should have known that her mother noticed, even from a distance. Her mother's hug and quiet words were just what Liz had needed to comfort her at that moment.

"So, what brings you four over here on this beautiful day?" Liz quietly inquired, to not awaken either one or both of the children.

"Your father is itching to see if there is something for him to do to help with setting up for the ceremony." Liz couldn't help but smile as she watched both of her parent's.

"Well, Dad, this time, you are off the hook for helping with the stage set up. Earlier this morning we finished all of the major painting. Now we have to allow it to have time to dry before we move on to the finishing touches." She noticed something in his eyes. Disappointment perhaps? Or maybe relief? "But, -"

"See, Mellie! I told you she would have something for me to do!" Jim gave her his all too familiar look with his chin lowered and his eyebrow scrunched. His corner of his mouth twisted, as he fought off a smile.

Liz laughed, momentarily forgetting the sleeping babies until they stirred unhappily.

"Oops!" She cringed, as Danny cried out. "Sorry." Liz said as she ducked down into the stroller and eased her nephew into her embrace. She nestled him close to her shoulder, gently patted his back and breathed in his scent. Baby. Then, she softly touched her lips to his fine head of light brown hair and kissed him. Danny seemed appeased by his aunt, yawned and returned to sleep. "Well, how about Danny and I show you what needs to be done?" She suggested with a much quieter voice.

Quiet conversation ensued as they leisurely walked along the path. Melissa pushed Mary in the stroller, needing Jim's assistance when the tiny wheel got stuck in a small depression in the ground. as they walked over to the field adjacent to the mess hall. The tent company had already erected the large tent for the reception. Jim noticed its size and figured it was double the size of the tent that had rented for after his dad's funeral last year. As they walked, Liz shared her vision of how the areas within the tent would be set up for the reception. Of course, everything was written out in her wedding binder.

When they got inside the tent, there were many familiar faces, and warm welcomes were exchanged. Andre and Natasha were among the first to walk over and greet Jim and Melissa. Then Blaine, Sasha, Jerry. Trisha, Julie, and Spud joined them and of course, they made a fuss over the babies. Both Jim and Mel watched Elizabeth, as she quietly spoke to her theater troupe, and made sure that Danny was not awakened from his peaceful slumber against her shoulder. Josh, Liz's assistant director, had stepped in for her overseeing the tent set up by using the diagrams, and her directions written on the pages in the wedding binder. It didn't take long for Jim to wander off with the stage lighting crew, who were taking care of the electronics and lighting, as well as tables and chairs set up.

Liz was glad that her dad felt comfortable to insert himself into the theater mix, and that her friends genuinely liked him, and accepted his assistance.

She briefly spoke with Josh, then gently eased Danny back down into the stroller next to his sister. Then, with a final satisfied gaze over the activity, she and Mel slowly walked back to the mess hall with the babies. Carefully, to not awaken their charges, they got the stroller up the stairs and into the building. Then, as if on cue, both children awakened, needing to have their diapers changed and to be fed. Liz covertly watched her mother, the family matriarch. Giver of life. A gentle smile eased onto Liz's lips as she listened to her mother gently speak to Danny, while she re-diapered Mary.

Liz knew how much still needed to be done before the wedding. Her life was as crazy as it was in the last days before opening night. Details. Glitches had to be worked out. Jitters. Liz drew in a deep breath. She honestly needed and was enjoying her day. Spending time with her mom, her niece and nephew interacting with them before they shut their eyes once again was helping to calm her nerves.

Once the children were back asleep, Liz got out the cart from the storage room and took it outside onto the porch. Melissa joined Liz outside and assisted her with taking the cart down the steps. Then they began the task of carrying out the cardboard boxes and plastic tubs that would be moved over to the tent.

By the time John arrived at the colony after work, most of the reception set up had been completed. Tables and chairs for dining had been arranged, the buffet tables were placed against the side, with electric run for hot food trays. Plus, a dance floor had been assembled, with Jim's assistance, earlier in the day. Lights were now being hung around the inside of the tent. John paused, as he stepped into the tent to allow his eyes to adjust to the difference in lighting from outdoor to inside the tent. He drew in a breath as he looked around at everything that had been done.

"Hi, John! Hey, here's the groom! Welcome! What do you think?" The barrage of greeting and questions pleasantly took him by surprise. He responded. But it was the hands sliding around his waist from behind, the body leaning into his and the quiet words that took his breath away. He turned while sliding his arms around Liz.

"Mm. Now this is a greeting I truly enjoy."

"Hey, you two, you're not married yet!" Blaine teased, as John's lips brushed against Liz's. They both sighed, while the onlookers teased.

Liz stepped out of John's arms, as she responded with deadpan seriousness in her voice and expression. "Blaine, you of all people should know that practice is necessary before any great performance."

"Touché!" Blaine simply shook his head, then laughed. "So, John, what do you think?" He was all smiles, quite proud of what he and everyone else had done for them.

For a moment, John was without words. He simply looked around the tent. Then he spoke. Liz heard the emotion in his voice, and fought back her own tear, as he said, "Honestly, you all have outdone yourselves. Thank you for all of your extra work that you each have done to make Liz's and my wedding day as near perfect as it could possibly be."

"Well, it's our pleasure." Didie, one of the new troupe members said. "I'm glad I accepted Andre and Tasha's invitation to come work up here this summer. Working behind the scenes, which I love to do, helping to make Liz and your wedding a dream come true. Well, I would not have passed this up for the world!"

Liz glanced at her watch, then out of the opening in the tent. She saw the caterer's approaching, and quietly instructed everyone to head over to the mess hall for dinner. Tomorrow was the wedding rehearsal and time for the finishing touches on the stage and in the tent. The hours were ticking by quickly. Liz was feeling the rush that she usually felt before opening night of a production. She smiled as John took her hand and they headed off with everyone towards the mess hall for dinner. In two days, they were going to be the stars of the day. Well, that is unless her nieces and nephews upstaged her. Liz knew with her family anything was possible.

Anything was possible, was an understatement for Liz's wedding day. Jim, unable to sleep, was up at the crack of dawn, showered and then get out of the way for the women in his family. Melissa was also up early. She had gone downstairs and busied herself in the kitchen, while Jim showered. With two hot cups of coffee in her hands, Melissa quietly eased back into their bedroom.

"Mm. My sweet Melissa, you are a precious gem! Thank you." Jim said, as he gently took the hot mug from her hands, and brushed his lips over hers.

"You're welcome." Mel took a sip of coffee from her mug. "Any word from Amanda?" She quietly asked, as she sat down on the end of the bed next to Jim, clad in a towel wrapped around his waist.

"Not yet. Phil sent me a text to let me know that he's back from Albany, and that Mandy sent him a text before the plane took off."

Melissa sighed as she leaned against Jim. He drew her close, while being careful that neither one, or both of them were burned by their coffee. "We owe Phil a debt of gratitude for helping us out, as he has and is doing for us throughout today."

"Yes, we do, Mellie." Jim cupped his hand around hers and gave it a gentle squeeze. He released a slow breath that became a heavy sigh. Then he yawned. He shook his head.

Melissa knew those subtle noises, mannerisms all too well. "Do you care to share what is on your mind?"

"Later. From the sounds outside of our room, I'd say that Liz and Jordan are up." Jim stood, slipped into a pair of sweatpants, then disappeared into their bathroom. Melissa listened and had a thought forming in her mind. She hoped that she was wrong. He emerged with a grin plastered on his face from ear to ear. "Time for a little fun!"

"Oh Jim, I'm not sure, -"

Melissa didn't have time to finish her thought, as Jim opened the door. Sure enough, Liz and Jordan were freely going in and out of the two bedrooms that they had slept in. Their quiet laughter and conversation touched both Jim and Melissa's hearts.

"Good morning, Dad, Mom!" They both were smiling, as they greeted their parents. It was then that they noticed water dripping onto the hardwood floor from alongside of their father. They gazed into each other's eyes, as they both understood what was happening. "No!" They exclaimed in unison. Their expressions when they turned back to their father and were blasted with ice cold water was priceless. Surprise. Disbelief. "Mom!" They wailed.

Melissa simply surrendered to the moment with her family. She leaned back against the wall, laughed, cried and thanked God for her crazy family that she would not change for the world.

Four hours later, no one attending the wedding would have ever guessed that Liz and Jordan had been soaked by their father with Nick's old water gun, that had conveniently been returned to the shelf in the closet. It was a private family memory that held deep meaning for the four who had participated in the early morning fun.

The small ensemble that would accompany the troupe for the summer were in place and began to play, when James Junior escorted his mother to her seat in the open auditorium under the late spring sunshine. The words of the song that Liz had chosen for her mother brought tears to Mel's eyes, as she took her seat.

Then, the curtain opened and everyone got their first glimpse of the stage. Gasps. Quiet words of amazement were audibly heard. The scene that Liz, John and their crew had created looked like they would be walking into a woodland garden by a creek somewhere further up in the mountains, or by a lake. Its simplicity and natural beauty was exactly right for them. Both Jordan and Samantha took their positions at the rear of the bleachers. They looked stunning in their light green tea length dresses, as they walked down the center aisle at the summer amphitheater to the music Liz had chosen from *West Side Story.* There were some sniffles from the guests, as they were met by the ushers and escorted onto the stage.

Eyes were once again centered on the rear of the auditorium and more gasps were heard, as Caitlin emerged in a forest green tea length dress. Only the Callison sisters knew that Cookie had sewn a secret in to each of their dresses. In each bodice of the dresses, touching their skin was a piece of cloth from their grandmothers wedding gown. Caitlin, fought to reign in her emotions with every step that she took. That special secret was something that Cait, and her sisters had not known until today when they were getting dressed at their parent's home. Of course, tears had freely flowed from each of the Callison daughters. Lizzie sure knew how to surprise them with a memory that they would share until their lives ended!

Elizabeth's and John's wedding ceremony was filled with surprises. Everyone had assumed that Elizabeth would immediately follow Caitlin down the aisle. No one had expected that Andre and Natasha would sing *All I Ask of You* from Andrew Lloyd Webber's Phantom of the Opera. While everyone's attention was focused on their duet, Elizabeth and Jim took their place at the rear of the aisle.

Jim swallowed back his emotions, as he gazed the stage that held three of his four daughters. Then, he glanced over at Elizabeth. Earlier in the day when she had stepped down the stairs and into the living room, Jim had allowed his eyes to mist. Elizabeth looked regal in the gown that had been created with pieces of fabric from his mother's wedding gown. Then much to Jim's surprise, he discovered that Liz's veil that now covered her face, had been his mother's. The old dry flowers had been replaced with fresh baby's breath and forget-me-not. Jim wished that his parents could be there with them, to see Elizabeth on her special day. Her face radiated her happiness, while her hand was gracefully poised on his forearm.

"Elizabeth Jeanne," he quietly said her name.

"Yes, Dad." She responded with equal quietness in her voice.

Her gaze reminded him of when she was his little girl. He swallowed, then quietly cleared his throat.

"Remember our conversation we had, as we sat by the creek on that hot summer day when you came home with all of your earthly belongings?"

"We spoke of many things when I came home."

"I mean about the bird?"

"Yes, Dad." She sighed.

"Well, my little bird, I'm proud of how you've allowed yourself the time that you have needed to be healed. Today you are ready to fly, ready to soar and go build your own nest with John Runner, a man whom I am going to be proud to call my son in law. I love you my Lizzie J." Jim's eyes were extremely moist. He sniffled.

"Oh, Dad!" Elizabeth fought back the tears that were right there ready to break over her invisible dam and tumble down her cheeks. "I love you, too!" Her lower lip quivered, as Jim carefully raised her veil and dabbed her eyes with his white cloth handkerchief. Then the song ended. Natasha and Andre took their seats on the left side of the house in seats directly behind the Callison family members that were not on the stage.

Once again, the music began with a very familiar song right out of Rogers and Hammerstein's *The Sound of Music*. Melissa stood, tears tumbled freely down her cheeks, as she watched Jim and Elizabeth make their way down the aisle and onto the stage, where he handed off Elizabeth to John. Then, as the music was winding down Jim took his place next to Melissa, and for the next half hour they were mesmerized by the sacred beauty that had been created by Elizabeth and John, as they exchanged their vows. Then to everyone's surprise they sang to each other *Love Changes Everything* from Phantom of the Opera. Needless to say, by the time the pastor announced that they were married and they kissed, well, many more tears were freely flowing, while others did their best to be discreet.

Even though the mood was festive for most people, gathered at the arts colony for the wedding celebration, there was an underlying current of uneasiness. Jim and Melissa stepped out of the tent away from the celebration with Phil Johnson. Phil's expression spoke before his voice.

"When?" Melissa quietly asked.

"Amanda sent me a text while we were eating. I stepped outside to call her and get the details for you."

"And?" Jim's expression matched Melissa's as they listened to Phil.

"Kevin's sister hung on until Mandy and Kevin got to the hospital. Mandy said that Kevin got to spend a few minutes alone with

Cora. Then Mandy, Cora's husband and their family joined Kevin and they all were with her when she took her last breath. Mandy's holding up as best as she can under the circumstances. She said that Kevin -" Phil sniffled, then sighed. "-Well, as you can imagine, he is a mess."

"Yes. I can imagine." Jim quietly breathed out, as his memory took him to a time long ago, a time when his brother had died during his tour of duty in the Vietnam War.

Jim drew Melissa into his arms as she openly wept. His eyes were red, strained by his holding the mournful tears at bay. Phil wasn't doing too much better. Then, their moment of grief was interrupted by very familiar voices.

"Phil, what's going on?" Stephen asked as his eyes honed in on his brother. He didn't like what he was observing, nor the treatment his younger brother had been giving him throughout the day. Something was gravely off, and Stephen intended to find out what was so important that it had taken Jim and Melissa away from their daughter's wedding reception.

"Uncle Jim, Aunt Melissa has something happened to my mom and Kevin?" Her gaze past between her aunt and uncle. "Uncle Phil, is that why they're not here?"

Jim looked at his niece in total amazement. Summer had a year to work on making amends with her mother, and now she was worried? A disturbing guttural sound came from Jim's throat. But, fortunately for Stephen and Summer, it was Phil who found his voice, as Jim continued to hold onto Mel, as she quietly wept. Perhaps they weren't too fortunate, after all, because Phil's expression was far from being joyful. In fact, it was filled with disgust and some other unmentionable things. The sound that came from his throat nearly matched Jim's. Then he asked, "Why do either of you even bother to act as if you care?"

Phil shifted his eyes to meet Jim's. As old friends, old officers of the law, they had their own communication that didn't need any spoken words. Jim nodded. Without a word he quietly eased Melissa away from his niece and her father. They had a party to rejoin. Heaven help him, if his sister discovered that they had collapsed into grief with her and Kevin, rather than celebrating Liz and John's wedding! And they did just that, while leaving Phil to handle Summer and Stephen.

"Uncle Phil, I came here with the hopes that I could begin to patch up my relationship with Mom, but if she is avoiding me, -"

"Tsk, tsk, tsk! You've had over a year to patch things up with your mom." He noticed the expressions change on both his brother and his niece's faces. "I know considerably more than either of think I do." With that statement Phil unloaded his disappointment with them. Then, as his cell phone indicated he had an incoming text, he told them exactly where they could go to find Amanda and Kevin. As Phil walked away from them, he heard Summer crying and Stephen consoling her. *Good*, Phil thought, as he responded to Amanda's text and returned to the celebration. He was on a new mission for Kevin, in his absence. Now, Phil hoped that Elizabeth would find him an adequate substitute for her real uncle as he danced with her.

"Oh, Aunt Amanda, everything was perfect! You and Uncle Kevin are the best!" Liz was grinning from ear to ear as she sat on the porch of her new home. Their cabin. She yawned.

"It sounds to me like you need some more sleep."

Liz heard the laughter and caring aunt tone in the older woman's voice. "I probably do need more sleep, but," Liz sighed in contentment. "It's a gorgeous day back up here in the mountains and I want to soak it all in."

Silence.

"I can understand that. There is something about those wonderful old mountains that draw you in to a place of sacredness."

Elizabeth listened, as her aunt shared images of what it means to be from, or reside in the Adirondack Mountains. "Oh yes, Aunt Amanda! I know exactly what you are saying. John and I thoroughly enjoyed our honeymoon, lying on the beach, soaking up the sun, swimming in the ocean. The day trips and night life to typical tourist attractions were wonderful. But to drive home from Albany International early this morning, seeing the silhouettes of our mountains, well, -" Liz sighed.

"It is home." Amanda completed Liz's sentence for her.

"Yes." Liz stretched and yawned. The squeaking of the screen door opening drew her gaze to John as he emerged from the cabin. Clad in a tee shirt, worn jeans, bare feet, unshaven and a mug of coffee in his hand, he quietly approached her.

"Ah, Aunt Amanda, I hate to end this, -" the sound of laughter made her pause.

"No, you don't!" Amanda was still laughing. "I heard the screen door. Trust me, I know what you want, and talking with me is no longer at the top of your list. Go enjoy the rest of your honeymoon! I love you, Elizabeth, and I'm glad that you are home where you belong."

Six weeks later, Liz remembered the very last part of the conversation that she had had with her aunt, as her summer theater troupe was busy creating the set and practicing for opening night of the musical *Damn Yankees*, an Alder and Ross collaboration. She was home, physically, emotionally, spiritually. Now, she needed to get finished with her work for the day and head home to John. Liz was straightening up her desk in her little office in the back of the mess hall, when she heard familiar voices entering the building.

"Hey, guys, I'm in here!" She called out. Placing her binder in her backpack, Liz glanced around to make sure everything was tidy. Then she quietly said, "See you two tomorrow. If you don't play any jokes on me during the night, I just might show you some pictures from my honeymoon." Liz quietly laughed as she felt the brushing as light as a feather against her neck. "Oh, and thanks for not scaring anyone this summer."

Liz closed the office door behind her, greeted Josh, her assistant director and Colleen, the high school volunteer who was his assistant and gofer. Colleen had aspirations for directing someday, and she was also someone Liz was mentoring throughout the year. At this hour of the day, Colleen and Josh reported in to Liz to go over any problems that had risen during the day, and things to be addressed during the next day.

With a smile, and satisfied with how things were going with summer theater, it was time to head home. Liz drove down the familiar road to Route 30. Rather than driving up the old road leading to the family cabin, as she had done for over a year, Liz continued on. She drove through Northville onto the county road that led her to their home. Earlier in the day when she had spoken with John, he said that things were relatively quiet. So far, people were respecting and following the fire ban. She slowed and pulled into the driveway, pleased to see that John was already home for the evening. By the time Liz shut off the motor, John was outside on the porch. He eased down the steps with lightness, that simply took Liz's breath away.

"Hey, beautiful," he said as he opened the door for her. His smile held promises of a life filled with love, and then he drew her into his arms. His lips caressed hers with promises of what was to come. "I was surprised when you texted me and said you were coming home early. Is everything alright?"

Liz was beaming with excitement, as her gaze held his. She eased her free hand into his, shut the car door with the other, then took a hold of the strap of the backpack as it rested on her shoulder. As they walked up onto the porch, John filled her in on how long it would be before dinner. Liz eased into the glider that they had installed on the one end of the porch, and waited for John to rejoin her with glasses of ice water.

"So, what's this?" John asked, as he pointed to the binder resting on Liz's lap.

Liz took a sip of water, then placed her glass on the small table at the side of the glider. "This is my play. It's finished and," her smile illuminated the porch. "I'd like for you to be the first to read it."

John tenderly looked into Liz's eyes. "Sweetheart, I'm honored, but, I'm not, -"

Liz gently touched his lips with her index finger. Her heart was in her words as she responded. "John, please. It means the world to me for you to be the first to read this."

There was something about Liz's expression that caused John to not say what he had planned to say to her. Instead, he agreed and picked up the binder. He read. He laughed. He teased her when he was reminded of their relationship in the two main characters. Then, he came to the ending. He drew in a breath, swallowed, and sighed, as deeper understanding of the plays ending came over him. A tear slid down his cheek. Then, his eyes met her misty gaze.

"Oh, my precious, Elizabeth." At some point his hand had moved and was now gently resting on her abdomen. "Are you really?"

"Yes, John. I'm pregnant and happier than witnessing the first light of a Sacandaga sunrise."

No words were needed to complete their scene, as their lips came together in sweet surrender. Their kiss was filled with love and joy, and as their evening progressed, well, they proved that a Sacandaga sunset wasn't too bad either!

FINAL
CURTAIN
CALL

May the road rise up to meet you,
May the wind be
always at your back.
May the sun shine warm
upon your face,
may the rains fall soft upon your fields,
And, until we meet again,
may God hold you in the palm of His hand.

-Irish Blessing

CPSIA information can be obtained
at www.ICGtesting.com
Printed in the USA
BVHW030839090821
613310BV00008B/7